Keeping Christmas

Rodeo Romance Book 7
A Sweet Contemporary Holiday Romance

by
USA TODAY Bestselling Author
SHANNA HATFIELD

Keeping Christmas
Rodeo Romance Book 7

Copyright © 2019 by Shanna Hatfield

ISBN: 9781705594636

*To the caregivers
who serve out of love...*

Books by Shanna Hatfield

FICTION

Chapter One

With a quick glance at her watch, Talilah King entered the time on the patient chart in her hand then moved into the hallway at the hospital.

She'd taken two steps toward the nurses' station when a friend and fellow nurse, Tonya, rushed her direction.

"You're needed in the emergency room, Tally," Tonya said, then pointed toward the elevator. "From the sound of it, you better hurry."

"What's going on?" Tally asked, shoving the chart at Tonya as they both strode toward the door that opened to the stairs.

"Just go." Tonya flapped a hand at her as though it could make her move faster.

Tally raced down two flights of stairs and ran to the emergency room desk where she slid to a stop. Her mouth dropped open and she gaped in surprise as she stared into the faces of two cowboys from her brother's ranch.

"What are you doing here?" she asked, placing a hand on Jared's arm. A feeling of dread settled over her like a soggy blanket on a frosty winter day.

"Trevor had a little accident, so we brought him in," Jared said, trying to give Tally a reassuring smile. It failed to bring her any comfort, though, since he looked every bit as concerned as she felt.

Tally shifted her focus to the nurse seated at the desk. "Where's Trevor?"

"They just took him into room three. Doctor Olsen is on his way."

"Thanks, Glenda." Tally turned to the men and motioned them to follow her to the waiting area. "Have a seat, guys. I'll be back as soon as I find out what's going on."

The cowboys nodded to her as she spun around and strode down the hallway. Doctor Olsen was one of their best surgeons. If he was coming in on his day off to see Trevor, Tally knew whatever happened had to be bad.

With a fortifying breath, she walked into the room. Her brother was on his back on a gurney, his skin a sickly, pale shade. Perspiration dotted his brow and he appeared to be struggling against a wave of nausea.

She moved next to the bed and placed a hand on his forehead. He opened eyes glazed with pain and gave her one of his lopsided grins.

"Fancy meeting you here," Trevor said, his words sounding slightly slurred. "I'm a day early for our weekly lunch date."

Trevor made it a habit to drive into town once a week and take her out to lunch. In the three years she'd worked at the hospital in Kennewick, Washington, they'd only missed their lunch date a handful of times.

"So you are," she said and forced herself to smile. "What happened to you?" Tally wet several paper towels with cool water and brushed them across Trevor's forehead and over his cheeks.

He sighed and appeared to relax slightly. "I was ready to head to town to help get things set up for the rodeo tonight, then I remembered I needed to move the water in that little pasture we still irrigate with tubes. After I yanked the dam and started running down the ditch, I discovered we have a badger out there. I stepped in one of his holes and went down. My knee hit the metal rod in the dam then I landed on the shovel. I don't know what I did, but I can't put any weight on it. Tony and Jared must have seen it happen, because they rode up on the four-wheeler before I could pull myself out of the hole."

"I'm glad they were there." Tally wondered what all he'd damaged as she glanced at his right leg. The denim of his jeans had been slit to his thigh and his knee appeared swollen and bruised.

"One of the best doctors we have on staff is coming to take a look at you. Glenda said he's on his way, so it shouldn't be much longer. Can I get you anything?" Tally asked, tossing the paper towels into the trash and bringing a pan near the bed in case Trevor felt sick.

He eyed the pan and shook his head. "I'll be fine."

Tally grinned at him. "You know, after you

rode broncs through high school and college, then competed professionally for four years, I always expected a horse to send you to the hospital, not a badger."

Trevor started to nod then clenched his jaw. "Stupid badger. I'm waging war against him when I get home." He tipped his head toward her. "I need you to do something for me."

"What's that?"

Before he could say anything, the doctor stepped into the room. The next thing Tally knew, Trevor was headed into surgery to repair a torn ACL and a shattered kneecap. Her brother wasn't going to like it when he woke up to find a plate, pins, and screws holding his knee together.

She returned to the waiting area and told Jared and Tony what was happening and encouraged them to head back to the ranch.

"We drove Trevor's rig since it was right there," Tony said, handing her the keys to her brother's pickup. "Do you want us to drive it back to the ranch?"

Tally knew when it came time to take Trevor home, he'd be much more comfortable in his pickup than her compact car. She shook her head. "No, I'll bring him home in the truck when he's ready. Maybe one of you wouldn't mind driving my car out there, so I'll have a way back?"

"Sure, Tally. We can do that," Jared said.

She hurried upstairs and grabbed her keys from her bag then brought them back to the two cowboys. "Thanks for taking care of Trevor this morning. He's lucky you two were close by when it happened."

"We were fixing a section of fence on the other side of the pasture. One minute, Trevor was running down the ditch and the next he just disappeared. We'll see about trapping that badger as soon as we get back to the ranch, then filling in the holes." Jared tipped his head to her then nudged Tony, who was a young cowboy fresh out of high school.

Tony tipped his hat to her and then the two of them left.

Tally returned to work, but her thoughts drifted to her brother. She sent up prayers for him while she took care of patients. The moment Trevor was out of surgery, Tally took a break and went to check on him. He was still out of it, but Dr. Olsen assured her with physical therapy, Trevor would have a full recovery.

Relief flooded over her and she blinked back tears before she thanked the doctor then called Judd, the older man who helped oversee the ranch operations and served as the cook for the hired hands.

"He'll be just fine, Judd. Can you let the others know?" she asked as she stood in the supply closet where she could have a moment of peace to gather her composure.

"Will do, Miss Tally. You tell that brother of yours we're all thinking of him and sending good thoughts his way. When will he be home?"

Tally shared the details she knew and offered suggestions of things the guys could get ready for when she did bring Trevor out to the farm. She also warned the old cowboy that Trevor would have to follow orders which meant no riding, ranching, or doing more than he should before the doctor released him back to work.

"We'll do whatever you think is best, Tally. You just get that boy healed up enough he can come on home."

Tally worked another hour before her shift ended and she went to Trevor's room. His color was nearly back to normal and he looked peaceful instead of in pain.

Quietly, she moved beside the bed, hoping she wouldn't disturb him, but Trevor's eyes popped open.

"This is not how I pictured spending this week," he said, weakly raising a hand to encompass the hospital room.

"I know. You planned to hang out with your rodeo buddies and wander down memory lane, reliving all your glory days as the bareback bronc riding hero of the local rodeo."

Trevor smiled. "You know it. I was even hoping to talk you into going with me one evening. You haven't been to the fair or rodeo for years."

"I'm usually working and if I'm not, I prefer the peace of the ranch to the craziness of the county fair."

He gave her a long look. "You are the only person I know who avoids fair food and all the fun that surrounds it."

"Maybe I'm smarter than the average idiot," she teased.

"What is it you hate so much about going? I think you were in college the last time I talked you into going."

Tally didn't even know where to begin. There were so many things she disliked about being there: the overpriced food that wasn't even all that tasty, the desperate girls chasing after men, the drunks that had no inhibitions, and the cowboys looking for a good time. She had no interest in attending.

Before she could think of a way to respond, Trevor cleared his throat.

"I need you to do something for me, Tal."

She gave him a speculative glance. Something about his tone let her know she wouldn't like whatever it was he was about to ask.

"I need you to go to the fairgrounds and deliver something for me to someone there."

"No." Tally shook her head and busied herself straightening Trevor's covers.

His fingers encircled her wrist with more strength than she would have thought he could possess in his weakened state. "Please, Tally. One of the guys sent me a text message this morning that someone stole his rigging right out of his gear bag last night. He's supposed to ride tonight, so I told him he could borrow my lucky rigging. Will you please take it to him?"

Tally shook her head again. "No. I'll get one of the guys at the ranch to run your errand for you. They'll all be at the rodeo, anyway."

"The rigging is in my pickup. Did Jared leave it here?" Trevor turned his head toward the window, as though he could scan the parking lot below. From his position on the bed, all that was visible was blue August sky and the top of a maple tree.

"He did leave it here, but I'm not taking it. Tell your friend to come get the rigging."

"He would, but he's driving up from a rodeo in Utah. If he's lucky, he'll make it with a few minutes to spare. You know bareback is the first event out of the chutes and it would be a big help if you'd just meet him there."

She was well aware of how the rodeo worked, having trailed after Trevor when he was competing more times than she could count.

"Please, Tally. All you have to do is take it to him. That's all. Just walk behind the chutes and hand it over. Nothing to it."

"No. No way! It's not happening, Trev." Tally glared at her brother as she gently adjusted his pillow in an effort to make him more comfortable. "I don't care what you think I should do. I'm not going, and you can't make me."

"But, Tally, please?" Trevor pointed to his injured leg and mustered a pathetic look. "I'd go myself if I could. Besides, I promised my buddy he could use my rigging. You know how I feel about keeping my word."

Tally ignored the imploring look on Trevor's face as she checked his vitals. He had to be feeling better since he'd resumed his normal, bossy older brother tone. She was grateful the surgery had gone so well, and Trevor would be fine in a few months.

But keeping him down and resting would be a monumental challenge. One she hoped the crew at King Penny Ranch could handle.

"Fine, if you won't do it, I'll take care of it myself. Didn't the doc say I'll be able to get up and around soon? Maybe you could spring me out of here early. Just bring me a set of crutches and I'll head to the rodeo." Trevor started to toss back his covers, but Tally grabbed his hand and stopped him.

Her gaze narrowed and she wished she could cuff him with the pillow she'd just fluffed.

"If you so much as even think about getting up before the doctor gives you the okay to do so, I'll tell that little blonde nurse you think is so cute that you need a big boy diaper before bedtime."

"You wouldn't dare." Trevor scowled, but his eyes, the same stormy shade of gray as hers, gave away his uncertainty that she might follow through with the threat. His head drooped in defeat and he sighed.

Tally hid her smile by turning away and pouring a cup of cold water. She held a paper straw to his lips as he took a sip.

After she placed the cup back on the table near the bed, Trevor took her hand in his and gave her a pleading look that had always gotten her to bend to his will. There were times she felt like the more mature of the two, but Trevor was six years older and ten times more stubborn, at least about most things.

"Who is it you want me to see?" she asked, straightening his covers again in an effort to keep from smacking the triumphant smile off his face.

"Gage Taggart. You remember him, don't you? He worked at the ranch one summer. Weren't you about nine or so?"

Tally had no intention of telling her brother she'd been twelve. Her young, almost teenage heart had nearly beaten its way out of her chest any time she got within ten feet of Gage. He'd been the same age as Trevor, eighteen, fresh out of high school, and so hunky that summer he worked on the ranch, she'd practically fainted with every smile he sent her way. Trevor had teased her about having a crush on him, but she'd denied it. Dad had noticed her interest, too, but he never said a word about it. From the time she'd first met Gage Taggart, she'd been in love with him, even if she'd never confess how many of her childhood hours were spent pining after the bareback rider.

"I remember Gage," she said, wondering if he'd changed much since then. Would the man he'd grown into be so very different from the boy she'd adored?

"It really would be a help if you'd take it to him, Tal. Please?" Trevor gave her another one of those looks that made her heart pinch.

"I don't have anything to change into, Trev. And I won't have time to run home and change." She glanced down at her scrubs. Since it was the week of the fair and rodeo, Tally and several others had worn farm-themed scrubs. Although her navy pants were plain, her pale blue top featured horses, sheep, cows, chickens, and pigs. "Surely, you don't expect me to go like this."

"You look great," Trevor said in a weary voice. Now that he'd gotten his way, his eyelids drifted down, like he couldn't hold them open any longer. She could wait him out, until he fell asleep, but she hated to disappoint him.

"If I do this, and that's a big if, you realize you

are going to owe me at least a huge favor, or six, don't you?"

"I am aware of that and will gladly pay up. Please, Tally? Take my phone and text Gage that you'll meet him there. You don't have to go to the rodeo if you don't want to. If he's nearby, you could even meet him at the gate and won't have to go in." Trevor's tone softened as he fought sleep.

Tally leaned over and kissed her brother's cheek. "The things I do for you, big brother."

"You're a good kid, Tal. Thank you." Trevor sighed and closed his eyes.

Chapter Two

Tally made sure Trevor was sleeping comfortably, or as well as possible in his condition, then took his phone from the bedside table and resigned herself to heading to the fairgrounds whether she wanted to or not.

She probably could have talked someone into going with her, but she planned to deliver the bareback rigging and leave as soon as humanly possible. She had no intention of hanging around, chatting with the cowboys at the rodeo, and especially not visiting with Gage.

Convinced she'd acted like a twitterpated ninny around him when she was younger, the last thing she wanted to do was see him. Embarrassment stung her cheeks just thinking of what a pest she'd probably made of herself that summer he'd worked on the ranch.

Maybe he wouldn't even remember her. The likelihood of that was far more reasonable than him recalling the silly little sister of one of his rodeo friends.

Tally drove Trevor's pickup to the fairgrounds and found a spot to park at the far end of a row of vehicles. It cost her ten dollars to park there, but the money went to one of the local service clubs, so she didn't mind. Cars were arriving in a steady stream since it was after five, and those coming after work appeared eager to get there.

Before she left the hospital, she sent Gage a text from Trevor's phone, asking if he could meet her at the gate. He texted back that he was still a few miles away and would meet her inside once he checked in at the rodeo registration table. Tally hadn't bothered to make it clear in her brief message that she was texting him and not Trevor. She figured the less said the better.

Filled with dread, she gave one more glance at her scrubs, tucked a strand of hair behind her ear that had escaped the knot she'd pinned at the back of her head, and walked across the parking lot.

She paid the admission fee, held her hand out to get stamped, and shifted the bag that held Trevor's rodeo gear on her shoulder. In no rush, she wandered down the main thoroughfare taking in the variety of booths. They hadn't changed much since the last time she'd been there. The aromas of burgers, cotton candy, and barbecue lingered in the air while the sounds from the carnival joined the cadence of excited voices and music being played on one of the small stages.

Tally stopped in front of a food booth. The proceeds would benefit one of the school groups, so it really was for a good cause. The food was ridiculously overpriced, but she did love a good corn dog and curly fries.

In spite of herself, she placed an order and found an empty bench in front of one of the stages. From the people beginning to gather there, she assumed a performance would soon begin.

She dunked the corn dog in a paper cup of mustard and took a bite. The crispy, golden breading was cooked to perfection and the hot dog tasted like it was made with beef instead of meat-like filler. The fries, sprinkled with just the right amount of salt, were some of the best she'd had in a long time. She sipped her soda and glanced around as she ate.

A couple with three adorable little girls took a seat on the bench in front of her. The two younger girls, one still in diapers, looked exactly like their father with light blond hair and pale skin, but the oldest resembled the mother with dark hair and eyes. The dad cuddled the youngest and teased a smile out of the middle daughter, but the oldest sat on the far side of the bench, quiet and subdued. The little girl couldn't have been more than five or six, but something about her made Tally long to give her a hug. The mother got up and headed for one of the nearby vendor booths. As soon as she left, the father glared at the oldest girl and said something that made the child's narrow shoulders curl inward while her head drooped despondently.

The way the man lovingly catered to the other two girls made Tally question if the child was even his. The mother returned with a box of food and served everyone first, herself included, before she handed the dark-haired child a hamburger. The little girl scooted over until she was almost falling off the edge of the bench and huddled over the burger as she ate it.

Concerned about what the poor little girl endured at home, Tally's heart ached for the child. While her brain scrambled for something she could do to help, the sound of tambourines and bells drew her attention to the stage.

A troupe of belly dancers swayed in front of the crowd. The women were far past middle age, out of shape, and not particularly a show Tally wanted to see. She gathered the remnants of her dinner and left. It was bad enough to watch the women gyrate on the stage with flabby folds of skin flapping in time to the music, but she really couldn't stand to watch the couple in front of her any longer.

Discouraged and heartsore for the little girl, she threw away her trash and wandered over to the barns where the 4-H and FFA students kept their animals. She watched two boys chase a wayward sheep, trying to catch it before it made a mad escape out the back of the barn. An older boy headed it off and the three of them managed to herd the animal back into its pen. Trevor had a similar experience with a steer, only he was in the show ring. The animal was a little bigger than he could handle, but he'd held onto the rope as it dragged him across the arena. Then it bumped into a horse one of the FFA girls was about to show. The horse started bucking and set off a domino reaction. It took what seemed like hours to get the animals under control. Tally had only been about five at the time, but she remembered it like it happened yesterday.

Oh, how she used to love to come to the fair and rodeo. It was a magical, wonderful place for a little girl, especially when her older brother plied her with ice cream and cotton candy anytime she asked for a treat.

Then one bad experience had soured her on attending.

Tally sighed and glanced down at her scrubs then rolled back her shoulders. At least no one had commented on her attire. Maybe everyone assumed she was there for a shift at the onsite medical station.

She'd just left the animal barns when Trevor's phone buzzed with a message from Gage.

Be there in ten minutes.

She glanced at the message and stuffed the phone back in her pocket. Gage was cutting it close. The rodeo would begin in thirty minutes. Under normal circumstances, that would be plenty of time, but he was missing a vital piece of gear and if he didn't find her before he had to ride, he was going to be out of luck.

With a few more minutes to kill, she started to walk through the door to see the floral exhibit, but a young couple pushing a stroller blocked the doorway. Although the stroller was too wide to fit through the open door, they kept trying, hitting the edge of the stroller against the doorframe over and over again.

Tally stepped forward and pulled open the other half of the double doors then waited as the couple pushed their way inside, not even bothering to thank her for opening the door.

What is wrong with people? she wondered as she strolled past displays of dahlias, daisies, and roses wilting in the heat. Between the idiots with the stroller, the horrible couple with the adorable little girls, and the fact she was there under duress, she wanted to turn around and leave. She could go back to her apartment, take a shower, and curl up in bed with a good book.

Instead, she left the flower building and made her way toward the rodeo arena. She was almost there when Trevor's phone buzzed again.

Meet me behind the chutes? Sure appreciate this, Trev.

There was no way on earth or beyond she was going behind the chutes. The last time she'd done that had cured her of rodeos and rodeo cowboys for life. She had no intention of repeating the experience. The very thought of going back there left her thoroughly disturbed.

She sent a text to Gage telling him to meet her near the ticket booth. It was only after she hit send that she realized she should have mentioned she was the one there, not Trevor.

Gage would figure it out soon enough, she supposed.

She leaned against the corner of the ticket booth, out of the way, and watched people coming and going. Through the crowd, she caught a glimpse of a face that looked familiar as a cowboy hustled her way.

Tally sucked in a gulp of air, unprepared for how much Gage had changed since she'd last seen him in person. The boy she'd had a crush on had morphed into a very handsome man. His dark brown hair was shorter, his shoulders broader, his body a finely-tuned machine of muscle. She noticed a scar on his right cheek that hadn't been there before, yet it only added to his rugged appeal.

But his eyes were the same magnificent shade of blue, and his lips still appeared incredibly kissable. When he looked at a little girl wearing a pink tutu over her denim overalls, his grin kicked up the left side of his mouth just as she remembered.

He didn't appear to have gotten taller than his already six-foot height, but he looked stronger and more capable than he had all those years ago.

Tally noticed several women eyeing him as he made his way through the crowd. He didn't even seem to notice them as he scanned the faces, no doubt searching for her brother. She stepped away from the ticket booth and headed toward him.

She tried to catch his eye, but he looked right past her, as though she didn't exist. Not that it surprised her. Guys like Gage weren't interested in girls like her — girls who would never be mistaken for a model, had brains in their heads, and held to an unyielding set of morals.

Nope. There was nothing about her that would be of the slightest interest to a cowboy like Gage.

Tally waited until she was standing directly

behind him to tap him on the shoulder.

"Gage Taggart," she said in a voice she used to subdue unruly patients. He jerked and turned around to stare at her.

She could see him struggling to pull her identity from his memories. Insulted he hadn't yet figured out who she was, someone jostled into her and she bumped against Gage. Something electric and completely unexpected arced between the two of them. Tally wanted no part of whatever it was and moved back.

Eager to get the torturous errand over with, she held the gear bag out to him. "Trevor sent me with this."

"Where's Trev?" Gage asked, taking the bag and looking around like her brother might suddenly materialize. "Who was I texting a minute ago if it wasn't him?"

"That would be me. I'm sure you don't remember, but I'm Trevor's sister."

"Tally? You're little Tally?" He held his hand down near his waist, indicating the height he thought she should be.

She nodded and Gage broke into a wide grin.

"You were always such a cute kid with those big gray eyes, sturdy little legs, and chubby cheeks." He reached out and playfully pinched her cheek. "You haven't changed a bit. Aren't you like, fifteen, maybe sixteen?"

Tally fought back the urge to roll her eyes or slug the clueless cowboy in front of her. "I graduated from high school six years ago, not that it matters. Trevor had an accident, but he wanted to make sure you got the gear you needed."

She would have walked away, but Gage grabbed her arm and propelled her out of the stream of humanity trying to get into the stands before the rodeo began. He stopped when they stood behind the ticket booth. Half a dozen people gathered in a circle talking there, but they didn't seem to pay them any mind.

"What happened to Trevor? Is he okay?" Gage asked, although he didn't release his hold on her upper arm.

Fiery spurts of heat spiraled from where his fingers curled around her bicep all the way up to her head before plunging down to her toes, leaving her more than a little disconcerted. Her gaze fell to his hand and he let her go.

"Is Trev okay?" he asked again.

Yanking her thoughts away from the way Gage's touch unsettled her, she nodded her head. "He will be. A badger hole got the best of him this morning. He's at the hospital right now, after having some hardware installed in his knee. He's going to be out of commission for a while, but he'll have a full recovery."

"Oh, man. I'm so sorry. I had no idea," Gage said. He gave her a look full of concern. "You're sure he'll be fine?"

"Yes. He's not going to like being stuck in the house while he recuperates, but he'll be back to his normal routine in a few months." Tally started to back away. "I know you need to get ready to ride, so I'll just be on my way."

"I've got a minute." Gage's gaze traveled from

the top of her head, over her scrubs, down to her sensible support shoes. Slowly, his eyes made their way back up to her face. "Either you're a nurse, or... you have a unique way of approaching fashion."

His comment piqued her ire. After all, he thought she was still a chubby teenager. With her ego deflated, she would have spun around and left, but someone knocked into her from behind again, sending her smacking against Gage. He dropped the gear bag and put both hands on her arms to steady her, but not before she felt the solid muscle of his chest.

What would it be like to be held there? Tally chased away the ludicrous question with a scowl and tugged free of Gage's grasp.

"You better go," she said, tipping her head toward the arena.

"Tell Trevor thanks for letting me borrow his rigging. Some lunatic snitched mine out of my bag last night. I ordered a new one, but it will take a few weeks to get it. Until then, Trev is really saving my bacon." Gage took a step closer to her. He raised a hand, like he intended to touch her.

If he pinched her cheek again, she really would slug him.

A frown furrowed his brow, as though he could read her thoughts, and he dropped his hand.

"Thanks for bringing this, Tally. It was sure nice to see you again," he said. "Are you going to watch me ride? I can get you in for free."

"Thanks, but I can't stay. I hope you do well, Gage."

He smiled at her and started to walk away. Tally released the breath she didn't even realize she'd been holding. Unexpectedly, Gage turned around and pulled her into a tight hug, making nerves explode in her stomach. The scent of his shaving lotion mingled with leather in a heady mixture that left her knees weak. And much to her combined delight and distress, it felt even better to be held tenderly against his chest than she'd imagined.

When he kissed her temple and stepped back, heat burned her cheeks. A crowd stared at them, as though Gage was about to embark on a scandalous adventure, and they wanted front row seats.

Tally wanted nothing to do with Gage, or the gossip that would certainly ensue. She knew how stories flew around the circle of rodeo groupies.

"Can I visit Trevor tomorrow?" Gage asked, with a sincere look that melted a bit of her reserve.

"Of course," Tally said, and told him how to find the hospital.

"Take care, Tally King. You always were the little queen of the ranch, you know." Gage tossed her another carefree grin, tipped his hat, and then raced off behind the bucking chutes.

Tally straightened her spine, inhaled a settling breath, and bought a ticket to the rodeo. No matter how much she tried to convince herself to leave, she felt an inexplicable need to watch Gage ride. No doubt, Trevor would expect her to stay at least long enough to report on how well Gage had ridden.

She found a seat on the end of an aisle and watched as the rodeo began. She hoped Gage would be among the first riders to compete, but he was the last bareback rider out of the chutes.

As Tally observed the athletes, both human and equine, she recalled all the times she'd gone with her dad to watch Trevor ride. She'd been about eight the first time she could remember seeing him compete in a high school rodeo.

He'd had raw talent then that he honed as he grew older and stronger.

She knew of all the events in the rodeo, bareback riding was the hardest on a body. The event had been compared to riding a jackhammer with one hand. Bareback riders endured more physical abuse and quite often carried away more long-term injuries than other rodeo athletes.

She watched as a rider adjusted his hold on his rigging, a piece of equipment made of leather that really looked like a suitcase handle on a strap. It was placed atop the horse's withers and secured with a cinch.

With one hand in the air, the cowboy gave a nod and the chute gate swung open. He kept both spurs touching the horse's shoulders until the horse's hooves hit the arena dirt after the initial jump out of the chute. The rider then pulled his knees up, rolling his spurs along the horse's shoulders as the horse went into a high buck. On the way back to the ground, the cowboy stretched out his legs, returning his spurs to the starting position, anticipating the next jump.

She knew the cowboy's score depended on several factors beyond staying on eight seconds. He was judged on his spurring technique, how far out his toes were turned while he spurred, and how well he handled twists and turns during the ride.

When the buzzer sounded at eight seconds, Tally guessed the cowboy had probably earned about an eighty-point ride. She smiled to herself when an eighty-one-score flashed on the big overhead screen.

"Next up is a cowboy who's been riding here for years. Let's give a big welcome to Gage Taggart! This cowboy is headed to this year's finals folks, I have no doubt about it," the announcer's voice boomed as Gage settled onto the back of the bronc.

From her seat, Tally could see the glove on Gage's riding hand wrapped with tape around the wrist as he took a grip on the rigging. He scooted back, snugged his hat down, and nodded his head. The all-white horse he rode burst out of the chute like a ghostly blur then bucked so high and hard, Tally held her breath, afraid the animal was about to flip right over on Gage.

She didn't breathe again until the buzzer sounded, and Gage smiled triumphantly. When a pickup rider she recognized as Shaun Price rode up beside him, Gage swung off the white horse, across the back of Shaun's horse, and landed on his feet.

"Look at that, folks! This cowboy has earned himself an eighty-eight-point ride and taken the lead," the announcer said as cheers echoed from the stands.

Gage waved to the crowd then jogged out of the arena, clearly pleased with himself and his performance.

Tally left the stands and marched back to her brother's pickup. When she slid onto the leather seat, she slapped the steering wheel twice in irritation. Seeing Gage again had been even worse than she'd envisioned. And watching him ride had been a stupid, stupid thing to do.

The crush she'd had on him all those years ago hadn't lessened at all. If anything, it was back with a vengeance and she wanted no part of it.

None at all.

Chapter Three

"I don't know what you said to my sister, but she was in here reaming my ears first thing this morning," Trevor said, grinning at Gage as he took a seat in the chair beside his hospital bed.

Gage shrugged and leaned back in the chair. "You didn't mention she'd grown up into a beautiful woman, Trev. I was expecting to see you last night. To see her instead caught me off guard. In my head, she's still fourteen and looking at me with hero-worship in her eyes. I think I've officially knocked myself off that pedestal."

Trevor chuckled. "That you have, my friend. She was fuming at me about making her go to the fair to meet you in the first place. She was even more worked up when she found out I'd never shattered your delusions that she was still a kid."

Gage had nearly swallowed his gum when the beautiful woman who said his name turned out to be Tally King. Recognition had set in an instant before

she said her name, but he was so overwhelmed by…
He didn't know what, exactly, but it left him feeling
short of breath while his stomach churned with
nerves. No woman had ever made him feel like that,
and he'd been around plenty.

Tally resembled the girl he remembered from
his teen years. The baby fat that plagued her as a
child had been replaced by more delicious curves
than a masterfully-built snowman could boast. Her
eyes swirled with whorls of gray, like storm clouds
moving across a winter sky. Her skin looked so
silky and smooth, he'd had to reach out and touch it,
even if it was to give her cheek a playful pinch. And
her lips. Oh, man. Those lips! Full and pouty, they
were positively made to drive a man to distraction.

Which was why he'd acted like a jerk and
pretended he thought she was still far too young for
him.

Tally King had grown into a gorgeous woman,
one Gage needed to stay far, far away from. She
wasn't a good-time girl like those who hung out
after the rodeo. No, Tally was a wedding dress,
porch swing, and grow old with me kind of girl.
That was the last thing Gage needed.

He was at the top of his career in the pro rodeo
circuit and he absolutely had to keep his focus on
being the best bareback rider in the business. Not
pining after a sweet girl.

In truth, Tally had caught his eye as soon as
he'd stepped into the crowd around the ticket booth.
He'd seen her leaning against the corner of the
building, but had no idea who she was, other than
an incredibly attractive young woman. Then, when

he'd realized who she was, he'd wanted nothing more than to pull her into his arms and hold her. Maybe kiss those amazing lips.

A sense of relief washed over him when he heard Trevor say she was miffed with him. Better that than to have her interested, not that he'd encourage it.

He was well aware of her crush on him when she was younger, but she was just a little girl and he'd been a boy teetering on the edge of becoming a man. Now, though, Tally was a woman any red-blooded man couldn't help but notice, even dressed in scrubs with her hair scraped back in an off-center knot.

Gage grinned at his friend. "Tally sure doesn't look like a kid. Your sister is gorgeous."

Trevor's humor faded and he gave Gage a warning look. "Don't you get any ideas about Tally. She is off limits. Understand?"

"Understood. I wouldn't think of doing anything to hurt her, Trev. She was always such a soft-hearted kid. I can't imagine that's changed."

"It hasn't. She wears her heart on her sleeve and would give anyone who needed it the shirt right off her back."

Gage wouldn't mind seeing her without her shirt but kept his thoughts to himself. "I'll leave her alone. You have my word I will not pursue your sister. I promise. Besides, I don't have time for women right now. I've got a world championship title to win."

Trevor relaxed against his pillows. "I can't believe you are sitting right there in the top three in the world. It's awesome, man. Congratulations."

"Thanks, Trev. I just need to hold onto that a few more weeks." Gage looked around the room. "How long do you have to stay here?"

"Tally's taking me home tomorrow. She's going to use a few weeks of vacation to stay at the ranch and help out until I'm a little more mobile."

Gage gave him a confused look. "She doesn't live at the King Penny Ranch?"

"No, not really. She has an apartment here in town she shares with some other nurses. They all work unbelievable hours. For the most part, Tally works three horrifically long days and then has three off in a rotating schedule. She generally comes out to the ranch when she's free." Trevor sighed. "I wish she'd stay out there all the time, but she has her own life to live."

"I think it's cool you and Tally are so close, especially since she's your half-sister." Gage rarely spoke to his lone sibling, but his brother thought he was wasting his life and talents by following his dreams.

"Regardless of the fact our mother couldn't stay with a man longer than a year or two at most, I've never thought of Tally as a half-sister, but just my sweet little sis. Dad always considered her his daughter, even if she wasn't his." Trevor shook his head, as though he wanted to dislodge his memories. He looked at Gage again. "You ever hear from your folks?"

"Not often. I think I told you they sold their business and moved to Florida. They claim they like the weather there much better and they have a variety of new wealthy clients to choose from with their financial investment firm."

"Is your brother still following in their footsteps?"

"Yep. He and his wife both work for an investment firm in New York. My niece is growing up to be just like them. The last time I stopped to visit them, all three of them sat with their cell phones glued to their hands throughout dinner and hardly said a dozen words. Fiona is barely eight."

Trevor gave him a sympathetic look. "You know you're always welcome to hang out at the ranch with us if you need a dose of crazy family."

"I do know that and appreciate the offer. I might even take you up on it sometime. Between you, Chase and Jessie Jarrett, Shaun and Brylee Price, and Cooper and Paige James, I've always got somewhere to hang my hat."

"Why don't you plan to stay with us the next few weeks, if you don't have other plans?"

Gage stood. "I won't be around much. I'm actually heading to a rodeo a few hours from here to compete tonight. But I'll be back tomorrow to ride again since I made the final round. Oh, and I hope it was okay, but I'm having the new rigging I ordered shipped to your place. It should be here before the Pendleton Round-Up."

"Of course, that's fine. I'm just glad I still had my old gear around for you to use."

"Me, too. Thanks again for letting me borrow it. I promise to keep it under lock and key, so it doesn't disappear."

"Any idea of what happened to your rigging?"

Trevor asked, shifting on the bed with a painful groan.

"I have a feeling an old girlfriend who didn't take kindly to me breaking up with her had something to do with it. She's been bugging me on and off the past several months, and she lives close to the rodeo I was at when my stuff disappeared."

"You ought to press charges."

"I would if I had any proof she took it. I reported it to the police and suggested she might be a person of interest, but there's not much else I can do." Gage glanced at his watch then reached out a hand to Trevor and patted him on the shoulder. "I better get on the road. Is there anything I can get you before I go?"

"Nope, but I appreciate you stopping by. Be careful out there and have a great ride at the rodeo tonight."

Gaged edged toward the door. "Will do. I'll drive out to the ranch on Sunday to check up on you."

"I'll look forward to seeing you then. Maybe we can talk Tally into grilling steaks for us."

"Sounds perfect," Gage said, then smirked at Trevor when a pretty little nurse breezed into the room. If he was a betting man, he would have put money on her being the homecoming queen and head cheerleader when she was in high school. Perky and personable didn't begin to describe her.

Trevor certainly seemed interested in her.

"How are you feeling today, Mr. King?" the nurse asked as she poured water into a cup for him.

"Fine," Trevor said. When the nurse wasn't

looking, he flapped his hand at Gage in a shooing motion.

"I think he's running a little fever." Gage said, grinning at his friend. "You might want to take his temperature. The old-fashioned way is probably best."

The nurse gave him then Trevor startled looks. Gage laughed, ignored the angry daggers shooting from Trevor's eyes, and strode out of the room. He walked down the hallway, grinned at the nurses sitting at the desk near the elevator, then stepped on. The feel of several pairs of eyes boring into his back made him turn around. He looked at the women and winked before the door closed.

Aware he was pouring it on a little thick, he couldn't help himself. He was a flirt and a tease and always had been. Unless he settled down with a woman, he supposed he'd always be that way.

Thoughts of settling down brought a picture of Tally King to mind, standing in her farm animal scrub top with Trevor's gear bag slung over one shoulder. As curvy as she looked in the scrubs, he wondered how she'd appear in something a little more formfitting. It was probably a good thing he wouldn't find out. Of all the women he'd dated, flirted with, kissed, and teased, she was the one who made strange, foreign feelings spring up inside him.

He didn't like it, though. Not in the least.

The fact he was still thinking about her didn't bode well. It was probably a good thing he was heading out of town and would be incredibly busy with a hectic schedule the next few weeks while he was in and out of the area.

Of course, he'd go by the ranch and see Trevor when he could. He'd just have to hope Tally wouldn't be there. Or he could continue to treat her like she was still fourteen and she'd be mad enough to take a wide swath around him. Either way, he had to keep her at a distance. Otherwise, he might just do something completely stupid, like pull her into his arms and see if those lips were as luscious as he imagined.

Last night, when someone bumped her from behind and knocked her into him, Gage had felt electricity sparking between them like a live wire. Unable to stop himself, he'd pulled her into his arms and hugged her before she left. For the sparse seconds he held her, it was like he'd finally come home.

Then he'd made the mistake of kissing her temple and almost lost his ability to step away from her. The fragrance of her, of something warm and soft that made him think of Christmas cookies and winter wishes, still haunted him.

And that was ridiculous. Wasn't it?

Truthfully, the most at home he'd felt in his life was the summer he worked at the King Penny Ranch. Gage was a city boy who grew up in Portland where his parents were too busy to pay much attention to him.

He'd been eight years old when a friend invited him to go with his family to the rodeo in St. Paul. Gage had been transfixed that day and his world spun in a different direction, guiding him onto a whole new path. The second the chutes opened, and the first horse bucked into the arena, he'd known what he wanted to do with his life. He was meant to ride broncs.

It hadn't been easy for him to pursue a career as a bareback rider, but he'd worked hard from that summer on. He started a business in his neighborhood of mowing lawns, raking leaves, and even hanging Christmas lights. With the money he earned, he sent himself to rodeo camps for youth and purchased the gear he needed. He talked his parents into sending him to a public school, instead of the private one his brother Tim attended, where he could join the rodeo team. His parents had no idea he was competing in rodeo until he came home with a broken arm. In spite of their insistence he stop, he continued to ride.

He earned a scholarship to Cal-Poly and competed on the rodeo team there while earning a business degree. Then he took his career a step further and joined the Professional Rodeo Cowboys Association and hit the road with Trevor as his traveling partner.

However, it was during his high school years of competing that he became friends with Trevor King. Trevor's father, Ross, often traveled with the rodeo kids to watch them compete. And in the summer, Trevor's little sister would trail along, shy but pleased as everything to be included in the fun.

The summer Gage graduated from high school, Ross had asked him if he'd like a job and he'd jumped at the opportunity to work on a real ranch. His parents had pitched a colossal fit, but he'd gone anyway.

The three months he spent at the King Penny

Ranch had taught him about ranching, rural life, and being a good man. Ross was so different than his parents and someone Gage greatly admired. For the first time in his life, he got a real sense of what it meant to be a family, to be part of a group of loving, caring individuals.

The ranch, located near the small town of Echo, Oregon, and the family that lived there came to mind whenever he thought of home.

Trevor had been Gage's traveling partner on the rodeo circuit from the moment they both started out professionally. Then five years ago, his friend received a call that his father's heart was failing. Immediately, Trevor left the rodeo world behind to return to the ranch.

When Gage received news of Ross's passing, he'd been across the country with five cracked ribs from an injury he sustained at a rodeo and couldn't get back in time for the funeral. His heart ached with loss and grief as though his own father had passed. He still mourned the loss of such a warm, wonderful man who'd given so much love and support to others.

After Trevor returned to the ranch, Gage decided to travel alone. It took a bit of adjustment, but he found he liked it. For all the jovial, life-of-the-party persona he portrayed around others, Gage enjoyed his solitude.

And solitude was what he needed to get thoughts of tempting Tally King straight in his head.

He walked through the hospital parking lot to where he'd left his motorcycle parked. In spite of the nearly hundred-degree heat, he pulled on a heavy leather jacket with reflective tape. He already had on a pair of jeans lined with Kevlar fibers as well as biker boots that hit him mid-shin. He took knee and hip protectors out of a saddlebag and stuffed them into the slots on the jeans. He'd rather sweat and be safe than ride without protective gear covering his body. Too many times he'd seen people seriously injured who rode without that extra safety precaution. He took enough chances on the back of a bucking horse in the arena. It seemed like he was pushing his luck to ride a motorcycle without doing what he could to prevent an injury.

A grin creased his face as he strapped on a helmet emblazoned with a bucking horse bursting through flames. Most of his friends thought he was nuts for riding a motorcycle, but it got great gas mileage and he loved being out in the open. The powerful touring bike he rode was made for the open road and included everything from cruise control to an audio system. Among the features that had sold him on this particular bike were four integrated hard-sided saddlebags that held all his gear, clothes, and travel necessities.

Trophies he won at rodeos were shipped to Cooper James's grandpa who held onto them until Gage could take them to a storage unit he rented in St. Paul, since he didn't have a home of his own. He didn't see the point in paying rent on a house or apartment when he was on the road almost fifty weeks out of the year.

A post office box and Nick James took care of anything that was mailed to him. The few bills he had, he paid online. And anyone who needed to get in touch with him knew his number or how to reach his friends.

The life of a rodeo vagabond had been all he'd known his entire adult life. Now that he was thirty and at the top of his game, he had no intention of changing things. Not even if he'd started thinking more and more about traveling less and setting down roots. A place to call his own sounded better all the time, but he didn't want to quit just yet.

When the time came to retire from rodeo, Gage planned to buy a piece of land, run cattle, and enjoy life at a slower pace. Goodness knew he had ample funds to do that thanks to his rodeo winnings, the money he'd earned as a model for Lasso Eight clothing, and smart investments. But he had no intention of retiring anytime in the near future.

Not when he had a shot at taking the championship title and winning the national finals rodeo.

Gage pulled on his leather gloves then checked to make sure his saddlebag boxes were all locked. The night his rigging disappeared, he'd stowed his gear, but didn't lock it while he watched a friend win the tie-down roping event. He returned to the bike to find his gear bag on the ground and his rigging missing. Regardless of who stole it, he was grateful Trevor had agreed to let him borrow his.

Ready to get on the road, Gage flipped down the face shield on his helmet and started his bike, enjoying the sound it made as he revved the engine and left the parking lot.

It didn't take long for him to enter the freeway

and head out toward the next rodeo. As he changed lanes and accelerated, he let his thoughts wander to Tally. What would she look like with her hair down? When she was younger it was unbelievably thick and wavy. The two King men had a hard time trying to help her comb it when she was too little to manage on her own. In fact, one summer he and Trevor had cut off her braid and Ross had spent the better part of an hour lecturing them about butchering a little girl's hair.

He was thinking about winding a strand of Tally's soft brown hair around his finger and tugging her close enough to kiss when a car roared up beside him. Without warning, it pulled into his lane as though he wasn't there.

Gage swerved to the left to avoid running into the side of the vehicle, but the rumble strip threw him off balance. In an attempt to keep from going down, he leaned the other way. He would have been fine, but the car was weaving all over the place. The back bumper caught his front tire and sent him into a long, greasy slide down the freeway.

Horns honked, brakes squealed, and Gage prayed he wasn't about to draw in his last breath. He was young with his whole life ahead of him. He wasn't ready to die. And surely not from an idiot driver who ought to have his driver's license revoked.

Agony seared up his right leg, bearing the brunt of the impact as he continued to slide on his side beneath the bike. The car that had caused him to wreck slammed on its brakes in front of him. He plowed into the back of the car, hitting his head.

Stars exploded behind his eyes and he heard a loud cracking noise.

The impact spun the bike around and tossed him into the next lane of traffic where cars were still trying to avoid crashing. Out of instinct or perhaps pure reflex, he threw out his left hand, trying to grab onto something to stop his momentum only to have a car run right over the top of it.

Overcome with pain, Gage closed his eyes and pictured Tally with her cute little farm animal shirt and the sun backlighting her lopsided knot of hair.

Chapter Four

"Tally! I've been looking everywhere for you," Tonya said as she raced up to her, out of breath.

"What's wrong?" Tally asked, placing a hand on her friend's shoulder.

"Emergency room. Need you now."

Tally shoved the charts in her hand at Tonya and ran for the stairs. Wasn't it just yesterday morning she'd done the same thing when Jared and Tony had brought in Trevor? As she clattered down the stairs, she prayed whomever was injured would be fine. Had something happened to one of the ranch hands? Or their loony aunt? Thoughts of Aunt Mary leaving them made a lump lodge in her throat.

She yanked open the door and rushed to the emergency room where Glenda grabbed her arm and hauled her into one of the examination rooms.

A man on his back on a gurney groaned in pain. Two nurses worked to remove his heavy biker boots while a doctor washed his hands at the sink, in preparation for an examination.

"He asked for you and mentioned Trevor," Glenda said. "He was on his motorbike. A car side-swiped him and caused him to wreck."

"Gage," Tally whispered, crossing over to him in a few strides. "Oh, my word."

"Hey," Gage rasped. He opened his eyes and tried to grin at her, but it looked more like a grimace.

"You know him?" Doctor Olsen asked as he pulled on a pair of gloves and moved beside her.

"He's friends with Trevor," Tally said, nodding at the doctor.

"You want to help us out a minute?" the doctor asked in a lowered voice. "It might be good to have a friendly face to distract him."

"Of course," Tally said. She grabbed a cloth and dampened it, then wiped the sweat, blood, and grime off Gage's face. "We need to get you out of those things, Gage, so the doctor can figure out what's injured. We'll be as gentle and careful as possible."

A grunt let her know he'd heard what she said as he closed his eyes.

Tally couldn't think about what might have happened to Gage if he hadn't been wearing the protective clothing. The right side of his leather jacket was nothing more than shreds riddled with holes. The same with his jeans. The fabric was tattered with holes and tears all up the right side. She could see Gage had a few spots of road rash, but it could have been so much worse. He had a few small cuts on his face that explained the blood, but no major gushing wounds. From the look in his eyes, though, she thought he most likely had a concussion.

The nurses let the boots drop to the floor with a thud and that was when blood began to drip off his foot.

"Doctor," one of the nurses said, pointing to a wet, lumpy spot on his leg that had been hidden by his boots.

"Cut those pants off. Now," Doctor Olsen said, shining a light in Gage's eyes then feeling along his head.

The nurses managed to cut up the legs of the jeans to the knees when something kept them from cutting further. Tally reached down and removed the protective pieces that covered his knees then felt along his hips. The one on the left side was whole, but the one on the right came out in splintered pieces.

She removed the glove from his right hand then reached for his left, but Gage yelped in pain when she lifted his hand.

"It's okay, Gage. It's okay." Gently, she removed his glove to see two fingers appear twisted with a bone sticking up on the back of his hand.

"At least it's not my riding hand," he said, although he kept his eyes squeezed tightly shut.

"Only a rodeo cowboy would say such a stupid thing," Tally muttered as she held his hand while one of the nurses cut up his sleeve.

When Tally finally returned upstairs to her floor, Gage was headed for surgery to repair two breaks in his leg as well as his hand.

After checking in at the nurse's station, she popped by Trevor's room.

"What's wrong?" he asked before she could even open her mouth to tell him about Gage.

Her brother had always been able to read her like a book written in large print. She'd never been able to hide anything from him or their dad, either.

"Gage was in an accident. He's in surgery right now."

"What?" Trevor shouted, then lowered his voice. "He was headed to a rodeo when he left here and that was only a few hours ago."

Tally moved closer to the bed and put a calming hand on her brother's shoulder. "From what I can gather, he was riding a motorcycle. A driver either didn't see him or wasn't paying attention when he changed lanes and caused the accident. Witnesses said the man pulled right into Gage. He swerved and the bike went down, sliding quite a distance before it hit the back of the car then spun into the traffic. A second car ran over his hand."

"It wasn't his riding hand, was it?"

Tally suppressed a scream and rolled her eyes. "No, it wasn't. But good grief, Trev. You can't possibly think he'll be able to ride after this, do you?"

"What's broken?" her brother asked, pushing himself up against his pillows as he waited for her answer.

"He has a concussion, road rash burns on his right side, two broken fingers and a broken bone between his middle finger and his wrist. Both his tibia and fibula are broken. The doctor hopes hardware won't be necessary for his leg, but Gage is definitely going to get pins in his hand. He's looking at two to three months of recovery time at minimum."

Trevor nodded. "In theory, though, he should be fine, shouldn't he?"

"In theory. He had on plenty of protective gear and he's in incredible shape, both of which worked in his favor."

Her brother scowled at her. "How much of his shape were you noticing?"

Tally felt tongue-tied and fussed with Trevor's pillows. She wouldn't admit she'd stared at Gage's hard abs and sculpted chest and arms when they'd pulled away the remnants of his clothes. She knew rodeo athletes who were on top of their game had to stay in shape. It took a strong core, outstanding arm and leg strength, and extreme flexibility to successfully do what they did for a living. The more limber they were, the more they were in shape, the less risk cowboys ran of injury.

That had definitely been a benefit to Gage with this accident. It could have been so much worse. In fact, when someone carried his helmet into the room, she felt lightheaded. Most of the paint had been scraped off the right side of the helmet on the asphalt, and a huge chunk was missing out of it on the left side, like it had struck something with unbelievable force, but it had done the job of protecting his head. It's a wonder he came through it with nothing more than a concussion.

"Tally, what's going on with you?" Trevor asked, grabbing her hand as she reached to adjust his covers.

"Nothing. It was a bad accident, Trevor. He could have been killed."

"But he wasn't and I'm sending up prayers of thanksgiving that he survived. If I know Gage, and he manages to stay in the top fifteen in the rodeo rankings, he'll do everything in his power to be in Las Vegas in December, competing with the best of them. He should be healed enough by then to do it."

"You're as nuts as he is," Tally said, throwing her hands in the air. "What sane person would climb on the back of a bronc when they're recovering from this type of accident?"

Trevor grinned. "I never said he was sane, I just said he'd most likely be there competing if he holds onto one of the positions. He's high enough up, it might happen, but there are still some big rodeos in the next few weeks that could really shake up the standings."

"Let's worry about him getting through today, not some idiotic plan to create permanent injuries by trying to compete in December. He's in surgery right now, but I'll let you know when he's out of recovery."

"Thanks. I'd like to go see him. Will he be on this floor?"

She nodded. "Yes. Just down the hall." Tally moved to the door then stopped and looked back at her brother. "Is there anyone in his family we should notify?"

"No. He's barely speaking to his brother and

his folks won't care. I'll text a few friends and they can spread the word." Trevor picked up his phone then glanced at her. "In fact, he's gonna need somewhere to recuperate for a while. Since you're already taking time off to help me…"

"No, Trevor. Absolutely not. I'll have my hands full with you." Tally couldn't even wrap her head around having Gage at the ranch the next several weeks. How would she ignore him if she was providing his care on a daily basis? "Besides, doesn't he have an entourage of girlfriends who can help him out?"

"Nope." Trevor grinned at her. "He just mentioned this morning he's been focused on rodeo instead of women this year."

"I find that hard to believe," Tally mumbled under her breath.

"What was that?" Trevor asked, although his knowing grin made her think he heard every word she said.

"I'll check on you later."

Before Trevor could offer more arguments or reasons why she should play nursemaid to both him and Gage, she returned to work, even if her thoughts remained on Gage.

He truly must have an entire fleet of angels watching over him to come through such a horrific accident with as few injuries as he sustained. She'd seen a photo of his motorbike. It was nothing more than a twisted chunk of metal now. She sent up another prayer of thanks that he'd survived with nothing more than a broken hand and leg. Bones would heal. But… no, she couldn't think about what might have happened. And she definitely wouldn't stop to examine the reason she cared about him. He was a friend of Trevor's. That had to be why she was concerned.

That was definitely it. It couldn't be because she couldn't get the picture of his teasing smile out of her head or the unique masculine scent of him out of her nose.

Chapter Five

"Shh. You'll wake him up and he needs his rest."

Gage heard the soft, feminine voice and tried to place it. The face that came to mind was Trevor's sister, but why would Tally King be in his room? That was something that would only happen in a fantasy, not reality.

Come to think of it, he wasn't sure where he'd spent the night. A hotel room? If so, it certainly had a strong scent of cleanser, or maybe it was disinfectant. Ugh. Why would his hotel room smell like a hospital room?

He remembered visiting Trevor at the hospital before he headed out for a rodeo. Did he ride? Had he gotten hurt? He wondered if he scored or placed.

He shifted and acute pain shot through his leg all the way to his head. It hurt so bad he had to swallow twice and clamp his jaw to keep from throwing up.

"See what you did," the feminine voice spoke again. "I told you to be quiet."

"You're the one yammering," Trevor's voice said.

Why was Trevor there? How could he go anywhere since he was in a hospital bed in Kennewick?

Suddenly, Gage popped his eyes open and stared at the King siblings. Trevor sat in a chair with a pair of crutches in his hands while Tally leaned toward him, holding a plastic dishpan, as though she was ready to provide assistance if it was needed.

"Where am I?" he asked, but his throat felt dry and his tongue thick.

"You're in the hospital, Gage," Tally said, setting down the dishpan and picking up a cup of water. She held a straw to his lips. "You had an accident earlier today."

He took a sip and she moved the cup away. A slight turn of his head made him swallow hard, again, as bile rose up his throat.

"Be still, Gage. You're probably going to feel a little nauseated and disoriented for a while." Tally brushed her fingers across his forehead.

That simple touch felt so soothing and good. He sighed and tried to relax.

Tally said he had an accident. That would explain why his head thumped in time with his heart and his leg throbbed. He held still, but took stock of what hurt and at that moment "everything" seemed to cover it. Even his toes and hair ached.

"What happened?" he asked.

"After an old geezer ran into you, your bike skidded along a hundred feet of freeway," Trevor said, leaning forward, arms propped through the handles of his crutches. "You're lucky to be alive, man, and I'm real grateful you are."

"Me, too," Gage said, accepting the straw Tally held out to him again. When she set the cup back on a table, he looked at her. "What's broken?"

"Your right leg and left hand. Earlier, you expressed your joy that it wasn't your riding hand." She gave him an indulgent smile that let him know she thought he was an idiot. "You've also got a concussion and a bit of road rash, but all things considered, you are very fortunate that's all that's damaged."

"I don't feel so lucky right at this moment." He lifted his head and moved his left hand to look at it. A wave of pain almost made his eyes cross.

"You don't have to suffer, Gage. We'll get you something to ease the pain." Tally disappeared from the room.

"I really am glad you're gonna be okay, man. You gave us, Tally in particular, quite a scare when they wheeled you in." Trevor gave him a long look. "Do you want me to let your folks or Tim know about the accident?"

"No." Gage didn't need to hear I-told-you-so from his parents or another long-winded lecture from his brother about why he needed to get his head on straight and stop playing cowboy.

"Look, Tally is going to use two weeks of her vacation time to help out at the ranch and keep an eye on me. Why don't you stay with us? We've got plenty of room and you'd have a nurse right there in case you needed one."

The thought of spending a few weeks around Tally held a great deal of appeal, but the few rational brain cells still functioning in Gage's aching head screamed it was a terrible idea. She was a distraction he couldn't afford, and he'd already promised to stay away from her, but at that moment, he didn't have many choices.

Chase and Jessie Jarrett would welcome him, but Chase was competing in all the area rodeos in the next month. Then there was the annual Lasso Eight photo shoot taking place at their ranch in two weeks. And he wasn't sure how much experience Jessie had as a caregiver, not that he'd let her do anything for him anyway.

Cooper and Paige James would take him in, but they were both in the area, staying in their travel trailer. Even if he could make it to their ranch in St. Paul, he hated to be a burden to Cooper's grandpa and their housekeeper.

Shaun and Brylee Price were another option, but they were as busy with the rodeo circuit as his other friends. Shaun was a pickup man and Brylee was doing her best to hold onto her title of world champion barrel racer. Neither of them had time for taking care of him.

No, his best option, other than checking into a hotel while his wounds healed, was to go home with Trevor. He'd just have to pretend Tally was still a starry-eyed teenager instead of a beautiful woman who stirred his interest more than any other female ever had.

She returned with a doctor and soon Gage was drifting off to sleep, dreaming of Tally's smile.

The next morning, in a flurry of papers, orders, and action, Gage found himself dressed in a tank top and a pair of basketball shorts Tally brought for him to wear. Before he could gather his wits, he was seated in the backseat of Trevor's pickup with his right leg propped up on the seat.

According to the doctor who signed his release papers, he needed to take it easy for the next week. Unable to use crutches with his broken hand, he would be stuck in a wheelchair until further notice.

The good news was that the doctor hadn't needed to put any hardware in his leg. A heavy cast that started above his knee and went clear down to his toes kept his leg immobile so it could heal, but he had an idea, from past experiences with casts, he was going to be miserable before it came off.

His broken hand looked like an experiment by Doctor Frankenstein. Pins poked out of it and a row of dark stitches crisscrossed the back. A nurse had used straps across his forearm and non-broken fingers to attach his hand to a soft foam board that would keep his hand protected and provide support.

Every movement of his head caused it to pound with pain, but he didn't want more drugs. He needed to stay alert lest he say something to Tally he shouldn't.

Part of him was so thankful Tally and Trevor had offered him a place to stay. The other part dreaded trying to keep his guard up around Tally for the next few weeks. Maybe he and Trevor would drive her nuts and she'd go back to work early, leaving the two of them to fend for themselves.

He doubted it, though. If she was anything like Ross and Trevor, her word was a bond she wouldn't break.

After she settled Trevor in the front seat with a pile of pillows to prop up his leg, she set his crutches in the back along with Gage's wheelchair and waved to the staff that had helped get them and their gear outside.

Someone had brought his belongings from his mangled bike. Thank goodness, the saddlebags had remained mostly intact, so other than a duffle bag with skid marks along the outside, everything was in good shape.

Tally climbed up into the truck and fastened her seatbelt. She wasn't short, but she wasn't tall either and Trevor didn't have running boards on his pickup. He'd watched as she used the steering wheel to pull herself onto the seat.

"Any jokes about my height and I'll leave you on the side of the road," she said, glaring from Trevor to Gage.

Trevor grinned but Gage closed his eyes, trying to ignore the effect she had on him.

He hadn't seen her all morning, but when she'd shown up in his room as the doctor was giving him a list of dos and don'ts, he lost the ability to listen to a word the man said. Tally's hair was pulled back in a thick ponytail, but a few tendrils escaped and framed her face. Instead of scrubs, she had on a flowing, long skirt, sandals, and a white summery blouse that accented her golden tan.

He opened his eyes and watched as she slipped

on a pair of sunglasses that made her look like a movie star in the making. She started the pickup, shifted into gear, and drove with ease through the traffic.

Gage fell asleep before they'd made it beyond Kennewick's city limits. He awoke when the pickup bounced over the cattle guard as Tally turned off the road onto the King Penny Ranch lane. They drove beneath an arch with a metal sign that bore the ranch's brand of a reversed K connected to a P.

Fat Angus cattle grazed in a pasture of verdant grass near the road. In the distance, he could see someone stacking big round bales of hay on the back of a semi-trailer.

"How was wheat harvest this year?" Gage asked, glancing at the fields covered in stubble that had not yet been worked up in preparation for next year. He wondered how Trevor would handle not being able to help with the autumn farm work. The King Penny Ranch encompassed several thousand acres, a good portion of which was wheat. Trevor also raised hay, corn, and ran an impressive herd of cattle.

"We had a great harvest and thank goodness it's finished, or I don't know what I'd do. The fields need to be worked up and our winter wheat planted, but we'll get it done, somehow," Trevor said. He glanced over the front seat as they followed the lane around a curve and the ranch house came into view.

Gage always liked the homey appearance of it. He knew it had been built back in the early 1900s and renovated several times, but the house sported a new roof from the last time he'd been there. A recently applied coat of white paint gave it a fresh appearance and contrasted sharply to the dark gray shutters, crisply framing the windows.

A porch stretched across the front of the house with a broad set of steps in the center that widened as they reached the front walk. The balustrade curved around to the sides, almost like a friendly smile.

Colorful flowers and bushes bloomed around the porch and the grass appeared to have been freshly mown.

A white-haired old woman in a hot pink dress with polka dots the size of golf balls stood in the middle of the lawn twirling a hula hoop around her waist. A vibrant red flower bobbed above her left ear and she held both hands in the air, giggling like a child.

"Aunt Marvella," Gage said. He watched the woman continue to send the hoop in perfect circles as though she was thirteen instead of an octogenarian. "I'd forgotten she was here."

Tally looked over her shoulder and smiled. "You must have whacked your head harder than we thought if you could forget about Aunt Marv."

Gage grinned at her then looked at her aunt. "How old is she now?"

"Eighty-two, but don't mention her age," Trevor said as Tally pulled around in front of the house. "She tells everyone she's barely seventy."

Three, or maybe it was four years ago, Trevor and Tally had moved Marvella Hawkins into a little guest house behind the main ranch house. The woman was really their mother's aunt. She possessed the sight of a hawk and could hear a pin drop at fifty yards, but the woman had the attention span of a snockered gnat. After a series of incidents that included catching her kitchen on fire when she left a pan of oil on the stove unattended, Trevor decided it wasn't safe for her to live on her own anymore. She refused to go to a care facility or move in with him, so Trevor had converted what had once been a storage barn for carriages into a home for Marvella.

Gage thought she was a hoot, because one never knew what she might say or do. She wasn't allowed to cook unless supervised, but she did clean house for Trevor and helped weed the flower beds and garden. Last he'd heard, Trevor had taken away Marvella's car keys when she'd almost caused a collision on the freeway. The concession was that she was allowed to drive into the small nearby town of Echo, but that was it. Everyone there knew to watch out for Marvella in her sable brown Cadillac Coupe deVille that she drove brand new off the showroom floor back in 1988.

Tally had barely stopped the pickup and shut off the ignition when Marvella tossed the hula hoop aside and scurried across the grass, waving both hands in greeting.

"You're home! You're home!" Marvella squealed when Trevor opened his door. She didn't even give him a chance to get out before she reached up and bracketed his cheeks with her palms and pulled his head down, leaving behind a smudge of orange lipstick where she'd kissed him on his forehead.

Gage wasn't sure he felt up to such an enthusiastic greeting and remained quietly waiting in the back.

Tally appeared beside her aunt and gave the woman a hug while gently nudging her out of the way then handed Trevor his crutches.

By then, the crew that worked on the ranch appeared and offered steadying hands to help Trevor navigate his way down the walk and up the front steps.

Tally started to heft the wheelchair out of the back of the pickup, but two cowboys Gage recognized took charge of it and got it set up in front of the passenger door.

"Ready to do this?" Tally asked, opening his door and motioning for him to scoot backward toward her.

"Whether I am or not, I can't stay out here all day," Gage said, offering her what he hoped was a teasing grin. His head hurt so bad, he couldn't quite see straight and that was a cakewalk compared to the pain shooting up his arm from his hand and burning across his injured leg.

She looked to the two cowboys. "You're going to have to lift him out and set him in the chair. I'll keep it steady. Then I'm going to need help getting it into the house."

"Yes, ma'am," Jared said, moving so he stood on one side of Gage.

"We'll try not to drop you," a young cowboy named Tony said.

"I'd appreciate it if you didn't," Gage said, smiling in spite of the pain. He settled his right arm across Jared's shoulder but couldn't lift his left one, so he held it against his chest.

He felt the two cowboys lift him out and set him in the chair. When he was seated, he released a long sigh of relief. Beads of sweat rolled down his forehead, but a lacy handkerchief that smelled like a mixture of menthol and lilacs wiped it away.

The next thing he knew, Marvella had kissed him on the cheek, leaving him branded with a lipstick smear similar to Trevor's.

"Welcome home, honey," she said, patting him on the head like he was five before she sailed down the walk and into the house.

"She hasn't changed a bit, has she?" he asked, glancing up at Tally.

"Nope. I wish I had even half her energy and sass," Tally said as she turned the chair and attempted to push it through the gravel to where the sidewalk began.

Jared and Tony lifted the front tires and pulled until they reached the walk then Tally pushed the chair right up to the front steps.

"We might need a little extra help for this," Jared said, eying Gage and the wheelchair. He dashed up the steps and disappeared inside the double front doors that had been opened wide. In less than a minute he was back with two more cowboys. One was a new face to Gage, but the other was an older man who'd worked on the place since before Trevor was born.

"Nice to see you again, Judd," Gage said, holding out his right hand to the man.

Judd shook it then gave Gage a long look. "If I

didn't know better, I'd say you and Trev had this all planned out to force Tally to take some time off work."

Gage grinned at the old cowboy then let his gaze settle on Tally. "No sir, but I sure can't complain about having a beautiful nurse around to take care of me."

"You just mind your manners, son," Judd said with a warning scowl. When each of the cowboys had their hands on a corner of the wheelchair, Judd nodded. "Lift 'em up, boys."

Tally stayed right beside them as they carried him up the steps and set him down on the porch. By then, Gage fought against the urge to throw up or pass out, in no particular order.

"Let's get him into the recliner there by Trevor's," she said, taking the handles of the wheelchair and pulling him over the threshold of the door with a soft bump.

Gage closed his eyes and focused all his energy on not losing his breakfast. He felt hands on him, lifting him up again, and then he was sinking into the soft cushions of one of Trevor's big leather recliners. Someone had covered it with a sheet that felt smooth and cool beneath his hand.

He opened his eyes and looked around at the faces hovering over him. "Thank you. I sure appreciate the help."

"Anytime," Judd said, nodding at him. "You two boys just rest up and we'll check in on you later."

Gage noticed Trevor propped up in the recliner on the other side of a wide end table made of reclaimed barnwood. His friend looked exhausted and his color didn't look quite right. He wondered if he looked as bad then decided he'd probably rather not know.

Tally disappeared but soon returned carrying a large tray. She set it down on the coffee table. Gage could see pill bottles, glasses of water, and a plate of cookies along with two bananas, some sliced cheese, and crackers.

"Do either of you want something to eat?"

Trevor shook his head, but Gage couldn't even manage to do that.

Tally glanced from him to Trevor with concern evident on her face. "Aunt Marv, you give this to Trevor, while I take care of Gage," she said, handing her aunt two pills and a glass with a straw.

"I'm not a baby, I can..." Trevor started to protest, but his aunt shoved the pills into his mouth followed by a straw.

Before something similar happened to him, Gage opened his mouth. Tally dropped the pills on his tongue then held a straw to his lips. He took a long drink, leaning back and closing his eyes.

The last thing he remembered before falling asleep was the feel of her cool, soft fingers, brushing against his skin then feathering through his hair.

When he awoke, the house was dark and quiet. A sliver of light illuminated the darkness to his left from what had to be a night light in the bathroom just down the hall. To his right, a ribbon of soft yellow glowed from the kitchen, most likely from a light located over the stove.

He stirred and failed to swallow back a groan at the pain the movement created.

"What do you need, Gage?" Tally asked, from the shadows. He hadn't noticed her across the room or Trevor asleep in the recliner near his. No wonder there had been sheets on the recliners when they got there. Tally must have known they'd fall asleep and spend the night in the chairs. He moved his right hand and felt a sheet covering his lap. It was then he realized the chair had been moved so it fully reclined, like a bed. He tried to sit up a little and grunted with the effort.

Gracefully, she rose from the couch and moved to stand next to his chair. She placed a cool hand on his forehead. "No fever. That's good."

If he hadn't hurt so badly, he surely would have developed a fever, but not the type she had in mind. The woman had no idea what her presence did to him. Just the gentle touch of her palm against his skin sent chills racing over him. How could that be? What was it about her that affected him so?

He decided it must be the medicine he'd taken for the pain. There really wasn't any other reasonable excuse for his reaction to her touch.

Maybe he was hallucinating and none of this had really happened. If he closed his eyes and woke himself up, he could be in a hotel room or a buddy's travel trailer. Gage squeezed his eyes and reopened them when the tip of Tally's braid brushed against his neck as she leaned over him.

He groaned again, but this time it wasn't from the pain.

"Eat this," she said, holding out a banana she'd

peeled for him. He took it in his right hand and ate it in a few bites. She handed him two pills. He placed them in his mouth then accepted the straw she held out for him. The cool water felt good as it slid down his throat.

"Thanks," he whispered when she set the glass back on the coffee table.

"Are you comfortable? Do you need me to move the chair?" she asked in a quiet voice.

"No. I'm fine," he said, taking in the fact she wore an oversized T-shirt and a pair of cotton lounge pants. The loose clothes hid her shape even more than the scrubs. He remembered when she was younger Tally had been self-conscious about her weight. She was bigger than most of her classmates, but he never thought she looked fat. He'd always thought of her as Trevor's cute little sister.

Now, as she tugged at her shirt, as though she wanted to hide behind it, he wondered if she was still insecure about her figure. From what little he'd seen, she had nothing to be embarrassed about. Tally was a beautiful, enticing woman. If things were different, she was one he'd definitely pursue. But he wouldn't, no matter how much he might want to.

He needed to spend the next several weeks focusing on healing as fast as humanly possible. If, by some miracle, he didn't get knocked so far down the standings that he wouldn't compete in Vegas, he had to be ready to ride in December. It would take every ounce of his strength and concentration to be ready to do that. Besides, even if that wasn't a factor, he'd promised Trevor he'd leave Tally alone and he wouldn't go back on his word.

She gave him a long look then disappeared into the kitchen. Gage closed his eyes and tried to go back to sleep.

"Gage," she whispered as she touched a cool, damp cloth to his face.

He opened one eye and stared at her.

She smiled at him. "I didn't want to startle you."

He closed his eyes and relaxed as she bathed his face and neck, then rubbed the cloth along his right arm and hand. She tucked his hand under the sheet then he felt the lightest brush of her lips against his forehead. "Go to sleep, cowboy."

Gage wanted to reach up and pull her down for a real kiss, but he was already falling back to sleep, ready to dream of a gray-eyed beauty who made him think of Christmas.

Chapter Six

Gage awakened with an odd sense of being watched. Unsettled, his eyes popped open and he tamped down a startled yelp when a face loomed just inches away. A pair of thick black-rimmed glasses covered blue eyes framed by wrinkles while the scent of menthol and lilacs drifted around him.

"Morning, Aunt Marv," he said, wondering what the wacky ol' gal was up to. He glanced over to see Trevor's empty chair and Tally no longer on the couch.

"Morning, sunshine!" Marvella beamed at him, although she continued to hover too close for his comfort. "Trevor's in the kitchen talking to Judd and Tally will be down shortly. Want to join us at the table for breakfast or have it in here?"

Gage was already sick to death of the recliner, so he carefully moved the chair into an upright position as Marvella shifted out of the way. "I'll come to the kitchen, but I might need a little help getting there."

"Not to worry, honey," Marvella said. She patted his cheek and then scurried off to the kitchen, setting the full skirt of her yellow and gray plaid dress swinging.

He shook his head and ran his hand through his hair then scrubbed it over his face, scratching over the stubble sprouting along his cheeks and chin. He needed a shave, and a shower. He tried to remember what the doctor had said about baths but couldn't recall what directives he'd been given. Tally would know, even if he hated to ask her.

"I hear you're ready to get up out of that chair," Judd said as he sauntered into the great room.

Gage nodded. "I am, sir. If I sit here too much longer, I might set down roots and never leave, and we can't have that."

Judd chuckled. "Nope. We sure can't." The older man moved the wheelchair as close as he could to the recliner and braced it. He held out a hand and pulled Gage upright then helped him pivot on his good leg and settle in the chair.

Although his head throbbed, it wasn't the intense drumming he'd endured the previous day. His leg didn't ache quite as badly either. He took that as a good sign as Judd wheeled him across the expanse of the large room toward the kitchen.

He knew down the hallway off the great room he'd find a bathroom and two bedrooms. An office that used to be a dining room was opposite the entry foyer. A big, sunny kitchen had a farmhouse table that could seat a dozen people in a nook that looked out on a pasture behind the house. Through the kitchen down a short hallway to the left was a master suite Trevor had added on when he'd remodeled the kitchen a few years ago. A mudroom, small bathroom, and utility room were down the hallway to the right. Through the mudroom, a door entered into a three-car garage Ross had built onto the house the summer before Gage worked there. Upstairs there was a sun-dappled bedroom with a private bathroom that had always been Tally's domain, along with a room that was full of books, board games, and comfy chairs.

Judd pushed Gage into the kitchen past the round bar made from a tree trunk cut right there on the ranch and the four stools surrounding it fashioned from antique cast iron tractor seats. The wooden plank floor came from an old granary that had been falling down. He'd been there when Trevor decided to reclaim the wood and helped pull all the nails from the boards. The cabinets were made of old wooden doors while the counters were poured concrete embossed with an acanthus scroll design and stained brown to look like leather. Many coats of sealant gave it a smooth, durable surface.

He was almost to the table when Tally bounded down the steps and came to a stop as she gaped at him in surprise.

"You're up. I didn't think we'd get you out of that recliner today," she said, smiling as she moved a chair out of the way so Judd could push him right up to the table.

Her scent ensnared his senses while he longed to reach out and wind a strand of her long, wavy hair, still damp from the shower, around his fingers.

The way the V-neck T-shirt and cotton shorts she wore fit her form made his mouth go dry.

He'd guessed she was curvier than most women he knew, but man alive, he hadn't expected her to be quite so... voluptuous. No wonder she kept all that hidden beneath her scrubs. If she didn't, she'd be chasing men off with a shotgun on a daily basis.

"You sleep okay?" Trevor asked, drawing him out of his musings about Tally and back to the moment.

"Sure did," Gage said, looking directly at Tally. She blushed and spun away, hurrying over to the stove where she pulled something from the oven. Marvella set the muffins in a napkin-lined basket and carried them to the table while Tally cracked eggs into a skillet and scrambled a pan full of eggs. She carried the skillet over to the table and spooned a serving onto each of their plates, then left the skillet soaking in the sink.

Marvella filled coffee cups while Judd set juice and milk on the table.

"What's your poison, son?" Judd asked, holding up a pitcher of orange juice in one hand and cranberry juice in the other.

"Cranberry," Gage said, draping the napkin next to his plate across his lap.

Judd seated Marvella by Trevor then Tally next to him before he took a seat at the table. He glanced over at Trevor who nodded, and they all bowed their heads as Trevor offered thanks.

When he finished, Tally took two of the muffins and broke them open. Steam wafted up around her face. Unable to look away, Gage watched her every move until she buttered the muffins and set them on his plate.

"You got this?" she asked, gently nudging his right arm with her elbow. "I could toss it all in the blender if you'd rather."

Gage grimaced. "That won't be necessary. Thanks for that enticing offer, though."

Tally smiled and her nose wrinkled slightly on the end, just like it had when she was younger and inordinately pleased about something.

He bit into one of the warm muffins, surprised to find it tasted of sweet cherries instead of the berries he'd been expecting.

"Cherry?" he asked and looked at Tally.

"Cooper and Paige brought a bunch to us the other day," Trevor said as he buttered a muffin and took a bite. "Tally promised she'd do something with them all."

"And I will," she said, taking a muffin from the basket for herself before she set it back in the middle of the table. "As soon as I get you two squared away for the morning, I plan to make pies to put in the freezer."

"How about to eat? Can you make a few of those, too?" Trevor asked, giving Tally a pleading look.

Gage would have joined in begging, but he wasn't sure that would help their cause at all, although Tally did seem to be in a good mood this morning. She wasn't nearly as frosty as she'd been the other night at the rodeo or even yesterday.

"These are good, Tally," Judd said, helping

himself to another muffin. "The boys won't like it that they had to fend for themselves this morning while I'm over here enjoying this."

"I made plenty. You can take some back to them," Tally said, smiling at the older man.

Conversation turned to the work that needed to be done on the ranch that day, if they had plenty of supplies, and what the weather forecast predicted for the coming week.

By the time he'd finished eating, Gage felt like he'd run twenty miles uphill in a hard rain. Exhausted beyond belief, he could barely keep his eyes open as he drained his glass of juice then wiped his mouth on his napkin.

"Before you drift off to dreamland, you better take these," Tally said, giving him his medication. She got a glass of water for him and he drank part of it before he set it back on the table.

"Recliner or bedroom?" Judd asked as he stood and rolled Gage away from the table.

"Recliner, I think," he heard Tally say, even if his eyes refused to obey his orders to stay open.

He tried to help when he felt hands moving him from the wheelchair to the recliner. A sheet settled over him and he fell asleep with a vision of Tally making him smile.

Chapter Seven

"Do we have more canning jars, Aunt Marv?" Tally asked as she pulled a peach cobbler from the oven.

"There might be some out in the storage shed," Marvella said as she peeled peaches and sliced them into a bowl. Marvella was a great help, as long as she kept focused on the task at hand.

Since Tally was home and in need of something to occupy her time between taking care of two injured cowboys, she'd gone to a local fruit stand yesterday after getting Trevor and Gage settled in their recliners. She purchased peaches, raspberries, and strawberries to go with the cherries Cooper James had left for them and had spent the past two days making jam, pies, crisps, cobblers, and muffins. She'd also put several bags of berries in the freezer to take out to use later.

A few gallons of peaches remained to use up and she wanted to can them, but they'd used all the jars she'd found in the house and garage.

"I'll run out and check," she said, wiping her hands on a dishtowel and leaving the cool air of the kitchen behind as she jogged across the yard over to the storage building where they kept everything from the Christmas decorations to rusty milk cans neither one of them could quite part with.

Tally turned the latch on the door and stepped inside, letting her eyes adjust to the dim interior.

"Jars, jars, jars," she muttered as she wiggled around a stack of storage tubs filled with Christmas lights and wreaths. She moved aside an old rocking chair wrapped in a frayed chenille bedspread, then weaved her way around various boxes and pieces of old furniture to reach the storage shelves on the back wall. A box full of canning jars caught her eye as she stepped over an old wooden apple basket.

She reached out for the box when a blur of green headed straight for her. Tally sidestepped just in time to avoid having a little frog land right on her. She hated the thought of anything crawling on her and shivered as she scowled at the frog that hightailed it behind an old ceramic pickle crock.

"You better hide, because I'd forcibly remove you if I wasn't busy right now." She picked up the box of jars and carried it outside, setting it down on a bench made from old iron wheels with a thick board running between them. She returned inside to see if she could find more jars in case she needed them. Unable to locate any, she was on her way back to the door when the frog launched another assault from the top of an old seeder. It landed at the base of her throat and hopped down the neck of her

T-shirt before she could blink.

While Tally wasn't one normally given to bouts of panic, she raced outside, screaming like her life was about to end while trying to fish the frog out of the front of her shirt. When she finally caught the frog, she flung it hard then looked up to see half a dozen men gaping at her like she'd lost her mind.

Trevor was halfway across the yard on his crutches and Gage was trying to get out the front door of the house in his wheelchair, like he considered hopping on one foot to her rescue.

Judd covered his mouth with one hand to hide his grin and cleared his throat twice before he moved closer to her. "You okay, Tally?"

"Yes," she said, snatching up the box of jars and kicking the door to the storage building shut with more force than necessary. Heat burned from the roots of her hair all the way down her neck.

"What happened?" Judd asked, holding out his hands to take the box of jars, but she refused to relinquish her hold on them.

"Apparently, an attack frog was defending what he viewed as his territory in there," she said, forcing herself to smile as she speed-walked toward the house.

The men chuckled and laughed then went back to work. She slowed her steps when she reached Trevor.

"Are you sure you're fine? I know you hate things that hop, crawl, or slither," he said as he took careful steps toward the house.

"I'm fine, it just grossed me out, Trev. And that frog better be careful because if it's still alive, it won't be if I find it back in there." She glanced at the storage building then back at her brother.

Wisely, Trevor didn't offer any comment as they made their way up the steps. She refused to make eye contact with Gage. He, too, seemed to sense the wisdom of keeping his thoughts to himself, but she could have sworn she heard him say, "wish I'd been that frog."

When she glared at him over her shoulder, his face was a mask of innocence, but Trevor couldn't hide his snickers.

"Men!" she huffed, then hurried inside the house, slammed the door behind her, and retreated to the kitchen.

"What was all the noise out there?" Marvella asked as Tally set the jars down on the counter with a thud that rattled the glass and sent a puff of dust into the air that caused her to sneeze.

"I had a little problem with a frog. Nothing to worry about," she said before racing upstairs. She took off her shirt, scrubbed every centimeter of skin the frog touched with a disinfectant wipe, then yanked on a clean shirt and returned to the kitchen.

Trevor and Gage returned inside and took a nap. When they awakened an hour later, they decided to sit on the front porch for a while. Aunt Marv served them both iced tea and cookies since Tally refused to speak to either of them.

She and Marvella had just finished taking the last batch of peaches out of the canning kettle when she heard shouting from the porch and Trevor banged his crutch against the wall.

"Go see what's wrong with those boys before

Trevor pokes a hole through the wall," Marvella said, yanking the potholders out of Tally's hands.

Tally raced through the house out to the front porch where Trevor was trying to push Gage over the threshold with one hand.

"You're going to end up in a chair with him if you don't stop that," Tally said, grabbing the handles of Gage's wheelchair and pushing him inside. "What's gotten into you?"

"Betty Brewster," Trevor said, looking out to where an old, rusty pickup rattled up the lane toward the house. "She's been trying to pair me up with that daughter of hers for years and you know it. Please, Tally, help us!"

Tally wanted to laugh at the desperate look on her brother's face, but she managed to subdue it while she wheeled Gage into the office since it was the closest room with a door. Trevor followed her inside and sank onto one of the chairs flanking the large desk.

"You two stay in here and keep quiet. If we're lucky, she won't stay long," Tally said, closing the door behind her then going to warn Aunt Marv that Trevor and Gage were resting, should anyone ask.

"If that Betty wasn't such a good cook and gossip, I'd never let her set foot inside the house," Marvella said with a wink. She snatched off her juice-splattered apron, whipped a tube of bright pink lipstick out of her pocket and applied it, then fluffed her white bobbed hair. "I'll get the door, sweetheart. You might want to wash your face."

Tally stepped into the bathroom off the kitchen and wiped a smudge of flour off her nose and a trail of cinnamon from her cheek. She unwound her braid, flipped her head over and tousled her hair, then pinched her cheeks.

Marvella was just welcoming Betty and her daughter, Arielle, when she walked into the foyer.

"Mrs. Brewster, how nice to see you," Tally said, forcing a welcoming smile. "And you, too, Arielle. What brings you ladies to the King Penny Ranch?"

"Well, we heard Trevor had a little accident and one of his friends is here, too. We thought you might have your hands full taking care of them, so we brought over some supper. Arielle, here, made the casserole all by herself. She's turning into quite a good cook."

The woman held out a box full of foil-wrapped pans.

"How kind of you," Tally said, taking the box and smiling at the two women. If Arielle had been twelve, she could see her mother bragging on her. But the woman was in her mid-forties and still lived at home. As far as anyone knew, she preferred sitting in the house reading to anything else. She'd never worked anywhere except on her parents' farm, and even the amount of work she did there was questionable.

For the past ten years, Betty had been trying to get Trevor to take Arielle out on a date. The fact her daughter was fifteen years older than him never seemed to enter Betty's thoughts, but she'd grown quite relentless in her pursuit of making Trevor her son-in-law. Tally wondered if it was the fact her brother was handsome and a former rodeo star, or the thought of getting her hands on the King Penny Ranch that spurred her on in her efforts.

However, Trevor had no interest in Betty's plans or Arielle. In fact, it had become quite a joke about the next time Betty would pop up and try to play matchmaker again.

Of course, with Trevor injured, Betty would pounce on the opportunity to find him trapped in the house and unable to get away. After all, he and Gage had only been home from the hospital a little more than forty-eight hours.

"Where is Trevor?" Betty asked, shoving Arielle forward and shutting the door behind her, making it clear this wouldn't be a quick visit. The woman craned her neck as though she hoped to get a glimpse of him. "Is his friend still here?"

"Both those boys are resting right now," Marvella said, looping her arm around Betty's and guiding her into the kitchen.

Tally waited while Arielle shuffled along behind her mother, head down, and shoulders slumped. It was hard not to feel sorry for the woman, but it was long past time for her to stand up to her mother and her meddling.

"You'll have to pardon our mess, we've spent the day baking and canning," Marvella said as she pulled out a chair at the table. "I do hope you ladies have time for a glass of lemonade and a slice of pie. Tally just pulled a cherry pie from the oven a little bit ago and it should be just about ready to eat."

Betty shook her head. "I can't abide cherries, but I'll take a glass of lemonade. You don't, by chance, have any of your chocolate chip cookies, do you, Tally?"

Tally had made a batch last night and Gage and Trevor hadn't eaten them all yet. She placed half a dozen on a plate and set it on the table while Aunt Marvella poured lemonade into two glasses and set them in front of Betty and Arielle.

"Did I hear Nancy June Ledbetter wants to get the town motto painted on the church?" Marvella asked as she took a seat at the table and slid the cookies toward Betty.

Tally sat next to her aunt and hid a grin behind her glass of lemonade. She knew Nancy June was Betty's sworn enemy, mostly because Nancy June's son had been in the chute to marry Arielle and ran off with one of the Baker girls three weeks before the wedding. Not that anyone blamed him, but from that moment on, Betty had turned on her friend and hadn't found a kind thing to say about her for the past twenty-odd years.

"That woman!" Betty fumed and went on to state her opinions on everything from why the motto didn't belong on the church to the fact Nancy June's front yard looked purely parched and she hoped her dahlias all withered into crispy brown straws.

"Well, look at the time," Marvella said, rising to her feet after she and Tally had listened to Betty's ranting for the better part of half an hour. "We better get that last batch of jam made before the boys wake up from their naps, honey."

Before Betty knew quite what had happened, Marvella had walked her to the front door with a promise to return any dishes she left behind at church on Sunday. Arielle strode ahead to the pickup and climbed in on the passenger side while Betty blinked in surprise as Tally leaned over her aunt's thin shoulder and waved goodbye.

"Thanks again for bringing over a meal, Mrs. Brewster. That was so nice of you," Tally called just before Marvella shut the door.

"Well, good riddance," Marvella said, brushing off her hands like she'd touched something filthy. She glanced out the window by the door to make sure Betty was truly leaving. Tally watched as Betty turned around and left in a cloud of dust.

"You're safe now," Tally said, opening the door to the office. Trevor sat in a chair with his leg propped up on the other while Gage sat on the other side of the desk. The two of them appeared to be playing cards.

"I win again!" Trevor crowed, tossing his cards on the desk.

"Well, you try playing one-handed and see how well you do," Gage said, throwing down his cards.

"I'm starving. I thought that bat would never fly off on her rusty broomstick," Trevor said as he picked up his crutches, pulled himself up from the chair, and headed toward the door.

"It's not a bat on a broomstick, honey. That would be a witch and all Betty needs is a black hat," Marvella said, leading the way back to the kitchen.

Tally pushed Gage's chair out of the office and up to the table. She hurried to clear away the glasses and napkins from Betty and Arielle's visit and set the table for dinner.

"Something smells good," Trevor said, leaning

over the box Betty had left.

"You shouldn't call her names if you're willing to eat her food," Tally said, pulling out a disposable foil casserole pan. She removed the lid to reveal a cheese-topped hamburger casserole. "I'll pop this in the oven to warm it up."

"Do you boys want lemonade or tea?" Marvella asked.

"Tea," they answered in unison.

"Tea it is," Marvella said, hurrying to pour four glasses and set them on the table.

"What else is in that box?" Trevor asked.

"Hold your horses and I'll see," Tally said, pulling out more covered dishes. "It looks like there are dinner rolls. Betty might be a blabbermouth, but she sure makes good rolls. I see sliced tomatoes and cucumbers, oh, and those." Tally's nose wrinkled in disgust as she set a bowl on the counter.

"Nope, not eating 'em." Trevor turned his face away and grimaced.

"What is it?" Gage asked, trying to see from his seat at the table.

"Brussels sprouts," Trevor said, looking like he might gag just saying the name.

"Yuck!" Gage turned up his nose, too. "Brussels sprouts taste like a rotten little cabbage had an unfortunate incident with a demented skunk. No thank you. A hard pass on those."

Tally grinned and Trevor chuckled, but Marvella picked up the bowl and set it on the table near her plate with a loud thud.

"I happen to like them, so more for me to enjoy." She glared at Trevor then Gage. "If you boys don't at least try one, I'll tell Betty you both would love to spend Sunday afternoon sitting on the porch with Arielle."

"No, no, no!" Trevor sank onto a chair at the table, picked up one of the offending little green orbs and popped it in his mouth.

Tally laughed as he squeezed one eye shut and tried to swallow the Brussels sprout. He glugged an entire glass of tea then held it out to Tally for a refill.

"As horrible as that was, it's better than getting stuck with Arielle," he said as she poured more tea in his glass.

"Are you going to take your medicine, too, or shall I go call Betty?" Marvella asked, pushing the bowl of Brussels sprouts toward Gage.

He glanced at Tally for help, but she just grinned at him as she held the tea pitcher and stood with one hand on Trevor's shoulder, waiting to see what he'd do.

"You're not serious, are you, Aunt Marv?" Gage looked at the old woman, expecting to see her smile and let him off the hook.

Instead, she fisted her hands on her bony hips and glowered at him. "It'll put hair on your chest."

"I've got plenty," he said, tapping a spot just above his heart.

Tally's gaze drifted from his blue eyes twinkling with humor down to his chest. He did indeed have a healthy crop of soft brown hair, visible as it peeked out from the top of the V-neck T-shirt he wore.

"Just try a bite, honey. You might change your

mind and decide you like it." Marvella speared one with a fork and held it out to him.

"You better pour a glass of lemonade for me," he said to Tally. "It might chase away the taste after I eat this. I'd like it noted that I'm eating this under duress and no other reason."

Slowly he took the fork from Marvella and studied the Brussels sprout from every angle.

Tally took pity on him. No one should be forced to eat something they disliked, especially when they'd only been out of the hospital for two days and were at the mercy of friends. She hated Brussels sprouts even more than Trevor. Aunt Marv knew better than to try and force her to eat one. The last time she'd tried that, Tally had been ten and lost her lunch all over the kitchen floor. After that, no one made her eat anything she didn't want to.

She poured a glass of lemonade and carried it over to Gage, setting it in front of him before she moved behind his chair.

"Oh, stop being such a baby," she said. She pulled the Brussels sprout off the fork, cupped her hand in front of Gage's face, and pretended to stuff the bite into his mouth. When she dropped her hand to her side, Gage played along. He spluttered and coughed then downed the glass of lemonade.

"Now, can we please eat and stop with the theatrics?" Tally asked as she crossed the kitchen and dropped the Brussels sprout in the trash before taking the casserole out of the oven.

She set it on the table, retrieved butter and jam for the rolls, and took a seat between Gage and Trevor. When they bowed their heads for Aunt

Marv to say grace, Tally cast a quick glance at Gage and winked. He grinned and reached under the table to squeeze her hand.

Heat shot up her arm and threatened to short-circuit her brain, but she sat perfectly still until Trevor's amen brought her back to the moment.

Tally gave Gage another look from beneath lowered lashes then moved her hand away from his. She was playing with fire and if she wasn't careful, she had no doubt he'd leave her poor heart in a heap of ashes.

Chapter Eight

"That's not fair!" Trevor whined when Gage came out of the doctor's office with his leg hooked into a hands-free crutch that gave him amazing mobility.

"Sorry, Trev, but with your kneecap busted, that type of crutch isn't an option," Tally said, smiling as she handed her brother his crutches and waited as he got to his feet.

Together, the three of them headed out of the hospital to the parking lot.

Gage was still adjusting to being upright and walking again, although the doctor made him practice for a good ten minutes before he turned him loose on the crutch. The doctor had to remove the original cast that went halfway up his thigh and put one on that reached just below his knee so he could bend his leg to use the crutch.

Wide bands fastened on his upper thigh and above his knee held the peg leg-style crutch in place. At knee level, a platform extended from the back of the contraption that kept his injured leg elevated and protected.

When he begged the doctor to do something to get him up and out of the wheelchair, he had no idea he'd leave the office upright. After a week of being stuck in the wheelchair, Gage was about to go stir crazy. He'd never had to sit still that long in his entire life.

If it hadn't been for having Tally around, he would have lost his mind. Instead, he'd found plenty of excuses to sit with her. And, if he wasn't mistaken, Aunt Marv was doing her best to put them together at every opportunity.

Tally treated him exactly as she did her brother. While it wasn't what he wanted, he'd take what attention from her he could get. It was better than chilly glances or being ignored altogether. He didn't know how he'd gone from being her hero to someone she clearly disdained, but he thought he'd noticed her frosty attitude toward him thawing slightly this week.

After all, she'd saved him from being forced to eat Brussels sprouts, something she hadn't even done for Trevor.

Gage grinned every time he thought about her pretending to stuff the nasty little veggie in his mouth. She'd also come to his rescue yesterday when Marvella decided he could help her choose an outfit to wear to a function the church ladies were hosting next Saturday. After watching the old woman model a dozen different dresses from what he was sure had to be as many eras, he was convinced Marvella had never gotten rid of a single article of clothing she'd ever owned.

When she walked into the great room wearing a pair of white go-go boots with a lime green and orange striped dress, he glanced toward the kitchen where Tally was making lunch, desperate to get away. Tally had told Marvella to wear the first dress she tried on and said she needed Gage to make a salad. He'd gladly chopped lettuce and cucumbers just to escape the fashion revue.

Gage felt like a new man, or at least not quite such a helpless one, as he walked behind Tally as she kept step with Trevor.

She wore her hair down and sunlight swept through the thick waves, creating golden highlights that begged for Gage to reach out and touch them. The urge was so strong, he slowed and let the King siblings get several paces ahead of him so he wouldn't be quite as tempted.

Tally opened the pickup door and helped Trevor onto the front passenger seat then glanced back at him.

"You doing okay, gimpy?" she asked with a teasing smile.

He nodded. "Yep. Just getting used to being upright again. It's an awesome feeling."

Trevor leaned his head out of the pickup and glowered. "Don't rub it in. I'm stuck with these dad-blasted crutches for who knows how long and there you are, practically ready to run a marathon."

Gage chuckled. "Let's not get too carried away, man. I won't be running anywhere until the doc gives me a full release, which can't happen a moment too soon."

"How about some lunch?" Tally asked, changing the subject as she closed Trevor's door and looked at Gage.

He glanced from his injured hand to the crutch attached to his leg, then at the back seat. He had no idea how to get in without removing the crutch and once he did that, he'd have a hard time getting it back on without help since he still couldn't do anything with his left hand.

"Come around to my side," she said, walking with him to the driver's side. She opened the door then placed her hands on his shoulder. "Turn and face me."

When he did, he wanted so badly to pull her into his arms and kiss her. Instead, he gave her a lopsided grin. "Now what?"

"Grab the bar inside and pull yourself onto the seat then scoot back until you can sit with your leg out to the side."

Gage reached inside and found the handle mounted above the door and used it to pull himself up. Tally stood with hands out, like she was ready to give him a boost or catch him. The idea of her doing either made him smile. He'd crush her if he fell out of the pickup. It was a good thing he had great upper body strength and could haul himself up with one hand.

She grabbed his leg and kept him from banging the cast against the door frame then gently set it down when he was settled on the seat. "You okay?" she asked.

Gage nodded and pulled the seatbelt around

him. "Sure am, Queenie."

Her gaze narrowed as she glared at him for using the nickname he'd given her when she was ten. He'd thought it was funny to call her Queenie since she was Tally King and reigned over the men at King Penny Ranch. Tally used to like it when he called her that, but she didn't appear to be quite as excited about it now.

She shut his door with a little more force than necessary then climbed behind the driver's seat. "Where would you two like to go for lunch?" she asked as she slid sunglasses on and looked back at Gage.

"Pizza?" Gage asked. "Or barbecue?"

"Definitely barbecue," Trevor said, placing a hand on Tally's arm. "How about that place near the mall?"

"Fine, meat eaters." Tally grinned at them both then drove to the restaurant. Since it was early, they weren't yet busy. The men told her what they wanted then found a table while she placed their orders and carried over drinks.

After lunch, Tally appeared ready to head home, but Trevor had other plans.

"Can you swing by the trailer place?" he asked as Tally started the pickup.

"Trailer place?" She looked over at Trevor as she put the pickup in gear and left the parking lot.

"The new stock trailer I ordered is ready to pick up. We'll swing by and get it before we head home."

Gage watched as Tally pulled into a parking space and stopped. Slowly, she lowered her sunglasses and looked over the top of them at Trevor. Even from the backseat, he could see her irritation as she scowled at her brother. "No. Get Judd or one of the boys to pick it up. It's not happening today."

"Come on, Tally. What's the problem? We're in town and it will save the guys a trip. It's a simple matter of swinging by and hooking it up, which one of the salesmen will take care of so you don't have to. Please?" Trevor gave her a look that made him appear like a little boy begging for a cookie.

Tally didn't move, just continued to glare at him for the length of several heartbeats.

Gage already knew they'd go pick up the trailer because Tally had never, not once that he'd witnessed, refused a request from Trevor when he pleaded with her like that.

Honestly, he didn't know what the big deal was. She was a country-raised kid, at least part of the year. Why on earth was she so hesitant to get the trailer?

Without saying a word, she pushed up her sunglasses, put the truck in gear and drove to the trailer dealership. Trevor got out and went to the office while Tally sat in the pickup and drummed her thumbs on the steering wheel in an agitated beat.

"Tally? What's the..." Gage snapped his mouth shut when she shot a look over the front seat that might have left lesser men stone cold dead. He widened his eyes in surprise but refrained from saying anything. Trevor made his way back to the pickup and managed to get himself and his crutches inside.

"It's the silver one, over there," Trevor said, pointing to a bumper-pull stock trailer.

"That's a nice one," Gage said. The trailer looked like it could haul anything from a horse to a couple of cattle with ease.

"I needed something smaller for running an animal or two around," Trevor said with a note of pride. "This one will be the perfect size."

The salesman motioned for Tally to back up to the hitch, which she did slowly and carefully. She hopped out and slammed the pickup door.

"I don't think she's very happy with you right now." Gage leaned forward and looked at Trevor.

"She's gonna be even angrier before we get on the road home." Trevor glanced in the mirror on his side of the pickup trying to see his sister.

Gage could see her talking to the salesman as the man hooked up the trailer, but he couldn't hear what they said. "Why's she so against driving with the trailer?"

Trevor sighed. "You know she only lived with us during the summers and on vacations, or anytime our mother got tired of her being around. I don't know if it was because we never knew how long we'd get to have her with us, depending on our mother's whims, or if it was because she's a girl, but there were certain things Dad and I never got around to teaching Tally."

"Like..." Gage prompted when Trevor fell silent.

"Like how to back up a trailer or how to drive the semi, and how to vaccinate an animal. She's figured out that last one on her own, though. The last time we tried to get her to back up a trailer it didn't go well." Trevor looked at Gage over the seat. "Enough time has lapsed since the previous fiasco, I'm sure she'll be ready to try again."

"Are you sure this is a good idea?" Gage asked. He remembered how he struggled to learn to back up a trailer when he was fifteen. The man who'd taught him was Ross King. Being a city kid, he'd never had a reason to learn and no pickup or trailer to practice with at home since his parents and brother drove cars.

"It'll be good for her," Trevor said, although he didn't sound particularly confident of the outcome.

"What do you have planned after we leave here?" Gage asked. "It might be best to just head on home."

As angry as Tally was now, Gage figured pushing her any further wouldn't be a great idea, especially when the two of them were basically at her mercy. Without her running interference, there was no telling what Marvella might try to feed them or make them do. At least with his new crutch, Gage had a small hope of outrunning the old woman.

Amused by the picture in his head of him in a footrace with Marvella and the old woman winning, the smile melted off his face like warm ice cream when Tally climbed in the pickup. She yanked off her sunglasses and shot daggers at Trevor then tossed a few at him for good measure before she slipped them back on.

She started the pickup and with exceeding care

drove out of the dealership. She was waiting at the stop sign to turn onto one of the major thoroughfares that would get them to the freeway and home when Trevor cleared his throat.

"Just one more stop, and we can head home," he said.

Tally pretended not to hear him as she turned onto the street and merged into traffic.

"Tally, please," Trevor said. "I need you to stop so we can pick up Remo."

She turned her head toward Trevor and Gage couldn't help but admire her profile. Tally was a beautiful woman, even when her chin was set stubbornly, and anger raised her shoulders closer to her ears.

"Who is Remo?"

"A new... friend."

"Friend, is he? Where'd you meet him?"

"Right here in town, about two months ago. I'm sure I mentioned him to you." Trevor gave her a charming smile.

Her scowl deepened but she turned onto a side street when Trevor pointed to his right.

"It's not far from here," he said. The street soon went from four lanes to two and in another minute, they were out of the city limits. Pastures and hayfields lined both sides of the road.

"Right there," Trevor said, pointing to a large metal sign with a picture of a bull cut into it.

"Let me guess," Tally said, her voice dripping with sarcasm. "Nemo has four legs. Is that right?"

"It's Remo, and yes, as a matter of fact he does."

"You better hope he's your friend because you're gonna be sleeping out in the barn with him," Tally muttered as she drove down a lane and pulled up near a big red barn.

Gage couldn't hold back a chuckle and looked out the window behind him when Tally turned around to frown at him.

"Just back up to the chute, there." Trevor pointed to a loading chute on the far side of the barn.

"Are you nuts?" she asked, whipping around to glare at Trevor. "You know I can't... that I... that it's..." She sighed. "There are days I really don't like you."

"Noted. Now back up to the chute," Trevor said. "Piece of cake. Just pull up there," he said, pointing his finger to a space in front of the barn, "put it in reverse, and back it straight up to the chute."

Tally pulled up where he said, took a deep breath, and appeared to be sending up a prayer or two before she shifted into reverse and started to back up.

Gage watched out the back window while Trevor kept his gaze fastened to the mirror on his side of the pickup.

"A little to the left," Trevor said in a calm voice.

"Now to the right a bit," Gage said when she overcorrected.

"Too far. Another nudge to the left," Trevor instructed, reaching out a hand toward the wheel. Tally slapped at him, rolled down the window, and stuck her head out, trying to better see what she was doing.

By that time, the trailer was at a thirty-degree angle from where it needed to be.

"Pull ahead and try again," Trevor said, reaching for the wheel a second time.

Gage thought Tally might slug her brother, but she pinched her lips together, drove ahead, and started over.

"Take it slow. Just keep it straight," Trevor said, watching in the side mirror.

"You're doing good, Tally. Keep on, nice and smooth," Gage said, wanting to encourage her. Both of her hands clenched the wheel so tightly her knuckles turned white as she glanced out the side mirrors. The trailer drifted to the right and she tried to correct it, but only ended up making it worse.

"Right! Turn right," Trevor said, sticking his head out the window. "You're gonna hit the barn if you don't…"

"Left! Left!" Gage yelled when the trailer continued going toward the barn.

By this time, a cowboy had ambled out to greet them and stood watching with a mirthful expression on his face.

"Turn it, Tally!" Trevor shouted.

"To the left! Go left!" Gage raised his voice.

Both he and Trevor were shouting directions when she slammed on the brakes, pulled forward and got the pickup lined up once again.

The cowboy observing the show looked like he might add his own thoughts on the matter, but one look from Tally quickly silenced him. He walked to the back of the trailer and opened the gate so it would be ready for loading.

Tally didn't look in the mirrors, keeping her gaze straight ahead as she backed up. Gage joined Trevor in calling out directions, but she acted as though she'd gone deaf. When she stopped the pickup, the trailer wasn't parked perfectly, but close enough they could load Trevor's new friend.

Tally rolled up the pickup windows, set the brake, and still refused to look at either of them. Trevor got out and made his way to the chute on his crutches. Gage opened the door and slid out. He almost lost his balance but caught the edge of the doorframe before he fell.

He looked up and caught Tally watching him in the mirror. He smiled at her and she looked away.

It only took a moment to load the bull and Trevor to sign a few papers.

"Let's head home," Trevor said when he and Gage were both seated back in the pickup.

Tally didn't speak to either of them as she put the pickup in gear and drove back to the road. She remained silent and the air inside the pickup cab crackled with tension when she merged onto the freeway.

Gage felt sorry for her as she sat forward, both hands holding the steering wheel in a death grip as she drove toward Echo. He noticed she was driving slightly under the speed limit and couldn't blame her, but Trevor kept looking at the speedometer and fidgeting, as though he wanted to push her foot down on the accelerator.

Not wanting to say or do anything else that

would upset Tally since she was clearly giving all her focus to driving the trailer and bull home without wrecking, he reached forward and gave Trevor's shoulder a light squeeze.

Trevor glanced back at him with a puzzled look until Gage motioned toward Tally then shook his head.

Trevor nodded and faced the passenger window, releasing a long sigh.

The trip that should have taken less than an hour seemed to drag on for days. Gage glanced at his watch as Tally took the exit at Echo and drove through town. The drive had taken five minutes longer than usual, but he would have sworn it had been two hours at the minimum since they loaded the bull.

When they reached the ranch, Trevor pointed to the pen by the barn. "If you just back up to the gate, we can let him out there."

"Just keep your eye on the back of the trailer, Tally," Gage said, trying to be helpful. "You can do this."

Without a word of warning, she slammed on the brakes in front of the house. Trevor reached for the dashboard while Gage grabbed onto the handle above the door and poor Remo bellowed his complaints at the abrupt halt. Tally popped the truck into neutral, stomped on the emergency brake, hopped out of the pickup, and ran down the walk then into the house.

Judd, who'd been walking from the barn to the bunkhouse, ambled over and leaned in the driver's side door.

"What did you boys do to our girl?" he asked.

"Apparently, she's still not quite ready to learn how to back up a trailer," Trevor said, grinning at Judd as the older man climbed inside and drove the trailer down to the pen.

Gage got out and opened the gate as Judd backed up. Together, the three of them watched the bull charge out of the trailer and check out his new surroundings.

"He's a nice-looking bull, Trev," Gage said, leaning his right arm on the fence. He looked over at his friend and smirked. "But I don't think your sister would agree."

Chapter Nine

Angry and embarrassed over the trailer-backing debacle from the previous day, Tally rose early while the house was still and quiet.

Eager to avoid encountering Trevor, and especially Gage, she dressed in a T-shirt and shorts, pulled on a pair of comfy sneakers, and went outside, intent on taking a long walk to clear her head.

She stepped outside, drew in a deep breath of sweet morning air, and choked. The stench of skunk was so strong, it made her eyes water.

It had to be close for the odor to smell that pungent. She cast the ranch dogs a warning look as they ran her direction from the barn and hurried back inside the house.

She turned the corner into the kitchen and smacked into a solid wall of muscle.

"Oh," she gasped, reaching out and grabbing onto Gage, afraid he might lose his balance.

"Hey, Queenie," he whispered, smiling at her in the muted light coming from the single light she'd left on over the stove. "What are you doing up?"

"I could ask you the same thing," she said, barely aware of anything beyond the fact Gage stood in front of her wearing only a pair of basketball shorts and his crutch. For a fleeting, ludicrous moment, she wondered what he'd do if she pressed her head against his chest and just rested there a while.

Suddenly aware that she clutched his biceps in her hands, she let go, although she didn't take a step back.

Gage studied her from the hair she'd pulled back in a ponytail to the toes of her well-worn tennis shoes. "Going somewhere?" he asked.

"I planned to go for a walk, but I don't want to tangle with the skunk lurking somewhere right outside."

"The dogs will chase it off soon enough, I suppose." He made his way to a barstool and sank down on it then set his injured hand on the counter.

"Are you hurting? Is that why you're up?" She flicked on the overhead lights and moved beside him, taking his hand in hers and examining the pins poking out of his skin. "It looks good. No infection."

"I'm fine. I thought I'd sleep better in a bed in the guest room, but I think the recliner kept me from moving around so much. I rolled over on my hand and woke myself up." Gage rubbed his right hand over his face then across his chest, drawing her gaze to the impressive muscles there covered by a soft mat of brown hair.

The itch in her fingers to feel his warm skin beneath her palms made her gently set his hand on the counter and step back.

"Since I'm up, any requests for breakfast?"

"Just one," he said, pointing outside the window over the kitchen sink where they could see Trevor's new trailer illuminated by the yard light.

She followed his gaze then shook her head. "No way. I'm not ever going to try that again."

"Talilah Jade King, I never thought I'd see the day you'd turn into a cowardly quitter."

She stiffened as she rose from taking a bowl out of a bottom cupboard and plunked it down on the counter. Slowly, she turned around to glare at him. "I'm not a coward or a quitter, but I'm never going to learn how to back up a trailer and that's just the way it is."

"Come on, let me teach you. If I can learn, anyone can."

"You mean all cowboys aren't born with the ability to back up trailers like magic, because that's how it always seemed to me," she said as she set out ingredients to make doughnuts.

"I was fifteen when a friend's dad finally taught me. You know who that friend was?"

At her curious glance, he smiled. "Trevor. Your dad was the one who taught me. I understand, Tally. Honest, I do. It's hard and intimidating, especially with two jerks yelling conflicting advice to you in the midst of backing up." She heard a soft thud and the uneven gait of his step as he walked behind her. The hand he placed on her shoulder nearly burned right through the cotton of her T-shirt, but she didn't turn to face him.

"Please? Won't you at least give it a try? We could go out right now while everyone is asleep." His voice was low and inviting, warming the skin below her ear as he bent close to her. "No one else even has to know."

The way he whispered that last part made goose bumps break out on her skin as she measured milk into a heavy saucepan and set it on to heat. Absently, she stirred the milk as Gage leaned against the counter next to her.

"I promise if I can't teach you in less than an hour, we'll never bring up the subject again. As an added bonus, I'll blacken Trevor's eye if he pulls another stunt like he did yesterday."

Tally grinned and held out a hand to Gage. He took it in his right hand, and she shook it. "That's a deal. I'm looking forward to seeing him with a shiner. He deserves it after humiliating me yesterday. You probably think I'm a useless city girl."

"Well, from one who used to be a useless city boy, no, I don't think that at all." Gage accepted the cup of coffee she handed to him and went back to the barstool. "Why didn't your dad teach you how to back up a trailer? Trevor said there were some things it might have been helpful for you to have learned years ago that they didn't teach you."

"Well, my theory is that Lulu was so flighty, Dad never really knew when she'd let me come visit, so he didn't want to spend the time I was here doing stuff like teaching me how to drive the semi or pull a calf or change my own oil."

Gage smirked. "Remind me how your mother got that name?"

"When Trevor was little, like four or five, he heard Dad talking to Judd, referring to our mother as a real lulu, meaning a doozy, and not in a good way. From that moment on, Trevor called her Lulu, and I did, too." Tally grinned, thinking of all the times her mother tried to get her to call her mother or at least Adelaide, her real name. "If it didn't fit so well, it wouldn't be nearly as entertaining."

"Where is your mom these days?" Gage helped himself to a fresh peach from the bowl on the counter.

He bit into it and Tally watched a bit of juice run down his chin. She had the strangest desire to go over and kiss it away. Instead, she turned her attention to the milk she was scalding. "Last I heard, Lulu is in Italy. She met a guy on a cruise last year about this time and married him before Christmas."

"And this is husband number what?"

"Seven, maybe?" Tally poured the milk into a bowl to cool then set the saucepan in the sink. "Honestly, I quit keeping track after the fourth one."

Gage raised his eyebrows and took another bite of his peach. "And your biological father? Have you seen him?"

"Nope. I've never met him and don't care if I do. He divorced Lulu when she was six months pregnant with me and he's not even listed on my birth certificate. I'm sure Dad was shocked when she gave me the last name of King since they'd been divorced several years when I was born."

"I still have a hard time wrapping my head around the idea of a mother just leaving her baby. Wasn't Trevor only a few months old when she took off?"

"Yep. She left Dad a note along with my brother and didn't even get in touch for several months. Then, I think it was only because she needed money between boyfriends. I'm not sure why Dad ever got mixed up with her in the first place." Tally stirred yeast into a bowl of water and set it aside. "I am grateful, though, Lulu only had Trevor and me. I wouldn't wish her on anyone, especially not another kid for her to mentally scar."

"But you had Ross." Gage finished the peach and wiped his fingers on a napkin then tossed it and the pit into the garbage can, shooting it across the room like a star player in the NBA.

"Yes, I did." Tally watched the napkin wad swish into the can then turned back to the milk, testing to see if it was cool enough to mix into the yeast. It wasn't, so she looked back at Gage. "He didn't have to treat me like a daughter, but he did. I think I was about seven before I fully realized he wasn't my birth father, but he always was and always will be my dad."

Tears burned the backs of her eyes as she thought about the man who gave her roots, supported her dreams, and loved her unconditionally. In the uncertain, ever-changing world her mother created, Ross King provided a solid place to land where Tally could relax, be a kid, and know what it meant to truly be loved. Around Lulu, she so often felt like the grown up who had to take charge and be responsible.

But at King Penny Ranch, Ross had doted on her, sheltered her, encouraged her, and made her feel like a princess. Trevor had been a wonderful big brother to her, never making her feel like she didn't belong there. He welcomed her to the ranch with hugs and big smiles each time she came and shared her heartbreak whenever her mother decided it was time for her to leave.

For the most part, she spent the summers and vacations from school with Ross and Trevor. There were a few times Tally ended up at the ranch for longer stays when her mother went off with the next man who fell for her charms and didn't want to be bothered with Tally.

When she was eleven, Ross even tried to gain custody of her, but Lulu fought him tooth and nail. Tally didn't think it had anything to do with her mother wanting her. It was more about making Ross angry and showing him Lulu was the boss.

At any rate, when she turned sixteen, she packed up her things in a used car Ross had helped her buy and moved in at the ranch permanently. She was old enough her mother couldn't force her to leave.

Ross might not have been her birth father, but he was the best dad she could ever imagine any girl having or wishing for. Except for not teaching her a few fundamentals a country girl really needed to know.

Tally sighed as she stirred the milk into the

yeast mixture then added sugar, eggs, salt, shortening and flour and mixed it for a few minutes before setting the bowl aside and covering it with a tea towel.

She set a timer, washed her hands, then turned to face Gage.

"If you can teach me to back up that stupid trailer before I have to come in and punch down this dough, I'll make anything you want for dinner tonight."

"Anything?" Gage asked, considering all the possibilities.

"Anything." Tally tossed aside the dishtowel in her hands and started toward the door. "Come on, gimpy. Let's get this over with. Do you still promise to deck Trevor if I fail at your lesson?"

Gage gave her a long look. "You're really gunning for me to hit your brother, aren't you?"

She smiled and tossed him a clean tank top from the basket of laundry sitting on top of the dryer she hadn't had time to fold. While he tugged it on, she opened the back door and held it then followed him outside. "Maybe. As much as I love Trevor, he deserves it."

"Maybe," Gage said, grinning as they walked together off the porch. Only a faint hint of skunk lingered in the air as they made their way over to where Trevor's pickup remained hitched to the new trailer by the barn.

"The guys will be out of the bunkhouse soon. Let's go somewhere I won't have an audience." She held the back driver's side door for Gage. With his crutch attached to his leg, he couldn't squeeze in the front seat with it, but he had plenty of room in the back. He settled himself in the middle of the seat while Tally climbed behind the wheel. She started the pickup and drove out of the ranch yard before anyone could question her. Before they reached the main road, she turned onto a dirt lane and followed it around the curve of what had once been the original homestead. It had burned to the ground in the late eighteen hundreds, but the foundation of the house, made from rocks hauled from the river, remained, as well as the rocks that marked where the chimney had stood.

"This is the old homestead, right?" Gage asked as she pulled around and stopped.

"Yes. Jedediah King came here in 1862. He was eighteen years old, an orphan, and completely alone in the world. He had three pennies to his name and a heart full of determination. Rather than continue further west to Oregon City, he decided to stay here. He got a job at the Indian agency and saved every penny he earned. Soon, he had enough to buy a piece of property. Then he saved enough to buy a little more, and a little more. By the time he married Larada Smith, he owned several thousand acres. They named the ranch King Penny because it all started with a dream from a man named King and a few pennies in his pocket."

Tally pointed to two massive rock cribs that once held up the entry gate to the property. "How about I try to back between them?"

"That's a good place to try," Gage said, leaning forward. "You can do this, Tally. I believe in you."

Unsettled by his proximity as he hooked his

right arm over the front seat, she wiped her clammy hands on her shorts and took a deep breath.

She reached up and took a tight grip on the steering wheel with both hands.

"Nope. You aren't going to be able to do it like that." Gage reached out and took her right arm in his hand, pulling it away from the steering wheel. Sparks raced up her arm and danced around her head, making it hard for her to concentrate on anything beyond the way his touch intrigued and unsettled her. "Got it?"

She'd missed his instructions letting her thoughts wander in places they shouldn't go. Sheepish, she looked over her shoulder at him. "Would you please repeat that?"

"Place your left hand at six o'clock on the wheel. And don't grab it like you have to strangle it to death. Just let your hand rest there."

She did as he said, and he released his hold on her right arm.

"Put it in reverse and go slow. You've got all the time in the world," he said.

Tally put the pickup in reverse, moved her foot off the brake and onto the gas while releasing the clutch. Slowly, the pickup started to move backward.

"Look in your rearview mirror and pick out a point on the trailer you can focus on, like the tire well, or even something on the end of the trailer. Then pick a focal point of where you are backing to, like the rock crib on the driver's side. Keep your focus on those two points."

Tally found her focal points, but the trailer was

veering too far to the left. She grabbed the steering wheel with both hands and whipped it to the right, causing it to go even farther off course.

"Stop," Gage said.

Tally applied the brake and shrugged in defeat. "I'm hopeless."

"No, you're not. You're just overthinking this." Gage pointed ahead of them. "Drive forward and we'll try again."

Tally pulled ahead, put the pickup in reverse and dropped her left hand to the bottom of the steering wheel.

"If you want the back of the trailer to go to the left, turn the steering wheel to the left. If you want it to go right, turn it to the right. Easy as that," Gage said, smiling at her as she gave him a dubious look.

"Easy as that," she mimicked, making him laugh.

Slowly, with her focal points lined up in her side mirror, she started backing up again. She turned the wheel slightly to the left and watched the back of the trailer go the direction she wanted. She eased it to the right and observed as the trailer went right where she wanted it to go.

"Gage," she whispered as she neared the rock crib. "It's working."

"Just keep going," he encouraged. "You can do this. Check your mirror on the passenger side. Do you have room over there?"

She looked and nodded. "We are good."

"Yes, we are," he said, leaning closer to her.

If she hadn't been so entrenched in backing up the trailer, she would have taken a moment to decipher if he meant something that had nothing to do with their early morning lesson.

Too excited to dwell on the possibilities, she successfully backed the trailer between the two rock cribs. When she stopped, she raised her hands and whooped in victory.

"Told you, you could do it." Gage grabbed her right hand and pulled it to him, kissing the back of it. "Mmm. You smell like Christmas cookies."

She pulled her hand away, not sure that was a compliment or not. "Thank you for helping me."

"You're welcome, Queenie. Let's try it again, just to make sure you've got it."

"Okay," Tally said. She pulled ahead and successfully backed between the cribs three more times before she glanced at the radio clock and gasped. "My dough will be ruined if we don't head back soon."

"Then let's go." Gage moved back so he rested against the seat and she drove them back to the house. Several of the ranch hands were outside when she pulled up near the barn and they all cheered when she backed the trailer into the spot where it had been earlier.

She jumped out and opened Gage's door, ready to help him if he needed it. He slid out and draped his right arm around her shoulders. "I'm so proud of you, Tally. Don't limit yourself. I know you can do anything you set your mind to. If Ross was here, he'd tell you the same thing."

Tally gave him an impulsive hug that nearly threw him off balance then ran up the back steps and into the house. Elated with her success, she cast

Trevor a smug glance when he walked into the kitchen a few minutes later.

"Guess what I did this morning," she said as she cut doughnuts out of the dough.

"Made a batch of doughnuts?" he asked, grinning at her as he plopped down at the table.

"Well, besides that." Tally beamed as she looked at him. "Gage taught me how to back up the trailer."

"What? How'd he do that?" Trevor glanced at Gage as he made his way into the kitchen.

"Apparently, your sister just needed the proper incentive." Gage smirked as he poured two glasses of orange juice and carried one to Trevor then retrieved the second one for himself.

"And what incentive was that?" Trevor asked, taking a swig of the juice.

"I promised if she couldn't do it, I'd sock you in the eye."

Trevor spewed juice across the table while Gage laughed and Tally rolled her eyes.

Marvella chose that moment to sashay into the room and shook an arthritis-gnarled finger at her nephew. "You're supposed to swallow that, Trevor. You're too old to be spitting juice at your friends."

"Yes, Aunt Marv," Trevor said, glaring from Gage to Tally. A grin finally kicked up the corner of his mouth. "I suppose, after yesterday, I might have earned a black eye."

"You certainly did, but you're safe, at least for today." Tally winked at Gage and returned to the doughnuts.

After Trevor and Gage had devoured the last

two doughnuts then complained about eating too much, Tally cleaned up the kitchen and went outside to work in the flowerbeds.

She spent the morning pulling weeds from among the dahlias, daisies, and delphinium then hauled the weeds to the compost pile behind the barn. Gage and Trevor came out on the porch mid-morning and wandered out to the barn to check on the new bull. When they returned, she made sandwiches for lunch, along with potato salad, and sliced melon.

Once they'd eaten and Aunt Marv had gone back to her house for a nap, the two men lingered at the table, discussing rodeo scores and arguing over who would rank where in the standings.

Tally turned to Gage when she finished the dishes. "Don't forget, I told you I'd make anything you want for dinner, so now is the time to speak up. I might need to run to the store or look up a recipe if it's something elaborate."

Gage looked at her with something in his eyes, something exciting and terrifying all at the same time. She took a step back and bumped into the counter.

"Well, Queenie, how about something incredibly difficult like grilled steaks, baked potatoes, and that cucumber salad you made the other day. And raspberry crisp for dessert, if you have any berries left. It sure would taste good with ice cream melting over the top."

Tally knew he was letting her off easy because she could grill steaks in her sleep, the potatoes were simple, and the salad would take less than five minutes to make. She could pull a raspberry crisp from the freezer because she didn't have enough fresh berries left to make one.

"Are you sure that's what you want?" she asked, knowing he wasn't a picky eater and liked a variety of foods.

"Well, there was something else, but this will be great."

"Just tell me what you want, and I'll make it," she said, moving closer to the table.

"Another day," he said, giving her a dismissive look as he turned to ask Trevor a question about the new bull.

Slightly miffed, Tally straightened the great room, changed the sheets on Trevor's bed and spread a fresh sheet over the chair Gage had claimed as his since he'd been staying with them.

The afternoon passed quickly as she caught up on housework. She spent a few minutes answering emails on her laptop and giggled at messages Tonya and Glenda had sent, asking if she was suffering greatly with a hunky cowboy to take care of. Those two had volunteered to come help if Gage or Trevor needed extra attention.

She messaged them back, letting them know she had everything under control before she went to the kitchen to start dinner.

Aunt Marv sat at the table flipping through a fashion magazine and drinking lemonade although Gage or Trevor were nowhere in sight.

"You scare the boys off again, Auntie?" Tally asked as she washed potatoes and wrapped them in foil.

"Nope. When I asked if they'd like to help me choose a new shade of lipstick, they disappeared so fast, I thought they might hurt themselves." Marvella grinned at her. "I think they've been out in the bunkhouse all afternoon."

"Probably there or the shop. It's too hot for them in the barn." Tally chatted with Marvella as she made dinner. The moment she pulled the steaks off the grill on the back porch, Trevor and Gage appeared, making their way up the steps and sniffing appreciatively.

"Sure smells good, Tal. I'll never turn down a good steak," Trevor said, following her inside while Gage held the door.

Conversation was lighthearted as they ate and Marvella volunteered to do the dishes since Tally did all the cooking.

Tally tossed another load of what seemed like never-ending laundry into the washing machine, folded the sheets she washed earlier, then remembered no one had gotten the mail. She walked down to the mailbox and retrieved it. She left the ranch mail on Trevor's desk in the office, handed Marvella two magazines and a catalog, then carried the rest of the mail out to the bunkhouse for the men there.

She wandered around the back of the house and decided to work in the garden for a while.

The herb garden she'd planted and dutifully tended on her days off had grown like gangbusters. Down on her knees, she pulled weeds from around the rosemary and mint plants. She glanced up as Gage settled with a grunt onto a bench over by the tomatoes.

"What are you doing out here?" she asked, brushing soil from her hands and looking at him.

He leaned back, at least as much as he could with his broken leg stuck out to the side with the crutch attached to it, and smiled at her. "Enjoying the view."

"We do get some pretty amazing sunsets," she said, flicking her gaze over her shoulder at the sun that had started its evening descent.

"That you do, but there are other spectacular things to see out here, too."

Her left eyebrow arched upward, but she continued pulling weeds, unwilling to discover if he was referring to her or the horses in the pasture.

Silence fell between them, interrupted only by the chirp of crickets, the sound of the horses swishing their tails to chase away flies, and the clank of metal as someone pushed a gate shut out by the barn.

"Gage?" Tally finally asked, unable to subdue her curiosity. She looked up at him to find his gaze focused on her.

"Yeah?"

"What did you really want for dinner?" She sat back on her heels and looked at him.

His blue eyes heated, and he gave her a half grin that would have sent even the most prudish heart into an excited rhythm. "What I really wanted, Talilah, was to take you out for dinner, just the two of us. Since that isn't feasible, steak was a good substitute."

She shook her head and tossed a weed at him.

"You shouldn't tease me like that."

"I wasn't teasing, Tally. Not at all."

From his tone and the look on his face, she knew he was serious, which disturbed her even more than his teasing.

As though he sensed her discomfort, he pointed toward a grouping of plants. "What's that?"

"Which one?" she asked.

"The one with purple flowers."

Tally broke off a small piece of lavender and carried it over to him. "English lavender. It's pretty, the bees like it, and it's a good culinary varietal."

"You eat it?"

She grinned. "You ate some in the blueberry coffee cake I made the other day."

"Huh. How about that," he said, rubbing the lavender between his fingers and sniffing. "Do you grow a lot of herbs?"

"I try. I don't always have a lot of time to take care of my herbs, leaving them at the mercy of Aunt Marv and Trevor." She plucked a few leaves from various plants and carried them back to him to smell.

"Mmm. What's that one?" he asked, holding a sprig out to her.

"Rosemary. It's great for adding a little pop of flavor to chicken dishes, especially." Tally went back to weeding while Gage worked his way through sniffing the herbs she left beside him.

"These smell really good," he said, holding out a piece of sage and mint.

"They do. Spearmint is probably my favorite." Content as she puttered among her plants while

Gage sat nearby, she wanted the moment to last. She could almost envision them in the future with a couple of brown-haired children running around in the background. But that was ridiculous and never going to happen. Not in a million years.

"Can't you just get all this stuff at the store?"

She shook her head and rolled her eyes. "I could, but it wouldn't be fresh like this. Besides, I enjoy working out here. It's peaceful. I think if every person in the world had an herb garden, there'd be a whole lot less fighting, stealing and killing. How can you be anything but happy with the scent of rosemary or mint tickling your nose?"

"Spoken like a true farm girl," Gage teased.

Tally threw a tarragon sprig at him then got to her feet and turned on the hose, giving the plants a gentle mist of water.

She moved on from the herbs to give a little extra water to a zucchini when a foot-long snake slithered out from the green leaves, right over her feet.

Her blood-curdling screams startled Gage so badly he almost fell off the bench on his injured leg. She launched into a series of dance moves that could have inspired the original performance in *Saturday Night Fever* while turning the nozzle on the hose to jet spray and hosing the snake down by the marigold border on the end of the row.

"Snake! Snake!" she screeched, trying to keep an eye on it while glancing around for the shovel she knew was nearby.

Gage hobbled over to the far side of the garden where a shovel leaned against a post and grabbed it.

He hurried back and attempted to kill the snake with it, but Tally had created a lagoon oozing mud and the snake used that to its full advantage.

"Don't let it get away," she said, pointing to where it tried to slither out of the hole.

"I think that's a worm," he said as she blasted the snake with the hose again.

"It's the snake! Kill it!" She danced a few steps and flapped the hand not holding the hose at him.

Gage stirred the murky water with the tip of the shovel, but he appeared to be struggling to handle the shovel with one hand.

"Give me that," Tally said, taking the shovel and handing him the hose. She started slicing into the water, trying to locate the reptile. Suddenly, the snake shot out of the hole, slithering back over her toes a second time.

She screamed again and shivered in revulsion. Much to her irritation, Gage started singing the chorus to "Stayin' Alive" by the Bee Gees.

Her agitation with him fueled her efforts to destroy the snake as she chased it through the garden. She finally nailed it with the shovel as it attempted to work its way under a watermelon.

"Got you!" she said, striking it twice more to make sure it was good and dead.

"That's a little overkill, don't you think?" Gage asked as she leaned on the shovel, panting from the exertion.

She glowered at him and pushed hair out of her face since several strands had fallen free of her ponytail in the excitement.

He smirked. "Pun intended."

"You're terrible," she said, trying not to smile. Now that the snake was dead, it did seem slightly humorous.

"Was it a rattler?" Gage bent over, like he intended to pick it up.

"Leave it alone. If it was a rattler, it could still inject venom even with a severed head." She sighed. "And no, it wasn't a rattlesnake. It appears to have been a bullsnake."

"Kill first, determine the variety later? Is that how you operate?"

"That's what Dad taught me. He said it was better to be safe than sorry and sometimes when rattlesnakes are small like this, it's hard to see the buttons." Tally scooped the snake into the shovel and headed for the burning barrel with it.

She returned to the garden and frowned at the foot-wide hole she'd made with the hose. The marigolds would never be the same, but none of her herbs were damaged. She hauled a few scoops of dirt to the hole and tamped it down, then called it a night.

"I'm all done and done in. My day started out being terrorized by a skunk, and then you with the whole learn to back up the trailer thing. Before it gets worse than a snake slithering all over my toes, I'm heading inside."

"I'll join you," Gage said, hobbling to catch up to her. "You suppose Trev left any berry crisp for me to enjoy?"

"If not, I know where to find more," she said, glancing over her shoulder at him. When he started humming "Stayin' Alive," she reached out and swatted him on the shoulder. "I'll eat it all myself if you're gonna be that way."

"Not if I get there first," he said.

Tally knew she could easily outrun him, but before she could take a step, Gage wrapped a muscled arm around her waist and lifted her off her feet.

"Put me down, you lunatic," she gasped, stilling her movements, afraid he might lose his balance at any second. "You'll hurt yourself even more than you already are."

He set her down but caught her hand and held it in his. "I doubt that, Queenie, but your wish is my command."

With the sun turning his skin into bronze and the evening light shimmering in his gorgeous summer-sky eyes, he had no idea what she truly wished or wanted. At that moment, her fondest desire was for him to hold her close and kiss her until she forgot all the reasons she needed to keep him at arm's length and pretend nothing existed between them but friendship.

Chapter Ten

"Tree! Tree!" Trevor shouted as Marvella careened down the road, headed toward town.

Gage closed his eyes, sent up a prayer, and grabbed onto the door handle, prepared to bail out if necessary. Since they left the ranch, she'd driven along the edge of the ditch twice, almost flattened a row of mailboxes, missing them by no more than an inch, and left a rut in the corner of someone's just-watered lawn.

Tally had to go back to work leaving Gage and Trevor's care in Marvella's questionable hands. Today, they both had physical therapy appointments. Although they considered having one of the hands drive them, Marvella assured them she could get them to Kennewick and home again.

Gage had plenty of doubts swirling through his head as he opened one eye and watched her swerve to avoid hitting a squirrel.

"Get out of the road, you fuzzy varmint!"

Marvella yelled, shaking a fist at the squirrel as it beat a hasty retreat off the road. The chunky pink beaded bracelets she wore rattled on her bony arm before she placed her hand back on the steering wheel.

Gage had to give it to the woman. She was colorful, if nothing else. Today, she wore an electric blue and bright pink paisley dress with shoulder pads so big, they looked like she'd stolen them from a linebacker. It appeared today was a trip back in time to the 1980s, at least from her choice of attire.

As she ran a stop sign in the little town of Echo, Gage tapped Trevor on the shoulder. "Maybe we should call this off," he suggested.

"You boys have to be there in an hour. It'll be fine," Marvella said, driving through town at a crawl.

Gage noticed a profusion of flowers blooming everywhere, along with big shade trees. It really was a pretty little town. He knew from past visits the community was quite proud of being named an America in Bloom Small City for three years in a row. They also boasted being Oregon's smallest Tree City USA designee.

When Marvella merged onto the onramp to the freeway, she buried her little foot into the accelerator with such force Gage braced his hand against the back of the front seat and prayed they'd all survive.

He and Trevor were both pale and wide-eyed by the time she pulled into the parking lot at the rehab center across the street from the hospital and parked in a space near the door.

Oblivious to the fact she'd nearly caused multiple collisions, ran over the curb three times, and scared a man on a bicycle so badly he'd flipped completely over in the crosswalk, she hummed to herself as she checked her lipstick in the rearview mirror.

"Do you boys need help getting out?" she asked, glancing from Trevor to Gage.

Gage shook his head, hoping his wobbly legs would hold him. He couldn't say for certain, but he was convinced Marvella had just frightened at least ten years off his life. With a deep, calming breath, he opened the back door and got out. Gage leaned against the car for support while Trevor got his crutches situated beneath his arms.

Thankfully, their appointments were back to back, which made it easier on everyone. Gage didn't know what he would have done the past few weeks without the King family. Trevor had provided a safe, comfortable place for him to stay as long as he needed. It was nice to spend time with his buddy and catch up on all the news they never seemed to get around to discussing when he popped in a day here and there during the year.

Then there was Tally. She'd made three delicious meals a day, given him the peace of mind knowing a nurse was handy if he needed one, and made him happier than he'd been for a long while.

Every time he pictured her dancing around in the garden, chasing after the little snake that was more the size of a worm, he broke into a broad grin. She'd been so cute when she'd gotten mad at him and he loved watching fiery embers spark in those mesmerizing gray eyes when she looked his way.

From what he'd observed, the woman had no idea she was beautiful. The thick waves of her brown hair offered almost more temptation than he could resist. Each time he saw her with it down, he wanted to touch it, bury his hand in it, and inhale the luscious scent of it.

Tally seemed to believe she was overweight, which she wasn't. Not at all. What she was, at least in his opinion, was blessed with delicious curves that made a man's mouth water just thinking about them. Her skin looked like silk. Her mouth — sweet mercy, but those lips of hers were just meant to be kissed.

It wasn't just the perfection of her face or the way he longed to run his hand over the curve of her waist. It went far deeper than that.

Tally had always been a nice kid when he'd known her years ago. She still had that sweetness mingled with innocence. And he'd watched her enough to know she truly cared about others, wanted to help others, and that's one of the things he admired the most about her. She would lend a hand to anyone who needed it, regardless of her personal feelings. He'd known from the moment she brought him Trevor's rigging at the county fair that she wasn't wild about seeing him again, but she'd given him the exact attentive, tender care she'd lavished on her brother.

In fact, she'd spent more time with him while she was at the ranch than she did Trevor. Those sunny, sweet summer days would be branded into his memory as some of the best he'd ever had, even with his injured hand and leg.

When Tally went back to work, the ranch seemed too quiet, too lonely, without her there. He'd missed seeing her in the kitchen, watching her watering the garden, or spying on her through the screen door when she sat on the porch and talked to the ranch dogs. He just plain missed Tally and wanted to be around her, spend more time with her. But she had her own life and Gage needed to focus on getting back to his.

If things were different, if he was different, he might pursue her with everything he had. But he wouldn't. Even if he wanted to make her his own, he'd promised Trevor to leave her alone and he would.

Yet, just knowing she'd never belong to him made something heavy and cold settle in his heart, leaving him sad and a little depressed.

For now, he'd have to be content with being friends. At least she'd allowed him to progress to that point. However, there were a few times while she was there in the past week that his control was stretched to the limits when she'd lean over him as she set something on the table, or she sat next to him on the couch.

The very hint of her fragrance kicked his temperature up a notch. Thoughts of kissing her kept him awake at night far more than the ache in his hand or his leg.

It was a good thing she had to get back to work this week or who knew what might happen. By the time she had another week off, Gage figured he'd be long gone down the rodeo road. He'd been letting his body rest and heal, but he looked forward to whatever the therapist had planned. He had to stay in shape, stay sharp, and stay focused on competing in Vegas in December.

By the time he finished his therapy session, Gage wanted to crawl in the back seat of Marvella's car and whine like a fussy baby. The therapist was a driven maniac who was determined to kill him. Or at least it seemed that way to him.

When Trevor came out of his session looking as pathetic as Gage felt, he knew he wasn't alone.

Marvella smiled and sashayed down the sidewalk between them as they returned to her car.

"Who's ready for lunch?" she chirped as she fastened her seatbelt and slid on a pair of rhinestone accented sunglasses.

"Maybe we should just head on home, Aunt Marv," Trevor said in a weary voice. He leaned his head against the headrest and sighed. "We can eat something when we get there."

"Nonsense. I know just the place for our lunch today." She put the car in reverse without looking behind her. The screech of brakes and a honking horn didn't even phase her as she pulled out of the spot and tootled through the parking lot.

Like a queen in a parade, she waved a hand out the window with her bracelets clattering and went on her merry way.

Gage closed his eyes and ignored the sounds of horns honking and people shouting as they drove through town. He pushed his left arm against his chest to protect his hand when the car ran over a curb and he bounced around the back seat like a pinball.

Finally, Marvella pulled the car to a stop and whipped off her seatbelt. "Let's go, boys!"

She was out of the car and halfway up the walk before Gage even registered the fact she'd brought them to a retirement center for lunch.

"Golden Oak Village," he said as he read the sign on the front lawn. "Perfect."

"This is gonna be bad," Trevor muttered as they gimped up the walk and through the sliding glass doors into the cool interior of the lobby.

Marvella waved her fingers at them, motioning for them to follow her as she turned down a hallway then disappeared around a corner.

"Is she going to make us eat lunch here?" Gage asked, glancing around at the gleaming tile floors, non-descript wallpaper, and the scent of oranges lingering in the air.

"I'm just spit-balling, but I think that's her plan," Trevor said, giving him a worried glance as squeals and laughter spilled into the hallway.

"Is it too late to go sit in the car?" Gage whispered as they made their way around the corner where Marvella stood in the midst of a group of old women of various sizes.

The second the women caught sight of them, they scurried their direction. One minute, Gage and Trevor were trying to figure out how to make a hasty retreat outside and the next they found themselves seated in the dining area, surrounded by blue-haired, denture-wearing octogenarians who had octopus hands and questionable motives.

The woman named Blanche sitting to Gage's

left kept reaching over and patting his thigh. Each time she did, it caused him to jump in surprise. He tried to move away from her, but it was impossible with a rotund little woman named Hattie plastered against his right side. Hattie squeezed his bicep and leaned against him, batting her sparse eyelashes every few minutes. Trevor sat across the table with two women pawing him. He looked equally as disgusted and terrorized as Gage currently felt.

Finally, food arrived at their table and Gage joined Trevor in attempting to eat their grilled chicken, seasoned rice, and salads in a hurry, but Blanche insisted on cutting his chicken for him and Hattie would have spoon-fed him if he let her.

Battling to keep the older women at bay was exhausting. From the way Trevor scowled at Marvella and shifted back and forth in his chair, Gage figured he was having an equally miserable time.

A prune-faced woman named Darla gave Gage a sly grin. "Do you have a girlfriend?"

"Not at the moment, ma'am," Gage answered honestly, although he hated to admit he was free and unfettered at the moment.

"Really?" Hattie asked, batting her eyelashes again and squeezing his arm.

"Really. I've been too busy to do much dating lately." He took a big bite out of a soft dinner roll so he wouldn't have to make any further comments.

"How about you, Trevor?" Darla asked him. "Any attachments?"

"Nope, unless you count Aunt Marvella. She's my best girl."

Marvella beamed at him, but none of the other women noticed. They all jumped up and hurried out of the dining area like a herd of gazelles being chased by a blood-thirsty lion.

In fact, Gage's eyes widened when he saw Hattie elbow a petite woman named Beulah in the side, making the woman lag behind her. Darla, the tallest of the bunch, looked like an Olympic hurdler when she jumped over someone's fallen walker as she raced toward the door.

"Let's get out of here," Trevor said, tossing aside his napkin and looking for his crutches. One of the women had left them propped against the wall behind them, out of Trevor's reach.

Marvella dabbed at her mouth with a dainty flick of her wrist. "I'm not finished with my lunch and there's no need to rush. You boys just cool your heels." Marvella picked up her fork and took a tiny bite of her salad.

"What are your friends doing?" Gage asked, glancing from Marvella to the doorway where the women had disappeared.

"Oh, they'll be back shortly," Marvella said, giving him a reassuring smile.

"That's what I'm afraid of," Gage muttered, looking at Trevor, who nodded in agreement.

Before he could figure out a way to bodily remove Marvella from the chair out to her car, the women returned, making enough noise to wake the dead and drawing odd looks from the other occupants of the dining room.

Some of them carried framed portraits, others had thick photo albums in their arms.

"Oh, no!" Trevor groaned, slumping in his chair.

Hattie and Blanche resumed their posts as sentries on either side of Gage while Darla plopped down next to Trevor and sneered at a woman named Judy who flanked his other side.

"You have to meet our granddaughters," the women said in unison. Photos of tall girls, skinny girls, chubby girls, smiling girls, and girls with hair of every color under the rainbow were held up for Gage and Trevor's inspection.

One photo looked like a senior portrait from the late 1980s. How old did these women think they were, anyway?

"This is my granddaughter Miranda. She's a dancer with a ballet troupe in Los Angeles. Isn't she gorgeous?" Blanche asked as she flipped an album page and showed off a spunky looking blonde with an infectious smile and legs that appeared to be a mile long. Gage admired the woman's beauty. The old Gage, the one who never shied away from a date or a good time, would have asked for the girl's name and number. But now, all he could think about was how the woman's smile wasn't as sweet as Tally's. He found himself comparing every single picture to Tally and finding them all flawed in some way.

Tally King was under his skin, in his head, and if he wasn't careful, she'd set up camp inside his heart. That would never, ever do.

But at the moment, he had more important matters to deal with, like Hattie about to leave permanent fingerprints on his arm and Blanche leaning on his thigh as she turned pages in the album.

Gage cast a quick look at Marvella's plate and noted she was almost finished eating. He caught Trevor's eye and he nodded in agreement. It was far past time to take their leave.

"It's been quite a memorable experience to have lunch with you lovely ladies, but we really do need to head on back to the ranch," Trevor said, tipping his head behind him toward the crutches.

With a bit of effort, Gage managed to disentangle himself from Blanche and Hattie and rose from his chair. He grabbed the crutches, handed them to Trevor, then pulled out Marvella's chair.

"Tell your friends goodbye, Aunt Marv. It's time to go." Trevor gave her a hard frown that didn't leave room for argument.

"Well, it was lovely to see all you girls," Marvella said as she hugged the women. "Perhaps, one of these days, you'll all come out…"

"Have a nice afternoon," Trevor said as he rose and propped the crutches beneath his arms.

Gage took hold of Marvella's arm in his right hand and nudged her out of the dining room, cutting off her invitation for the women to join them at the ranch before she could utter the words.

"Well! That was rather rude, Trevor. What's gotten into you?" Marvella lifted her chin in the air and glared up at Trevor then at Gage. "You boys hardly gave me time to say goodbye."

"Time to go, Aunt Marv." He sighed as they made it outside without being waylaid. "I couldn't abide one more minute of looking at granddaughters or having those old women squeeze me like a piece of ripe fruit."

"Oh, fiddle-faddle. They were just happy to have someone new to talk to." Marvella unlocked the car. Gage opened her door for her and waited as she slid behind the wheel before closing it. He settled on the backseat while Trevor took the front passenger seat. Marvella started the car then gave them both a long look. "If you aren't in too big of a toot to get home, I'd like to drive by the old place, just to see how it looks."

"Sure, Aunt Marv. We can do that." Trevor smiled at her and patted her shoulder. "I haven't been out there for a long time."

Marvella took side streets, then back roads out of Kennewick to a farm located at the end of a lane surrounded by hay fields. A rusty sign hanging from a rotting fence post let them know they'd arrived at Roamin' End Ranch.

"Who lives here?" Gage asked, looking at a sturdy red barn and outbuildings in the distance. Marvella pulled the car around in front of a house painted the color of freshly churned butter and trimmed in white.

The gray roof looked fairly new, as did the front door, but the window box hanging beneath the front window appeared to have been there a while. No flowers bloomed in it, but Gage could imagine it filled with colorful blooms.

Five white posts held up the overhang that stretched from the front door around the side of the house, creating a small porch. He could picture a rocking chair or two out there to enjoy the evening breezes that stirred through the big, old trees that shaded the house.

"This is my house, darling," Marvella said as she put the car in park and turned off the ignition. For a moment, she sat staring at the house before she smiled and scurried out of the car.

"Her house?" Gage asked as he got out and walked with Trevor along the slate stones that made the front walk.

"Aunt Marv wasn't ready to sell when she moved out to King Penny Ranch, so she rents the acreage. One of us generally checks on the house every few months to make sure it's in good shape." Trevor tipped his head toward the house. "A tree fell on the roof back in the spring and punched a hole right through, so we had a new roof put on and did a little work inside."

"It's a nice place," Gage said, liking the quaint appearance of the welcoming house. "How much land does she own?"

"She's got a half section of land, most of it in hay. The farm has good water rights, though, and a creek runs through the property on the other side of that hill." Trevor motioned for Gage to follow Marvella inside the house once she unlocked the door.

Hardwood floors, though a bit dusty, were in excellent condition. Sunlight shimmered through the windows and made the space seem much larger than it probably was. Built in bookcases flanked a marble fireplace in the living room. Rounded doorways attested to fine craftsmanship from a bygone era.

"When was the house built?" Gage asked as Marvella wandered into a kitchen that would catch the morning light.

"My husband's parents built this house in 1928. He was their only son, a farm boy through and through. When we married, he wanted to do something different, so we moved to Alaska for twenty-five years. Richard worked a variety of jobs until he finally landed a position with an oil company. He made good wages and we saved what we could. His father passed away and his mother wanted to sell the farm, so we moved back and bought it from her." Marvella sighed and ran her hand over the scarred wood of an old farm table. "Richard and I made many beautiful memories here. I sure miss him."

Trevor handed Gage one of his crutches then pulled Marvella into a hug. "I miss Uncle Rich, too. He was a fine fellow."

"He was," Marvella sniffled and moved back, dabbing at her tears with a lacy handkerchief she pulled from her pocket. "Enough of that, though. The house appears to be in good shape. I'm going to go check the bedrooms then I'll be ready to go."

"That's fine, Aunt Marv," Trevor said, taking his crutch and making his way to the back door. Gage opened it and let in some fresh air.

Although the house was stuffy, it didn't have any odd moldy or overrun by rodent smells. In fact, it appeared Richard and Marvella Hawkins had taken great care to preserve and restore the home. He could picture it as it may have looked when it was first built, especially since there was a Hoosier cabinet pushed against the far wall and a deep cast-iron sink set in the countertop.

"Marvella and your uncle never had children of their own?" Gage asked Trevor as they stood in the kitchen.

Trevor shook his head. "No. They wanted them, of course, but they just never had any. Aunt Marv said she used to dote on Lulu until she went nuts, which was supposedly around the time I was born."

"I guess I didn't realize your mother was from around here. And Ross was her first husband?"

"Yep. Her first husband. Victim. Whatever you want to call it." Trevor sighed. "Aunt Marv thinks Lulu might have had a really bad case of post-partum depression that went unchecked and led to her running off and leaving us."

Aware of the tension settling on his friend's shoulder at the mention of his mother, Gage changed the subject. "So, what does Marvella plan to do with this place?"

"She says when the right buyer comes along, she'll sell it, but until then, a neighboring farmer rents the ground and keeps an eye on the buildings. I try to drop by and check on the house once in a while, and Tally does, too. There's a swing out in one of the maple trees that was a favorite place for her to play when she was little. I think she comes and sits out here sometimes when she needs a quiet place to gather her thoughts."

Gage tucked that tidbit of information away and meandered through the house. Marvella was sitting on an antique maple bed staring out the window, so he left the room without disturbing her. He took in a larger master bedroom with a connected bathroom. A smaller bathroom was in the hallway between the room where Marvella wandered through her memories, and what was most likely a linen or storage closet.

He returned to the living room and looked around, taking in the details of the room, including the high ceiling.

In his mind's eye he could see a Christmas tree, decked with old-fashioned lights, and a record player cranking out holiday songs from vintage albums. Tally beneath the tree with a warm smile on her beautiful face and a dark-haired baby on her arm.

Gage sucked in a gasp as awareness slammed into his chest with a brutal force.

This house, this place, felt so comfortable and right. And the notion that he wanted Tally there with him felt just as good, just as perfect. Was this the little farm he'd always dreamed of owning? Was Tally the woman he was meant to marry? The one who would finally give him roots?

Nah. Surely not. It was loony to feel this attached to a place, to her. Wasn't it? If he voiced his thoughts to Trevor, he had no doubt his friend would tell him he'd lost his mind.

Maybe he had.

Or maybe he was just starting to find it.

He went outside and looked through the barn, the shop, storage shed, and garden shed. An old Johnny Popper tractor in the back of the shop made him grin. He'd always wanted to tinker with one.

Full of questions, none of which he wanted to answer, he made his way back to the house as Marvella and Trevor stepped outside. Marvella locked the door and, with a wistful sigh, sauntered to the car.

"Is she always like this when she comes here?" Gage asked as he and Trevor made their way down the walk.

"Yes. She calls it her happy-sad time. She's happy to see the place, but sad Uncle Rich is gone, and she no longer lives here. She knows she can't live alone anymore, but I think she truly misses being here. She and Uncle Rich lived here for thirty years before he passed away and then she stayed on a few more before she almost set the place on fire."

"I didn't notice anything charred in the kitchen," Gage said as they neared the car.

"She wanted it all repaired, so it was." Trevor nodded to Gage in thanks as he opened his car door for him. "Are you done tripping down memory lane, Aunt Marv?"

"I am, honey. Get in the car and let's go home. I'm tired." Marvella gave them a distant smile, as though her heart and mind lingered somewhere far away before she put the car in gear and drove them home.

Gage thought about how much she must have loved Richard Hawkins, how much she loved him still, if he'd guessed the reason for her quiet, subdued attitude on the way home. She didn't even hit any curbs, run through stop signs, or nearly drive off in the ditch.

Love could certainly do strange things to a person, as Gage was slowly discovering, even if he wasn't yet ready to admit it.

Chapter Eleven

"I'm still not convinced this is a good idea," Tally said as she stopped the pickup at a crosswalk so Gage and Trevor wouldn't have far to walk to enter the Pendleton Round-Up. Pedestrians swarmed in front of her, running across the street as they waited for the main gates to open.

"We'll be fine," Trevor assured her as he hurried to position his crutches beneath his arms and turned to glance back at her. "We'll meet you at the gate. Just text me when you're ready to go in."

Tally nodded as Trevor and Gage shut the doors and Gage placed his hand on Marvella's elbow, guiding her through the crowd. She didn't like the idea of anyone bumping into Gage or Trevor, possibly causing damage to their injuries, but the two men were so stubborn. The other night she'd argued with Trevor until she'd gotten a pounding headache about skipping the rodeo this year, but he refused to listen to reason. Gage wasn't any less mule-headed than her idiot brother.

As a compromise, they agreed they'd skip the first two performances and only attend on Friday and Saturday. Of course, Aunt Marv didn't want to be left out and came along.

Yesterday, Gage and Trevor assured her they could walk no matter where she parked. She ended up in a lot several blocks from the rodeo grounds. By the time Gage and Trevor made it to their seats, they looked exhausted, especially after they insisted on going early to watch the parade. Tally had brought seats for them, but she knew the long walk had worn on them. Marvella was nearly as wilted as the two men by the time they all got home that evening.

Today, Gage told her to stop in front of the gate and let them out. He and Trevor assured her they could keep an eye on Marvella until she got back from parking the pickup. She hoped they were right. Marvella had been acting strangely, even for her, since the day she'd taken Gage and Trevor to their physical therapy appointment the previous week.

Trevor had called her that evening and given her an earful about never again allowing Marvella to drive anywhere. Tally agreed, but there wasn't much she could do about it when she was at work.

Thankfully, her schedule of three long days at the hospital left her free to attend the rodeo. Truthfully, she'd enjoyed being there yesterday and looked forward to the performance today. It had been a long time since she'd gone to the Round-Up and had forgotten just how much fun it could be.

Part of her enjoyment, if she cared to admit it,

came from sitting with Gage and Trevor. The two of them kept up a running commentary on the events, who they thought would win, all while cracking jokes and playing off each other.

Tally looked forward to sitting with them again today. She parked the pickup in a lot several blocks from the rodeo arena, paid the fee to stay there for the day, then headed out.

A smile tickled the corners of her mouth as she thought about Aunt Marv tagging along with Trevor and Gage. One of these days, she was going to have to talk the woman into letting her help sort out her clothes. She was certain Marvella had dresses she'd worn back in high school and they progressed through each decade.

In fact, she was sure the outfit Aunt Marv chose to wear today had been one she'd purchased in the 1950s. The cream western-cut blouse and split skirt were embroidered with red roses. Aunt Marv wore a cream cowboy hat that looked a size or two too small as it perched on top of her head at a jaunty angle. A red leather belt with a silver buckle and red boots accented with white roses on the shafts completed the ensemble.

Gage had complimented Marvella on her snazzy attire before they left the house, making her aunt blush like a schoolgirl. While Marvella pranced outside to the pickup, Gage had leaned close to Tally and whispered in her ear that he thought she looked stunning in her burgundy blouse and dark blue jeans. She knew he was just being kind, but she'd wanted to spin around and kiss Gage. Somehow, she resisted the urge.

Honestly, she couldn't get the man out of her head, even at work. It seemed like he was there, lingering in her mind while the scent of him — that masculine combination of leather, sunshine, his aftershave and something that was uniquely Gage Taggart — haunted her day and night.

Thank goodness she'd been so busy at work or who knows what kind of trouble her thoughts might have gotten her into. She loved her job, but she missed being on the ranch, being with Gage all the time.

After spending two weeks with him, she supposed it was natural to miss him, to miss his laugh and the silly faces he made, the way he joked and teased, and put everyone at ease.

More than a few times, she'd gotten up in the night to check on both him and Trevor. But Gage was the one she watched while he slept, taking in the way his thick, dark eyelashes shadowed his cheeks, how his jaw created such a strong, rugged profile, how much she wanted to kiss those tempting lips.

As she crossed the street, she pulled her wayward thoughts back to the moment. Today, she wouldn't worry about Gage, or her growing feelings for him. She'd just enjoy the rodeo and hanging out with friends.

On her way to meet the guys and her aunt, Tally stopped in a vendor booth that captured her attention and looked through the clothing and accessories. A cute little top screamed at her to purchase it, but Tally didn't want to have to pack it around with her and she certainly didn't want to make the hike back to the pickup, so she bypassed it and continued on her way. Maybe she'd stop after the rodeo and see if it was still there.

She waited for a lull in traffic and crossed the main street with what seemed like a hundred other people, all eager to make their way into the stands for the rodeo.

Tally took out her phone and called Trevor, but it went to voice mail. She waited a moment and tried again, unable to reach him. She called Gage, since he'd programmed his number into her phone last week before she went back to work, insisting she might need to get in touch with him sometime.

Now, she was glad he had. It only took a moment for him to answer.

"Hey, beautiful. What can I do for you?" he said. She could hear the smile in his voice as he spoke as well as something alluring and teasing that made her knees threaten to wobble.

"To whom do think you are speaking?" she asked, wondering how many women were chasing after him at any given moment in time. Maybe he assumed she was one of them. That thought left her with a bitter taste in her mouth and an ache in her stomach.

"I'm speaking to the prettiest girl here today, Queenie. Do you think I answer the phone like that for just anyone?"

"Yes," she blurted, before she could stop herself.

Gage laughed. "You are mistaken, Tally. The guys wouldn't appreciate it and I'm not giving any of these whackadoodle girls who somehow got my number any encouragement or bad ideas."

"Good to know," she said, with a sense of relief. "Where are you?"

"We're almost to the main gate. Trevor ran into a bunch of people he knows then your aunt saw some friends, so we're just now heading that way."

"Okay. I'll wait for you right outside the main gate."

Tally disconnected the call and stuffed her phone in the little bag she carried. She watched the crowd, made up of an interesting mix of people. Some clearly excited to be there, smiles broad on their faces as they hurried to the gate and presented their tickets. There were a few who looked angry they had to deal with the crowds. A few harried parents tried to keep antsy children from running off or descending into full-fledged tantrums.

She leaned against the brick wall near the main gate and observed a group of middle-aged women in scanty attire as they attempted to flirt with a good-looking cowboy who was closer to Tally's age. He offered the women a tight smile while he looked around like a helpless animal caught in a trap, as though he sought a means of escape.

Tally didn't know what got into her, but she raised her hand and waved to the man. "Hey, honey, I've got our tickets," she called. Her voice was loud enough for him to hear over the crowd.

His gaze locked on hers and he smiled broadly, returning her wave. "Hi, darlin'! I thought I'd lost you in this crowd," he said as he hurried over to her, wrapping her in a hug.

Unaccustomed to being hugged by strange

men, especially when they fit in the category of tall, dark, and undeniably handsome, she tried not to stiffen and just enjoy the experience.

"Are they gone?" he whispered as he held her to him.

Tally glanced over his shoulder to see the women scowling at her before they marched off. "Yep, you're safe."

She stepped back and he let go, tipping his hat to her with an engaging smile that she was sure left a bevy of breathless women in his wake.

"Thanks for the save. I owe you one."

Tally grinned. "It's the least I can do. Enjoy the rodeo."

"I plan on it. You have a good time and if you need a rescue, here's my card." The man took a business card from his pocket and gave it to her before he moved into the line of people entering the gate.

"What were you doing?" Gage asked from behind her.

Tally spun around and gaped at him. She hardly recognized him with his forehead all wrinkled into a frown, his jaw clenched, and mouth set in a firm, hard line.

"Who was that?" His voice sounded accusing and angry as he balled his right hand into a fist, watching the cowboy she'd helped go through the gate. "Why were you hugging him?"

If she didn't know better, she might have thought Gage was jealous, but that was impossible. As far as she could tell, he still thought she was Trevor's chubby little sister. Nothing more.

Certainly not someone he'd considered dating.

Not that she wanted him to. Okay, maybe she did, but that was stupid at best and something that was never, ever going to happen.

"He was having a little trouble getting away from a pack of man-hungry cougars, so I gave him a hand. That's all."

Trevor chuckled and motioned for her and Marvella to go ahead of them in the line. "They are prowling everywhere. I've decided any male wearing jeans and boots is fair game."

"Good thing you are wearing shorts, then," Tally said, grinning at her brother over her shoulder. She knew it had irritated Trevor to wear anything but boots and jeans, but with his cast, shorts were far more practical, especially in this heat. It felt more like mid-summer outside than heading into fall as the forecast threatened to edge close to ninety-five degrees today.

However, Gage refused to go to the rodeo if he couldn't wear jeans and a boot on his left foot. Yesterday, she'd split the seam up the leg of an older pair of his jeans so he could get them on over his cast. He'd tossed them in the washer last night when they got back to the ranch and wore them again today with an aqua and navy striped shirt that made her want to swim laps in his incredible blue eyes. A black cowboy hat only heightened his good looks.

It was no wonder women swarmed around him like hummingbirds to a feeder dripping with sweet nectar. Even with one leg encased in a cast and strapped into his walking crutch and his left hand held together with pins, he was still one of the most attractive men she'd ever encountered.

She drew in a breath, catching a hint of his scent on the breeze as she handed her ticket to the person at the gate then held out her small purse for inspection. Once she was cleared, she went through the gate right behind Marvella and waited for Trevor and Gage to join them.

Her brother, in cargo shorts with a dark gray T-shirt showcasing the muscles of his chest and arms and an NFR ball cap on his head, drew plenty of attention from women, too.

Amused by the fact she was at the rodeo, accompanied by two men some women would pay money to be with, she looped her arm around Gage's and grinned at her aunt. "What would you like for lunch today, Auntie?"

Marvella chose a corn dog while Trevor and Gage both wanted Philly cheesesteak sandwiches and curly fries. Tally got herself a brisket sandwich and purchased two bottles of water and two of Dr Pepper before she carried all the food over to where the men and Marvella had secured a table in the shade beneath the stands.

"That looks so good," Trevor said as he dug into the fries then slid them toward Gage. Tally took a few and then tucked into her sandwich.

She felt someone glaring at her and turned slightly to see the group of women who'd been bothering the cowboy outside the gate watching her.

One of them sneered and tossed her hair over her shoulder. "How does a fatty like that hang out with such hot guys?"

"How do you think?" one of the other women said, moving her eyebrows in a suggestive manner.

A third one spoke up. "Well, I can think of a few ways and they all end up with a good time, at least for her. The guys probably have second thoughts when they wake up and sober up," the woman said, implying any number of things that weren't true as they walked off.

Gage and Trevor were busy talking to a rancher they both knew and missed the conversation, but Marvella placed a hand on Tally's back and gave her a comforting pat. "Don't you listen to a word those fork-tongued witches said, sweetheart. They are just jealous and being spiteful."

"I've got nothing for them to be jealous of, Aunt Marv." Tally sighed, no longer hungry as she pushed her half-eaten sandwich away and wiped her hands on a napkin. Most of the time, the fact she'd never been a skinny girl didn't bother her. She was healthy and strong and was careful about eating a nutritious, balanced diet. Sure, she made treats when she was at the ranch, but that was more for Marvella and Trevor than her own enjoyment. She never over-indulged and limited her sweets and carbs even if she did enjoy a piece of cake or sweet roll from time to time.

But today, with thin, beautiful women all around her, many who could have posed as models for Lasso Eight, she wished she hadn't taken after whoever passed on the DNA with excessive curves, heavy hips, and a full face. Just once, she wondered what it would be like to be thin and willowy.

Since she'd never know, she released a long

breath and took a drink of water from the bottle in front of her.

Marvella wrapped her arm around Tally's waist and gave it a squeeze. "My darling girl, I hope the day arrives when you see yourself as others do. Not catty women like those nitwits, but people who know you and love you. You are beautiful, inside and out. And if you hadn't noticed, there's more than one or two cowboys around here who've been checking you out."

Tally blushed. "Don't be silly, Aunt Marv."

Marvella reached across the table and lightly tapped Gage on the arm to get his attention.

"We are in need of an expert opinion," Marvella said, tipping her head toward Tally. "On a scale of one to ten, how would you rate Tally? Ten being the best, of course. And you have to be honest, Gage Taggart. No teasing or fibbing."

"I don't fib, Aunt Marv," Gage said, raising one eyebrow at her before fixing his gaze on Tally. His gaze roved over her from the brown curls she'd fashioned in her hair, across her face, down her neck and chest to where the table hid the rest of her. "As for Talilah King, she's about the prettiest, sexiest, classiest girl I've ever met, and that's saying something. On a scale of one to ten, she's at least a twelve."

He winked at her and turned back to Trevor's conversation with the rancher.

Tally's cheeks burned with heat and she couldn't help but stare at Gage. Had he been teasing her? Did he mean anything he said? Surely not. He was probably just trying to be nice and make her feel better.

About to be overcome with heat and emotion, Tally rose from the table. "I'll be back in a few minutes."

"Don't wander too far, honey," Marvella said. "We'll be ready to make our way to our seats soon."

Tally nodded and walked into the crowd, just wanting to blend in and not be seen. She walked the length of the area where vendors sold food outside the arena then turned and started back. Someone jostled into her from behind and the cowboy she'd helped earlier reached out a hand to steady her.

"It seems I'm destined to bump into you today," he said, slowly releasing her arm with a warm smile.

"So, it seems," she said, smiling at him then taking a step back. "Are you sure you're safe out in the open like this?" She glanced around, like she watched for predators that might be stalking him.

He laughed and shook his head. "Most likely not, but I thought I'd brave it for some of that barbecue over there. Is it any good?"

"Yes, but I like the brisket over there better," she said, pointing to the booth where she purchased her sandwich.

"Thanks for the tip. Maybe I'll see you later."

She smiled. "Maybe." Tally turned to leave and heard a whistle.

"Now that is one fine caboose," a male voice said directly behind her.

Tally looked over her shoulder to see the cowboy with another young man and both of them appeared to be watching her. Although she tried to act nonchalant, her gaze darted around, searching for the person they were talking about. The crowd in the immediate vicinity included three couples, all closer to Aunt Marv's age, a girl who looked like a punk rocker with spiky hair and slouchy jeans, and a pregnant woman with two cranky toddlers swarming around her legs, crying.

Covertly, she glanced back at the cowboy again and he winked, pointing a finger at her and nodding his head to let her know she was the one his friend had whistled at.

A blush started at the roots of her hair and traveled down the neck of her blouse as she hurried away into the crowd and headed back to where she'd left the men and Marvella. In spite of her embarrassment, she felt better than she had when she'd walked away from the table. Admittedly, it stoked her ego to have someone who wasn't living under her brother's roof tell her she was attractive.

Maybe those women who'd been so rude were like all the snarky girls she'd gone to school with over the years. Her mother had moved around so much, Tally never tried to make friends because she knew she'd just have to leave them behind. But it was hard being the new girl in school, especially when she was shy, chubby, and came with a backpack full of insecurities. She supposed a part of her would always feel like the shy misfit with braces, someone the popular kids shunned or criticized for being too fat to be in their clique.

She wouldn't have joined them if she'd been rail-thin, but that was neither here nor there.

Here was at the rodeo with her aunt, brother,

and Gage waiting for her so they could go up to their seats and enjoy the final performance of the Pendleton Round-Up.

Tally returned to the table to find Marvella finishing the last bite of her corn dog and the men visiting with Chase and Jessie Jarrett. Tally had met the couple a few times, since they lived less than thirty minutes away. Chase rode bulls and had been a friend Trevor stayed in touch with, even after he left the rodeo circuit. He'd married his wife in a publicity stunt a few years ago, but it was easy to see the two of them were very much in love. Jessie was a little shy and quiet, yet someone Tally found easy to be around.

"Hey, Tally! How are you?" Chase asked, giving her a welcoming nod. "These two worn you to a frazzle yet?"

Tally offered him and Jessie a friendly smile. "Not yet, but they're working on it."

"Need any help getting to your seats?" Chase asked as he handed Trevor his crutches when he rose from the table.

"I think we can make it, but the more the merrier," Gage said, motioning for Tally and Marvella to precede them. Tally led the way, keeping a hand on Marvella's arm, guiding her up to their seats.

Tally didn't know how Trevor had acquired them, but he'd managed to get four tickets on the end of the second row in a section with a great view of the bucking chutes. He'd also purchased two seats in the front row, so he and Gage had somewhere to rest their legs without them being in the way of others. Marvella slid into the row first followed by Trevor. Gage sat down next, leaving Tally on the end so she could be their official errand girl without having to climb over anyone to get out.

Chase and Jessie sat down behind them, joining a group of friends.

"Well, the gang's all here," Cort McGraw said with a laugh. "How are you doing, man?" he asked, coming down from his seat two rows back and holding out a hand to Trevor then Gage. "The two of you look like the twins of misery."

Everyone around them laughed. Tally glanced back and smiled at Cort's wife, Kaley, and their best friends, Tate and Kenzie Morgan. Cort and Tate both knew the rodeo way of life better than most since Tate had been a world champion saddle bronc rider before he retired and Cort had been a steer wrestler before an injury left him sidelined. The two couples each had a son and daughter and the four youngsters giggled and wiggled as they excitedly waited for the rodeo to begin. Tate came down and spoke with the men and was joined by Shaun Price who worked as a pickup man but wasn't working at this particular rodeo. Shaun's wife, Brylee, was with him as well as her teenage brother. Tally knew Shaun and Gage were good friends and she recalled meeting Brylee years ago. Brylee was still beautiful, but now she wore an unmistakable glow of love as Shaun kept her tucked close to his side.

"Are you racing today?" Tally asked Brylee. The woman had been number one in the world last year and she was working to hang onto that title this year.

"I sure am. I just came up to sit with the gang for a while, then I need to get Rocket ready to run." Brylee looked at Shaun with a smile that lit her whole face, then glanced at the sky. "At least today promises sunshine and no rain."

"That's right. Last year you took quite a spill in the mud," Tate said as he joined the conversation. "I hope you win it this year, Brylee."

"I'm going to give it my best shot," she said, then kissed Shaun's cheek and waved. "I'll be back in a bit. I just want to check on Rocket."

The group visited for a few more minutes then all of them greeted Paige James as she made her way into the stands. The woman was married to Cooper James, rodeo clown and barrelman extraordinaire. She also ran her own ad agency and her top client was Lasso Eight apparel. Gage had gone over to Chase and Jessie's ranch on Monday to model for the holiday campaign photo shoot. Even with his injuries, Paige had still wanted him to participate since he'd been a model from the beginning of the company's launch. Cooper had given him a ride and Tally could only imagine the conversations that took place in the vehicle on the way there and back.

In truth, Tally had nearly drooled over the print ads she'd seen of Gage modeling jeans and shirts for the clothing company. Last year, he and Shaun had been in several promotional pieces together and she recalled seeing one with the two of them and Brylee. But it was always Gage that drew her eye and interest. That hadn't changed since she'd first met him back when she was a little girl with pigtails.

"Maybe next year, you'll agree to be part of our photo shoot," Paige said as she stopped beside Tally and offered her a warm smile. "The founder of Lasso Eight is working on a new clothing line for women and you'd be a perfect model." Paige handed her a business card. "Let me know if you're interested."

Gage bumped her with his elbow and nodded toward Paige. "You should do it, Tally. It's a lot of fun, the pay is amazing, and you'd be a smokin' hot model."

Heat seared her cheeks until Tally felt like her skin was aflame, but she managed to smile at Paige. "I'll give it some thought. How are you doing?"

Paige rubbed a hand over the small mound of her stomach and got a sweet, wistful expression on her face. "Wonderful. I can hardly wait for the baby to be here."

"When are you due?" Tally asked, eyeing Paige and guessing her to be about four or five months along.

"Mid-January. Cooper is relieved the baby shouldn't be making an arrival during the finals. If he had to miss the rodeo, I think he'd spontaneously combust," Paige said with a grin that made the others laugh. "And I can't miss the fashion show or getting things in order for the Lasso Eight booth."

"Do you know if you're having a boy or a girl?" Tally asked, smiling up at the pretty woman.

"No. We decided we wanted to be surprised." Paige grinned and leaned down, lowering her voice to a conspiratorial tone. "I think the surprise will be if Cooper survives the experience. He's been fussing over me since I gave him the news we're having a baby. And his grandpa isn't much better."

"I'm sure it's all coming from a place of love," Tally said, feeling a pang of envy. Paige had a husband who not only doted on her, but truly loved her. She wanted that. Wanted to be looking forward to the arrival of her first child. To be loved and accepted by a group of close-knit friends.

The past several years, she had avoided being around Trevor's rodeo friends. Now that she'd spent time around them, she decided perhaps she'd been missing out on friendships with some truly kind and good people. From what she could tell, the members of this tight group were all kind, generous, and full of fun.

She watched as Cort McGraw picked up his daughter and Tate's then carried both little girls off to get a snow cone while their older brothers trailed behind him, talking a mile a minute.

"Can I get you guys anything?" Shaun asked as he maneuvered past Paige on the steps and glanced at Gage and Trevor.

"We're good, but thanks, man," Gage said.

"Okay, but if you change your mind, let me know." Shaun hurried out of the stands.

Paige patted Tally on the shoulder. "Think about modeling for Lasso Eight for the spring line. You really would be perfect."

"Thank you, Paige. I'll give it some thought."

Paige slid onto the bleacher next to Jessie Jarrett and sighed as she settled into her seat.

A moment later a loud "bang" signaled the beginning of the rodeo. Cheers erupted along with whistles and claps from those who'd been counting down the seconds until the event began.

After a brief introduction, the first horse bucked out of the chute in the bareback riding event. Trevor and Gage both watched with interest, but Gage seemed particularly intent on studying each movement of every ride.

Tally noted he cheered for each competitor, but the two he clapped the loudest for were the cowboys at the top of the rankings. Gage had slid from second to seventh place the last few weeks and Tally wondered what he'd do if he fell below fifteenth in ranking. That meant no trip to the finals and no shot at winning any titles this year.

In spite of something that had to be eating him alive with concern, he seemed carefree and happy as he clapped for his competition.

"Way to go, Tim!" Gage cheered as the rider in the arena earned eighty-four points on his ride.

"That's nice of you," Tally said, leaning toward Gage so he could hear her over the noise of the crowd.

"What?" he asked. He turned so fast to look at her, it left their faces mere inches apart. She had to battle the urge to press her lips to his.

Quickly gathering her wits, she smiled and leaned back. "Cheering for the riders. If it was me, I'd secretly hope none of them score."

He chuckled. "The odds of me holding onto a ranking that will take me to the finals are slim at best. I might as well accept the inevitable and support my friends."

She nodded, amazed by Gage's attitude and integrity as the last rider hung on for eight seconds, but received no score for not marking out the horse.

"Oh, that's too bad," she said, as the rider walked out of the arena with slumped shoulders.

"He really could have used the win," Gage said, pointing toward the chutes. "If he'd scored on that ride, he might have even taken the first slot. He's a good kid with a lot of potential. If he doesn't give up, he's got a shot at being a champion someday."

"Did you see him ride last month at..." Trevor launched into a conversation about riding techniques and styles which Tally tuned out completely. By the time the saddle bronc event finished, everyone was thirsty and wanting snacks, so she stopped by the restroom then made her way to the vendor booths. She had a box full of drinks, pretzels, and popcorn when a cowboy accidentally bumped into her as he left a booth selling strawberry shortcake.

"Sorry about that," he said, "I should... Hey! It's you again."

Tally smiled as the cowboy she'd helped earlier and then run into with his friend grinned at her.

"Fancy meeting you here," she said, moving out of the way as people tried to get in line around them.

"Are you feeding a small army?" he asked, glancing at her box.

"My brother and his friends," she said, hefting the box and starting in the direction of her seat.

"Here. Let me carry it," the man said, trading his shortcake for the box and keeping step beside her. "I don't think I caught your name earlier. I should at least know it if we're going to keep seeing each other today."

"Tally," she said, looking up at him. Wyatt, or so the name on his business card had said, was handsome, polite, and had a sense of humor. But he wasn't Gage.

"Well, Miss Tally, it's been the highlight of my day running into you."

"It has been fun," Tally said, meaning the words. If nothing else, the cowboy provided a diversion from dwelling over what would never be with Gage.

It was nice to know at least a few cowboys at the rodeo found her attractive or interesting.

"This is me," she said, pointing to the section where her group was seated. She took the box from him and nodded to the steps.

"Take care and enjoy the rest of the rodeo," he said, giving her one more grin before he strode away with his shortcake.

Tally walked up the steps and turned toward the seats only to see that same group of horrible women crowded around Trevor. They noticed her, pointed her way, and laughed.

She had no idea what they said, but Trevor glowered at the women. Aunt Marvella looked like she was ready to snatch them all bald as she rose to her feet with fury oozing from every pore.

"Listen you two-bit floozy, our girl has heels higher than your standards," Marvella said in a loud voice that carried over the crowd, shaking a bony finger at the woman who seemed to be leading the group. "Furthermore, my boys wouldn't want anything to do with the likes of you. If you'd get a gander at yourself in the mirror, you'd realize you are chasing after the wrong crowd. Try the senior citizen center for men closer to your age, or the prison release program for someone interested in what you have to offer."

The big-mouthed woman pulled back her hand, as though she intended to slap Marvella, but Paige stood and moved in front of Marvella before Tally could race up the steps or Trevor could grab his crutches and rise to his feet.

"I wouldn't do that, if I were you," Paige said, glaring at the group of women as Jessie Jarrett stood beside her. Without a word, the women turned and marched out of the stands then disappeared down the steps.

"Are you crazy?" Tally asked as she rushed up to her friends. Jessie gave Paige a hand climbing back up to her seat.

"I did marry Cooper, so probably," Paige said with a cheeky smile.

"Well, thank you for that. I don't know what they said to get Aunt Marv so worked up but thank you for stepping in like that." Tally handed the box of food to her brother then gave Paige a hug.

"I assumed even they wouldn't hit a pregnant woman, so it seemed like I was the most logical choice," Paige said, accepting the cold bottle of water Tally handed to her.

"Where is Gage?" Tally asked, settling into her

seat although her nerves felt tightly wound after the incident. She had no idea what she'd done to make the women dislike her so, but whatever it was, she hoped she didn't run into them again.

"Restroom," Trevor said, handing Aunt Marv a bag of popcorn and a bottle of water.

"I hope he makes it back unscathed. The cougars have sharp claws today," Tally said, drawing laughter from the friends around her.

"And really big, yellow teeth," Paige added, nudging her playfully from behind.

Gage returned a moment later. Tally moved out of the way so he could take his seat next to her. When he turned to look at her, he placed his left forearm on her leg and leaned close to her.

"I don't know what's wrong, but something is bugging you. If it has anything to do with those disgusting women I saw making their way out of the stands, don't let them bother you. They aren't worth your time, Queenie." Gage kissed her cheek and turned to accept a pretzel and bottle of soda from Trevor.

Tally watched out of the corner of her eye as he took a long swig of the cold Dr Pepper. Even that simple, everyday act seemed more... fascinating when it involved Gage.

She sighed and wondered how she'd survive until he was well enough to leave. Then she wondered how she'd survive without the hope of seeing him on her days off. Tormented and conflicted, she jumped when something cold touched her neck.

Gage held the bottle of pop there and grinned at

her. "Have a drink. It'll make you feel better."

She unscrewed the cap on the bottle and took a long sip. It wasn't until she handed the bottle back to him that she thought about what she'd done, sharing his soda.

Placing her lips where his had been seemed a rather personal, intimate thing. One that made a little thrill of excitement sizzle through her although she hid it by snitching a piece of Gage's pretzel and popping it in her mouth.

Tally had calmed down considerably by the time the rodeo volunteers hurried into the arena to move the fencing for bull riding. Suddenly, the sounds of the opening strains of "Stayin' Alive" began to play over the speakers.

Cooper James strutted into the arena with a six-foot long plush toy snake draped around his neck like a feather boa.

When the words of the song started, he grabbed the snake's head and held it in front of him like a microphone, doing a few disco moves as he sang along to the song.

Gage looked at Tally and winked.

"I can't believe you told Cooper, of all people, about the snake." Tally glared at Gage then looked back at Cooper.

The barrelman's head bobbed in time to the music as he danced his way around the arena.

"Cooper still has the moves," Gage said, glancing back at Paige.

She smiled. "What they are is the question," she said, as those around them laughed.

"Sing along!" Cooper shouted when the song

reached the chorus. The crowd joined in, clapping in time to the beat.

Near the end of the song, Cooper ran over to their section, vaulted over the fence and into the stands, then tossed the snake into Tally's lap. He gave Paige a quick kiss then jumped back into the arena and boogied his way over to his barrel.

Tally thought she might die from embarrassment as she picked up the snake's head and whacked Gage on the shoulder with it.

He laughed and reached over to pat her arm with his right hand. "You know it's never a dull moment with me around."

"That's putting it mildly," Tally said as she rolled her eyes.

"Let's all give a hand to Super Cooper James for that impromptu performance," the announcer said before the bull riding began.

After the rodeo, Tally held onto Marvella's hand as she, Trevor and Gage waited to cross the street. The men assured her they could make it to where she parked the pickup with no trouble, so she agreed to let them walk.

They'd only gone a few feet down the block when Tally heard someone call her name. She turned to see Wyatt step out of a vendor booth and hurry toward her.

"Hey. It's you again," she said, smiling at him.

"I just wanted to thank you, again, for earlier. It really was fun to meet you." He gave her a long look then noticed Trevor and Gage. He held out a hand toward the two men. "Wyatt Nash."

"Trevor King." Trevor shook his hand.

"You ranch out near Echo, don't you?" Wyatt asked.

"That's right. Nash? You related to the folks who own Nash's Folly?"

"Yep. My sister and her husband took over, but it's been in my family for generations."

"It's a nice place, one of the top wheat producers in the area," Trevor said with a hint of admiration. He gave Wyatt a long glance. "You also rodeo, don't you?"

Wyatt grinned. "Tie-down roping. I would have been competing this weekend, but I hurt my hand a few weeks ago. Just waiting for it to heal up." He held up his right hand then turned to Gage. "We've met a few times, Gage. I'm sure sorry to hear about your accident. You were a sure thing for the finals."

"Thanks." Gage sidled closer to Tally and she wondered why. He couldn't possibly be jealous of Wyatt, could he?

No. That was completely ridiculous.

Tally placed a hand on Wyatt's arm and gave him another friendly smile. "It was nice to meet you today."

Wyatt kissed her cheek. "The next time I need to be rescued, I hope it's by a girl even half as sweet as you." He tipped his hat and backed up a step. "You all have a nice evening."

Tally nodded and continued toward the pickup. When she glanced down, Aunt Marv gave her a long wink then squeezed her hand. "I want to hear every detail about you meeting that hunky cowboy, honey, and don't you dare skip a word."

"Yes, Aunt Marv." Tally glanced over her

shoulder, aware of Gage's dark scowl. Maybe a little jealously on his part wasn't so far-fetched after all.

Chapter Twelve

Autumn arrived slowly at King Penny Ranch, as though a master artist wanted to linger over painting each leaf in a spectacular jewel-toned hue.

The temperature at night dipped down to frosty levels, making Gage grateful he had somewhere warm to stay for the time being.

Truthfully, he felt like he'd been a burden to Trevor and Tally the last six weeks, but they'd both assured him that wasn't the case. He and Trevor had fallen back into a routine of easy friendship they'd enjoyed the summer he lived on the ranch.

However, Tally was an entirely different matter. She treated him exactly like she did Trevor — as a brother. She teased him, laughed with and at him, and argued with him. But not once did she provide any indication she saw him as more than just Trevor's best friend.

It annoyed and irritated him that she shoved him into the friend category, even if it was for the best. After visiting the doctor yesterday, Gage knew he was in for a few more weeks of wearing his cast. Until it came off, there wasn't a whole lot he could do for himself.

He'd been looking for a vehicle to purchase, although it would be a while before he could drive one. After his accident, he decided to give up the nomadic biker lifestyle and purchase something that would protect him better on the open road. A tank seemed like overkill, so he'd been eyeing a new pickup. Of course, he told Trevor he was looking at a brand he knew his friend held strong opinions against just to debate the finer points of each vehicle.

A picture of driving the pickup, Tally in the seat beside him and snow falling around them made him smile and think of the winter days that would soon be approaching. Would he still be in Echo then? Or would he head south as he'd done in past years? There were a number of rodeos in warm climates where he could get back into competing and start working toward claiming the championship title for the following year.

Disappointment stabbed at him when he thought of how hard he'd worked all season only to have his chance to compete in Las Vegas plucked out of his hands by a senile old goat who should never have been behind the wheel of a car. He'd found out when police questioned the man who caused his wreck, the crotchety man blamed Gage, saying he deserved to get hurt for riding a motorcycle on the freeway.

Furious, Gage had wanted to punch or kick

something. Instead he'd gone out on the porch and watched Tally work in the flower beds. It wasn't being on the ranch that calmed him, although he liked being there better than anywhere else. It was Tally. She was the balm that soothed his soul and diminished his troubles.

Whether she realized it or not, whether he wanted to admit it or not, he cared for her. Deeply.

The day at the Round-Up when he'd seen her hug some good-looking cowboy, he'd wanted to pummel the guy until he was black and blue. Gage wasn't given to outbursts befitting a cavedweller, but he didn't want anyone touching Tally unless it was him.

And that was not something she'd likely welcome.

There were times he turned and caught her watching him with something in her eyes that gave him hope, then she'd look away and he'd think he imagined it. The woman was driving him daft and had no idea he was confused, intrigued, and so fascinated with her he could hardly hold two thoughts together in her presence.

The day was coming soon when the doctor would clear him to drive and he'd be well enough to leave the ranch. Gage dreaded it. He enjoyed being at the ranch where he'd learned so many life lessons from Ross. He liked hanging out with Trevor and strengthening their friendship. Marvella was a kick in the pants that kept him entertained with her antics. But Tally was the reason he didn't want to leave.

It wasn't like she was there every day, but as

soon as her shift ended at the end of her three-day run, he knew she'd be home and he'd have three days to spend with her before she'd leave again.

He'd miss her like a body missed air to breathe or water to drink — as something vital and necessary to his existence. Yet, no matter how much he wanted or needed Tally, she didn't feel the same.

Years ago, he'd been aware of her crush on him. He'd thought it was cute at the time. But somewhere along the way, she stopped looking at him like he was a prince about to sweep her away into a fairy tale and started seeing him as nothing more than as Trevor's good friend.

He supposed part of that was his fault. It's not like he made a point of connecting with her in the past several years. When he'd been at the ranch, Tally had always been working. She didn't attend rodeos with Trevor. The only way he would have seen her is if he'd been at the hospital.

Considering how badly his hand still hurt he didn't like the option of making injuries that required hospitalization a common occurrence. He'd been banged up plenty riding bucking broncs, but nothing that involved hardware holding him together.

In spite of how uncomfortable he was, how much he looked forward to being healed, he was glad he'd gotten hurt where he had. He could have been hundreds of miles away without anyone nearby to help him. He would have been at the mercy of strangers, or even worse, his parents or brother, to care for him.

Tally was an excellent nurse, and an even better

friend. Gage supposed there were worse things than being in love with a woman you respected, admired, and liked more than anyone you'd ever met.

"I'm in love with her," he said, surprised by this admission. The air whooshed out of him. He scooted back against the pillows until he was propped against the headboard of his bed. Air slowly filled his lungs and he took a deep breath. Love? How could he be in love with his best friend's little sister?

Gage had been in any number of relationships. He'd chased after girls, and run from many, but love had never been part of the equation.

Not once had he even been close to falling in love, but he knew he'd been in love with Tally since the day she'd brought him Trevor's rigging at the rodeo. Even in her goofy farm animal scrubs, he'd taken one look at her and lost his heart.

The problem was that he seemed to be alone in his feelings and doubted anything he did or said would alter that.

Stunned by the revelation he wanted to change that, to change her mind and make her fall in love, Gage got out of bed and dressed for the day. He'd grown adept at managing with only one hand, even if he still couldn't tie his shoes. Luckily for him, Marvella was more than happy to help when he needed it.

Quietly, Gage left his room and went to the kitchen where he made a pot of coffee and listened to see if anyone else was awake. It was early and he didn't want to disturb anyone, so he poured a cup of the dark, fragrant brew and took it outside. He hiked one hip on the porch railing and watched the darkness of early morning begin to take on the muted tones of coming daylight.

"You're going to freeze out there without a coat," Tally said from behind him.

Caught by surprise, he choked on the sip he'd just swallowed and coughed. Tally whacked his back a few times then moved back inside the warmth of the kitchen.

Gage followed her and sat on a stool at the bar. "I hope I didn't wake you."

"You didn't. I wasn't sleeping, so I figured I might as well get up and make breakfast." She smiled at him and Gage felt his heart trip before it began to beat at an accelerated pace. "Any requests?" she asked.

He shook his head. "Everything you make is delicious, so surprise me. Or, you could make those cinnamon rolls we had a few weeks ago. They were amazing."

She smiled. "Cinnamon rolls it is. They sound good on a cold autumn morning. If you and Trevor don't eat them all, you can have some later with that apple cider I brought home yesterday."

"I thought Marvella was going to get sick on it," Gage said, taking a sip of his coffee.

"Me, too. I guess it's been a while since we had any." Tally measured milk into a saucepan to scald then gathered the other ingredients she'd need to make the rolls. "Do you have any plans for today?"

Gage wondered what she'd do if he said his only plans involved figuring out a way to finagle a kiss out of her. Instead, he shook his head again.

"Nope. Trevor thought between the two of us, we might be able to finish going through the ranch accounts and get everything updated on the computer."

"It's nice of you to help him with that. He hates doing the bookwork and I'm not much better."

"I don't mind it," Gage said, leaning back in his chair and toying with his now empty cup. "I've always had a head for figures."

Tally glanced over at him and raised an eyebrow. "Figures? As in female, perfect size two?"

He smirked. "No, ma'am. I meant numbers and investments, that sort of thing. For the record, my preference in figures of the female variety leans toward those with a lot more shape than a broomstick. Take you, for instance."

"What about me?" Tally asked in an uncertain tone as she stirred milk into a big bowl so it would cool.

"Those curves of yours are killer, Queenie. I'm talking knock a cowboy out of his boots and right onto his backside kind of curves that leave a fella gasping for air, but what a way to go." He tossed a rakish grin at her and she shyly glanced away. "Any man in his right mind would rather hold you in his arms than some scrawny girl who survives by eating carrots and those cardboard-tasting diet bars. I'm here to tell you, girls like that are cranky. They give hangry-angry a whole new meaning."

Tally smiled, although he observed the color that stained her cheeks was a perfect shade of pink. His teasing words embarrassed her, but he hoped she knew he meant them. The first time he saw her in snug boots with jeans, he thought he might have to ask Marvella for a bib so he didn't soak his shirt when he started to drool.

Although she didn't seem to realize it, Tally King was a gorgeous woman, one with a figure that put men in mind of classic Hollywood stars who once graced the big screen. He hated she believed what the idiot women at the rodeo, and others like them, said about Tally being fat.

He'd dated women of every shape, size, and color. All women were pretty to him, until they weren't. Women could be so cruel, hurtful, and catty with their comments about each other, especially when someone didn't fit the mold they deemed to be acceptable. He had nothing against skinny girls, if that's the way they were born. It was the women who starved themselves so they were thin that bothered him. So did the women who didn't care enough about themselves to stay healthy and got so heavy their health was at risk.

However, there was a world of difference between being obese and being a well-endowed beautiful woman that men couldn't help but notice. Tally was oblivious to their interest as well as the truth that she intimidated some women and they were, in turn, incredibly jealous of her.

That naïveté, though, was one of the many things he admired about her. Tally didn't play games, leading men on. She didn't snub other women. She was a genuinely kind, thoughtful, caring person, even if she didn't have a clue how much he was attracted to her, how much he longed to love her.

For now, he'd have to be content with making her smile. "I bet if you got all dolled up, someone might think you were a time traveler from the golden age of Hollywood."

She gave him a warning look, followed by a pleased smile. "You are laying it on a little thick, Mr. Taggart. I'll have to go pull on a pair of rubber boots to wade through your malarkey if you don't put an end to it soon."

He got off the barstool and walked over to the coffee pot which just happened to be near where she was stirring yeast into the milk. He used his body to block her in as he reached around her with his right hand and got the coffee pot.

"Just sayin', Queenie." He whispered in her ear in a low voice.

A shiver made goose bumps pop out on her skin and he grinned. Perhaps he might affect her more than she let on. When she looked at him with liquid eyes full of yearning, he tossed her a rascally smile and moved back.

If he didn't, there was no telling what might happen. The first time he kissed her, he wanted to be able to bury both of his hands in that mass of glorious hair.

"I was thinking, if you and Trevor don't have anything pressing to do today, we could pick up a few bushels of apples and pears. You boys could help peel them."

Gage's eyes widened. "Well, gosh, as much fun as that sounds, I'm sure I've got, um…"

She giggled. "You've got nothing going on and no excuses. Admit it. I bet if I asked you to be a taste-tester for pies, you'd be all over that request."

"I'd be all over something," Gage mumbled as Tally bent over and searched inside a cupboard across from him. The view that afforded him made his shirt collar feel like it was about to strangle him, especially when she wiggled around to reach something in the back.

She pulled out a large baking pan and set it on the counter then looked over at him.

"Are you okay?" she asked, walking over to him and placing the back of her hand on his forehead. "You look flushed, but you don't seem to be running a fever."

Gage would have argued with her that he was about to incinerate, but he kept his thoughts to himself. If she waggled her cute backside at him just one more time, he would have refused responsibility for what might have happened. It was a good thing she found that stupid pan when she did.

"I'm fine, Tally." His voice sounded raspy even to his own ears.

"You sound like you're coming down with something. Maybe you should rest. Want me to make you some tea and toast and bring it to you in bed?"

The thought of her bringing him breakfast in bed caused another spike in his temperature and left him off balance.

"That won't be necessary. I think I'll walk on down to the barn and see if Judd needs any help." Gage grabbed the old cowboy hat he left by the back door and slapped it on his head.

"Don't be gone too..." Tally stopped talking at the sound of a vehicle coming down the driveway. "Who could that be?" she asked, leaning over the sink to peer out the window.

Gage swallowed hard and turned away before he reached out and slid his hand over one of her curves. "I'll go find out. You might tell Sleeping Beauty to roll out of bed."

"I don't think we need to wake Aunt Marv," Tally teased.

Gage rolled his eyes. "You know who I'm referring to."

"What's going on?" Trevor asked as he made his way into the kitchen. His hair stuck up every direction, but he was dressed, even if he still looked half asleep.

"Someone's here. Gage is going to go see who it is and what they need."

"I'll go with you," Trevor said, grabbing his hat and settling it on his head before he followed Gage outside in the brisk morning air.

Gage's grin broadened when three cowboys spilled out of a pickup pulling a horse trailer.

"I heard there's a couple of down-on-their-luck cowpokes in need of a hand," a cowboy named Garrett said as he reached out to give Gage a thump on the back. "How are you, man?"

"Getting by." Gage returned the thump on his friend's back. "What in the world are you doing here?"

"We heard about Trevor's surgery and your accident," Garrett said. "Figured y'all might need some help with a little fall work and decided we'd stop by on our way through the area. We're heading to California, but we don't have to be anywhere until Thursday." Garrett motioned to the other cowboys with him.

"That is awesome, man." Trevor said, bracing himself on his crutches so he could shake Garrett's hand. "All three of you are welcome, although you don't have to work."

"We want to help. In fact, you'll have more help than you know what to do with by the time the day gets rolling." Garrett grinned as another pickup drove down the lane and more cowboys got out.

"I better tell Tally to make more food for breakfast." Trevor turned around and headed into the house.

Gage grinned at his friends, trying to understand what they were doing.

"What's going on, guys?" he asked as he waved at more of his friends.

"Nothing, except we really did want to help out. We just figured a little assistance with fall work might be appreciated." Garrett smirked at him. "And we heard there's a girl who may have caught your eye."

Gage scowled. "What did you hear?"

"Just that you were pretty chummy with a girl at the Pendleton Round-Up. Is she here? Can we meet her? Or have you dumped her and moved on already?" Garrett asked.

"You guys leave her alone." Vertical lines pinched Gage's brow as he growled at his friend. "She's not like... well, she's different from the girls I typically date and I don't want any of you scaring her off."

Garrett laughed and thumped him on the back. "You'll take care of that soon enough on your own. We'll be on our best behavior."

"Is that a promise?"

Garrett grinned. "One you can take to the bank."

"In that case, come on in and have some coffee. She's making cinnamon rolls for breakfast." Gage took a step forward then glanced back to see his friends sharing knowing looks.

"So, she is staying here with you?" Garrett asked as they headed for the door.

"Not like you think. She lives here. Trevor is her brother. He's threatened to end my sorry life and leave my body where even the coyotes won't find it if I do anything to hurt her, so keep that in mind." Gage gave them all warning looks before he led them inside the house.

Tally looked like a deer caught in the headlights as five cowboys she'd never met before strolled into the kitchen, yanked off their hats, and gave her their most charming smiles.

"Tally, these are some of my rodeo buddies. They're just passing through but offered to help out around the ranch today. This is Garrett, Tom, Cody, Nick, and Hank."

"It's nice to meet you all," she said with a wary smile. "Is anyone else coming?"

"Oh, there'll be about twenty of us, but don't worry about lunch," Garrett said. "They're bringing it."

Tally dropped the saucepan she'd just pulled

out of the cupboard and bent over to pick it up while the men all studied her.

Gage would have socked Garrett in the nose for ogling Tally's form if he'd had two good hands and didn't think she'd be appalled by his behavior.

"Twenty?" she asked on a squeak, slowly turning around to face them. "Who is coming?"

"Tate Morgan, Cort McGraw, Chase Jarrett, Shaun Price, and a few others are coming." Garrett looked to Trevor. "Hope you don't mind."

"Are you kidding? That's awesome. It'll be just like old times," Trevor said, appearing more excited than he'd been since before his accident.

"Did a badger really do that to you?" a cowboy named Hank asked, pointing to Trevor's cast.

"Rotten, stinking beast certainly did. But Judd made sure they caught him, and the boys filled all the holes out there in the pasture." Trevor sighed. "I'm just glad it was me and not one of the horses that found that hole."

Tally shook her head and Gage winked at her as she went about making breakfast preparations. She'd just pulled an egg and sausage casserole from the oven when Marvella sailed into the kitchen. The elderly woman wore a plaid skirt of autumn colors with a bright yellow sweater that looked like she'd dipped it in the same can of paint used to identify school buses.

"Morning, Aunt Marv," Trevor said, greeting her. "Some friends came over to help out today."

"Well, howdy do, boys. Welcome to King Penny Ranch," Marvella said in an exaggerated twang.

She dominated the conversation during breakfast. Gage sat back and observed Tally as she attempted to stay in the background by refilling coffee cups and pouring juice. Little did she know every time she bent over to set down a cup or glass, a half a dozen men watched her every move.

They'd just finished eating when more pickups and horse trailers arrived.

"I better run into town and pick up some things for lunch," Tally said as Gage set an empty platter on the counter by the sink where she did the dishes.

"The guys said it's covered. Don't worry about cooking for them." Gage kissed her cheek and followed the others outside, ignoring the scowl Tally shot his way or the grins from his friends.

He and Trevor waved as Tate and Kenzie Morgan got out of their pickup. Kenzie picked up their daughter, Marley, while Tate hefted a box full of food and carried it into the house.

Kaley McGraw handed her daughter, Grace, a bag of food then she and Cort both carried in boxes of food.

"I hope you brought plenty! We'll be starving by the time lunch rolls around," Cooper James yelled as he drove up and parked with the other rigs by the barn.

"You're always hungry," Paige commented as she got out of the pickup and carried a basket toward the house. Jessie Jarrett fell into step beside her while Brylee Price hurried to catch up with them.

"Just tell us what you need help with, and we'll do our best to get it done today," Chase Jarrett said as he moved next to Trevor and shook his hand. Tate and Cort joined him while the other men greeted one another.

"I can't believe you all are here to help today. It's amazing and so appreciated," Trevor said. "We've been working up the ground so we can get the winter wheat planted. The cattle need to be worked, too, and the spring calves should have been weaned a few weeks ago. Judd has been trying to find time to finish burying a ditch out in the pasture. The pipe's out there, it just needs to be placed and covered. Anything you want to do to help would be great."

Cort glanced at Tate and the two of them divided everyone into groups. Those who knew how to run a tractor went with Judd to get the ground worked up. The men willing to work on the ditch went with Jared and Tony, and the rest of them started taking their horses out of the trailers to go round up the cattle.

Gage looked up when Tally and Brylee came out of the house together. Tally had changed from a pair of knit leggings and a long tunic top into jeans, dusty boots, and a dark burgundy shirt topped with a denim jacket. The hair she'd twisted into a messy knot on top of her head now hung in long waves down her back, held away from her face with a small clip.

"Planning to join in the fun?" Gage asked as the two women approached him.

Tally tipped her head back toward the house. "They kicked me out of the kitchen and told me to come have fun with the boys. Brylee offered to come keep me company."

Gage was surprised the women had somehow talked Tally into coming outside, but he was glad they had. From the past weeks of living at the ranch, he knew she loved to ride but rarely had time. He just hoped she wouldn't act withdrawn as she tended to do when she was around Trevor's rodeo friends. She was never that way as a kid, but he had no idea what had changed, why she'd changed.

For now, he just wanted her to enjoy the time outside on a beautiful autumn day, with a group of good-hearted people.

"I'll meet you by the barn," Brylee said as she headed toward her horse trailer where Shaun was leading out her horse.

"You doing okay?" Gage asked as Tally drew in a deep breath, as though she needed to steady her nerves.

"I'll be fine, Gage, but thanks for asking. This is all a bit overwhelming," she said, looking to where half a dozen pickups were parked and people rushed around, joking and laughing. "I can't believe they'd all do this for Trevor."

Her gaze narrowed and she studied his face. "Did you arrange this?"

Gage shrugged. "I merely mentioned to Shaun and Cooper that Trevor could sure use a hand." He glanced down at the pins in his left hand then smiled at her. "Preferably one that functioned. No one told me they were coming for sure, though. I had no idea they'd all be here today."

"You never cease to surprise me, Gage Taggart." Tally threw her arms around him and gave him an impulsive hug.

Taken by surprise, he wrapped his right hand around her waist and held her close before she pushed against his chest and stepped back, obviously uncomfortable. Her scent that always made him think of winter and Christmas cookies filled his nose and he savored the fragrance.

"I better go saddle my horse," Tally said, backing toward the barn.

"Have a good time, Queenie. Enjoy it enough for both of us." Gage waved at her then retreated to the porch where he watched his friends mount their horses and ride off with Chase and Shaun leading the way to gather the cattle.

Trevor joined him on the porch and eased onto a chair. "I can't believe this, man. It's so nice of everyone to give up their time to be here today."

"It's pretty great, but then we have some pretty great friends." Gage grinned and slapped Trevor on the back. "Since we can't do anything to help out here, how about we go inside and make sure Marvella doesn't burn the house down or scare the babies."

Trevor chuckled. "That's probably a good idea. If they need more food, I could order some and send Tally to go pick it up."

"I think you should let her play cowgirl today. She'll enjoy visiting with Brylee and she loves riding."

"I know, and I feel bad she doesn't get to do as much of it as she'd like." Trevor used his crutches to pull himself up out of the chair and followed Gage inside.

"Hey, just who we were looking for," Kenzie said with a smile and handed Trevor a vegetable peeler. "You are on spud duty, my friend."

Trevor groaned, but winked at the women as he took a seat at the counter and started peeling potatoes.

"What can our one-handed organizer do?" Marvella asked, placing a hand on Gage's arm.

"Keep the girls entertained?" Kaley asked, motioning to where Grace McGraw and Marley Morgan sat at the table eating jam-slathered toast. Marley sat on a stack of books, since she wasn't yet three, and Grace, who was almost four, sat on a chair, barely peeking over the edge of the table.

"Maybe I better head back outside," Gage said, taking a step toward the door before Paige and Jessie turned him around with a laugh.

"You're the designated babysitter this morning, Gage. No side-stepping your duties," Paige teased. "If you need help, let me know. I'm trying to get in all the practice I can."

"You'll be a great mother, Paige. I have no doubt about that at all. Cooper, now…" he grinned. "How's *he* gonna be a parent when he still acts like an overgrown child most of the time?"

Paige smiled; aware he was teasing. "That remains to be seen, but I have a feeling he'll be a great dad."

"I know he will be." Gage gently squeezed her shoulder then made his way to the table and sat down with the two little girls. "So, did you two bring a unicorn with you?"

"No!" Grace said, smiling up at him with big

gray eyes that put him in mind of Tally. "But we gots good things to eat!"

"You do?" Gage leaned forward and playfully tugged on Grace's pigtail. "Do you think you'd share with me?"

"Yep! Mommy made lots and lots."

"Well, that's good to know." Gage smiled at Grace then turned to Marley. "Do you need help eating that toast, Marley? It sure looks good."

"No! All done!" She stuffed the last bite in her mouth then held up sticky hands.

He tossed a helpless look at the women who laughed at him. Kenzie lobbed a wet dishcloth his way. Gage caught it and started wiping mouths and hands.

It was gonna be a long morning.

By the time everyone returned at noon, Gage was exhausted from trying to keep up with two active little girls. Trevor had tried to sneak outside multiple times, but each time he did, one of the women found something else for him to do inside the house.

Gage had a sneaking suspicion Tally had asked them to find indoor jobs for him and Trevor so they wouldn't be tempted to get in the middle of things and chance an injury. He didn't appreciate being mollycoddled, even if he did understand the reasoning behind it.

The scents of barbecued beef and yeasty rolls filled the kitchen with such a delicious aroma, Gage could hardly wait to dig into the food. It looked like there was enough to feed an army, or three, by the time the women piled it all on the table and counter.

Trevor asked a blessing on the meal then plates were filled, and people found seats in the great room, the kitchen, and a few even went outside to sit in the sunshine and eat.

Gage felt a prick of irritation as Garrett and Hank somehow managed to flank Tally as she sat on the couch. When Garrett leaned close to her and said something that made her laugh, anger stung like bile up Gage's throat. He swallowed hard and turned to Cooper and Paige, asking them about their plans for the baby and which room at the house they'd converted to a nursery.

"I haven't spoken to Nick for a while," Gage said, referring to Cooper's grandfather who shared his home with the couple. "Is he getting excited?"

"Excited doesn't even begin to describe Nick," Paige said with a smile. "He's been offering suggestions on baby names for weeks. He even climbed up in the attic and brought down a set of baby furniture that looks like it should be in a museum. It's truly beautiful."

"If the baby is anything like Cooper, it will probably gnaw through the crib and be racing around the house, laughing at his own jokes." Gage ducked when Cooper threw his napkin at him.

"Just wait until it's your turn, dude." Cooper warned.

Thoughts of marriage and babies drew Gage's gaze to Tally. He scowled when Hank brushed a lock of hair away from her face and gave her a smile meant to turn women's knees to jelly. Gage had seen his friend use it often enough, and with success, to want to toss the man outside on his ear.

Frustrated he couldn't do anything with his injuries hampering his every move, he leaned back in his chair and frowned.

Shaun leaned around Brylee who was sitting on Gage's other side and gave him a knowing look. "You've got it bad."

"Got what?" Gage asked, scowling.

Shaun grinned and lowered his voice so no one else could hear. "A case of falling in love with a beautiful girl, if what I'm seeing is any indication of what's happening here at King Penny Ranch."

Since Shaun was correct, Gage couldn't argue with him, but he didn't like that his friend had figured out his feelings for Tally when the woman appeared so clueless.

"I think she likes you, too," Brylee whispered.

Gage turned from glowering at Hank to give Brylee a questioning glance. "What makes you say that?"

"She talked about you quite a bit this morning and when she says your name, her whole face lights up." Brylee grinned at him. "And if you weren't so busy trying to kill Hank and Garrett with those glares of yours, you'd notice she keeps looking at you when she thinks no one is watching."

"Really?" Gage asked, feeling marginally better. "Maybe I've got barbecue sauce on my face." He wiped his napkin around his mouth.

"Dude, get a clue. She's into you and you are into her." Shaun's grin broadened. "And now we sound like we're back in junior high passing notes in study hall."

Gage chuckled. "Agreed. How about you two

tell me how things are going at the Price ranch? And how's Birch doing? Did you say he joined the rodeo team at school?"

After the men returned to work and the women took care of the dishes, Gage wandered outside with Trevor and over to the pens where the cattle were being sorted and worked.

Tally had stayed in the house to help with dinner preparations, but the girls must have kicked her out because she wandered over to where he and Trevor leaned against the fence.

"I can't believe how much work they've gotten done this morning," she said, motioning to a field in the distance. "It would have taken Judd and the guys until Thanksgiving to get this much done."

"It's incredible," Trevor said in a thick voice, obviously overcome with emotion.

Gage settled his right hand on his friend's shoulder and gave it a brotherly pat. "You'd do the same for any of them. In fact, I know you have for some of them, Trev. Just take the gift of friendship and pay it forward when you can."

Trevor nodded as Tally stepped next to him and wrapped her arms around his middle, giving him a hug.

"The ladies oust you from the kitchen again?" Gage asked when Tally moved back from her brother.

She nodded. "They insisted they had everything under control. I feel like I should be in there helping, but they assured me they can take care of dinner without me. Brylee wanted to play with Marley and Grace before they went down for naps, so here I am."

"I bet if you wanted to help sort the cattle, they'd be glad to have a hand," Trevor said, pointing inside the pen.

"I don't know. It's probably best if I stay right here or go back inside and demand they give me something to do."

Gage smiled, envisioning Tally marching into the kitchen and barking orders. It wouldn't ever happen.

Brylee jogged over to them and grabbed Tally's hand. "Come on, Tally. Let's show these boys a thing or two."

Tally glanced back at them with a helpless look as Brylee pulled her over to where they'd left their horses. When Tally swung onto the back of a sleek black mare Trevor called Velvet, Gage's mouth went dry. He watched her ride off with Brylee, hair bouncing against her back, perfect form as she sat tall and straight in the saddle.

He wasn't sure how it happened, but he was sure Tally got prettier by the day. Was that possible?

Trevor bumped his arm, holding out a blue bandana handkerchief. "You need this?" he asked.

Gage frowned and shook his head. "No. Why?"

"Thought you might need it to wipe away all the drool dribbling down your chin." Trevor gave him a hard look as he tucked the handkerchief back in his pocket. "Don't forget that's my baby sister and you made me a promise."

A sigh rolled out of Gage. He clenched and unclenched his right hand before he rested it on the top rail of the fence, gaining control of his thoughts and emotions before he spoke. Slowly, he turned to face Trevor. "I haven't forgotten, and I won't go back on my promise."

"Good. Now, how about we mosey over there by the chute? I think between the two of us, we can at least help get the vaccinations ready to hand to them."

"Lead the way, Trev," Gage said, waiting while Trevor got his crutches propped beneath his arms. "Anything is better than letting Grace and Marley play beauty shop with me again."

Chapter Thirteen

"I need you to take Aunt Marv on a date."

Gage raised an eyebrow and lifted his gaze from the screen of his laptop computer he'd set on the kitchen table. Tally had been busy baking something that filled the whole room with the delicious scent of chocolate. He could have found somewhere less distracting to work as he reviewed his investments and made a few tweaks for the last quarter of the year, but he liked being near her.

After Trevor's reminder last week of the promise he'd made to leave the man's sister alone, he'd tried to stay away from Tally, but it was impossible. It was like a magical magnetic force pulled them together. Honestly, he didn't want to be anywhere other than where she was.

Although he'd been trying to work, he'd been watching Tally out of the corner of his eye, listening to her hum softly as she mixed something in a big bowl.

"Why in the world do I need to take Marvella on a date?" Gage asked, curious, but also hesitant. Anything that involved Marvella was generally a recipe for trouble if not disaster, although she'd been well behaved when his friends descended for a work day at the ranch.

"Today's her birthday and I want to make it special for her. I managed to track down a bedding set she wanted. If you could go with her to town for just an hour or so, I can redecorate her room while she's gone and surprise her when you come back. I've got a chocolate cake in the oven and I'm making all her favorite foods for both lunch and dinner." Tally wiped her hands on a dishtowel and crossed the room until she stood beside him at the table. "Please, Gage? Would you do this tiny little favor for me? You only need to keep her away for an hour minimum."

"Is this the bedspread I heard you spend hours on the phone trying to order a while back?"

Tally nodded and rolled her eyes. "Aunt Marv fell in love with a bedding set from a magazine she unearthed that is ten years old. If she hadn't just raved about how much she wanted it, I wouldn't have tried to track one down, but I found one, still in the package, never been used. I know she'll love it, even if it was a major pain to order. The seller charged me extra for rush shipping, but seemed to have sent it via slow boat from China since it just got here yesterday."

"Sweating a few bullets?" Gage asked with a grin.

She smiled. "Maybe even a bucket full." She

reached out and squeezed his right hand between hers. "Please, Gage? Would you distract her? I really want this to be a nice surprise for her."

"I'd be happy to help. How about we go to Echo? She can take me to the museum and give me her version of the town's history."

"Perfect. She'll love that." Tally hugged his neck and kissed his cheek before she rushed over to the oven and pulled out three round cake pans that would turn into a layer cake.

Gage couldn't concentrate after that hug or the kiss on his cheek, so he closed his account files, shut off his computer, then went to his room to change. He needed to mail a few documents to his insurance company and could use that as an excuse to go into town.

Not for the first time, he was truly thankful he had good health insurance. So many rodeo cowboys either couldn't afford the ridiculous premiums some companies charged or were refused coverage at all. When they were injured, and nearly all rodeo cowboys sustained a major injury at some point in their career, it left them scrambling financially. He was glad there was a crisis fund to help out those who needed it most, when they needed it.

He returned to the kitchen with two envelopes in his hand and found Marvella licking a spoon full of white frosting.

"Miss Marvella, would you do me the honor of driving me into town? I forgot to have Judd stick these letters in the mail this morning and I need to send them to my insurance company." Gage offered the old woman a charming, boyish smile.

"Of course, I'll drive you, darling. Let me get my purse and I'll meet you at the car." Marvella dropped her spoon in the sink and rushed out the back door. If Gage didn't know better, he'd say she even had a spring in her step.

"Thank you for doing this," Tally whispered as he walked past her on his way to the door.

"My pleasure, Queenie. It'll be fun. I haven't seen my life flash in front of my eyes since the last time Aunt Marv drove me to town. I'm about due for a rerun episode."

Tally laughed. "Surely it's not that bad riding with her."

"You ought to try it sometime." He grabbed his hat and grinned at her. "But only if you're willing to lose five to ten years off your lifespan."

"Oh, get out of here," Tally said with a laugh, waving him out the door.

In a good mood, Gage made his way down the steps with his crutch secured around his leg. He had an appointment tomorrow with the doctor that he hoped would rid him of both the crutch and the cast. If the stars all aligned, maybe he'd get the pins out of his hand, too.

He reached the end of the walk as Marvella pulled up in her vintage car. Someone had given it a wash and shine, since the glass gleamed in the windows and not a speck of dust covered even the tires.

"Need a ride, handsome?" Marvella asked with a grin when he opened the door and settled onto the front passenger seat.

"I appreciate you taking me, Aunt Marv." She

smelled of lilacs without the menthol today and was dressed in an outfit that put him in mind of June Cleaver from the old television show *Leave it to Beaver*. From the snappy little hat on her head to the pearls around her neck and the crisp gloves on her hands, she looked quite proper and retro.

He leaned over and kissed her papery cheek. "Happy Birthday to you. Are you twenty-nine again?"

She laughed and put the car in gear, creeping down the lane to the main road so she wouldn't get the car dirty. At least with the slow pace, the threat of running off the road drastically decreased. "I gave up being twenty-nine about forty years ago, sweetheart. I'm eighty-three years young today."

"Wow! Congratulations!" Gage leaned back and studied her, taking in the wrinkles along her neck and around her eyes that time had etched across her skin. She really did look young for her age and acted much younger than her age, too. He would have guessed her to be in her early seventies if he didn't know better.

Marvella Hawkins might be a little on the harmlessly loony side, but she had a huge, caring heart and she was one of the most upbeat, positive people he'd ever encountered. It was easy to see why Tally and Trevor both adored her. Gage loved her like she was his own aunt or wacky grandmother.

"Is there anything fun you'd like to do while we're in Echo?" he asked. "We could run by the historical museum or go to Fort Henrietta Park."

Marvella smiled at him. "I'd like to walk

around and look at the flowers. They're always so lovely."

"A stroll for flowers it is," Gage said, offering her another smile. "That's a nice outfit you have on there. I like the pink color and the hat that matches your dress."

Marvella glanced down at her dress and smiled. "My husband bought this outfit for my birthday the fifth year we were married."

"He had good taste," Gage said, wondering how the woman had preserved so many decades worth of clothes. Perhaps even more perplexing was the fact she still fit into them.

"The year Richard bought me this, we were living in Alaska and I was so homesick. He came home early from work that day, gave me this dress, hat, gloves, and there used to be a matching pair of shoes, but I wore them out years ago. We went out for dinner and then walked home beneath the stars. It was such a beautiful day; one I'll always remember. Richard was a wonderful husband. I miss him every day," Marvella said, reaching up to brush away a tear. The charms dangling from a bracelet she wore clinked together, drawing Gage's interest.

"Tell me about that bracelet. I don't think I've seen you wear it before."

Marvella wiggled her wrist, making the charms jangle. "Richard gave me the bracelet for our twenty-fifth wedding anniversary. It's silver, you know. The anniversary, I mean, although the bracelet is, too. Silver is the proper gift for twenty-five years. Anyway, Richard bought this bracelet and every year for our anniversary he gave me another charm to add to it."

She held it out for Gage to study. The bracelet was so loaded with charms it was a wonder it didn't crack Marvella's tiny wrist. The charms included a teapot, a heart, a Cinderella carriage, a horseshoe, a hot air balloon, a flower, a set of measuring spoons so small he had to lean closer to figure out what they were, a dress, a shock of wheat, a cow, and many others. The one that caught his eye, though, was a pair of baby shoes.

"What did this one represent?" he asked, pointing to the shoes.

Marvella sighed. "That one he gave me on our twenty-seventh anniversary, as a reminder." She fell silent for a long moment, but Gage didn't push her. She released a long breath and glanced at him before turning her attention back to the road. "We tried for years to have a baby. Richard didn't want to adopt, so we gave up on having a child of our own. One summer day when I thought I was past the age of having children, I discovered I was expecting. We didn't tell anyone, wanting to hold that wonderful secret to ourselves for as long as we could. When I was five months pregnant, I was walking across the street with two friends and a drunk driver hit us. Of course, I lost the baby. The baby shoes were Richard's way of reminding me that God has plans we can't begin to comprehend, even if that precious little bundle would have been the most-loved baby ever born."

Gage's heart ached for Marvella, for a loss that happened through no fault of her own. He had no idea what to say to the woman for something that obviously still caused her pain and grief. "I'm so sorry, Aunt Marv."

She patted his leg and shook her wrist, as though she shook off the painful memories. "See the charm that looks like a daisy?"

He tipped his head and located the charm. "Yep, it's right there between the dog and the saddle."

"Tally gave that to me when she was about five or so. She and Trevor talked their father into taking them shopping. She knew I had this bracelet, so she asked if she could get that charm for me. Ross bought it and even had it gift-wrapped. Tally was as proud as punch when she gave me that gift. It's one of my favorite charms, because it reminds me of such a special, happy day."

"Ross was an amazing man." Gage glanced at her then back at the road. For once, Marvella didn't seem to be driving in the ditch or the opposite side of the road. Much to his surprise, she kept the car heading right down the center of her lane.

"Ross was one of the best. He sure didn't have to take in Tally like he did, but he loved that girl like she was his own. In a way, I guess she was, since he cared for her from the time she was a baby."

"What do you mean?" Gage turned in the seat and stared at Marvella.

Rather than answer, Marvella pulled up in front of the post office and stopped. "Want to mail those letters?"

"Yes, ma'am. I'll be right back." Gage got out

of the car and went inside, dropping the letters in the outgoing mail slot, then returned to find the car empty and Marvella waving to him from across the street where she talked to a woman he recognized as someone she knew from church.

He returned her wave and crossed the opposite street, heading into a store that sold hot coffee along with gift items. The scent of cinnamon and apples tantalized his nose, so he ordered two hot ciders. He was on his way out of the shop when he spied a display of charms. He browsed through them and nearly whooped in excitement when he found one perfect for Marvella.

Convinced she would love it, he took it to the cash register, then charmed the girl behind the counter into wrapping it in tissue and placing it in a tiny gift bag for him. He tucked it into his shirt pocket then hurried outside and over to where Marvella spoke with Nancy June Ledbetter.

"Hello, Mrs. Ledbetter. Beautiful day, isn't it?" he said, smiling at the woman.

"It is a lovely day, Gage. Marv was just telling me she brought you to town to take care of a few errands. Any word on when the doctor is going to take those horrid pins out of your hand?"

Gage handed the cup of cider to Marvella and shrugged. "Nothing for sure, but I'm sure hoping he'll take them out tomorrow when I go see him."

"Well, I certainly hope he does, for your sake. Poor boy. You've had those wretched things in your hand for what seems like months."

"Seven and a half weeks, but who's counting."

Nancy June patted Marvella on the back. "Have

a wonderful birthday, Marv. I hope it's full of delightful surprises."

"Oh, I'm sure it will be." Marvella sipped the hot cider and gave Gage an appreciative nod. "That sure hits the spot. Shall we go for a stroll?"

Gage held out his arm and Marvella wrapped her thin hand around it, smiling at him as they made their way down the street, admiring a profusion of colorful flowers.

"They really are quite something," Marvella said, admiring a grouping of mums that ranged in color from bright yellow to blood red. "I think the colors this year are more vibrant than I've ever seen."

Gage had thought the same thing, but then again, he rarely stayed in one place more than a few days, a week at most, so it was hard to compare his past autumns to the one he'd experienced in the little community of Echo. He also wondered if being in love for the first time in his life had heightened his awareness of certain things, like the beauty crafted by the Creator's hand.

Marvella made her way to a park bench and sat down, smoothing her skirt with one hand as she continued sipping the hot cider.

"Tell me more about Tally," Gage said, hoping Marvella would go back to her earlier comment. Had Ross really raised Tally from a baby?

"Adelaide, or Lulu as everyone calls her these days, used to be a sweet girl, or so I thought. Maybe she was always a nut-job and I didn't want to see it because she was the closest thing I had to a daughter. Anyway, when she married Ross, I just knew she'd found a special man who'd be as devoted to her as Richard had always been to me. And I was right. Things seemed fine until she had Trevor. I went to visit when he was about two weeks old and Lulu completely ignored him. She let him cry, his diaper hadn't been changed for hours, and he'd lost weight because she didn't like to get up at night to feed him. Ross wanted to help, but Lulu refused to let him, telling him he knew nothing about taking care of a child."

Marvella scoffed then looked at Gage. "Ross had more sense than most, except when it came to Lulu. Anyway, I don't think it was a shock to anyone when she took off when Trevor wasn't even yet three months old. She left Ross a note letting him know she wasn't cut out for motherhood or being tied down. He hired a private investigator who tracked her down, but by then, she'd already gone through two boyfriends. Once the divorce was final, Ross filed for sole custody and Lulu gladly gave it to him. She came back for Trevor's first birthday, but I think the reason was because she'd run out of money and men and needed a break from her new lifestyle."

Gage had heard most of Lulu's past from Trevor and Ross, although Marvella added a few details that he didn't previously know. Rather than push her to get to the part about Tally, he leaned back against the bench and took a long drink of the cider.

Marvella sipped her cider and went on with the story. "When Trevor was five, Ross found out Lulu had married a guy she met on the subway in New

York. Apparently, she'd only known the man a few days, but she married him. Personally, I think he was a mobster. She sent me a photo of them together in a note at Christmas that year. Something about him just looked evil to me, and he was a heavy, squatty man, although he was handsome enough, I suppose. Tally bemoans her full-figured tendencies, and I'll tell you they came from his side of the family."

"Tally should embrace her size and figure. I think she's beautiful." Gage didn't mean for the words to slip out, but they had. And the last person in the world he wanted to hear them was sitting beside him.

The old woman smiled and patted his leg, as though he was the class dunce who'd finally figured out the answer to a simple question. "Of course, you do, darling."

Marvella watched a bird land on the gazebo railing and waited until it flew off to continue her story. "Lulu's husband left her when she told him she was pregnant. I don't know if there was a divorce or if he was killed off by fellow gangsters, but he disappeared completely. She only ever mentioned him once and what she had to say confirmed my thoughts about his career choice. Anyway, she arrived at King Penny Ranch with a newborn baby and not a dime to her name. Ross took her in, because that's just the kind of man he was. He could hardly stand the sight of Lulu, but the moment he took Tally in his arms, it was as if she was his child. And he never thought of her in any way except as his daughter. Tally was about a month old when Lulu cleaned out the cash in Ross's wallet and left. Ross tried multiple times to get custody of Tally, but Lulu refused to give it to him, even though she didn't want her. Truthfully, she used that poor girl as a bargaining chip to control Ross. I think her plan was to come back to the ranch and make Ross fall in love with her again. She didn't count on the fact she'd destroyed his heart so completely the first time she ran out on him that he'd never love again. Lulu finally came back and got Tally when she was about six months old. I thought Ross was going to die when she took that baby away from him. Over the years, she'd get tired of taking care of her and send her to the ranch. Then Lulu would meet a new man, marry a new husband, be excited for another of her get-rich-quick schemes and tear Tally away from the people who loved her most in the world. When she turned sixteen, Tally brought herself to the ranch and refused to leave with her mother. I just wish Lulu hadn't been so selfish all those years. Tally's life would have been so different if she could have just stayed with Ross."

"It certainly would have been." Gage could picture Tally as he first saw her, a chubby, shy girl who didn't seem certain about where she fit into the world, or even the ranch. It would have been hard to feel at home when her mother made sure she always had one foot out the door. If she'd been raised on the ranch, by Ross, would she be as confident and settled in life as Trevor?

"What are your intentions, Gage?" Marvella asked, fixing him with a pointed look.

"Intentions?" he asked, puzzled. "I figured we'd finish our cider then head back to the ranch, unless there's something else you wanted to do while we're here."

"No, not that," she said, lightly smacking him on the leg. "I'll be ready to head home after we finish this delicious cider. But that's not what I meant. I want to know what you intend to do about your feelings for our girl."

"What?" Gage asked, his tone louder than he intended. No one else was in the park, so it didn't really matter, but he dropped his voice when he spoke. "What are you talking about?"

Marvella giggled. "Denial, is it?" She raised a bony finger and shook it at him in a scolding manner. "My eyesight might not be what it used to, but I'm not blind, son. You're in love with Tally and have been for a while. I want to know what you intend to do about it."

Gage gaped at her for a long moment before he slumped back against the bench. If even Marvella knew he was head-over-heels in love with Tally, he had to wonder who else had noticed. His friends had certainly razzed him the other day, but he chalked that up to their love to tease and Tally had been a bit of a surprise to several of them.

Did Tally know? Did she care?

His doubt and worry must have shown on his face because Marvella reached out and placed a hand on his arm, patting it gently. "She feels the same way, even if she isn't ready to admit it."

"She does?" Gage asked, perking up at this bit of news.

"Perhaps I should take you to the eye doctor, Gage Taggart. Anyone with even a smidgen of vision can see she's in love with you." Marvella studied him a moment. "What are you going to do about it?"

Gage sighed. "Nothing. I promised Trevor to leave her alone."

Marvella laughed. "Oh, darling. No one would hold you to that promise, even Trevor. What he wants for Tally, more than anything, is for her to be happy. You do that. She's been happier than I've ever seen her these last several weeks."

"I'm no good for her, Marvella. I'm not ready to give up rodeo and Tally deserves someone who'll be around to love her all the time, not just in passing."

Marvella shrugged. "Perhaps you ought to ask Tally her opinion instead of assuming to know what she wants or needs."

"No. I don't want to hurt her and once that door is opened, we can't stuff everything back inside and pretend it never spilled out." Gage gulped the last of his cider and tossed his cup in a nearby trash can. "Please don't say anything to her."

Marvella sipped her cider and remained silent.

"Please, Aunt Marv? Please?"

He gave her such a pleading look, tears glistened in her eyes and she finally nodded her head.

"I promise I won't say anything now, but that comes with a condition. If you haven't told her how you feel by Christmas Eve, I'll tell her myself."

"Marvella, that's not…"

She held up a hand to silence him. "That's the deal. Take it or I'll tell her when we get back to the ranch."

"You're a ruthless, conniving ol' biddy, you know that?" Gage grinned at her to soften the words.

She cackled with laughter. "I do know that, although no one but you has been brave enough to say it to my face. I like you, Gage, and I think you are just the man to help Tally reach her full potential in life."

"But she's a great nurse and from what I can see, she loves her job."

"She is great at it and she does love it, but that's not what I meant." Marvella stood and tossed her cup in the garbage then looped her arm around Gage's when he stood. "When two hearts belong together, they bring out the best in each other. I see that in the two of you. Tally has always been so unsure of herself, uncertain where she belongs. With you, she is more confident and definitely more joyful. It has nothing to do with her career choice, darling, and everything to do with her heart. Just like you seem settled and content when she's around. She's softened you in ways you never anticipated or expected."

Gage had no idea what to say to that since what Marvella said was true, even if he couldn't have put it into words quite like she had. He had felt settled and content and deliriously happy the past eight weeks.

Under normal circumstances he would have been fuming over his injuries, losing out on the opportunity to compete at the finals in Las Vegas since he'd dropped to number sixteen in the standings, and having to stay in one place for more than a few days. But Tally made him want to be at the ranch. She'd caused him, albeit unwittingly, to start thinking of a future on a ranch of his own where they could raise their kids and spend the rest of their lives wading deep in wedded bliss.

"Come on, honey, let's head back to the ranch. It'll be lunch time when we get there, and Tally is making ham quiche for lunch along with coconut cream pie." Marvella squeezed his arm where her hand rested as they crossed the street back to her car. "I know you've got a lot to think about but consider what your life would look like if you told Tally how you feel, and then picture it if you keep that secret to yourself."

Gage mulled over his conversation with Marvella on the way back to the ranch. She must have been feeling more like herself, because she almost drove into the ditch twice. The second time she did it, she turned and winked at him, causing him to ponder if she drove like a maniac on purpose.

"You are something else, Marvella Hawkins," he said as she parked her car in the little carport next to the guest house. Gage got out and opened her door for her, giving her a hand as she rose to her feet.

"Always be an authentic, irreplaceable version of you," she said, then raised her chin a notch and waved at Tally as she stepped out of Marvella's front door.

Marvella was so excited about the new bedding set, complete with matching curtains and cushions for the chair she had in her bedroom, she squealed with joy and clapped her hands like an animated child.

Lunch proved to be a lively affair with Marvella gushing about the bedroom makeover and how much she loved it. The food, as always, was delicious and Gage had a second helping of the pie.

Several of Marvella's friends dropped by throughout the afternoon bearing gifts, bouquets of flowers, and birthday wishes. Tally served them tea and meringue cookies shaped like roses. Gage and Trevor snatched a handful then headed out to the barn to hide out until all the women left.

After dinner, Marvella opened her gifts and laughed at the charm Gage selected for her.

"I figured that little crutch would remind you of the time you helped take care of me and Trevor," he said when she held up the tiny little trinket and smiled.

"I can put that on your bracelet for you, Aunt Marv," Trevor said, taking the charm from her and easily attaching it to the bracelet.

Marvella gave her wrist a shake and beamed at him. "It's perfect, Gage. Thank you."

Once they'd sung "Happy Birthday" and watched Marvella blow out enough candles the frosting should have melted, they ate thick slices of chocolate cake with ice cream.

Worn out from the excitement of the day, Marvella hugged and kissed Trevor then Gage before bidding them goodnight. Tally went with her to tuck her in.

Gage smiled as he listened to them walk out the door with Marvella chatting nonstop about it being one of the best birthdays she'd ever had.

"You did good today, bro," Trevor said, thumping him on the shoulder. "Aunt Marv thinks the world of you, you know."

"The feeling's mutual. She might be an acquired taste, but I'd do anything for that ol' gal."

"And the young one who went out the door with her?" Trevor asked with a hint of caution in his voice.

Gage refused to be baited into saying something he preferred not to. "Same goes for her."

He went to his room and sat in the darkness, trying to figure out how he'd ever work up the strength to tell Tally goodbye, because regardless of what Marvella said, he couldn't ask her to be tied to a man who'd never be home. She'd had enough of that growing up with her unbalanced, horrible mother.

Chapter Fourteen

"Are you okay?" Gage asked as Tally tried to lift the laundry basket and set it back down with a thump.

"Dandy," she said, turning away to hide a grimace of pain. She didn't know what had happened but at some point yesterday she'd pulled a muscle in her chest. Vaguely, she recalled twisting and lifting the chair in Marvella's room when she was rearranging the furniture. A muscle had twinged then, but she didn't give it a thought.

Not until she woke up this morning, couldn't lift her left arm, and it hurt to take a deep breath. She figured she'd probably strained a chest muscle, but she was embarrassed to admit as much to anyone, particularly Gage.

"What hurts?" he asked, moving in front of her and lifting her chin in his hand.

She looked into his eyes, those incredible pools of blue, and forgot the question.

"What hurts, Queenie? I know something does. You're talking to an old injury pro, you know." He smiled at her and she felt the corners of her mouth lift as she returned it.

"I'm fine, Gage. Truly. I just um… maybe pulled something yesterday."

"Why didn't you say something? We could have eaten cereal for breakfast instead of you slaving away in the kitchen, and we would have helped more with the dishes."

She took a step back, unable to stay so close to him and retain a bit of sense. He smelled like leather, sunshine, and a tantalizing fragrance that was solely him. He'd shaved that morning and the scent of his aftershave along with his taut, tanned skin so close to her threatened to scramble her brains like the eggs she'd made for breakfast.

"Where does it hurt?" he asked, reaching for her hand. He lifted it slightly and she held back a yelp of pain, wincing with the effort. "Your arm, obviously. What else?"

"It hurts to breathe, the area is swollen, and I've had a few muscle spasms this morning."

Much to her shock and dismay, he reached out and placed his right hand on her upper chest, near her left armpit. "Right here?" he asked, gently massaging the area.

If Tally hadn't worn a long-sleeved shirt, she was sure his hand rubbing against her skin would have seared it right off the bone.

She nodded and would have pulled away, but he placed his hand on her shoulder and offered a sympathetic look. "I think it's a pulled pec muscle.

Those are painful and there isn't a lot you can do for them other than put ice on it and wait it out."

"Thank you, Dr. Taggart, for that diagnosis. I'd already concluded that myself."

Gage grinned. "How on earth did you do that? I thought you were busy baking and cooking for Marvella's birthday all day."

"I rearranged the furniture in her room. It must have happened then. It didn't hurt until I got up this morning."

"Then stop trying to use it and give it time to heal, Nurse King. You, of all people, should know better than to continue to strain it."

Gage took her right hand in his and led her out of the kitchen into the great room and guided her to the couch. "Sit there and rest a while. I'll get you an ice pack."

"You don't have to wait on me," she said, starting to rise, but Gage settled a hand on her shoulder again, pushing her back against the soft cushions of the couch. He leaned down until his face was just a few inches away from hers. She studied the dark lashes rimming his eyes and considered the injustice of a man having such long, thick lashes. "Sit there and don't move for at least ten minutes. That's an order. I'll be right back with that ice."

Tally would have argued with him, but she was afraid he'd lean close to her again and her willpower to resist kissing him had nearly evaporated. One more encounter with his hand touching her or his lips taunting her as they lingered close enough to kiss, and she couldn't be blamed for any crazy thing she might do.

She drew in a deep breath to calm herself, forgetting about her pulled muscle. Pain seared through her chest and drew tears to her eyes. Rapidly blinking them away, she was taking shallow, tight breaths when Gage returned with an ice pack wrapped in a towel. Rather than hand it to her, he reached down and placed it against her chest, tucking it into her armpit.

"That's cold," she whispered, although her body felt like someone had poured liquid fire into her veins.

"Here," he said, snagging a throw off the back of the couch and draping it over her lap. Even though he could only use one hand, he'd grown quite adept at managing.

In fact, he managed a little too well as he tucked the blanket in around her hips and down her legs.

"That's fine, thank you," she said, wondering if a body could die from longing. If so, she would be dead within the hour if Gage didn't step back and leave her alone. Desperate, she glanced at the clock on the wall. "What time is your doctor's appointment today?"

"Two and Trevor's is right after that. I figured we'd need to leave right after lunch. Maybe I could get Judd to drive us, since you really should stay here and rest."

"No, I'll take you guys. It won't hurt anything just to drive." The smart thing would have been to accept his offer to get someone else to drive them. The less time she spent with Gage, the better.

Over the past weeks, she'd gotten past her dislike of Gage, even if she didn't yet trust him. He'd been isolated on the ranch and injured. What would happen when he returned to the rodeo circuit with beautiful women flocking around him? She had no doubt what the answer would be. She'd be setting herself up for heartache if she allowed herself to admit her feelings for him. He wasn't the type to settle down with one woman. Gage Taggart would never want to give up the rodeo and stay in one place.

Tally had all she could stand of living a nomadic lifestyle growing up with Lulu. What she needed was roots and the assurance that the man she loved would be beside her, not across the country at a rodeo with half a dozen women propositioning him on a nightly basis. Nope. That wasn't how she envisioned her future.

She wanted a home and kids, and a husband who adored her enough to set down roots, too.

Sadly, Gage was not that man. No matter how much she enjoyed their friendship, no matter how much she'd come to love him, she wouldn't give him her heart. Not when he'd just break it.

She looked up and realized he was standing beside the couch, waiting for her to answer a question he'd asked.

"Don't worry about it. I'll take you both. There are enough leftovers from yesterday, we can heat them up for lunch and I'll ask Judd to make dinner. How's that?" She offered him a toothy smile that felt as fake as it had to look.

He shook his head, rolled his eyes and took a

step back. "I'll ask Judd to make dinner, leftovers are fine, and Trevor and I will finish up the laundry you started. Can I bring you anything? A book? A cup of tea?"

"I'm fine, but thank you." She gave him a genuine smile as he took another step back then turned and left the room.

She released a long breath, remembered her injury and drew in a shallow one. Annoyed with herself for getting hurt, she hated for Gage to see her slightly incapacitated. Around him, she needed every drop of confidence she could muster, and it was hard to do that when she couldn't even lift her arm. At least she had two more days to recuperate before she had to return to work.

Tired from work, from a busy day yesterday, from running away from her feelings when it came to Gage, she closed her eyes, just for a moment.

The feel of something moving against her, brought her instantly awake. Aunt Marv held the now-warm ice pack and smiled at her.

"I didn't mean to startle you, sweetheart, but the boys and I have lunch ready. Do you feel like eating something?"

"Oh!" Tally tossed aside the blanket and lunged to her feet then plopped back down when a wave of dizziness swept over her.

"Stood up too fast, didn't you," Marvella said, giving her a knowing look. "I've done that a few times myself. Let's take it a little slower this time."

Tally took the hand Marvella held out to her and walked with her aunt into the kitchen. The table was set, and steam rose from the dishes of food.

"Thank you for doing this," Tally said, uncertain who'd been in charge, but grateful to whoever it was who'd let her sleep. She hadn't realized how worn out she'd been.

"Gage gets the credit. I was out in the barn most of the morning and Aunt Marv has been busy on the phone. It seems everyone who didn't call with birthday wishes yesterday, made it a point to get in touch today."

Tally smiled at her aunt and took the seat between her and Gage. Trevor asked the blessing on the meal. She ate in silence while Trevor and Gage discussed the bull Trevor had made Tally drive home and his plans for increasing his herd the following year.

When she finished eating, Tally set her dirty dishes in the dishwasher then hurried to her room. She changed her clothes, tugging on a pullover sweater while holding her breath against the pain it caused. She applied a little mascara, released her hair from the ponytail she'd forced herself to fashion that morning, and added a bit of styling product to hold her waves in place.

She stepped back and gave herself a critical look in the mirror. Not fabulous, but it would do for a trip to the doctor's office and home again. After tamping her feet into boots and looping a scarf around her neck, she started to leave her room, then turned back and gave herself a quick spritz of her favorite perfume. The scent always made her think of Christmas and happy times spent at the ranch, which was why she loved it. Quickly grabbing her purse, she left her room and made her way back to the kitchen.

Aunt Marvella was just placing the last dish in the dishwasher while Gage wiped off the table and counter with a wet dishcloth.

"Ready to go?" she asked, glancing at the clock. They had plenty of time, but she didn't want Gage to be late for this appointment. If all went well, he'd get his cast off today. The doctor had also mentioned taking out the pins, if Gage had healed sufficiently.

"I am ready. Trevor went to change his clothes. He'll be back in a minute." Gage rinsed out the rag one-handed then dried his hand on a damp dishtowel.

Marvella took it from him and hung it up to dry. "I'm in need of a little rest this afternoon. I'll see you kids when you get back."

She disappeared, leaving Gage and Tally alone in the kitchen. Tally had gotten used to Gage being around and felt comfortable with him, for the most part. For some reason, though, she felt awkward around him today. Maybe it was the fact she'd pulled a muscle and he'd been trying to play nursemaid to her. The reversal of roles didn't set well with her. She didn't like being in need of assistance, especially not from him.

Gage already saw her as the goofy, chubby little sister of his good friend. She didn't need to add weak and helpless to the list of flaws.

"I'll bring the pickup around," she said and left the kitchen before she did something dangerous, like beg Gage to hold her, just for a few minutes. His touch earlier that morning, even if it was brief and innocent, had ignited something in her that she didn't want to subdue. But she would.

Outside, she placed her right hand to her chest where it ached as she drew in a breath of autumn air, tinged with the fragrance of spices and loamy earth. She caught a whiff of horses and manure then waved at Jared as he rode by on his way to the pasture down the lane. Every season was unique and beautiful in its own way on the ranch. Tally had tried to decide which one she liked best, but she'd never been able to choose. She loved the rich, deep colors of autumn and the smell of apples and wood smoke lingering in the air. She liked winter days when she could stay curled up in the ranch house with a good book and watch snow blanket the world in white. Spring brought new life through the animals, trees, flowers, and plants. She looked forward to the warmer days and the feeling of renewal that came with its arrival. And summer was filled with gorgeous sunsets, busy days, peaceful evenings, and skies a fabulous shade of blue.

Blue like Gage's incredible eyes.

"Agh!" She opened the door to Trevor's pickup with a jerk and climbed inside. She had to close it with her right hand, but when she did, it slammed loudly inside the garage. She backed out and continued backing around the corner, coming to a stop at the end of the front walk.

Gage and Trevor made their way down the porch steps and hobbled toward her, although she had an idea their off-centered walk was due more to casts and crutches hampering them than their injuries. For their sakes, she hoped the doctor would remove the casts today.

Trevor climbed in the front while Gage slid onto the backseat. "Let's go," her brother said, tapping the console between them with his hand.

Tally didn't say much as she drove them to town. Trevor had to help her shift a few times since she couldn't lift her left hand high enough to hold onto the steering wheel. Other than that, though, they had no problem reaching the doctor's office well before Gage's appointment. She went in with them and took a seat only to have the two men sit on either side of her, blocking her in like bookends.

She took her electronic reader out of her purse and turned it on. Before she could get back into the story she'd been reading, Gage pulled it out of her hand and read the page that was open.

"Romance?" he asked, handing it back to her.

"As a matter of fact, it is. Got a problem with that?" she asked, daring him to disparage the genre she loved to read. She got enough drama at work and she'd never been one who particularly enjoyed fantasies, since Lulu seemed to live in one after another. But a good romance with a handsome hero and a strong heroine always helped her relax and she loved reaching the happily-ever-after at the end of the book.

"Not a problem at all. What's this one about?" Gage asked, leaning back in the chair.

"Let me guess," Trevor said, joining the conversation. "There's some hunky dude chasing a pretty girl and she eventually lets him catch her. Am I right?"

Tally rolled her eyes at Trevor and shook her

head. "It's a tragedy you aren't nearly as funny as you think."

Trevor and Gage both chuckled, but Gage pointed to her e-reader. "Seriously, what's it about?"

"There's this guy who wants to play professional football, but he's had an injury and he's trying to work his way back onto a pro team by playing for an arena football team. The girl is a bit of an uptight executive and her boss makes her attend a game since his company is a sponsor. Anyway, the football player and the girl are complete opposites, which makes the book so fun."

"Do you think opposites attract?" Gage asked. The look on his face said he genuinely wanted to know her answer.

"I suppose they can, it just depends on the people and the circumstances."

"What about true love?" Gage's eyes held interest as he asked the question.

"What about it?"

Trevor leaned around Tally and scowled at Gage. "Yeah, what about it?"

Tally pushed Trevor back and turned to Gage.

He cleared his throat but held her gaze. "Do you believe in it? What do you think true love really is?"

If someone told Tally she'd be sitting in a waiting room between two cowboys discussing the meaning of true love, she would have called them nuts. Yet, here she was having that exact conversation with her brother and his best friend, no less.

"I don't think true love is like you see in the movies, you know, where everything ends perfectly and they ride off into a glorious sunset," Tally said, deciding to be brave and speak from her heart. "I think true love is when two people complete each other, make each other better just by loving them. It's encouraging one another and being there for each other and bringing out the very best in that person — not by changing them, but accepting them and loving them because they have changed and grown. It's not about moonlight and flowers, although those are nice things to dream about. True love is knowing your heart is in someone else's hands and they'll do everything in their power to shelter it, nurture it, protect it, and cherish it. True love doesn't mean everything is perfect, it just means that no matter what might come, you have someone to stand beside you who'll hold your hand and lend you strength as you weather every storm and celebrate every victory."

Gage appeared stunned, staring at her without uttering a word. She glanced at Trevor, but he appeared deep in thought. A woman sitting across from them grabbed a tissue from her purse and dabbed at her eyes. "That was one of the most beautiful things I've ever heard."

Tally gave her a shy half-smile. "Thank you."

Fortunately, a nurse appeared at the doorway and called Gage's name. It wasn't until he disappeared down the hall with the nurse that Trevor nudged her with his elbow.

"Did you mean all that about true love, Tal?" he asked.

She tipped her head back and met his gaze. "I did."

"And have you found true love?"

Something in Trevor's tone made her study him before she offered an answer. She couldn't say what it was, but he seemed concerned and even a bit scared.

"Not yet," she said, honestly. True love meant your feelings were reciprocated and she was definitely alone in her infatuation with Gage. "Maybe I never will."

"Why on earth would you say that?" Trevor asked, placing his arm around her and giving her shoulders a squeeze. "You're smart and have a good job that you're passionate about. You're a great cook and know how to take care of a home. In spite of what you tell yourself, you're a very pretty girl, Talilah King. I wish you wouldn't be so hard on yourself all the time."

Tally fought the tears that burned the backs of her eyes. Trevor wasn't one given to sentiment or flowery compliments, so his words meant more to her than he realized.

He gave her another squeeze before he let her go. "Any guy would be lucky to win your heart, Tally, but the right man, the one who truly loves you, will discover he has a precious treasure in you, one he can cherish his whole life through."

Unable to speak around the lump that lodged in her throat, she leaned her head against Trevor's arm and waited for the emotion to subside.

"I love you, Trev. You're the best big brother in the world," she said when she could finally speak.

"Right back at ya', kid. As annoying little sisters go, you never were one. I always liked having you around and I'm so happy you've stuck around, spending time at the ranch when you aren't at work."

"You know I love it there, more than anywhere else." She brushed away a teardrop that managed to escape and slide down her cheek. "I don't know what I'll do when you finally get around to falling in love. You won't need me there in the way."

"Hey, none of that," Trevor said, holding her chin in his hand, forcing her to look at him. "You will always, always have a place at the ranch. Besides, you own part of it."

"No, I don't." Tally knew her dad left her forty percent of the ranch in his will and Trevor had the other sixty, but she'd never felt like she could accept the gift.

"You know if it ever came down to it, I'd split everything with you fifty-fifty."

She shook her head. "No, Trevor. The ranch is yours. It's been in your family for a hundred and fifty-years. I'd never take that away from you. Not ever."

"You're wrong, Tal. The ranch has been in *our* family that long. You might not be blood relation to the King family, but you are my family and Dad always considered you his daughter. Whether you like it or not, you are a full-fledged King and own part of the ranch."

"Then why do I always feel like an imposter?" Tally whispered, unable to meet Trevor's gaze as she turned away.

"Imposter? What nonsense are you blabbering about?" he asked, jiggling the foot that wasn't in a cast, a sure sign he was getting frustrated or upset.

"I've never fit in anywhere. Not at the ranch, not with Lulu and her many men, not at all the schools I attended. I'm not even sure I fit in at the hospital because even though I love my job, when I'm there, all I think about is being at the ranch. Yet, when I'm there, I think about the moment someone will realize I don't belong."

"You belong on that ranch every bit as much as I do and you know it," Trevor said, his voice taking on a bit of an edge. "I don't understand where this is coming from."

"It comes from the fact that although I lived at the ranch and Dad let me learn some things, like how to ride a horse or help irrigate, there were all kinds of things he taught you that he didn't teach me. Do you have any idea how many times I asked if he'd teach me to drive the truck? Or let me run the haystacker? Or show me how to pull a calf? I feel like an outsider half the time because I don't know how to do things that come second-nature to you, things others assume I should know, and I don't."

"Dad just wanted you to have fun on the ranch and you liked tagging along to irrigate or he wouldn't have let you do that much." Trevor sighed and ran a hand through his hair. "I'm sorry, Tal. Whatever it is you want to learn, let me know and I'll teach you. I had no idea you felt this way, like you didn't belong. I'm sorry and Dad would be, too.

He only ever wanted you to be happy, to feel special."

"He did make me feel like a princess, but sometimes, I just wanted to trade in the glass slippers for a pair of dusty boots."

Trevor grinned. "Well, just wait until spring work begins and I'll put you smack in the middle of it."

"I'll hold you to it," Tally said, feeling lighter for having spoken the truth to her brother.

"Miss King?" a nurse asked as she stood at the doorway that led back to the exam rooms.

Tally stood. "Yes? Is there something wrong with Gage?"

"No, not at all. He mentioned you have an injury and would refuse to seek treatment for it on your own." The nurse motioned for her to follow her.

Tally rolled her eyes and hurried to fall into step with the nurse. "I'm a registered nurse and I know what's wrong. It's just a pulled muscle."

"Still, we have a doctor available thanks to a no-show, so you might as well let him take a look while you're here." The nurse led her into an exam room and motioned for Tally to take a seat on the table. It felt odd to be on the receiving end of answering questions and having her blood pressure and pulse checked.

When the doctor stepped into the room, she told him what she thought was wrong. It didn't take long for him to confirm her suspicions and tell her to rest for a few days, use ice for the swelling, and he gave her a few sample packets of a muscle relaxant to help with the muscle spasms.

Tally was annoyed Gage had tattled to the staff about her pulled muscle. She planned to give him an earful and returned to the waiting room only to find Trevor had been called back for his appointment and Gage was still at his.

Too worked up to focus on the book she'd been reading, she moved to a seat that allowed her to look out the window and waited. And waited. She tried to catch one of the on-duty nurses between patients, but they appeared swamped and busy as patients continued to stream in for appointments. The no-show today was likely the only time some of them had a break in what she knew had to be a long day. Working fourteen, sometimes even sixteen hours on her shift, Tally understood better than most why they sometimes seemed rushed and inattentive. Tally felt more fortunate than many. She worked three days on and three days off in a rotating schedule. Which meant every once in a while, she enjoyed a three-day weekend.

But on her days off, she could sleep in a bit, catch up on her rest, and spend time at the ranch. And spending time there had become a top priority since Gage's accident. Whether she wanted to admit it or not, she looked forward to every minute she could spend with him. She knew he'd be gone soon and likely only stop by between rodeos when he was in the area, but she didn't want to think about what might happen tomorrow. She only wanted to enjoy today when she knew he wasn't going anywhere.

A sound at the doorway drew her attention to

two smiling faces as Trevor and Gage both stood looking at her. The casts were gone and Gage no longer had hardware attached to his hand.

Tally forgot about being mad at him and jumped up, hurrying over to them. "Oh, my goodness! Look at you two!"

"I feel like going dancing," Gage said with a grin as he took a hesitant step forward. "But I might need a while to practice walking normally again."

"Me, too," Trevor said, grinning as the two of them made their way to the door. Tally pulled it open, but Gage held it and motioned for her to go ahead of them.

"I'm so happy for you both," she said, once they were all seated in the pickup. Gage claimed the front passenger seat, saying he'd been stuck riding in the back for almost two months.

Trevor stretched out on the back seat, propping his leg up with a relieved sigh. "I might just take a little siesta on the drive home." He tipped his hat so it covered his face and began breathing deeply before she even pulled onto the freeway.

"Did the doc take a look at your...um... muscle problem?" Gage's gaze fell to her chest. Color trickled up his neck, staining it red all the way to his ears. If she didn't know better, she would have thought he was blushing, but she couldn't remember him being embarrassed about anything in all the years she'd known him.

"He told me exactly what I already knew, Mr. Busybody." She pinned him with a scolding look, one she used on patients who wouldn't follow her orders. "But he did give me some muscle relaxant to use if I have more spasms."

"That's good. So, it's a pulled pec muscle?"

She nodded. Thoughts of pectoral muscles weren't exactly the first thing that came to mind when she considered her physique.

Covertly, she glanced at Gage's sculpted chest, outlined by the soft cotton shirt he wore. Talk about pec muscles to spare. He could be the official poster boy for a gym or fitness company.

"I've pulled mine a few times," he said, drawing her attention from his form to his face. "It hurts like the dickens the first day or two, but if you rest it, you'll feel like new in another week or so."

"Thanks. I'm hoping for a speedy recovery since I have to be back at work on Monday."

"Take a sick day or two if you need to."

She shook her head. "No. They are counting on me, and besides, I just took an unplanned two-week vacation when you guys came home from the hospital. I've used up my share of time off recently."

Gage looked like he wanted to argue with her, but instead he looked out the window and pointed to a pumpkin patch. "Do you get many trick-or-treaters at the house?"

"No, although we always buy candy. I usually wait until right before Halloween to purchase it, otherwise it magically disappears long before the end of October."

"You've got the house all decorated nice for fall. Do you always do that?" Gage turned and looked at her.

"I enjoy decorating for the different seasons.

We'll take down the fall decorations Thanksgiving evening and put them away. Trevor usually hauls all the Christmas decorations down for me on Black Friday while I take Aunt Marv to town."

Gage's eyes widened. "You take her to the crazy sales?"

"No," Tally smiled, picturing Marvella fighting someone over a toaster on a door-buster sale. "She spends the weekend with her friends at the retirement village, supposedly helping them decorate. Honestly, I think they mostly sit around drinking tea, eating cookies, and bossing around the crew that comes in to set up the decorations, but she loves it."

Gage laughed. "That I can imagine." His gaze seemed to rove over her, and he grinned. "Do you wear cute little Christmas scrubs, like the farm animal set you had on that day at the fair? Most of the time you have on plain colored scrubs."

She worked to keep her mouth from falling open. Gage had noticed her ridiculous scrubs. Not just noticed them, but thought they were cute? Maybe he was teasing her again.

"I do have some holiday scrubs I wear."

"With gingerbread men and elves?" He gave her one of those half smiles that turned her insides into melted butter.

"Snowmen, reindeer, and one set even features the Grinch."

"I bet you make them all look awesome."

A blush covered her cheeks and she looked away. Desperate to change the subject, she asked him about his hand and leg, what the doctor had said, and the recommended therapy now that he could move without the hardware or cast hampering his movements.

He looked out the window, then did a double-take. "Wonder what that guy is hunting? Deer?"

"Probably." Tally leaned forward and looked out the window. "At least with those orange vests on, they're easy to spot."

"Orange vests?" Gage's brow puckered in confusion. "He's dressed in camouflage. Can't you see that big rifle he's packing?"

"Rifle? I can barely see the two guys in orange. How can you possibly see what type of weaponry they're packing?" Tally scowled at him. "Are you colorblind? How did I not know this?"

He scoffed and pointed to a spot in the distance. "I'm not colorblind, woman. There's a guy in camo walking there on the ridge. The rifle he's carrying is silhouetted against the skyline. Right there," he tapped on the glass of the pickup window. "See him?"

Tally did see a man walking on the ridge and the outline of his gun. She grinned and motioned to a spot about a hundred feet below the ridge. "Down there, what do you see?"

Gage shifted his view from the ridge down the hillside and grinned. "Two hunters dressed in orange. And here I thought you'd already taken one too many of those muscle relaxants and gone loopy on us."

"You took drugs and are driving?" Trevor asked in a cranky tone from the backseat.

Tally huffed. "I've not taken anything besides

two ibuprofens. Both of you can just calm down. Good grief! Do you think I'd drive if I wasn't completely with it?"

"Well, I'm not sure you've ever been completely with it, Tal," Trevor mumbled, then grunted in feigned pain when she let go of the steering wheel long enough to whap his arm.

"Careful there, Queenie," Gage said as the pickup started to drift to the left.

She straightened it out and tossed one more glower at her brother before she exited the freeway and drove through Echo.

"Anyone need anything in town?" she asked as they passed city hall and the post office.

"Nope," Trevor and Gage said at the same time.

They arrived home to find Judd fixing barbecue pork for dinner while Marvella served tea and leftover pie to the pastor's wife and Chase Jarrett.

"Chase! What brings you to the ranch?" Trevor asked, shaking the man's hand as he rose from the table and greeted them with broad smiles.

"I ran down to Baker City to look at a horse Shaun and Jason Price think I should buy and thought I'd stop on my way home to see how you all are getting along. Miz Marvella insisted I stay for a slice of pie, which was excellent by the way." Chase motioned to Trevor and then Gage. "Looks like you two are on your way to being back to normal, or at least as normal as you get."

"Very funny, man," Gage said, thumping Chase on the back. "So, are you gonna buy the horse?"

The men wandered off in the direction of

Trevor's office while the pastor's wife finished her last bite of pie, thanked Marvella for the refreshments, gave Tally a hug, and left.

Gage tried to talk Chase into staying for supper, but he assured them Jessie had something ready and he needed to get home.

Once he left, they all went to the bunkhouse to eat with the ranch hands where Judd served barbecue pork sandwiches, spicy baked beans, potato salad, and pears he'd filled with sugar and cinnamon and baked in the oven.

"These pears are killer, man," Gage said with a nod to Judd as he helped himself to a second serving.

Tally had noticed he enjoyed anything made with fruit. She assumed he didn't get a lot of fresh home-grown produce out on the road.

After dinner, Marvella went back to her cottage, Trevor and Gage went out to the barn with Jared to look at a calf with a sore on its hip, and Tally stayed to help Judd put away food and clean the dishes.

He shooed her away when he realized she was hurting, and she returned to the house. She turned on the gas fireplace and snuggled into a big chair next to it with a soft afghan Aunt Marv had crocheted out of chunky yarn. She set her e-reader on her lap but couldn't focus on the words or the story.

The house seemed so quiet without Trevor and Gage there, laughing over a sit-com or good-naturedly arguing over something they heard on the news.

Tally gave up trying to read and stared into the flames of the fire, watching them burn and flicker. A hand on her shoulder startled her and she jumped, swallowing back the pain the sudden movement brought.

"Hey, I'm sorry. I didn't mean to scare you," Gage said in a quiet voice as he stood next to the chair. "It's just such a nice evening out, I wondered if you'd like to go for a walk, now that I can actually, you know, walk."

She smiled up at him and set the afghan aside then uncurled her legs from where she'd tucked them up in the chair beneath her. "That sounds nice. Let me grab a jacket."

They went through the kitchen to the back door where she pulled on an old wool coat and he grabbed his coat, jamming his arms in the sleeves.

"It's so weird to be able to move my hand without worrying about catching the hardware on something," he said as they walked down the porch steps and across the yard.

Tally stopped. The spectacular night sky captured her attention. "Oh, it's lovely," she said. The sun had set and a full bright moon loomed above the tops of the trees. Smoke from the wood stove in the bunkhouse, silage from the corn the men had cut that day, and a lingering hint of barbecue from dinner wafted in the air.

Gage stepped closer to her and his scent chased away the others, tantalizing her senses. Then his hand settled at the small of her back and her entire body began to tingle.

Rather than move away from him, which was

her first inclination, she continued walking, staring up at the moon that seemed to increase in both size and luminosity by the minute. She meandered past the outbuildings to where the pasture's pole fence was hidden in the shadows cast by the barn, shielding them from prying eyes.

She leaned her back against the fence and looked at Gage as he stood in front of her, unmoving. He seemed tense, anxious, but she had no idea what could be bothering him. He'd been in an amazing mood all afternoon and through dinner, as he should be after getting rid of his cast and the hardware in his hand.

With the moon shining directly on him like a spotlight, she could easily picture an artist capturing the rugged lines of his face, the pure masculinity of him, in a marble statue. A giggle threatened to work its way free of her throat when she thought about him posing while someone chiseled his likeness into a chunk of stone.

"What are you thinking?" he asked with that knee-weakening half smile.

"Nothing important," she said. There was no way she'd tell him she'd been envisioning him personified in a statue in a Tuscan villa's garden.

He took a step closer and she felt the all-too-familiar pull to him, like something magnetic that defied explanation wanted to bring them together. Although they remained invisible to the naked eye, she felt sparks arc between them in the autumn stillness.

Another step brought him so close, his breath mingled with hers, turning to silvery wisps in the night air. The front of his coat brushed against her chest while his gaze entangled hers. Powerless to move, to yank herself out of a fantasy she'd dreamed of dozens of times, she tilted her head back and studied Gage.

The man was handsome, and knew it, but he was also funny and sweet and kind. He'd been amazing with Marvella, treating her like she was royalty and making her feel special. Not just anyone would dote on her loony aunt.

Gage had spent a great deal of time the past several weeks making Tally feel special, too. When she was at the ranch, he went out of his way to pay attention to her, to compliment her on her cooking or something she wore. Not once had she allowed herself to consider the possibility that he might think of her as anything more than Trevor's little sister.

But tonight, beneath a moon that bathed them in a soft yellow glow, as Gage continued to look at her as though she was someone extraordinary, she wanted to believe it was true. Wanted to believe he cared about her as more than just a friend. Wanted to believe what she saw in his eyes was a yearning similar to what she felt for him.

Could it hurt, just for a few wild moments, to let herself pretend she was the woman Gage loved?

Her head screamed that it would in fact not be beneficial for her to spend even another second alone with Gage.

She stiffened and glanced back in the way they'd come. It might be best if she just headed back to the house now before the moonlight and her own ridiculous longings pressed her into doing something she knew she'd regret.

Gage seemed to sense her unease as he shifted and gave her a studying glance.

"What do you have against rodeo cowboys in general and me in particular?" he asked. His fingers gently cupped her chin, forcing her to look at him instead of turning away.

Tally considered ignoring his question or offering a flippant reply. Instead, she told him the truth.

"The summer I was eighteen, Dad and I went to all the rodeos we could where you and Trevor competed."

"Your dad was always good to come out and support us, and you, too, when you were at the ranch." Gage dropped his hand and gave her a questioning look. "So, how does that translate into the distrust, or maybe it's disgust I see in your eyes sometimes?"

Tally sighed, not wanting to tell Gage the truth, but realizing it was time. She'd never told anyone why she quit attending rodeos and began avoiding Trevor's friends. Perhaps sharing what had happened would help Gage understand why it was so hard for her to trust him.

"You and Trevor were both riding at the Horse Heaven Round-Up and you both placed, although Trevor took first that night." Tally turned and braced her arms on the fence.

"I remember that. You and Ross cheered for us both." Gage leaned on the fence beside her. "You had on a red shirt that made it clear you were all grown up. I think that was the first time I realized you were no longer a child."

She gave him a surprised look. "I thought you had no idea I even existed."

"Oh, I knew, Queenie, but you were my best friend's little sis, and I was way too old for you." He grinned at her. "But it doesn't mean I didn't notice when you changed from a cute kid into a beautiful young woman."

Rattled by his words, Tally focused on the moon as she gathered her thoughts.

Gage bumped her arm with his elbow. "So, what happened?"

"Dad told me I could go behind the chutes to congratulate you both. That was an eye-opening experience," she said, continuing to stare at the moon rather than the handsome man beside her.

"I can imagine," he said on a chuckle. "Ross always kept you away from there so you wouldn't be corrupted."

She couldn't stop her smile. "Dad sometimes sheltered me more than was necessary, but he might have been right on that count." She sighed. "I could see you and Trevor gathering up your gear, but before I reached you, Trevor disappeared. I stood there and watched you kiss one girl after another, telling each one how she was special, and you'd save her a dance later. I had no idea, until that moment, you were such a…" Tally struggled to find the best word to use.

"Player? Idiot? Jerk?" Gage supplied.

"Those words did come to mind." She glanced over at him then looked back at the pasture bathed in moonlight. "I had all these hopes and dreams about you, Gage, and in that moment, they were all crushed. I realized I'd been quite naïve and childish and was embarrassed I'd even considered the possibility of you one day noticing me. I was Trevor's chubby little sister with confidence issues. I couldn't begin to compete with the worldly, experienced women flocking around you. Now, I wouldn't want to even try."

"But, Tally…" Gage placed a hand on her shoulder, but she shook her head and slid away from him.

"No, Gage. It's fine. I needed that reality check even if it shattered my illusions." She took a deep breath then continued. "I turned to leave but two drunken cowboys grabbed my arms and dragged me away from the stands. Even if I'd screamed, no one would have noticed with all the noise."

"What?" Gage's voice sounded harsh in the evening quiet.

A shiver rolled through her as she relived that horrible moment when she'd been terrified of what might happen to her.

"What happened?" Gage asked, taking her arms in his hands and pulling her around to face him. "Were you hurt? Did they…" He swallowed hard, unable to voice his question.

"I struggled against them, but they were strong and mean. One of them slapped me so hard, my ears started to ring. I kicked and clawed at them, desperate to escape. In a moment of what I'm convinced was divine intervention, a stock contractor drove his horses straight at us. It startled the two drunks and gave me the chance to run away from them. I rushed back to Dad, told him I felt sick, and went home. That was the last time I attended a rodeo, until I brought you Trevor's gear bag."

"I'm so sorry, Tally. I had no idea." Gage pulled her to him, hugging her tightly as he held her. "I'm so, so sorry and I'm glad those horses kept you safe. If something had… If they'd…"

His lips pressed a soft kiss to her temple then he let her go. Cold seeped through her and she felt bereft without his arms around her.

"Do you want to tell me who those two cowboys were? I'll hunt them down and teach them a lesson they won't ever forget," he said, giving her a dark look she'd never seen on his face.

She shook her head. "I didn't recognize them. They might not even have been competitors, just guys there for a good time, but it ruined rodeo for me all the same."

"But you know not everyone is like that."

"I know, but being nearly abducted was only part of the issue." She looked away from Gage.

He released a frustrated breath. "The other part was seeing me act like a first-class donkey's patootie."

Tally grinned and nodded. "That did have something to do with it. I know it was stupid and silly, but I had such a crush on you back then. You were my hero and all those delusions I'd created around you died that day. It was hard to watch you topple off that pedestal you'd been on from the moment I met you."

"For the record, I've grown up a lot since then." Gage took a step closer to her.

"I noticed," she said in a quiet voice, wishing he'd take her in his arms again. Everything seemed so right when he held her.

"You might be interested to know that I only date one girl at a time and I haven't even had a single date for months. In fact, since a certain foxy nurse dropped off her brother's gear bag back in August, I haven't given any other women a second thought or look."

She would have turned away from him, but he caught her chin in his hand again and took another step closer. "In case you need me to clarify, I'm referring to you. You're gorgeous, sassy, fun, hardworking, and loyal. You've got a body that drives men completely wild and the fact you have no idea about the effect you have on the male species just makes you even more desirable."

Tally felt heat searing her cheeks. "You shouldn't say things you don't mean," she whispered, unable to look away. Not when her dreams danced in the reflection of his eyes.

"I never say things I don't mean or make promises I can't keep." Once again, he moved so close not even air could sneak between their coats.

"Gage," she said in a voice that sounded breathy and uncertain. She looked up at him, desperate for him, for his affection, in a way she was far too afraid to acknowledge let alone put into words.

"Talilah King, what have you done to me?" he asked in a husky tone as he slid a rough, callused hand across her cheek and buried it in her hair.

She didn't have an answer, wasn't sure she even understood the question. Her eyes drifted shut, seeking to memorize every tempting, tormenting second of this unexpected encounter with Gage. His left hand slowly threaded into her hair then she felt his breath on her face as he moved so close to her, the breeze had no space to blow between them.

"You are so beautiful, Queenie," he whispered. Hesitantly, or perhaps it was more a matter of restraint, his lips lightly brushed across hers. "I've been thinking about this moment, about kissing you, since you handed me Trevor's gear bag at the fair."

"You have not," she said, popping her eyes open, sure she'd find an impish grin on his face and a teasing gleam in his eye.

However, the gleam he sported was miles away from teasing. It looked like desire, raw and pure, and his mouth... Oh, that mouth. It had nothing to do with joking and everything to do with the wobbly state of her knees.

"I have, Tally. I wouldn't joke about something this serious," he said, moving his right hand just enough that he could brush his thumb over her cheek. "Not when I've spent hours lying awake at night wondering what it would be like to hold you in my arms and taste these ripe, luscious lips."

Tally hoped the darkness hid her blush as his head dipped toward hers again. "I'm gonna kiss you, Tally. If you have any objection at all, then you've got two seconds to run back to the house."

"I'm not running anywhere, Gage." She smiled and lowered her lashes as his lips brushed across hers again softly, tenderly, exploring and discovering.

In a state of complete rapture, she leaned into him and sighed in pleasure as her arms wrapped around his back. She didn't even notice the ache in her left arm and chest as she embraced him. She was too involved in the most delicious, decadent kiss she'd ever experienced in her life.

No doubt existed in her mind that Gage had plenty of practice kissing girls and women. Regardless of his experience, and her relative lack of it, nothing prepared her for the fervent blending of their lips as he thoroughly captivated her with his powerful, masterful kisses.

Long minutes passed as the kiss deepened. Her resolve to stay away from him weakened. Then the world disappeared until nothing but them and this moment in time existed.

Finally, when she was sure her legs would no longer hold her upright, Gage kissed her forehead and pulled her into a tight hug. His cheek rested on top of her head as he held her, just held her, not saying anything.

She didn't know how long they remained like that until Gage bracketed her face with his hands, as though he sought to memorize every detail about her.

"Tally, girl, you are..." He smiled at her, his mouth kicking up slightly on the left, making it a struggle for her to remain standing on bones that felt as though they'd liquefied. He bent down and kissed the tip of her nose then spoke in a raspy tone while heat emanated from him. "You are the sexiest, sweetest, most beautiful woman I've ever known. Don't ever forget that. Own it, Queenie."

"Gage, you know I'm…"

His mouth moving on hers silenced her protest and anything else she might have said. When he pulled back, she was too breathless to speak and too witless to form words even if she wanted to.

Gage took her right hand in his, kissed each one of her fingers with slow deliberation, then unsnapped his coat, placing her hand over his heart. "You feel that? My heart's beating so hard and fast it feels like it might explode, and that's because of you. You do that to me, Tally. You make me want to be more than I am, better than I've been. You're an amazing, intelligent, passionate, strong woman and I hope you'll always remember that."

"Thank you," she said, unable to think of anything else to say when his words stroked places in her heart that she'd never allowed anyone to touch. "Gage, I… I want you to know that I'm glad you've been here since your accident. I'm sorry you got hurt, but I'm not sorry we got to spend time together. I've enjoyed having you here. You're an incredible man, one I'm proud to know. I hope you'll always feel at home and welcome here." *And in my heart,* she thought.

He grinned and kissed the inside of her wrist, sending tendrils of warmth twirling through her. "The closest I've ever come to calling a place home is right here, on King Penny Ranch. And you've made it a welcoming place to be, Tally. Thank you for taking care of me these past weeks. I wouldn't have healed half as well without your help."

"Yes, you would have, because I know rodeo cowboys do whatever it takes to heal as quickly as possible." She smiled at him, although warning bells started to clang in her head. This conversation wasn't going anything like she planned or expected. Instead of being a declaration of feelings, it seemed more like a prelude to him saying goodbye. Gage couldn't leave, not now when everything inside her felt like it was coming to life and he was the only one who could help her bloom.

"Tally, I'm truly thankful to you for your care, and your friendship, and for this stolen moment. I'll never forget how dazzling you are, standing there surrounded by moonlight. You look like something from a dream, one I never want to wake from." He tugged her back into his arms and kissed her again with a hunger and need that met her own. When the kiss ended, he stepped back and took several deep breaths.

"That was...I... It..." Tally couldn't come up with a word incredible enough to describe what she felt in her heart, how she felt in his arms.

"Spectacular, magnificent, and the best kiss I've ever had seem inadequate to properly verbalize just exactly what that was, baby." Gage grinned at her, the moonlight reflecting off his white teeth. "Come on, Queenie, before I have my way with you right here in the pasture. Let's get back to the house or Trevor might actually notice we're missing and that won't go well for anyone."

She smiled and wrapped her right arm around his waist while he settled his left arm around her shoulders and snuggled her close to his side. He kissed the top of her head as they headed to the house.

At the back door, he stopped and cupped her chin, kissing her with such tenderness it brought tears to her eyes.

"Have sweet dreams, Talilah. I know who'll be in mine tonight."

Tally practically floated inside then went to her room lest Trevor see something had happened between her and Gage. Tomorrow would be soon enough to tell him they were in love, to discuss the possibilities of what might be, to make plans for the future.

Tonight was made for dreams, dreams of the cowboy who'd finally claimed her heart.

Chapter Fifteen

Trevor strode into the kitchen, realizing he was the first one up. After making coffee, he poured a cup full and sat down on a barstool at the counter, enjoying the peacefulness of the morning.

He thought about what the day might bring, trying to plan ahead. Water ran above him, letting him know Tally was up. He recalled her pulled muscle, and grinned as he remembered something his dad used to make for her when she was sick.

He hauled out the toaster and popped in two pieces of bread. While it warmed, he dug around in the drawer where Tally kept her special baking supplies. He took out several jars of sprinkles and one that said edible glitter. When the toast popped up, he coated it with chocolate-nut spread then smothered the bread with sprinkles and glitter.

Proud of his efforts, he located a china plate and set the toast on it, then filled a delicate china cup with hot chocolate. He'd just set the plate and cup on a tray when Tally bounded into the kitchen.

Joy radiated from her smile while her eyes sparkled with happiness. She pecked his cheek and gave him a tight hug. He sucked in a breath, wondering when she'd turned from his awkward little sister into such a beautiful woman.

He didn't know exactly what was different about her this morning, but she seemed full of more life and energy than he'd ever seen in her. And that bothered him. Greatly.

The reason for the change in her no doubt started and ended with Gage.

Trevor swallowed back a primitive growl and forced a smile as Tally spied his efforts at making her breakfast.

"Princess toast?" She looked at the tray then at him. "I haven't had that in years. Thank you, Trev." She lifted the cup of steaming hot chocolate and took a sip. "Mmm. So good. Just like Dad always made it."

"Yep. Nothing is too good for my favorite sister."

One eyebrow rose as she stared at him over the rim of the cup. "I'm your only sister, unless Lulu has another child hidden away I don't know about."

"Bite your tongue! I wouldn't wish Lulu on anyone," Trevor said, placing an arm around Tally and giving her a hug.

She set the cup back on the tray and looked from the toast to Trevor. He tried to keep his face impassive, but she shook her head then crossed her arms over her chest and leaned back against the counter.

"What's going on? You're being awfully nice to me, and Dad only made princess toast when I was sick or disaster had struck." Tally's eyes widened. "Nothing happened to Aunt Marv, did it? Please tell me she's…"

"Ready for breakfast," Marvella said as she marched into the kitchen, rubbing her hands on the arms of her chunky sweater to ward off the cold. "This cold air makes me hungry. Are we having toast?" she asked, pointing to the toaster on the counter. "I can make eggs to go with it."

"That's fine, Aunt Marv," Trevor said, giving his aunt a glance as she pulled a skillet forward on the stove and dropped in a glob of butter.

"Scrambled okay?" she asked.

"Scrambled is great, Aunt Marv," Tally said, smiling at the older woman then turning back to Trevor. "Where's Gage? He's usually up before the chickens. Did he go outside to help with chores? He should be careful with his hand for a while."

Rather than answer, Trevor turned his back to her and took a long drink from his rapidly cooling coffee.

Tally stepped around in front of him, hands on her hips in a stance that testified to her mounting irritation. "Fess up, Trev. Something is going on. I can see it in your face and there's no use denying it. You might as well just rip off the band-aid and get it over with."

"Gage is gone," Trevor said quietly.

"Gone? Like out in the barn gone?" Tally asked, glancing out the window in the direction of the big red building.

"No, Tal. Like packed his stuff and left. That kind of gone." Trevor hated to tell her, hated to see the wounded look in her eyes and the sudden slump to her shoulders.

"He left? Without a word? After all the… and the…" Her shoulders inched upward as indignation joined forces with her fury. "After last night… the moonlight…" She pinned Trevor with a gaze full of anger and hurt and something he had no idea how to describe. "He's truly gone?"

"Yep. I had Judd drive him to Pasco to the airport. He had something come up he needed to take care of." Trevor didn't think his sister needed to know the thing that came up so suddenly were Gage's feelings for Tally. "He did say goodbye and left a note for both you and Aunt Marv. They're on the table."

"A note? A note!" Tally's voice rose and she stamped her foot. "I don't want a note, I want an explanation, in person, from that… that… cowboy!" She said cowboy as though it was the most disgusting word in existence.

"Now, Tally, don't get all worked up." Trevor tried using a placating tone.

When Tally spun around, hands clenched into fists at her sides and nostrils flaring like an enraged mama cow ready to wipe out anyone in her way, he took a wide step back, out of her reach.

"Worked up? You think this is worked up? You haven't even begun to see worked up!" Tally closed the distance between them and poked Trevor in the chest with her index finger. "Why, exactly, did Gage leave so unexpectedly?"

"I told you," Trevor said, grabbing the finger trying to puncture his lung. "He made a promise he had to keep, so he left."

"Where did he go?"

Trevor shrugged. "It was late when he decided to leave. I'm not sure I heard his travel plans."

"Agh! Men are so... so..." Tally kicked the clothesbasket that was sitting near the doorway with such force it slid all the way across the room before she thundered up the steps to her room. The slamming of her bedroom door made the windows in the kitchen rattle and Trevor cringe. He hadn't seen her so angry since... Come to think of it, he'd never seen her this angry. Ever.

He turned around to find Aunt Marv standing in front of him looking nearly as out of sorts as his sister.

"What did you do?" Marvella demanded.

Slowly, he backed away from her. "What makes you think I did anything, Auntie? Maybe I'm the good guy who helped Gage get a ride to the airport. Or saved his sister from a lifetime of heartache."

"What! Did! You! Do!" Marvella accentuated each word she spoke by poking him with a bony finger in the exact spot Tally had abused a few minutes ago.

"Ow!" he said, taking Marvella's hand between his and holding it gently. "Aunt Marv, it's for the best. Just let it be."

"What, exactly, is for the best?" she asked, giving Trevor a push so he plopped down on one of the barstools at the counter.

"Gage leaving before Tally falls in love with him. That's the direction it's headed. Don't tell me you haven't seen it happening."

Marvella narrowed her gaze and appeared to be considering if some demon had taken possession of her beloved nephew. At least he hoped he was still beloved.

The old woman sighed. "Of course, I've seen it happening, you nitwit. I've done everything I could to encourage it. If you'd accurately assessed the situation, you'd have seen Gage and Tally are perfect together. They've been in love since the moment they set eyes on each other."

"What? No…" Trevor glared at his aunt, then wondered if she could be right. "Surely they aren't…" He switched gears, hoping to make his aunt understand why he'd agreed when Gage said he needed to leave. "Aunt Marv, you have no idea how Gage is with girls. He's out for a good time. The longest he ever had a girlfriend was three months, and that was only because she was in Texas and he was in the middle of the summer rodeo season traveling all over. He's never going to be the guy who settles down with a wife and family, at least not anytime soon. He's my best friend, but he's not right for Tally. She needs a man who'll commit to her, be home every night, and cherish her."

Marvella grabbed a newspaper that had been left on the table, rolled it up, and whacked Trevor on the arm.

"Hey! What's that for?" he asked, jerking back before she could hit him again.

"For being so stupid, Trevor Ross King! How dare you decide what's best for your sister!" Marvella fumed. "As for Gage, you forget I've been here many times when he's been passing through. I've seen him in action with girls, but this was different. He's different. Only a blind dolt would miss the fact he's in love with our girl."

"No, Aunt Marv. He'll just break her heart." Trevor didn't know how to make his aunt see reason. "He promised he'd leave Tally alone. Gage is honest and he'd never back out of a promise. He always keeps his word. Last night, he and Tally went for a walk and when they came back, Gage told me if he didn't leave, he wouldn't be able to keep that promise, to keep away from her. So, I helped him go."

"Oh! You're a pitiful dunce, Trevor! How could we have raised such a ninny?" Marvella swatted him again. "Gage would keep his promise to you, even if it means breaking his heart and Tally's. Call him. Tell him to come back. Release him from that ridiculous promise. Go tell your sister what you've done by meddling in things that are none of your concern."

"Now, hold on there, Aunt Marv." Trevor yanked the newspaper away from her before she nailed him a third time. "I only had Tally's best interest in mind when I extracted that vow from Gage. I didn't want him to hurt her, to leave her heartbroken. Everyone knows she had a crush on him when she was a kid. I worried she might still like him, even though she refused to be here if he was around since she graduated from high school.

With Dad gone, it's my responsibility to protect her and keep her safe."

"To the point you ruin her life, Trevor? What if Gage is the one she's meant to love for a lifetime and you made him choose a promise to you over his love for her? Hmm? Can you live with that, knowing you chased away your sister's chance at true love?"

True love. Those words echoed in his thoughts after Tally had given such an eloquent description of what it meant to her just yesterday. He'd known she was falling for Gage. He could see the way she lit up when Gage walked into a room, the way her eyes sought his across the table, the way she seemed attuned to him without needing to say a word.

However, Gage had hidden his feelings for her well. Until his friend had come to him last night, confessed he was falling in love with Tally, and agreed he needed to leave, Trevor had hoped Gage wouldn't play his sister along like he had so many women. It wasn't that Gage set out to break hearts, but women had certain expectations when a handsome, rugged man dated them, especially if he dated them enough times they considered themselves a girlfriend. From there, wedding bells began ringing in their heads and that was when Gage cut things off with a brief word of goodbye and few explanations.

Trevor had done the same thing plenty of times. Too many times, if he cared to admit it, but that was neither here nor there.

The immediate problem was the two women who kept Trevor fed and comfortable in his home were both so mad at him he was surprised they hadn't started spewing venom.

"Look, Aunt Marv, we all knew Gage had to leave sometime. It's best he did it now before Tally's head or heart gets any more tangled up with these silly thoughts of romance."

"Silly thoughts of romance!" Marvella screeched. Faster than he would have given her credit for being able to move, she snatched the newspaper from him and smacked him twice on the shoulder with it then tossed it in his face.

"You march up those stairs, confess what you've done, and make this right, Trevor. Right now!" she demanded.

"No," he said, wadding the newspaper into a ball and tossing it in the trash. He silently dared Marvella to dig it out and hit him with it. "It's for the best and eventually both of you will see that. Tally's not like other girls. She's naïve and too trusting and I won't stand by and watch her get her heart shattered. I won't. And that's the last I want to hear about it," Trevor bellowed before grabbing his coat and storming out of the house.

It was bad enough he'd had to send his best friend off like a thief in the night, but now Tally and Aunt Marv were both so upset it might be Christmas before they spoke to him again.

No matter what anyone said, he'd only wanted to keep Tally safe. A little heartbreak now was better than a huge heartbreak later, wasn't it?

Chapter Sixteen

Tally ached.

She'd been working for twelve hours and had at least another four before she could call it a day. Her feet ached. Her back ached. Her head ached.

But none of that compared to the ache in her heart. It hadn't stopped throbbing with pain since the morning she'd awakened to find Gage gone from King Penny Ranch.

Trevor had tried to assure her it was for the best, as though he understood she'd completely and hopelessly fallen in love with his friend.

But how could he even begin to comprehend the depths of what she felt for Gage? It went beyond longing, beyond a physical attraction, far beyond reason. She felt as though some part of her very soul had connected with Gage's and unless they were together, nothing would be right in her world.

Strangely, Aunt Marv had been very close-mouthed with her opinions on the matter, but she offered Tally plenty of hugs and had gone out of her way to be on her best behavior the past several weeks.

Now that December had arrived, Tally just wanted to survive the holidays and hope she could start the new year with a fresh outlook. Maybe by the time January rolled around, she wouldn't cry herself to sleep and wake up dreaming of being in Gage's arms.

She couldn't fathom what kind of promise would have pulled him away from the ranch at such a pivotal time in their relationship. In retrospect, Gage hadn't said he loved her, or offered a single word of commitment.

But he'd made her feel beautiful, desirable, smart, and witty while treating her like a queen. He'd been so sweet and supportive when she told him the secret of why she'd avoided rodeos and him. And then he'd kissed her with more passion and longing than she'd ever imagined possible.

Even now, just thoughts of those fervent kisses they shared made her lips tingle while her insides melted.

How could he have kissed her like that if he didn't care?

Then again, Gage was used to kissing girls and moving on. Maybe he'd just played her for a fool.

The sensible part of her brain refused to believe that, though. Gage had proven time and again he was trustworthy, honest, and a man of integrity.

Why, then, had he run from her the moment she'd finally allowed herself to accept her dreams of a future with him weren't far-fetched fantasies?

Trevor refused to give her any details and Tally would rather walk through the mall naked than call Gage and ask for an explanation. Since he was the one to leave her, she felt it was up to him to make the first move and reach out to her.

In the six weeks he'd been gone, she hadn't heard a single peep from him. Of course, he and Trevor were in frequent contact.

It might help matters if she'd finally read the note he left for her, but she wasn't ready to accept his excuses, whatever they may be. Aunt Marv had read the note he left her and cried for two days afterward, bemoaning his absence. She'd forced Tally to read what he'd written, and it brought tears to her eyes, too. Gage had been so sweet in thanking Marvella for spending time with him, driving him around, and providing a listening ear. He assured the old woman her husband had been a lucky man and promised the next time he was in the area they'd go to Echo and get an ice cream cone at the cafe or another cup of hot cider.

Tally wondered if he'd promised the same to her, but she wasn't curious enough to break the seal on the envelope and read it.

Part of her wanted to write Santa a letter and beg him to place Gage on his permanent naughty list for leaving her just when she was ready to finally surrender to her feelings for him. The other part of her wanted to beg the jolly old man to bring Gage home for Christmas. Home to her.

Conflicted and weary, she made her way to the cafeteria where she hoped to grab a bite to eat and rest her feet for a few minutes on her break.

She fixed a cup of tea and got a bowl of chicken and wild rice soup then made her way over to a table where Glenda and Tonya took a break.

"Hey, girl! How's it going?" Glenda asked as Tally set her tray on the table then took a seat.

"It's going," Tally said, working up a smile for her friends. "How are you both doing?"

"Fine. Looks like it will be a long night, though," Tonya said, pointing to Glenda's tablet screen and grinning.

"What are you looking at?" she asked lifting a spoonful of soup.

"Photos of celebrities when they were young," Glenda said, turning the tablet so Tally could see it.

Tally choked on the bite of soup and coughed.

"Are you okay?" Glenda asked, setting the tablet on the table and patting her back.

"Who is that?" Tally croaked, pointing to the screen as she took a sip of tea.

Tonya smiled. "That is a young and very handsome Marlon Brando. Why?"

"He just looks so much like..." She stopped herself and took another sip of tea.

"Gage?" Glenda and Tonya asked in unison.

Tonya smiled again while Glenda fanned a hand in front of her face. "Well, no wonder you've been pining after that cowboy. He's one hot tamale," Glenda said.

"I haven't been pining after him," Tally said, then noticed the knowing glances the two women shot her way. "Okay, maybe I have been."

"The only time I saw him was the day he came into the emergency room, and he was covered in blood that day," Glenda said. "Does he really look like Brando?"

Tally nodded and lifted the tablet, scrolling through to a photo that showed the actor bare-chested with a teasing grin on his face. "Oh," she whispered, wondering how she'd never noticed the resemblance between Gage and the man before. Then again, she rarely had time for watching television, let alone seeking out old movies.

"Wow. Lucky girl," Tonya said, studying the image on the screen. "I bet your burning hunk of rodeo cowboy is even more handsome, though."

"He's not mine," Tally said, and picked up her spoon again.

"But he could be, couldn't he?" Glenda asked, placing a hand on Tally's arm. "You never really said what happened, just that he left."

"He left in the night, like some cowardly, spineless, worthless, cheating, low-down…" Tally took a deep breath. "He left without a word of goodbye and I haven't heard a single peep out of him since. It was stupid and foolish to think he'd ever be interested in a girl like me."

Tonya crossed her arms over her chest and leaned back in her chair. "A girl like you? Now, what is that supposed to mean?"

Tally swept a hand at her side that encompassed the hair escaping from the messy bun at the back of her head, the dark purple scrubs that hadn't appeared fresh for several hours, and the support shoes on her feet. "What would a guy like Gage want with a girl like me when he could have anyone he wanted? I'm nobody special and on top of that we all know I'll never win any beauty contests."

"Only because you're too shy, modest, and humble to enter them," Glenda said, giving Tally a one-armed hug. "If Gage had even two brain-cells bumping against each other, he'd be able to see you're quite a catch, Tally King."

"Glenda's right, Tally," Tonya said. "You're gorgeous, even if you don't realize it. You're smart, funny, kind, and one of the best nurses I've ever met, not to mention a wonderful friend. Any guy would be blessed to win your heart."

"You both are sweet, but…"

"No buts about it," Tonya interjected. "If you'd spend a few minutes looking in the mirror, you'd see what the rest of us do."

"And that's a beautiful person with an amazing heart," Glenda said. She picked up her tablet and tapped a few keys, then sucked in a gulp. "That's your Gage?"

"I told you he's not mine," Tally said, glancing over at the tablet Glenda held. There was Gage, with his killer smile, mesmerizing blue eyes, and thick brown hair that her fingers suddenly itched to run through. He had on a blue paisley shirt that enhanced the color of his eyes and accented the width of his shoulders. The way he stood, with his arms crossed in front of him, showcased his bulging biceps.

Tally wondered if the shot was one taken at Chase and Jessie Jarrett's place for a Lasso Eight fashion shoot. There was snow in the background while a pine garland draped across the fence behind

Gage.

"He models for Lasso Eight?" Tonya asked, tapping the screen to enlarge the image which had a Lasso Eight logo in the corner.

"Yes. He's done that since the company started," Tally said, forcing her gaze away from Gage. From her dreams. From her longings.

"Are you insane?" Glenda asked, holding out the image of Gage. "If you don't call this hunky cowboy right now and demand to know why he left, I'll do it for you."

"No, you won't." Tally looked at her friend, knowing she and Tonya were teasing and only wanted to make her smile. "Now, tell me if you've heard what plans are in the works for the staff holiday party."

By the time Tally finished her shift, she was utterly exhausted. She returned to her apartment and fell asleep a minute after her head hit the pillow.

The next morning, before she had to be at work, she sat at the kitchen table eating a bowl of oatmeal, mulling over her options. She could go on being livid at Gage, never read the letter he left, and refuse to ever speak to him again. Although that had been her go-to move the past six weeks, she was tired of it. Tired of being furious. Tired of letting the hurt rule her heart and life.

A better, and more mature option, would be to read the letter he left her, and, after reading it, forgive him for leaving so abruptly. Even if it was going to take a long time for her heart to heal, she could at least let go of her anger and move on.

Since she'd left the letter at the ranch, there

wasn't a lot she could do until she went out there Thursday. It was the first night of the national finals rodeo and she'd promised Trevor and Aunt Marv she'd watch it with them even though at the time, she'd been loath to do so.

For the first time since he'd left the professional rodeo circuit, Trevor wasn't going to Las Vegas for the rodeo. She didn't know if he dreaded walking around on his still recovering knee or if he'd changed his plans in deference to her feelings.

They hadn't discussed it, although she had mentioned in passing she hated to see him miss out on the only vacation he took each year.

Before she could change her mind, Tally typed in Gage's name on her laptop. She was shocked to discover he'd made it to the national finals, after all. The article that popped up mentioned his wreck and being bumped down to number sixteen in the standings. It appeared the bareback rider who'd been at number twelve in the standings sustained an injury that left him unable to compete and shifted everyone below him up a notch. That meant Gage was going to be in Las Vegas, riding with his barely healed hand and leg.

The man was crazy! What if he reinjured his leg or a horse trampled his hand? He could end up crippled for life.

"Stupid, stubborn, idiotic man!" she fumed and closed her laptop. She gave it a shove across the table, harder than she intended. The computer would have crashed to the floor if one of her roommates hadn't entered the room and caught it.

"Good morning to you, Miss Merry Sunshine," Susan teased as she set the laptop beside Tally and poured a cup of coffee. "The only thing that could put me in such a foul mood this early in the day is an empty coffee pot or a man. Since you've got a steaming cup in front of you, I'm guessing it's that cowboy you took care of all autumn."

"He's competing at the national finals rodeo in Las Vegas. I'm concerned he's going to cause permanent damage to his healing injuries."

"So, why don't you buzz down there and be his personal nurse?" Susan asked, giving Tally a teasing look over her coffee cup.

"Then you better catch a pig and harness it because they'd have to be flying before I'll do that." Tally dumped out her cereal, gulped what remained of her coffee, and picked up her laptop. "Have a good day, Susan. If you want, I can help put up the Christmas decorations when I get back tonight."

"Thanks. I shouldn't be too late. Maybe we can put on some holiday tunes, drink a little eggnog, and deck our halls."

Tally nodded from the kitchen doorway. "That sounds great. See you later."

She finished getting ready and went to work, feeling marginally better than she had the previous day. Normally, she loved the holidays and everything about them. Perhaps she just needed to get into the spirit of the season and completely forget about Gage.

Throughout the day, anytime her thoughts started to drift toward one gorgeous rodeo cowboy, she hummed a Christmas carol. By the end of her shift, she didn't feel as tired in body or mind as she had for a while.

On the way back to the apartment, she stopped at a craft store and purchased a few supplies.

Once there, she and Susan hung garlands and wreaths, and even decorated the small fake tree they'd all chipped in and purchased two years ago.

When they finished, they sipped eggnog while watching a Charlie Brown Christmas special on TV.

Tally went to bed smiling instead of in tears for the first time in weeks.

She was nearly finished with her shift at the hospital the following evening when Tonya ran up to her and grabbed her arm, dragging her into a nearby patient's room.

Her friend pointed to the television. "Is that him?"

Tally's mouth dropped open as she gaped at an advertisement for Lasso Eight. Horses and snow were barely visible in the background, although it was unlikely anyone would notice them. Not with Gage leaning on his forearms against the wall of a bunkhouse, shoulders stretching the fabric of an aqua blue shirt flecked with diamond shapes of darker blue. The hue of the shirt made his eyes pop with intense color. His short hair looked tousled and tempting while his slightly parted lips would have tantalized any red-blooded woman into giving him a kiss, should the opportunity arise. The way the photographer had posed Gage, with his arms braced against the wall, one rested higher than the other and kept his injured hand out of the image.

No wonder Paige invited Gage back to model

each season's new line. He looked beyond amazing.

"Oh, my," Tally whispered, taking a step closer to the television.

"Do you know that handsome cowboy?" an elderly lady asked as she rested in the hospital bed.

Tally nodded. "He's my brother's best friend."

"Well, aren't you a lucky girl," the woman said with a laugh. "If I was forty years younger, I'd be for making him my good friend, too!"

Tonya laughed and settled a hand on Tally's shoulder. "I thought you'd want to see that."

"Thanks," Tally said, distracted by the advertisement and Gage's appearance.

"He is a mouth-watering morsel, isn't he?" the old woman asked, although it was said more as a statement than a question.

"Mmm, hmm," Tally mumbled, not paying attention to anything except the way Gage looked. When he winked and smiled at the camera, she reached behind her and braced her hand on the end of the bed.

"Yep, I can see you are totally over him," Tonya said with a giggle.

The commercial ended and Tally turned to glare at her friend. "Oh, hush!" She smiled at the elderly woman then hurried out of the room.

Before she could leave after her shift, her supervisor asked if she could cover for someone who was sick the following day.

Tally hated to say no, so she agreed to put in another long day. When she left the hospital the following evening, the air was moist and cold, as though it might snow, although they hadn't had a single snowflake fall all season. At this rate, it might be a brown Christmas and she hated to think of that. At the very least, she hoped to get a thick frost to turn the world white.

Trevor texted her and asked her to pick up something for dinner on her way to the ranch, so she swung by a barbecue restaurant and got an order to go before she drove to King Penny Ranch.

She sat between Trevor and Aunt Marv on the couch in front of the television as the three of them waited for the first night of the rodeo to begin.

"Why aren't you there, Trevor?" Marvella asked, pointing to the television screen with her fork as two commentators discussed their thoughts on the evening ahead. "You always go."

"It just didn't seem right to be there this year," he said, glancing at Tally.

"If you missed out on your only vacation of the year on my account, you shouldn't have." She bumped her shoulder against his. "It's not too late. You could still go."

"No. I'll sit this year out. Gage..." Trevor gave her a quick look. "My friends understand."

Tally shrugged. "Then they comprehend you far better than I do."

"Hush! The Lasso Eight commercial is on," Marvella said, flapping her fork at the screen again.

This commercial showcased Shaun and Brylee Price. She sat on a pole fence wearing a long blanket coat while Shaun rested his arm on her thigh and gazed up at her with such a look of love, Tally sighed dreamily.

"They are just the cutest couple," she said. "I'm

so glad they got back together."

"Being around those two is almost like getting a sugar high from all the sweetness," Trevor groused, but he winked and smiled, letting her know he was happy for his friends, too.

"Oh, look at the kids," Marvella said as the Morgan and McGraw children ran into the shot, each carrying a brightly wrapped package.

"They're adorable!" Tally smiled as Shaun lifted little Marley Morgan up and she kissed his cheek.

"She's gonna be a heartbreaker. Tate better buy an extra shotgun and stock up on ammo to keep the boys away," Trevor said, then took a bite of his brisket sandwich.

"Cort better be careful with Grace, too," Tally said, watching as the little girl posed next to her brother with an extra dose of sassy flair.

"That child has got too much of her daddy and aunt in her," Marvella said. "The boys might need to run from her."

Tally laughed and they all relaxed, prepared to enjoy the evening. The rodeo began and they watched the bareback riders compete, chatting about the scores. All three of them sat in tense silence, though, when the horse Gage was riding roared out of the chute. She held her breath as she watched him spur, legs moving front to back, left hand up in the air while he made it the full eight seconds. A pickup man rode up beside him and Gage swung off, waved his hat in the air over his head then did a fist pump when he scored an eighty-seven-point ride, which turned out to be the high score of the evening.

"He did good," Marvella said, then went back to eating her supper.

"That he did," Trevor said with a grin.

Tally didn't comment, but she was proud of Gage for doing so well, even if she worried about the toll competing would take on his body, particularly his recent injuries. She knew he'd wrap his arm, wrist, and leg with sports tape and do all he could to minimalize the wear and tear on his body. Even so, she worried about him.

The fact she did made her consider how much she still cared about him, even if he had destroyed her heart. The first time she thought he'd broken it back when she was eighteen was nothing compared to what she felt when she realized he'd left without telling her goodbye. She'd been childish, silly even, to assume he felt the same way about her.

The kisses they'd shared in the moonlight that October night might have rocked her world off its axis, but obviously, she was nothing more than a temporary diversion for Gage. In spite of that, she believed he had, at that moment, found her beautiful and attractive.

One thing she did know about Gage is that he wouldn't lie to her, even if he omitted the detail he was planning to leave that very night and disappear from her life.

Trevor mentioned a few times that Gage asked about her, wanted to make sure she was well, but he did the same for Marvella. The thought of her meaning no more, or less, to him than her aunt left Tally with a bitter taste in her mouth. No longer hungry, she handed Trevor the remainder of her meal and watched the rest of the rodeo in silence.

When it ended, Marvella kissed them both on the forehead and announced she was going to bed.

Trevor had already texted Gage right after his ride to tell him congratulations, but he called his friend as he walked off toward his room. From the one-sided conversation, she could tell Gage was excited and pleased with his first night's ride. He'd earned the right to celebrate his victory and she truly was glad for him, even if she was still mad at Gage.

Tally went to the kitchen and placed the few dirty dishes left in the sink into the dishwasher, turned off the lights, and made her way upstairs to her bedroom. With a deep, determined breath, she opened a cedar keepsake box Ross had given her for her sixteenth birthday and took out the letter Gage had written to her back in October.

Slowly, she broke the seal of the envelope, pushed back the flap, and removed a single sheet of paper. When she unfolded it, she caught the barest whiff of Gage's scent. She closed her eyes and inhaled, savoring it as she pictured him as she so often thought of him, with that knee-weakening half-grin on his face.

She opened her eyes and focused on the words written in Gage's bold hand.

Dear Tally,

I don't even know where to begin, so I'll start with an apology. I'm so sorry for leaving without saying goodbye in person. It's not what I want to do, but what is necessary. Due to a promise I made, I have to leave. However, I don't want you to think, even for a second, that it's because of something you said or did. It is only because of that promise.

If circumstances were different, I'd stay right here on King Penny Ranch and never leave. I've told you before, but I'll say it again — it's the closest to a home I've ever had, and I love being here. Especially with you.

Tonight, out there behind the barn, I felt like a king, because I held you in my arms, Queenie. Thank you for the most amazing kisses I've ever experienced. You took my breath away and left me so rattled, I'm surprised I managed to walk you back to the house without saying or doing something stupid.

Tally blushed. "Considering all the women you've kissed, I highly doubt my kisses ranked that high for you, cowboy," she whispered to herself, even if she was secretly pleased by his words.

I know you don't realize it, but you are gorgeous, sweet, and wonderful. Don't ever change who you are. Not for anyone.

No matter what happens, you'll always be in my heart and my thoughts.

Again, I'm sorry for leaving you so suddenly, but it couldn't be helped. I hope you'll forgive me. The last thing I want to do is hurt you, Tally. Not when I'd much rather hold you.

"If that's true, then why'd you run off, Gage?"

she asked aloud. Her mind played over any number of ways he could have said goodbye without allowing her to find out from Trevor he'd left.

If you ever want to talk or just need a friendly ear, you've got my number. Call me anytime.

Keep Trevor and Aunt Marv out of trouble, or at least do your best!

Yours always,

Gage

"Yours always?" she questioned. "What's that supposed to mean?"

Tally read through the letter a second time before she folded it, tucked it back into the envelope and set it inside her keepsake box. Gage hadn't made any professions of undying love, but his words did seem sincere. If she wasn't reading more into the note than he meant, he truly did seem to care for her. But if that was true, how could he just leave like that and not call her, even once, in the long weeks since then.

She was still mad at him for kissing her until nothing in the world existed except him and then leaving without a single spoken word. In spite of that, though, she thought she might be ready to forgive him. After all, he had left the note and she could have read it the morning after he left, instead of waiting weeks to open it. If she had, she might not have felt so tormented and maudlin the last six weeks.

Confused and heart-sore, she got ready for bed and slid between her cool sheets. Before she clicked off the light, she grabbed her phone and sent Gage a text, congratulating him on his ride.

She turned off the light, rolled onto her side, said a prayer, and fell asleep, wondering if he'd really meant what he wrote.

Chapter Seventeen

Gage fought the urge to pinch himself as he sat with the other winners at the first go-round awards ceremony of the national finals rodeo. He couldn't believe he'd not only made it to the finals, but also won the first night of competition.

After his motorcycle accident and spending so many weeks unable to compete, he knew he'd lost out on the chance to ride at the finals this year. Then one of his friends had an unfortunate accident that pulled him out of the competition. Gage had risen to number fifteen, squeaking into the finals. Although he felt bad for his injured friend, he was so grateful to have the chance to participate.

He'd spent hours and hours practicing while he stayed with Cooper and Paige James after he left King Penny Ranch. Cooper's grandfather, Nick, made arrangements to use the arena in St. Paul with real bucking broncs, so Gage could get back into the rhythm of riding.

Now that he was here in Las Vegas, it almost seemed surreal. For the first time since he'd been coming to Vegas in December, Trevor wasn't with him. He missed his best friend, but Trevor hadn't felt like he could attend with things so unsettled with Tally.

Gage understood, even if he didn't like it.

If he could magically snap his fingers and have anything he wanted, he'd be sitting with his arm around Tally, looking forward to having her close beside him for the next ten days. Instead, he hadn't heard from her since he'd left without a single spoken word of goodbye.

After kissing her in the moonlight that October evening, he realized two important details. The first was that he loved her to the very depths of his soul. The second was that if he didn't leave right then, he'd never be able to walk away from her. And he'd made a promise to Trevor that he had no intention of breaking.

Truthfully, he'd hoped Trevor would release him from the promise he so rashly made. Instead, when he'd gone inside the house that evening and told Trevor he wasn't going to be able to leave Tally alone if he stayed, his friend had practically shoved him out the door in his haste to get rid of him.

Gage would have done the same thing if Tally had been his sister. He wasn't mad at Trevor. However, it didn't stop him from being disappointed in the circumstances and himself. He knew better than to spend time with Tally, to let her sweetness soothe the tumult in his heart and her gentleness smooth his rough edges.

He loved everything about her. Her smile lit up his whole world. Those gray eyes of hers could change in a blink from looking like ice in a winter lake to stormy, like lightning scorching across a summer sky, to soft and tender, like when she doted on Marvella. Tally was devoted and caring, hardworking and strong, smart and sassy, funny and beautiful.

Just thinking about her curves made him feel overheated. He took a long gulp of his icy-cold soda. Tally had always been a cute little girl, even if she was a bit on the chubby side. But that baby fat had gone away, leaving behind the kind of luscious figure that was the stuff of dreams.

Gage would know, since he'd dreamed of holding her dozens of times since he'd seen her in August at the rodeo.

As the awards ceremony continued around him, his thoughts drifted to the first time he'd met Tally at a high school rodeo. She'd been with Ross and clung to his hand, so shy and uncertain, but she'd been adorable with her hair in dark pigtails, wearing a pair of denim overalls with a pink shirt that sparkled in the sunlight.

Anytime he'd been at King Penny Ranch during his teen years and even into his early twenties, she'd followed him around like a besotted pup. Then she'd just disappeared. Trevor always made excuses for why she wasn't at the ranch, and Gage hadn't given it a lot of thought until now. He'd missed her even if he hadn't realized it at the time.

At least he knew why she stayed away from him and Trevor's rodeo friends. Not that he could blame her. If he ever found out who the two idiots were who tried to abduct her, he would hunt them down and leave them staked in the desert as buzzard feed. He probably ought to be left out there with them, too, since he'd destroyed Tally's delusions that night so long ago. She said he'd broken her heart then, but he considered what she felt after he left her back in October.

Would she hate him forever? Ever speak to him again?

He couldn't blame her if she pretended he no longer existed. He'd wanted so badly to tell her how he felt, to confess his love for her, but he couldn't. Not when he was bound by a promise to Trevor, and not when Gage knew Tally deserved someone so much better than him. She needed a man who would be home every night. One who could offer her the world.

But the thought of anyone getting close to her made Gage want to punch something.

The buzzing of his phone drew him from his musings. He took it from his pocket and glanced at the text message, shocked to see it was from Tally.

Congrats on the great ride tonight. You've got this, champ.

A smile stretched so wide across his face, people sitting around him gave him strange looks, but Gage didn't care. Tally had reached out to him and that was a miracle he hadn't counted on. The fact the message was upbeat and encouraging didn't escape his notice, either. Then again, that was Tally. She was the kind of person who did her best to lift others up, even if it came at a painful cost to her.

Gage started to text her back then decided against it. He needed to compose just the right message, not send whatever popped into his head.

He drained his glass of soda, tucked his phone back in his pocket and made his way to the door when the ceremony came to an end.

"Hey, come to the concert with us, handsome," a throaty blonde said as she sashayed up to him and slipped her arm around his waist. Another blonde pressed herself to his other side hemming him in like over-perfumed, drunken bookends.

"Sorry, ladies, I've got plans, but thanks for the invitation." Gage managed to squirm away from them and rushed over to a group of his friends, planting himself between Cooper and Shaun Price.

"Do we look like your bodyguards?" Cooper asked, glancing over his shoulder at a trio of women hustling toward them, teetering in their high heels.

"Yes. Yes, you do," Gage said, grinning at the rodeo barrelman. "Just don't let any of them latch onto me. I'm not interested."

Cooper raised an eyebrow at Shaun. The pickup man shook his head. "He's done for man. Might as well hang out a 'this seat is taken' sign so the single girls know to keep right on looking."

A laugh rolled out of Cooper as he slapped Gage on the shoulder. "We can make an escape together. Paige was too tired to stay up, so I'm heading straight back to our room. If you want, we can share a taxi."

"If you don't mind being cramped, we can give you a ride," Brylee Price said from the other side of her husband.

"It's okay, Brylee." Gage smiled at the petite woman. "I don't mind catching a taxi. Besides, didn't I hear you say you wanted to stop back by the venue and check on Rocket?"

"She did, but we could drop you off then drive back," Shaun offered.

"No, man. We'll be fine, but thanks for offering." Gage looked at Cooper who nodded his head in agreement.

Brylee and Shaun bid them goodnight when they walked outside and headed off toward the parking lot while Cooper and Gage got in the taxi line. Cooper struck up a conversation with an older couple in front of them.

Gage listened as Cooper discussed the couple's ranch in Wyoming and the fact they came to the finals every year as a special getaway.

"Enjoy the rodeo, folks," Gage said, tipping his head politely as the couple climbed inside a taxi and left. He moved to the front of the line with Cooper as a valet motioned for the next taxi to drive forward. "How's Paige doing? She looked good when I saw her at the Lasso Eight booth this morning."

"She's doing great for an eight months pregnant woman who really should be at home resting with her feet up instead of chasing all over Vegas with me. She's been in a frenzy for the past two months, like a lunatic hyped up on triple-shot espressos, trying to get all her work done so she can take two months off when the baby arrives." Cooper slid into the taxi and gave the driver the name of their hotel.

"Are you going to take time off when the baby comes, too?" Gage asked as he settled into the seat and looked at his friend.

Cooper grinned. "You bet your life I'm taking time off. I'm not letting PP have all the fun with our newborn. And I don't want our baby to think there is anything more important than me being home with my little family. I've got several rodeos lined up to work starting in March, but I don't plan on leaving home until then."

"You might have to fight Nick if you think you're going to get much time holding that baby."

Cooper laughed. "He is pretty excited about being a great-grandpa. Between Paige's sister, Gramps and Irma, I might have to take Paige to a hotel just to have some time to ourselves with the baby."

"Good luck keeping them away from Junior when he arrives." Gage smirked. "Did you and Paige ever decide on baby names?"

"Not yet. It would probably help if we knew what we're going to have, but she wants the gender to be a surprise. So far, she's shot down all the names I've suggested except for Jaelin."

"For a girl, right?" Gage asked.

"Yep. I don't care if it's a boy or girl, as long as the baby and Paige are healthy, but it might be fun to have a little girl to spoil."

Gage raised an eyebrow. "And what are you

gonna do when that little girl is sixteen and the boys are pounding on the front door, wanting to take her out. Think of what you were like at that age."

"Our baby isn't gonna be allowed to date until he is twenty-one, and only then if it's a boy. No rotten boys are touching my little girl!" Cooper huffed and glared at Gage, making him chuckle.

"I can see Paige is going to be the reasonable one," Gage said, paying the driver when the taxi stopped in front of their hotel.

"Reasonable? She decided if the baby is a girl, she won't be allowed to leave the house by herself until she's thirty."

Gage's chuckles turned into a laugh as they walked through the lobby and onto the elevator. He pushed the button for his floor and then Cooper's. "I wish you luck, man. Tell Paige I said hello and I'll most likely see you both tomorrow."

"I will, Gage, and congrats, again, by the way. You had a great ride tonight. Keep showing 'em how it's done, man."

Gage knuckle bumped Cooper when he stepped off the elevator. "Have a good night."

Uncertain if it was his win, spending time with friends, or the text from Tally that had him in such a good mood, Gage was too wired to sleep. He ordered a burger from room service, turned on the television and flipped through the channels as he waited for his food to arrive. When it did, he settled back to watch an old black and white version of *A Christmas Carol*.

When Ebenezer Scrooge promised he would "honor Christmas in my heart, and try to keep it all the year," it struck a chord with Gage.

His childhood years had never been filled with happy Christmas celebrations. Both of his parents thought celebrating Christmas meant buying a few ridiculously expensive gifts, attending a Christmas Eve party thrown by their friends, and getting takeout Christmas day. Half the time they refused to even bother with a tree.

As an adult, Gage had never really had a place of his own to decorate or any traditions tied to the holiday. Wherever he happened to be on Christmas Eve, he attended a church service, and generally had a nice dinner. Christmas Day he mostly spent alone, unless friends invited him to join in their celebration, but it wasn't the same as being surrounded by loved ones. When he was just out of high school, he spent a few Christmases on King Penny Ranch and they were the best he could recall. Ross had gone out of his way to make Gage feel included, even filling a stocking for him.

Gage realized in that moment, the gifts or food weren't what made the holiday special. Christmas was so much more than a commercialized event that came once a year. It wasn't just a feeling of peace or goodwill that rolled around near the end of December. Christmas wasn't about presents and decorations, lights and Santa.

It was forgiveness and grace, hope and faith, tied together with mercy and wrapped in a beautiful gift of love.

Love was the reason for the first Christmas and should be the reason for the celebration each year.

What would it be like to keep that wonderful

holiday feeling the whole year through? To focus, with intention, on matters of the heart by keeping Christmas and all it represented with him every day.

"I'm gonna give it a try," he said quietly as the final credits rolled on the movie. After saying a silent prayer, lifting up his heart in gratitude for his many blessings, he decided a good place to start would be to reply to Tally's text message. He took his phone out of his pocket and sent a brief message then went to bed, feeling better than he had for weeks.

Chapter Eighteen

Tally awakened and stretched in bed; glad she didn't have to work a shift at the hospital today. The peacefulness of the ranch was exactly what she needed after putting in so many long hours the past four days.

She sat up in bed and glanced at her phone. Her eyes widened in surprise to see a text from Gage in reply to the message she'd sent him last night.

Thanks for the congrats, Tally. I sure miss Trevor being here to cheer me on. And I miss being at the ranch with you more than you can know. Have you decked the halls yet? Give Aunt Marv a hug from me. Have a great day!

A smile tickled the corners of her mouth as she read the message a second time. Did Gage mean he missed being at the ranch and missed her, or did he just miss the ranch and everyone there in general?

Rather than analyze the message to death, she showered and dressed then headed downstairs to make breakfast.

Marvella was already in the kitchen, sitting at the table while she sipped from a cup filled with fragrant holiday tea. Tally leaned over and kissed her cheek and breathed in the spice-laden steam.

"That smells so good, Aunt Marv. I think I'll have a cup while I whip up a batch of cinnamon pancakes."

"I can make bacon or sausages to go with them," Marvella offered. "You know how your brother is about eating meat."

"How about sausages?" Tally asked, taking a package of links from the freezer and handing them to her aunt, then mixing the pancake batter.

By the time Trevor came in for breakfast, the kitchen smelled like Christmas, since Tally had made an entire pot of tea.

"Boy it sure smells good in here," Trevor said as he washed his hands then carried the plate of sausages to the table. "Smells like Christmas."

"Yes, it does," Tally said, taking a seat and bowing her head. Marvella asked the blessing on their meal then they dug into the food. Tally filled her aunt's teacup and her own, then offered a cup to Trevor.

He accepted it and took a long drink. "That is good, for girly tea."

"So, I was thinking, we really need to finish decking the halls around here. I know I wasn't much in the mood the day after Thanksgiving when we usually decorate, but I'd like to get everything out this weekend. Does that sound okay?" She looked from Trevor to Marvella.

"I'll haul all the boxes in as soon as I finish eating," Trevor said, smiling at her. "I'll even stay and help, at least for an hour or two. The vet's coming later this morning to check on that calf that got tangled up in the fence yesterday, but until then you can put me to work."

That evening, they watched the second performance of the rodeo with the glow of tree lights in the background and the scent of spices and evergreen filling the air.

"Now this is more like it," Trevor said, leaning back in his recliner with a mug of hot chocolate in one hand and a sugar cookie in the other. He glanced over at Tally. "I'm glad you found a little Christmas spirit."

"Me, too," she said, smiling at her brother.

"Here he comes!" Marvella excitedly pointed to the television screen as the camera zoomed in on Gage.

The announcers discussed his accident in August that left him sidelined and him barely making it to the finals due to one of the other contestants having to drop out because of an injury.

"I think he's got a good shot at winning, at least if his ride last night is any indication," one of the commentators said.

"Of course, he has a good shot at winning," Marvella said, scowling at the television. "I wish they'd hush up and get on with the action."

Trevor winked at Tally then they both turned their focus to the TV, watching as Gage nodded and the gate swung open on the chute. He made the mark out with ease then gave an amazing ride on the horse he'd drawn, which had won the bucking horse of the year award two years ago.

Unaware she'd been holding her breath until she released it when Gage was safely on the ground, she cheered when he received an eighty-seven and a half score for the ride.

She and Trevor both pulled out their phones, but she stopped before she tapped out a message. Instead, she took a photo of their Christmas tree and sent it to Gage along with a short message.

Look at you, Mr. Champ! Way to go! And yes, our halls are officially decked and I'm ready to slip right into the spirit of the season. #KeepingChristmas

Trevor nodded at her and returned to watching the rodeo.

The next day, Tally spent the morning baking what seemed like a hundred loaves of pumpkin and cranberry bread with Marvella. After wrapping them in cellophane, they stored the loaves in the freezer for the holiday bazaar planned the following weekend.

The past several years, she and her aunt had a table selling the bread. They donated all the proceeds to a local charity to help purchase clothing and gifts for children in need.

It was much easier on Tally to bake the bread in advance and freeze it rather than try to make it the evening before after a long day at work.

The three of them watched the rodeo again that night and when Gage placed second, both she and Trevor sent him encouraging text messages.

The commercial break left her practically drooling as she watched a Lasso Eight commercial with Gage and two other cowboys walking through the snow while they led horses. Gage had on a blue plaid shirt that again made his eyes pop with color. The camera was angled to hide the crutch attached to his leg when they filmed the spot back in September.

There could have been a stampede of horses, a circus in the background, or the president delivering a speech and she wouldn't have noticed. She had eyes only for Gage.

"Need a napkin, darling?" Marvella asked, handing Tally a tissue from a box on the end table.

Trevor chuckled as Tally blushed and glanced at her phone when it chimed again with another message from the cowboy she'd been ogling on the screen.

That tree is sure pretty. Wish I was there to see it in person. Tell Trevor to eat a cookie, or dozen, for me. I like your hashtag, Miss Queenie. #KeepingChristmas is part of my holiday plan, too.

Tally had no idea where these text messages would lead, if anywhere. For now, she didn't care. She was grateful to be in contact with Gage again, even if it remained only as friends. From the past six weeks of having no contact with him at all, she'd rather be his friend than push him completely out of her life. She knew she'd never love anyone like she loved him, but for the moment, she wouldn't think about it. She just wanted to enjoy the holidays and that meant keeping in touch with him.

Even when Tally went back to work on Monday, she made sure to be near a television about the time she knew the bareback riders would compete and sent Gage a message each night, supporting and encouraging him. He'd scored every single night, even though Tuesday evening he only got a seventy-nine. The horse didn't perform well and that seemed to really throw him off his game.

Now that it was Wednesday and nearing the end of the rodeo, she knew he'd do better. If he wanted to take the title, he had to. He was sitting in second place and anything could happen in the next few days, but she had faith in him and his talent.

Tally left work with just enough time to hurry out to the ranch before the rodeo started. She parked her car, grabbed her purse, and raced into the house, surprised by the cold nipping at her nose and toes. The weather had been unseasonably mild. Even though she hated to be cold, thanks to the years her mother made her live in the warmer southern states, it would feel so much more like the holiday season if it was cold. Snow would be even better, although she didn't look forward to driving to work on bad roads. Then again, the hospital was only a mile from her apartment. If the roads were that bad, she could bundle up and walk.

Thoughts of snow and holidays made her smile as she breezed into the house where the scents of pine, spices, and the holiday scented plug-in she'd left in an outlet in the kitchen greeted her. She took a deep breath as she removed her coat, left her purse on the bench by the door, and hurried upstairs to take a quick shower to wash away the filth of working in the hospital all day. Once she was clean, she dressed in a pair of worn jeans and a soft sweater. She towel-dried her hair on her way down the stairs and tossed the towel into the hamper before stepping into the kitchen.

She grabbed the sandwich someone had left for her on a plastic wrap covered plate and rushed to the great room where Aunt Marv and Trevor were already settled into their favorite spots, watching the commentators discuss that night's rodeo.

"You're just in time," Marvella said, patting a spot beside her on the couch.

Tally sat beside her aunt, removed the plastic wrap from her plate, said a brief prayer, then took a bite from the sandwich made just the way she liked with extra cheese and no lettuce.

The three of them watched as the first bareback rider came out of the chute with a no score.

"He didn't mark out," Trevor said, pointing to the screen as they watched the instant replay.

"Tell me what that means again, honey," Marvella said.

"In bareback and saddle bronc riding the cowboy has to have the rowels of his spurs in front of, and touching, the break in the bronc's shoulders on the horse's first move out of the chute," Trevor explained. "If he misses that, he gets flagged and doesn't score."

"Oh, that's right," Marvella said, flapping a

hand at the screen. "Isn't that the boy you beat out the last year you competed?"

"Yep, that's him," Trevor said with a cocky grin. "I'd cheer for him tonight, but I want Gage to win."

"As we all do," Marvella said, reaching over and patting Tally on the leg as she ate her sandwich.

She'd just taken the last bite and set her plate on the coffee table when the camera panned to Gage. He had on a blue Lasso Eight shirt and a black hat snugged down close to his ears as he pushed his gloved hand into the handle of the rigging, adjusted his grip, yanked on the fingers, adjusted it again, then leaned back.

At the nod of Gage's head, the gate to the chute swung open. Tally held her breath and leaned forward, willing him to have a great ride.

"Look at that," Trevor said with a bit of awe in his voice as Gage executed a perfect ride. "He nailed it!"

The buzzer sounded and the commentators added their thoughts that it would be a high score.

Tally and Trevor sat bolt upright at the same time, frozen in fear as Gage got hung up in the rigging. He couldn't get his hand free and the horse continued wildly bucking across the arena. The pickup men hustled to help him, but they had yet to get close enough to be of assistance. Suddenly the horse lunged forward then twisted to the side, throwing Gage off to the left while his hand was hooked on the right. He dangled like a rag doll with his hand still caught in the rigging.

His body served as a dead weight, pulling on

his arm as he frantically tried to work free while avoiding the kicking hooves of the horse tossing him around as though he was a play toy.

"My stars! That beast is going to kill our boy!" Marvella shrieked.

Tally slid an arm around her aunt's shoulders while Trevor punched numbers on his phone then held it to his ear. Evidently all his friends were too involved watching the spectacle to answer.

Finally, one of the pickup men managed to get a rope on the horse and slow it down long enough for two bullfighters to boost Gage back onto the animal and pull his hand free. Gage fell off the other side and landed on his belly with a resounding thud. The horse added insult to injury by stomping on his thigh as he bucked past him.

The cameras zoomed in on Gage as the sports medicine team raced into the arena, ready to provide help. Three men hunkered around his unmoving form. Slowly, Gage rolled over. It appeared as though he couldn't get his breath and his face was a pale, ghastly shade somewhere between white and puce green. Blood smeared his face and his eyes looked glassy.

Tally and Trevor jumped to their feet and sprang into action without the need of discussing a plan.

"I'll get the suitcases," Trevor yelled as he ran from the room.

"I'll call the airline," Tally said, grabbing her phone and searching for the number. She raced into the kitchen and booked their tickets. They'd have to hurry, but they could catch a flight and be in Las

Vegas before midnight.

Trevor sprinted into the kitchen carrying three suitcases. He tossed one up the stairs toward her room and left a second next to her before he hustled off toward his room.

Tally turned to see Marvella standing in the kitchen, looking at her uncertainly.

"Aunt Marv, we've got to hurry. We need to leave for the airport in fifteen minutes," Tally said, giving the suitcase a push toward her aunt.

Marvella blinked twice and sniffled. "You mean you aren't leaving me here? You'll let me go along?"

Tally wrapped her arms around the woman she loved like a mother, grandmother, and aunt rolled into one. "Well, of course we're taking you, auntie. But only if you get that suitcase packed and are ready to go in..." Tally glanced at the clock on the wall, "twelve minutes."

"I'll be ready, darling!" Marvella grabbed the suitcase and hustled out the door faster than Tally had seen her move in years. She had no idea what outlandish clothes Marvella would pack and right now she didn't have time to care.

She ran up the stairs to her room two at a time, tossed clothes and toiletries in the suitcase, then took a quick minute to swipe on mascara and run a brush through her hair. She shoved her feet into a pair of cowboy boots, packed two pairs of shoes, grabbed a coat, and then tossed a light jacket into her stuffed suitcase. With effort, she zipped it shut and hauled it to the kitchen.

Trevor was there, tamping his feet into his

boots. "I'll go warm up the pickup. Will you grab my rodeo tickets from the office? I couldn't bring myself to get rid of them and now I'm glad I kept them. If Gage isn't dead, he'll force himself to ride tomorrow and I want to be there to watch it."

"Tickets," Tally repeated then ran to the office, rifled through Trevor's desk drawer, and snagged the envelope. He had two season tickets and usually found someone to give the second ticket to, since Tally always refused to attend. Now, she was glad he had those tickets and she could sit with him. Of course, they'd have to figure out a ticket for Marvella, but all that was contingent on Gage's state of health.

The way he looked in the camera's up-close shot, he might be in the hospital at this very moment. Tally stopped in the hallway, took a deep breath, and sent up a prayer he'd be okay. She scurried through the house, turning off lights, unplugging electrical cords, and locked the front door.

In the kitchen, she stowed the tickets in her purse, then wrote a quick list of things Judd would need to take care of while they were gone.

Trevor came in with Judd behind him.

"Can you take care of these?" she asked, handing the man the list.

He grinned and nodded his head. "I sure can, Tally. You kids go on and don't worry about a thing. I'll hold down the fort until you get back. I'm assuming that will be Sunday."

"Yep, unless Gage is badly injured then we'll be back sooner." Trevor shot Tally a quick glance then pointed to his watch. "We need to hit the road. Where's Aunt Marv?"

Judd glanced outside and pointed to Trevor's pickup where Marvella had already climbed into the backseat. "Looks like you two are last to the party."

Trevor grabbed Tally's suitcase and his and hauled them to the pickup while Tally gave Judd a hug then jogged down the steps and settled into the front seat. Trevor broke at least half a dozen traffic laws on the way to the airport. They barely made it through security in time to dash to their gate and catch the plane.

When they were all seated on the plane, Tally released a long breath. Trevor looked as traumatized as she felt, but Marvella, bless her heart, sat in her seat with a wide grin on her face as she looked all around. The woman appeared to think they were on a grand adventure and Tally certainly wasn't going to correct her.

The moment they landed, Trevor started texting his friends to see if anyone knew how Gage was doing. All he found out was that Gage earned a ninety-two-point ride and no one had heard how he was doing since he'd been taken to the hospital.

"That's not good," Tally said when Trevor relayed the information.

"If he's not at the medic trailer and was transported, it had to be bad, right?" Trevor asked.

"Not necessarily. They might just be taking extra precautions because of his recent injuries."

Trevor guided them through the airport to claim their baggage then led them outside to get in line for a taxi. They didn't have long to wait until they were nearing the front of the line.

"Where are we going? Hospital? Hotel?" Tally asked when there was only one couple in front of them in line.

"Hotel. I know where Gage is staying," Trevor said as they moved to the front of the line. A taxi pulled up and he started stuffing the luggage in the trunk of the car. "Cooper and Paige, Shaun and Brylee, and some of the others are there, too. We can get Aunt Marv settled and then figure out what hospital Gage is in, if he's still there. I've been trying to get in touch with Cooper, but he hasn't been answering and Shaun's phone goes straight to voice mail, too."

Tally helped Aunt Marv into the back of the car then slid in beside her. Trevor took a seat up front and gave the driver the name of the hotel.

The driver took them on side streets, avoiding the busy strip traffic and soon they were getting out in front of a swanky property. A valet gave Tally a hand then held one out for Marvella. The old woman batted her eyes at him and offered him a big smile.

"Thank you, sweetheart."

"You're welcome, ma'am," the young man said, before he moved to the trunk to help Trevor with the luggage. A porter stacked their bags on a cart and promised to meet them with it at their room before another valet held open the door to the lobby for them.

"I'll get a room if you want to try and track down someone who might know something," Tally said quietly, trying not to gawk at the gorgeous lobby decked to the nines in holiday decorations as they walked across it. She'd been holding onto Marvella's hand, but the old woman pulled out of her grasp and pointed to an arrangement of couches and chairs near a towering Christmas tree decorated in burgundy and gold.

"I'll wait for you right here, darling. I'm too tired to stand in line."

Tally nodded. "Just don't run off, Aunt Marv."

"I won't." Marvella perched on a chair like she was of royal blood and watched people come and go.

Tally hurried to the front desk, noticing Christmas carols playing in the background and a hint of cinnamon and citrus in the air. The festive atmosphere was welcoming and cheerful as she plastered on what she hoped was a charming smile since it was an older man standing on the other side of the counter.

"May I help you?" he asked in a pleasant tone.

"I hope so. We need three beds. Those can be in two rooms or a suite. We'll take whatever you have available." She gave him an imploring look. "I do so hope you'll be able to help us."

He gave her a long glance then looked down at the computer screen in front of him. "I'll see what we can do."

Tally almost whooped in glee when he said he had a suite with three beds available. He took her credit card, gave her two keys, and offered directions for finding the room. "Enjoy your stay, Miss King."

"Thank you, sir. I intend to." She gave him a

grateful nod then walked over to where Trevor had joined Marvella. They both looked exhausted. Tally felt like she could collapse on a bed and fall immediately asleep, but she wouldn't allow her body to rest until she saw Gage.

"Did you find out anything?" she asked, holding a hand out to Marvella and pulling her upright.

"Yes. Gage is back in his room. Shaun gave me the room number." Trevor followed her to the elevator. "What floor are we on?"

"Fifteenth. Room fifteen-ten." Tally pushed the button for their floor.

"Gage is in room fifteen-twelve. How handy is that?" Trevor said, grinning as the doors opened and they stepped into the hall. He took the room key Tally held out to him and unlocked the door to their suite. He flicked on the lights and motioned for her and Marvella to precede him inside.

"Oh, my gracious!" Marvella said, gingerly stepping into the living area. "This is quite extravagant."

"I'll say," Tally said, gazing around the well-appointed room that looked like something she'd see in a reality show of the rich and famous.

Trevor whistled. "I hope you put this on your credit card and not mine," he teased.

She playfully swatted his arm. "You can pay me back later."

Trevor turned on the light in the kitchen area and had started down the hall toward the bedrooms when a knock sounded at the door. Tally opened it and the porter wheeled the cart in with their luggage.

Once it was unloaded, he smiled at them. "Anything else you'll need this evening?"

"No, thank you," Tally said, taking a ten-dollar bill from her purse and handing it to the man. They'd have to find somewhere to get cash tomorrow because she'd spent all she had in her wallet and she thought Trevor probably had wiped out his supply on the taxi driver.

"Thank you, miss. Have a pleasant night," the man said, tipping his head to her, pushing out the cart, and quietly closing the door.

"Okay, Aunt Marv. Let's get you into bed, then Trevor and I are going to see if we can find Gage."

"I'd argue with you to go see him, too, but this old body needs some rest." Marvella looked like she was on the verge of collapse, so Trevor helped her into a spacious room with two queen-sized beds while Tally rolled in their suitcases. They had an adjoining bathroom while Trevor had a king-sized bed and his own bathroom across the hall.

"I'll try to get in touch with Gage while you get Aunt Marv tucked in."

Tally nodded and helped Marvella prepare for bed, getting her a drink, and making sure she took her nightly medication that, thank goodness, her aunt had remembered to bring with her. Marvella gave Tally a hug and kissed her cheek before she climbed into the bed and released a weary sigh.

"You kids go on and do what you need to. I'll be fine right here." She closed her eyes and was nearly instantly asleep. Tally clicked off the bedside lamp, but left a light on in the bathroom and closed the door except for a small crack so she could see where she was going when they got back. She closed the bedroom door then met Trevor in the living room.

"Did you get in touch with anyone?"

"Gage answered his phone. He sounded pretty drugged, but he was awake." Trevor opened the door to their room and motioned Tally into the hotel's hallway. "I didn't tell him we were here, just that we were worried about him."

"Oh," Tally said as Trevor took a few steps down the hallway and knocked on Gage's door. They waited. And waited. When no one answered, Trevor knocked again with more force. Tally was afraid he'd wake up everyone in the surrounding rooms, but most of them probably hadn't yet turned in for the night. After all, it was just a few minutes past midnight.

The sound of the lock turning drew their gazes to the door before it swung open and Gage stared at them bleary-eyed. In fact, one eye appeared black and was partially swollen shut. He looked like he'd been used as a punching bag, which wasn't surprising in the least considering a twelve-hundred-pound horse had basically thumped all over him. Since all he wore was a pair of plaid pajama bottoms, Tally could see bruises of varying shapes and colors forming across his abdomen and arms.

"Trevor?" Gage asked through thick lips. His bottom lip was swollen and had a cut on the right side. He blinked several times, as though he attempted to clear his vision. He looked at Tally and blinked again. "Queenie?"

"Hey, man. We saw you get hung up and got here as fast as we could." Trevor put his hands on Gage's shoulders and eased him back into the room.

Tally followed and shut the door. Gage's room was every bit as large and spacious as their suite. She recalled him saying something about Lasso Eight paying for the rooms of the models who participated in the fashion show. She assumed that's why Gage was staying at this hotel, close to the rest of the Lasso Eight gang.

"You flew all the way here tonight?" Gage asked, sounding slightly dazed. "Because I got hurt?"

"The moment we saw you hit the dirt, Tal and I decided to come check on you. We even brought Aunt Marv along." Trevor grinned and looked like he wanted to help as Gage painfully limped across the room to the couch and sank onto it with a groan.

The nurse in Tally took over. She hurried to Gage's side, placed the back of her hand on his forehead and grabbed a throw pillow, sliding it behind his back. "What hurts? How can I help?"

"Everything hurts and you can kiss it all better if you want." Gage gave her a rascally grin. Or at least it would have been if it hadn't looked so pathetic with his cut lip.

Trevor snorted and plopped onto the chair beside the couch. "Reel it back, Romeo, or we'll leave you to your own defenses."

Gage rolled his head to look at Trevor. "I'm sure glad you both are here. Shoot, I'm even glad you brought Aunt Marv. Where's she at?"

"Unless she was pretending to be bone-tired and snuck out to a casino, she's snoring in our room just down the hall," Trevor said, leaning back in the chair.

Tally moved back and studied Gage for a moment. He favored his right side, as though something still caused him a great deal of pain.

"Did they take you to the hospital?" she asked as she snagged two more pillows from the other end of the couch and propped up his right leg on the coffee table.

"No. They were going to insist on it, but I assured them I'd be fine. The docs were worried I'd done something to my leg and both hands." He wiggled the fingers of his left hand then the right. "I dislocated my shoulder and cracked a rib. No biggie. It's nothing that will keep me from riding."

Tally straightened and scowled at him. "Are you insane? You can't ride with a cracked rib. What if it punctures your lung? What if you do more damage? How could you possibly ride with a dislocated shoulder? What if…"

Gage reached out and caught the hand she'd been waving in the air, emphasizing her questions. The moment they touched, she felt sparks shoot from the point of contact throughout her entire body. Her temperature started to rise, and her knees felt weak when he gently rubbed his thumb in slow circles across her palm.

Unwilling to be distracted, she tugged her hand away and pinned him with a glare. "Did they get your shoulder back into place?"

"I guess so. The intense pain went away, and I

can move it now." He rotated it then grimaced.

Tally placed her hands on his shoulder and gently felt around. It was in place, but likely to be sore for a while. She glanced at his side and moved her hand down to feel along his ribs. "Which one did you break?"

"It's not a break. Just a crack. It's the next to the last rib," he said, staring at her with a look in his eyes that had nothing to do with injuries and everything to do with the wild currents arcing between them. He shifted slightly, and she felt his skin warming beneath her hands.

Under other circumstances, that didn't involve him being hurt or Trevor observing her every move, she might have indulged in the pleasure of exploring Gage's taut skin. She'd seen hundreds of men without their shirts on, but they'd all been her patients and of no interest to her at all. But seeing Gage without his shirt had always left her discombobulated. Tonight was no exception.

"Trev, would you go get some ice, please?" Tally straightened and took a step away from Gage and temptation.

"Sure. How much do you need?" Trevor rose from his seat and headed toward the kitchen area.

"A bag or two to start with," she said, then looked up as Trevor tugged a resealable bag from a box on the counter. He quickly filled it using the refrigerator's icemaker. Trevor sealed the top then carried it over to her.

"Well, that's helpful," she said, carefully setting the ice against Gage's side.

"The doc sent those bags. Thought they might

come in handy," Gage said. He sucked in a gulp then winced at the pain it caused.

"Easy," she whispered, holding the ice in place. She glanced up at Trevor. "Can you get a bag of ice ready for his leg and another for his shoulder?"

"I can do that," Trevor said, filling the bags and handing them to her. She gently placed them on Gage.

He watched as she adjusted the one on his shoulder. "I know I should have been sitting here with ice, but I was too tired to care. I'd be asleep, but my brain won't shut off."

"Did you hear about your score?" Trevor asked.

"Ninety-two points. Can you believe it?" Gage grinned, then rubbed at his lip, as though that simple action made it hurt. "That moved me into the number one position. All I have to do is hold onto it for three more nights."

"You can do it," Trevor said, crossing his hands behind his head. "We all believe in you."

Gage nodded once then glanced at Tally, as though seeking her support.

She smiled at him, even though she thought he was pressing his luck to keep riding when he clearly needed to let his body heal and rest. "We absolutely believe in you. We'll all be there cheering you on."

"Good," Gage said, then leaned back his head and closed his eyes.

"When was the last time you had a pain pill?" Tally asked as she continued to keep the ice on his side.

"Probably about eight-thirty or nine," he said,

sounding sleepy.

"Trevor, please get him a drink and bring that medicine bottle I see on the counter over here." Tally tipped her head toward the kitchen.

Trevor filled a glass with water, retrieved the bottle and handed both to Tally. She read the label on the bottle, gave Gage a pill, then the water. He drained the glass and leaned his head back on the couch again, closing his eyes.

"Where is everyone?" Trevor asked as he returned to his seat. "It took forever to get anyone to answer the phone and what little info I got out of them wasn't exactly accurate. Tom told me they'd hauled you off to the hospital."

"Paige was feeling a little tired, so Cooper told everyone they were taking a night off and not to bother them unless the arena was on fire. Shaun checked on me a couple times, but Brylee won tonight, and they went to the awards ceremony. A few of the other guys popped in. Tate and Cort helped bring me back to the hotel, though. Those kids of theirs are something else. Grace told me I looked like a chew toy their dog had shaken and slobbered all over."

Tally giggled. "She isn't entirely wrong."

Gage opened the eye that wasn't black and glared at her. "I'm not covered in slobbers. Maybe a little horse snot, but no slobbers."

She wrinkled her nose. "Is that what smells?"

"I took a shower when I got back, smarty." Gage reached out and placed his hand over hers. "Thank you both for coming. It means the world to me that you're here. But you've got to be worn out." He opened both eyes and focused on Tally. "Especially if you worked at the hospital today."

"I did, but one of us can stay with you, if you want. Or you could sleep in our room so we can keep an eye on you. Aunt Marv and I are sharing a room. You could have my bed and I'll sleep on the couch."

"Or you can have my bed and I'll take the couch," Trevor offered.

"No. I'll be fine right here. Knowing you two, though, you'll want to check on me. I've got a spare room key in the bedroom on my nightstand. Just take it when you go."

Trevor nodded and Tally moved back. "Is there anything you need right now?"

The gleam in his eyes spoke volumes although he merely shook his head. "No. I think I could go to sleep now."

Trevor stood and helped Gage to his feet and to the bedroom while Tally set the bags of ice in the freezer section of the refrigerator. She found a salt shaker in the cupboard and mixed a spoonful with a cup of warm water and carried it to the bedroom where Trevor tossed throw pillows into a corner then yanked back the covers.

"Here. Rinse your lip with this," she said, holding the cup out to Gage. He hobbled into the adjoining bathroom and she heard him grumbling after he spit out the salty liquid.

"What was that? Fire juice? My lip feels like you poured hot sauce on it," he groused as he limped to the bed and slid between the sheets.

"Salt will help. Trust me," Tally said, snagging

two of the pillows Trevor had tossed aside and bringing them back to the bed. She placed one beneath Gage's right knee then used the other to brace his shoulder and arm. "How's that?"

"Good, thank you. Do I get a bedtime story, too?"

"No, you do not," she smiled and stepped closer. Of their own volition, her fingers feathered through his hair a few times, then trailed along the side of his jaw. She bent down and pressed a light kiss to his forehead. "Sleep well."

She grabbed the keycard from the table beside the bed then left the room. Trevor joined her and together they turned off lights before closing the door to Gage's suite behind them.

In their suite, the sound of Aunt Marv's soft snores made them both smile. Trevor gave Tally a hug and went to his room. Tally set the alarm on her phone to awaken her in three hours then fell into bed, exhausted.

It was almost three-thirty when she let herself into Gage's room. She wished they'd left a light on so she could see where she was going. She made it past the couch then banged her shin on a table, sucking air through her teeth as she grabbed the lamp to keep it from toppling to the floor.

She backtracked until she found the light switch by the door and flicked it on then hurried down the hall to the bedroom door. Quietly, she turned the knob and pushed it open. The light spilling in from the living area allowed her to see Gage on the bed. His covers were twisted and the pillow she'd left beneath his knee was hanging off the bed near his foot.

On tiptoes, she crossed the room, adjusted the pillow, and straightened his covers. For a moment, she watched him in the muted light, admiring the angular lines of his face, the strong jaw and determined chin, the straight nose, the kissable lips, even if one of them bore a nasty cut. Her index finger traced the scar on his cheek then she bent down and pressed a light kiss to it.

She straightened and started to turn away, but a hand grasped her wrist, keeping her from leaving.

"What are you doing, Queenie?" Gage asked in a voice heavy with sleep. It sounded raspy and husky, and caused every cell in her body to tingle.

"I just wanted to make sure you were okay," she whispered, moving closer to the bed.

His grip on her relaxed, although he didn't let her go. "Will you stay a minute?" he asked sleepily.

"Of course," she said, gingerly sitting on the edge of the bed. She brushed her fingers through his hair and softly hummed "O Little Town of Bethlehem."

"Another one?" he asked when she finished humming the song.

"One more." Rather than hum, she quietly sang "I Heard the Bells on Christmas Day." By the time she sang the last line of the song, Gage had fallen asleep. She kissed him once more then left the room and returned to her own bed where visions of Gage's smile filled her dreams.

Chapter Nineteen

Gage started to stretch in bed but pain that began at his right shoulder and radiated all the way down to his ankle made him stop. He opened his eyes and recalled getting hung up in his rigging the previous evening at the rodeo.

In those moments when the horse continued to buck, dragging him along as though he was an afterthought, Gage considered what he'd do if the horse left him crippled for life, or worse. Was it worth it? Was he stubbornly continuing to ride just to prove to his parents he could? Was he really willing to toss away his future to pursue a dream that started when he was just a boy?

As the horse yanked him around like a limp dishcloth, he thought of Tally and how much he loved her, how much he missed her and longed to be with her. Even if the promise to Trevor didn't stand in his way, she deserved so much better than him. He'd done more than his share of things he regretted, now that he was older and far wiser than he'd been as a cocky twenty-year-old kid.

Even if he could offer financial stability and would be faithfully devoted to her until he drew his last breath, she deserved a man who'd be home with her every night, someone without the baggage that trailed along with him that came from his cold, uncaring family. He tried to picture his parents as doting grandparents to any children he might have, but the image wouldn't gel. He'd seen the way they were with his niece — reserved and demanding. The last thing he'd do is subject Tally or a child to the torture of being around his family.

Then, hands were there, lifting him back on the horse as he frantically worked his hand free. The horse bucked again, hitting his midsection with the handle of his rigging and knocking the air out of him. He'd fallen to the arena floor and struggled to breathe, but he was alive and the searing pain in various body parts assured him his limbs were still functioning.

The whole time the doctors were checking him over, he alternated between sending up prayers of gratitude and wishing Tally was there. Her cool hands were so comforting and her smile could have cured him of any number of ailments.

But she wasn't. The doc must have given him some good pain meds because he could have sworn she and Trevor had appeared at his door last night, but that was ridiculous. Nearly as silly as imagining Tally sat beside him and brushed those gentle fingers through his hair while she sang Christmas songs to him.

Perhaps he'd had a reaction to the medication and been hallucinating. That made as much sense as anything.

Gage glanced at the clock and forced himself to get out of bed. Today was the Lasso Eight fashion show and Paige was counting on him to be there. As long as he could walk without limping too badly, he'd go.

He took a shower and shaved with an electric razor. He'd started using it when he broke his hand back in August and had brought it along, in case he needed it, which he did today since it hurt to raise his right arm any higher than waist level.

Awkwardly, he combed his hair with his left hand and dressed, albeit with several groans of pain and winces. He shoved his phone and wallet into his pockets, snagged his best cowboy hat and moved into the hallway.

He'd taken only one step toward the elevator when the door to a room in front of him opened and Trevor walked into the hall.

Gage stopped and gaped at him as Tally and Marvella joined him.

"Oh, darling! Are you okay?" Marvella asked, placing a hand on his left arm and giving it a pat. "Have you had breakfast?"

"I'm fine, Aunt Marv, and I was just on my way to find something to eat." Gage gave the woman a hug then turned to Tally. "So, I didn't just dream you guys were here last night?"

She smiled at him and shook her head. "No, we came as quickly as we could once we knew you were hurt. Are you sure you feel up to being out and about today?"

"I'll walk off my aches and pains," he said, grinning at Trevor. "Today is the Lasso Eight fashion show and Paige would place my head on a platter if I didn't show up."

"All things considered, I think she'd understand," Tally said, looking up at him with questions in her eyes.

Questions Gage couldn't quite interpret and didn't want to answer.

"Why don't you all come with me? There's a nice lunch there and I can get you in. In fact, Paige might be glad to have a few extra hands to help if you want to get behind the scenes."

"Definitely count on our help," Trevor said, starting to thump Gage on the shoulder then remembering his injury before he touched him. "Do you have a car, or do we need to take a taxi?"

"I drove down with Cooper and Paige, but I've been catching taxis everywhere. If we hurry, we can snag breakfast on our way," Gage said, leading them through the hotel to an adjoining retail center with a food court. They ordered their food then took it with them to get in line for a taxi. Since it was early, they didn't have long to wait and ate their breakfast wraps on the way to the fashion show.

Hundreds of women were already lining up to get inside the big ballroom at the venue when they arrived. Gage guided them through a side door that would take them behind the stage where Paige oversaw fashion show details from a tall stool pulled up to a high table while Cooper hopped around like an elf who'd eaten one too many candy canes, doing her bidding.

Paige waved at them and smiled as they approached.

"Gage, I'm so happy you made it. Are you sure you feel up to modeling today?"

"I can do that much," he said, smiling at the woman. He didn't know if it was her diminutive size or what, exactly, that made her appear to be approximately fourteen months pregnant or on the verge of giving birth to twin elephants. Her belly stuck out nearly two feet in front of her, although the rest of her looked as lovely as ever.

Cooper joked that the baby was going to arrive half-grown, but Gage wasn't sure he was far off in his assessment if Paige's circumference was any indication.

She rested a hand on the mound of her stomach and smiled at Tally. "I'm thrilled you all are here. I've got some extra luncheon tickets. Tally, I could sure use your help, if you'll stay."

Tally nodded.

Paige's smile broadened. "Wonderful. Now, Marvella, you can sit at a table near the stage with Celia Kressley and Jessie Jarrett. Trevor, would you like to help out behind the scenes or sit out front?"

"I'll stay back here, if no one minds, as long as I get some food," Trevor grinned at Paige. "I can take Aunt Marv to her seat, though."

Paige handed him a ticket and pointed to a doorway that would take him into the ballroom. She motioned to Gage. "The guy's dressing room is the same as last year. When you get changed, I think we better do a little makeup on that black eye of yours.

Jamie is set up over there. Just go see her when you're ready." Paige wiggled her pencil toward a table where a woman had makeup spread out and one of the models on a stool in front of her as she dusted her face with powder.

"Got it." He started to walk off then heard Paige ask Tally to find Brylee Price to show her where to change.

"Change?" Tally asked.

Gage turned around and watched as Tally stared at Paige.

"Well, sure. I had a model call in sick and you're the perfect size to take her place. Her clothes are on the rack right next to Brylee's. It's just two outfits." Paige took Tally's hand in hers and gave her a pleading look. "Please? Would you model for me? I know you'll make the clothes look amazing."

Gage liked that Paige said Tally would make the clothes look good, not that she'd look good in the clothes. In his opinion, Tally could wear a paper bag and still look incredible. He'd studied her as they left the hotel this morning. The jeans and sweater she wore set off her killer curves. Not to mention those lips that were a hard temptation to resist. Truthfully, she was more beautiful than he remembered. It was hard not to reach out and touch her, to feel that smooth, soft skin beneath his hand.

"Gage, clothes!" Paige said with a laugh, pointing toward the men's changing area.

"Yes, ma'am." He hobbled up to Tally and placed a hand on her back. "You should model, Tally. You'll have fun and you really will make the clothes look good."

She blushed but nodded her head at Paige. "I guess I can try, if you're certain you need my help."

"Oh, I do." Paige waved her hand at Cooper and he jogged over to her. "Could you show Tally where the girls are getting ready? Brylee can help her find her clothes."

"Will do, PP." Cooper kissed his wife's cheek then guided Tally off to get ready.

Gage smiled at Paige. "Did you really need her help?"

"I really did have a model cancel on me, but I've been wanting to get her to model since I first saw her. She'd be perfect for the new line Elliott is working on. Maybe after today, she'll join Lasso Eight."

"Maybe, but she hates to be in the spotlight. It could take a lot of convincing." Gage left Paige then went to change. It took Jamie a considerable amount of time to hide the worst of his black eye with makeup. Gage felt like an idiot wearing it, but he supposed it wouldn't show up too much on the stage.

"Don't you want her to do your eyelashes, too? Maybe some lipstick," Trevor said as he stepped beside him.

"Just shut it, bro. It's for a good cause, you know." Gage closed his eye as Jamie rubbed more concealer around his eye.

"I do know. Paige said when you are finished here you could grab a bite to eat. I'm going to help Cooper as her personal errand boy." Trevor grinned and took a step back. "Don't break a leg out there, man."

"I won't."

Gage listened as the luncheon began and bowed his head as a grandmother of one of the rodeo contestants offered an invocation. He helped with the models and tried to keep Jacob McGraw and Gideon Morgan entertained as they waited their turn to go out on stage and walk the runway.

Gage walked out with Shaun and the two of them provided quite a show as they danced their way to the end of the runway and made their way back to the stage. Gage had just stepped to the side to wait with the other models when Tally walked out with Brylee.

She had on form-fitting dark blue jeans, a T-shirt with the Lasso Eight logo across the front and a lacy black vest that swung out when she turned at the end of the runway. Gage thought it was like waving a red flag in front of a bunch of bulls. Several men in the crowd stared at Tally's backside as she walked back toward the stage. Two cowboys who'd imbibed a little more wine with lunch than they should have whistled, and when one called out a suggestive remark, Gage started toward him. Shaun stepped in front of him, shook his head, and motioned toward Tally who was already off the stage.

"What's gotten into you?" Shaun asked as they went back to the men's dressing room to change clothes.

"Nothing," Gage said, unwilling to admit Tally had him tied in so many knots he could be a macramé project on Aunt Marv's wall.

"Sure seems like something. You looked like

you were gonna rip ol' Clovis' head clean off when his mouth got away from him." Shaun smirked at him as he fastened the snaps on his shirt and stuffed the tails inside the waistband of his jeans.

"She's not a piece of prime beef." Gage grumbled as he tamped his feet back into his boots after he'd changed jeans and shirts for the next go-round of modeling.

"No, she's not, but she's sure a pretty girl. Sweet, too. Brylee thinks she's really nice and I agree." Shaun patted him on the back. "I understand the misery you are in my friend. Rather than try to fight it, you might try just giving in to it. You'll be glad you did."

Gage knew Shaun spoke from experience. The man had been so loopy over Brylee at last year's rodeo, he could hardly walk in a straight line let alone form complete sentences.

"There are a few very good reasons why that is never going to happen, but that's a story for another day. Come on. Let's get out there before Paige sends Coop and Trev in here to bark more marching orders." Gage headed for the door, but Shaun put a hand on his arm, drawing him to a stop. "What?"

"If you ever need to talk about what's going on with you and Tally, you know I'm always here for you."

"I know, man, and I appreciate it. Now, come on. Let's go give these ladies the show they're expecting."

"You know my wife told me now that we're married it was no longer suitable for me to continue as Shakin' it Shaun." Shaun grinned as they took their places to go out on the stage again.

"Yeah? Well tell that to the women out there." Gage listened as nearly a thousand women whistled and clapped while a group of male models danced down the runway.

He and Shaun walked out with Chase Jarrett and Kash Kressley. The four of them played off each other and offered a fun performance for the women to watch as they returned to the stage and took places on the sides as they waited for the women to come out. They were there to offer a hand if any of the ladies needed it stepping on and off the stage onto the runway.

Brylee sidled up to Shaun when she came out and kissed his cheek when he gave her a hand as she went down the steps in high heels. More women came and went, but Gage's eyes widened and his heart thundered in his chest as he watched Tally step from behind the curtain.

The burgundy lace dress she modeled made his mouth go dry. Tiny little sleeves seemed to caress her upper arms, leaving a lot of creamy skin exposed from her chin to the heart-shaped neckline of the dress. The bodice nipped in at her small waist then glided over the curve of her hips before it fell straight past her thighs and fanned out at her knees. A hand-stamped silver concho belt encircled her waist while a matching pendant called attention to the swells rising just above the gown's neckline.

"Eat your heart out Sofia Vergara," Shaun whispered beside him, referring to the voluptuous actress. "Tally is a knock-out, man. Go get 'er, Tiger."

Gage glared at Shaun but stepped forward and offered Tally his hand. Her hair had been pulled up and pinned at the back of her head, but wispy curls encircled her face. Those full lips that haunted his dreams were the same shade as her dress, and her eyelashes were so long, they looked like fans against her cheeks when she lowered her gaze and placed her hand in his.

A jolt rocked through him, like he'd grabbed onto a hot wire fence, but he held on, admiring how graceful she looked as she lifted the front of her skirt in one hand, just enough to make it safely down the steps and reveal the shiny black boots on her feet.

She released his fingers and glanced back at him once with eyes that looked like a stormy December sky before she pasted on what he knew was a fake smile and walked to the end of the runway. When she turned around and began the walk back to the stage, Clovis hopped out of his seat and started toward her. Tate Morgan intercepted him and escorted him from the room while another guy on the other side of the runway released a long wolf-whistle. A blush nearly as dark as her dress stained Tally's cheeks, but she kept her head held high and never faltered in her steps as she returned to the stage. Gage took her hand and refused to let it go as he helped her up the steps then accompanied her off stage.

"You put all the other girls here to shame, Queenie. You are the most gorgeous woman I've ever seen," he whispered as he bent his head close to hers and walked with her behind the curtain.

"Don't tease me, Gage. My knees are shaking so bad, I'm glad I had a long dress to wear to hide it. If you hadn't given me a hand, I'd probably have fallen face first up the steps back there." She offered him an impish smile. "Did someone really just whistle at me?"

"Yes, and if it happens again, I'll knock out all his teeth," he growled, placing his hand possessively at the small of her back. "For the record, I was not teasing, Talilah. You look incredible, like someone who just stepped out of one of those old Hollywood movie screens. If Paige offers to let you keep any clothes, make sure you hang onto that dress. It was made for you."

Her blush deepened and she remained quiet as he walked her to the dressing room door. Trevor was there, standing guard.

"You look great, sis! How'd it go?" Trevor asked, giving Tally a hug.

"Fine, I think," she said, smiling at her brother then turning back to Gage. "Thanks, again, for giving me a hand."

She disappeared inside the dressing room and Gage would have followed her if Trevor hadn't stepped in his way. "Are you feeling okay, man? You look a little flushed. Do you need Tally to take a look at anything? She probably has something she could give you if you're feeling feverish."

There was no way Gage could tell his best friend the reason for his fever started and ended with the way Tally looked in that dress. The whole building suddenly felt tropical. Gage popped open two snaps on his shirt and backed up a few steps.

"I'm fine, but thanks for asking. I'll change and be back in a few minutes. The show will be wrapping up soon." Gage hurried to change into his street clothes then peeked around the curtain to see Aunt Marv excitedly talking to Celia Kressley who was photographing the event.

He was on his way back to where Trevor waited outside the women's dressing room when Cooper intercepted him.

"You doing okay today?" he asked, shaking his hand.

"I've been both worse and better," Gage said with a grin. "Paige put on a great show, as always. I'm glad I could be a part of it."

"Me, too. By the way, I happened to notice the way you had your eyes glued to Tally King. If I didn't know better, I'd say she's at the top, bottom, and every line in between on your Christmas wish list," Cooper teased. "She's a nice kid, Gage. Don't break her heart."

Gage scowled at his friend. "I wouldn't do that, Coop. It has already been established we will be nothing more than friends. Ever."

Cooper gave him a long look, since he knew him nearly as well as Trevor did. A slow grin lifted the corners of his mouth and he thumped Gage on his shoulder, making him wince since it was the one that had been dislocated the previous night.

"Sorry," Cooper said, his smile widening. "But you can't fool me. You've got it bad for that girl. Just be careful. Falling in love ain't for sissies."

Gage's scowl deepened and he would have said something, but Trevor walked up to them with

Marvella hanging onto his arm.

"Well, Miss Marvella! How are you doing?" Cooper asked, kissing her hand and making the old woman titter like a schoolgirl.

"Wonderful. This has been such a lovely experience. Between Celia and Jessie, they made sure I had a great time." She turned to Gage and gave him an odd look. "Did you see our girl in the fashion show, darling? I thought some of the men might break into a brawl over who'd get to walk her out of here today."

"I saw," Gage said, trying to keep his tone smooth, his face impassive.

Marvella winked at him and shifted the conversation to the upcoming arrival of Cooper and Paige's baby, giving Gage a moment to collect his wits before Tally appeared beside them dressed in her own clothes. She did carry a large shopping bag with the Lasso Eight logo on it.

"You find something to take home with you?" Cooper asked, eying the bag.

"Yes. Paige insisted I take a few things. She's so generous."

Cooper grinned. "That she is, but you enjoy the clothes. Paige wouldn't have given them to you if she didn't want you to wear them. In fact, she's mentioned you modeling for the line a few times. I hope you'll consider it."

"I... um..." Tally appeared to consider her response. "I'll give it some thought."

"Great! Well, I'm sure you all have things to do today before the rodeo tonight, so we'll see you there, if PP feels up to going." Cooper gave them a wave then jogged off.

"We need to get Aunt Marv a rodeo ticket," Tally said as the four of them headed toward the doors.

"I can get one for her," Gage said, pulling his phone from his pocket and texting someone. His phone soon buzzed with a response and he looked at Marvella. "A ticket will be waiting for you at the front desk when you get back to the hotel. It won't be right next to Trevor, but you'll be in the same section of seats."

"Why don't I take that one and Aunt Marv and Tally can sit in my seats?" Trevor asked as they moved into the line for taxis.

"That's a good idea," Tally said, smiling at her brother. She looped her arm around her aunt's and guided her forward until they reached the front of the taxi line. "Where are we headed next?"

"How about one of the vendor shows?" Trevor asked, glancing at Gage. "Are you up to it, or would you rather go back to the room and rest?"

"Let's do one of the smaller shows and then we can all take a break before the rodeo."

"Good plan," Trevor said, telling the taxi driver where they wanted to go when they all got into the car. Trevor sat up front with the driver, while Gage squeezed into the back with Tally squished against his side, leaving his entire body tingling from her proximity. Her fragrance, something that would forever bring to mind Christmas, filled his nose while his fingers twitched in an effort not to wrap around her and pull her onto his lap or bury themselves in her rich hair.

He grinned, thinking of the hashtag they'd exchanged several times. He'd give just about everything he owned if *#KeepingChristmas* meant he got to keep her with him always.

In what seemed like no time at all, they arrived at the vendor show. Trevor paid the taxi driver then the four of them made their way inside.

Gage fought back a smile when Marvella clapped her hands like a gleeful child when she saw all the booths.

"Oh, wow," Tally said, trying to take it all in. "This is bigger than I expected," she said.

"This is one of the smaller shows. Wait until we go to the big one tomorrow," Trevor said, placing a hand on her shoulder. "What would you like to see first?"

"I have no idea." Tally glanced down at Marvella then back at Trevor. Finally, she looked at Gage. "Why don't we just meet you both back at the hotel? That way you aren't waiting around for us if we get serious about shopping."

"Works for me," Trevor said, glancing at his watch. "Let's plan to meet in two hours at the hotel. Does that sound okay?"

"Yes! Let's go," Marvella said, grabbing Tally's hand and pulling her over to a clothing vendor.

"Want to wander around or is there something else you'd like to do?" Trevor asked.

"I don't mind wandering for a little while. I have some Christmas shopping I need to take care of anyway."

"Me, too. What do you think I should get Aunt

Marv?" Trevor pointed to a booth selling vintage Christmas signs.

"Oh, I see just the thing," Gage said, guiding him down the aisle.

Chapter Twenty

Tally sat on the edge of the seat with her aunt's hand tightly gripping hers. Gage was next up to ride and she could only hope all the tape he'd wrapped around his injured body helped him make it through the ride unscathed.

"He'll be fine," Trevor said, leaning forward from his seat directly behind her and whispering in her ear. "Don't worry, Tal."

Unable to speak around the lump in her throat, she nodded her head and watched as Gage finished adjusting his hold in the rigging handle then folded his chaps back, pulled his hat down with his free hand, and leaned back, wiggling slightly to adjust his seat.

He lifted his free hand, nodded his head and held his spurs in position as the big roan horse named Blue Crush bucked out of the chute when the gate swung open.

Marvella squeezed Tally's hand, but she didn't

notice. She was too focused on watching Gage. To her, it seemed he rode in slow motion. The fringe on his chaps slapped against his legs, dust puffed up around the horse's hooves, and she could almost hear the creak of leather as he rode.

At six seconds into the ride, she saw Gage wince after Blue Crush twisted and kicked to the left. Gage made it to the buzzer, but Tally knew it wasn't his best ride, although it was better than what some of the others had done.

"He'll get at least an eighty," Trevor whispered in her ear.

"Look at that folks," the announcer boomed. "Give ol' Gage a hand. This cowboy went through the wringer last night but he's back and still showin' ya how it's done. Gage Taggart, that's an eighty-point-five ride tonight!"

The crowd cheered and clapped. Marvella beamed and waved when Gage looked their way and waggled his fingers at them before he made his way out of the arena.

"He did good, didn't he?" Marvella asked, looking back at Trevor as he sat beside Cooper and Paige.

"He sure did, Aunt Marv." Trevor smiled at her. "He won't take first tonight, but he'll probably hang onto third place."

Tally watched the remaining bareback riders, anxiously awaiting the score for those who rode the full eight seconds. Only one scored higher than Gage which left him in second place for the evening.

She glanced back at her brother and he nodded

with a happy grin as they saw the final bareback scores.

"Well, he might be held together with duct tape and twine, but he still did a great job out there," Cooper said. "Are you all planning to attend the awards ceremony tonight?"

"I don't think so," Tally said, glancing back at Cooper then tipping her head to Marvella. Although the woman wouldn't admit it, Tally knew she was exhausted. They'd been on the go since they got up that morning.

It had been so many years since Tally had attended the rodeo, and then it was just over the weekend with her Dad, she'd forgotten how tiring it could be.

"Yeah, I think we better head back to the room after this. We were up late last night and up and on the go early this morning." Trevor placed a hand on Tally's shoulder and squeezed. "And this one turns into a pumpkin at midnight."

Tally glared at Trevor while everyone in their group laughed. She liked that they had a fun group and enjoyed being around Trevor's friends. In fact, she'd struck up a friendship with Jessie Jarrett and Paige. Jessie lived less than twenty minutes away from the ranch and it was easy enough to meet her in Hermiston for lunch on occasion. Twice, they'd even had dinner together, once at King Penny Ranch and once at Chase and Jessie's place.

Tally looked at the families seated around them and felt a sense of well-being, of belonging. There was the Price family, the Morgans and McGraws, and Jessie with Chase's aunt, uncle and cousin.

She'd heard Ashley Jarrett refer to Gage as danger in a pair of cowboy boots and wondered what that meant, but decided she didn't really want to know.

At any rate, she was glad to be there amongst friends and excited to see Gage ride two more nights and hopefully claim the title. He certainly had a shot at it, if he didn't sustain more injuries.

The rodeo was just wrapping up when Gage appeared out of nowhere and offered Tally a hand as she rose to her feet. "Ready to go?" he asked, helping Marvella onto the steps that would take them out of the arena.

"I'm pooped, honey." Marvella held onto Gage's arm while Trevor stepped behind Tally. "But it was sure something to see you ride. You did good."

"Thank you, Aunt Marv. I'm glad you were here to watch my ride. Did I hear you cheering for me?"

"Of course, you did, darling!" Marvella squeezed his arm then let go of him as they reached the doors that would take them outside. "You and Tally run ahead and save us a place in the taxi line. Trevor can help me down there." She let go of him and took hold of Trevor's arm.

"Yes, ma'am," Gage said, with a grin. He grabbed Tally's hand and gave her a slight tug. "You heard your aunt. Let's go hold a place in line."

Tally glanced back at Trevor, but he was focused on helping Aunt Marvella onto the escalator. She hurried to keep up with Gage as he started jogging down the steps. He had his gear bag slung over his left shoulder as they raced down the steps. There were only about thirty or so people in front of them when they reached the taxi line.

"It won't take long for these to go through. I hope Trev and Aunt Marv catch up to us before we reach the front of the line," Gage said, continuing to hold onto Tally's hand.

She should pull her fingers free and step back from him, but people were crowding into line and she liked the way it felt with his fingers entangled with hers. It felt right and good, like they belonged together. Just thinking about the warmth of his callused palm against hers made tingles dance their way up her arms, like a chorus of jingle bells at a Christmas performance.

"You look beautiful," Gage whispered, leaning down so his lips nearly brushed her ear. She could feel the warmth of his breath on her skin and smell the mint of his gum.

A shiver skidded down her spine when he pulled back and smiled at her. Not just any smile, but the half-smile that made her knees feel like they were made of Jell-O.

"Is that a new top?" he asked, fingering the fabric of her sleeve.

Tally glanced down at the black silk blouse patterned with dark red roses she'd purchased that afternoon. She'd loved it the moment she saw it and Aunt Marv told her she had to buy it. It made her feel pretty and feminine. The fact Gage noticed it pleased her immensely.

"It is," she said, smiling up at him.

Someone bumped into her from behind and she

caught herself on Gage's chest. The solid muscles beneath her hands along with the glorious scent of Gage — of horse and leather and that woodsy, outdoorsy scent that was uniquely him — left her so befuddled she could hardly think straight.

He chuckled and wrapped his arms around her, not letting her move away.

"I think you're fine right where you are," he said, looking down at her with the grin on his face growing wider. "In fact, how are you not freezing? It's nippy out tonight," he said, rubbing his hands up and down her arms.

Each motion of his big hands brushing over her sleeves inched her internal temperature up another notch. If he continued, she wondered if her new blouse might actually spark and catch fire.

Without turning her loose, he edged her backward when the line began to move. She would have resisted except she was enjoying being close to him far too much to do anything that might end this unexpected interlude.

"There you are, darling," Marvella said as she wrapped her bony hands around Tally's arm. "I started to think we'd never find you."

"Here we are," Tally said, moving away from Gage as she turned and wrapped an arm around her aunt's shoulders. "Are you warm enough, auntie?"

"I'm doing fine, sweetheart. We shouldn't have long to wait before we're on our way," Marvella said, pointing to the rapidly moving line.

"That's a fine looking outfit you have on, Aunt Marv," Gage said, causing Marvella to turn to him with a beaming smile.

"I bought this in 1956," Marvella said, brushing a hand over the front of her blush-colored split skirt. She wore a matching blush and white western blouse with a blush short jacket, accented with dark pink roses on the yoke.

"Not everyone can keep their girlish figure like you have all these years, Aunt Marv," Tally said, guiding her aunt forward in line. "You are blessed with a fantastic metabolism."

"I have been. I could eat a horse for dinner every night and not gain an ounce. Lulu is the same way, which is probably where Trevor gets it." Marvella glanced back at him. "I swear that boy puts away enough food for ten people."

"Eleven, but who's counting," Gage said, giving Trevor a playful punch to the arm.

Tally turned toward her brother, but he had a strange look on his face as he glowered at Gage then at her.

Unaware of what had him upset, she held up four fingers to indicate there were four members of their group and a volunteer directing traffic pointed them toward a van with a big taxi sign on top of it.

Trevor helped Marvella climb inside the taxi. The sound of girls squealing drew Tally's gaze around to Gage. A group of girls who couldn't have been more than their late teens or early twenties held out programs for Gage to sign, all talking at once. She watched as he treated them politely, signed their programs and tipped his hat to them before climbing in the van and shutting the door.

"Let's go before we get mobbed," he said, tapping Trevor on the arm since he sat in the front seat. "You could have warned me they were approaching."

"Where's the fun in that?" Trevor said, grinning at Gage then telling the driver where they'd like to be dropped off.

Marvella was nearly nodding off when they got back to the hotel, so Tally left Gage and Trevor talking in the doorway, making plans for tomorrow while she helped her aunt get ready for bed.

The following morning, after Gage met them for breakfast in one of the hotel's restaurants, they caught a taxi to the large vendor show at the convention center.

"Are you girls ready to shop?" Gage asked as the taxi let them out and they walked inside.

Tally couldn't believe how many vendors were lined up in aisles in front of them. She wasn't sure Aunt Marv would make it past the first fifty.

"Come on, darling, let's go!" Marvella pulled on her hand. "Christmas time's a comin', and I have gifts to buy!"

Tally laughed and looked back at Trevor and Gage. "How about we check in with each other in an hour?"

"Works for me," Gage said, glancing at his watch. "I have an autograph session at one. Maybe we can grab some lunch before then?"

"Sounds perfect." Tally felt her aunt tug on her hand again, so she gave Trevor and Gage one parting look before joining the people steadily streaming into the aisles and got caught up in the fun.

An hour later, she carried half a dozen bags of

her own and just as many for Aunt Marv. Her arms and feet were both tired, but she was having a wonderful time. She'd even taken a selfie of her and her aunt at a booth selling one-of-a-kind squash blossom necklaces and sent it to Tonya and Glenda. Her friends messaged back that she could bring them each one for Christmas.

She laughed and told them they weren't that high up on Santa's nice list, since the least expensive necklace she saw cost several thousand dollars.

Tally had just purchased a large tote bag from a vendor selling kitchen goods, along with a few gift items for her friends, when her phone chimed with a text. She stuffed all her purchases into the tote and checked to see a message from Trevor telling her to meet him and Gage at the escalators half-way down the convention hall so they could all head upstairs where events were taking place throughout the day.

"Let's go, Aunt Marv. The boys have summoned us," she said, taking Marvella's elbow in her hand and guiding her through the crowds along the wide center aisle.

"But I'm not done shopping, darling. Did you see that leather duffle bag back there? Wouldn't it make a wonderful gift for Gage?" Marvella glanced up at her with a twinkle in her eye. One Tally chose to ignore.

"Maybe we can look at it later." Tally wouldn't admit that a few of the things she'd purchased that morning were for Gage. No one needed to know he was constantly on her mind and in her thoughts. Especially not Aunt Marv, who couldn't keep a secret even if her life depended on it.

She caught sight of Gage and Trevor as they waited for them near the escalator and was nearly to them when a strong hand gripped her arm and pulled her around.

"Honey, I'm home!" A tall, dark, and handsome cowboy engulfed her in a hug.

At first, Tally was so shocked, she remained speechless. Then the cowboy pulled back and she laughed.

"Wyatt Nash! What are you doing here?" she asked, squeezing his hand.

"I'm right pleased you remembered my name, Tally. I figured you'd forgotten all about me and the way you helped me out at the Pendleton Round-Up," Wyatt said, smiling at her like she'd hung the moon and stars in the sky.

"Oh, you aren't an easy one to forget," Tally said. With a teasing grin, she glanced around to see if he was being stalked then stepped closer to him. "You aren't in need of being rescued again, are you?"

"Not at the moment, but maybe you should give me your number, just in case."

"Now that's a smooth line if I ever heard one," Marvella said, beaming at the cowboy. "I'm Tally's aunt, Marvella Hawkins. If she won't give you her number, you can have mine."

He chuckled. "I remember seeing you in Pendleton, Miz Hawkins. It's a pleasure to run into you again." Wyatt tipped his hat to her. "Are you ladies here alone?"

"No, we were just meeting my brother," Tally

said, pointing to Gage and Trevor as the two men approached, sporting matching scowls.

"Hey, there. Nice to see you again. Congrats, Gage! It's great to see you made it to the finals after your accident. I hope you win," Wyatt said, holding out his hand in greeting.

Tally wondered what had gotten into Gage and her brother when they both frowned at Wyatt.

Gage finally shook the hand the man had extended. "Thank you. I appreciate the kind words."

Trevor shook Wyatt's hand then moved so Tally was sandwiched between him and Gage. "We better get going. Enjoy your time here, Nash."

"You all have fun," Wyatt said. He slipped Marvella one of his business cards with a wink and walked off.

Marvella clasped it in her hand as though she held a priceless jewel, then wrapped her arm around Trevor's. "Lead the way, Trevor, dear. What are we doing upstairs?"

"Cooper talked us into participating in one of his special events," Trevor said, glancing at Gage. "It should be entertaining."

"It's not a hiney-shaking dance-off is it?" Tally asked, having heard from Paige all about the tricks Cooper played on her when she was searching for the first Lasso Eight model.

"No dancing is involved, but there are horses," Gage said, placing a hand on Tally's back as they stepped off the escalator. He guided her toward the arena that had been hauled in upstairs. It was where junior rodeo stars competed as well as other events took place.

Although there wasn't an entry fee to get in, attendees were asked for a donation to help the crisis fund.

Gage took Tally's hand and led her to a section of seats straight away from a gate. "You just keep your eye on that gate," he said, then held out a hand to Marvella and helped her up to the bleacher seat. "We'll see you girls in a bit."

"And don't worry, we won't get hurt," Trevor said over his shoulder as he and Gage jogged down the bleacher steps and disappeared.

"I wonder what trouble they're about to get into?" Tally mumbled as she set down her tote bag and glanced at her aunt.

Marvella held out Wyatt's business card. "I think you should call that very nice boy, Tally. Maybe you could go out on a date while you're here."

"Aunt Marv! I don't have time for dating. We'll be at the rodeo tonight and tomorrow night and besides, I don't... it isn't...." She was grappling for excuses, but her aunt just gave her a knowing look.

"What could it hurt to at least send him a text message?"

Frustrated, Tally sighed. "Fine. One short message."

She took the card from her aunt, entered Wyatt's cell phone number in her phone and sent him a brief text, simply stating it was nice to run into him and wishing him a fun time while he was in town.

Only a few minutes passed before her phone

chimed with a reply from Wyatt.

Running into you was the best part of my trip here. If you'd like to have lunch or dinner, or even just hang out for a few minutes, let me know. My schedule is wide open.

Marvella leaned over her shoulder and read the message. "Text him back and tell him you'd like to meet for ice cream this afternoon. People do still eat ice cream, don't they?"

Tally rolled her eyes. "Yes, Aunt Marv. But I'm not going to set up a date with a man I barely know. Besides, we're here for Gage. I don't..." She couldn't very well tell her nosy aunt she had no interest in dating anyone when her heart belonged to Gage, even if he didn't want it.

She tried to recall the last time she'd been out on a date. It had been in the spring, but she couldn't recall the year. Man, she really did need to get out more. Between work and the ranch, she didn't have a lot of free time, even if she had met someone she liked enough to endure the trials and tribulations of an awkward first date.

From her seat, she could see a group of women encircling a few cowboys and realized one of the men being patted and ogled was Gage.

With a longsuffering sigh, she read the text from Wyatt again then sent him a message.

My aunt said we should meet for ice cream this afternoon. What do you think? You're not lactose intolerant, are you?

Either he'd appreciate her attempts at humor, or she wouldn't hear back from him. Her phone chimed with a response almost immediately.

LOL! No, I'm not lactose intolerant and I love ice cream. Do you like gelato? I know a great place. Meet me in the front lobby here at 2?

Tally had eaten gelato a few times and enjoyed it, but she was mostly looking forward to going on a date. Even if Wyatt wasn't Gage, he seemed like he'd be fun and nice. What could it hurt to enjoy an afternoon with a ridiculously attractive man?

See you at 2!

"Good girl," Marvella said, patting her on the leg. "I hope you have a grand time with that nice man."

Tally grinned. "I thought he was a boy. My, he's grown up quickly into a man."

"Oh, hush, sassy britches." Marvella bumped against her then pointed to the arena where Cooper rolled out a barrel with the Lasso Eight logo on the side. He had on his clown costume, complete with full makeup.

Tally waved to Jessie and Ashley Jarrett as the two women looked around for a place to sit. Paige was right behind them with Brylee Price, Celia McGraw, Kenzie Morgan and Kaley Peters. Jessie waved back and the group made their way up to where they were sitting.

"Hey! How are you girls today?" Tally asked as Kenzie and Kaley wrangled their children and Jessie and Ashley helped Paige to a seat in front of them.

"Doing good," Paige said, glancing back at Tally. "I heard my husband talked your brother into this showcase of shenanigans."

Tally grinned. "Yes, he did. If nothing else, it should be fun to watch."

"Oh, that's guaranteed," Jessie said, smiling over her shoulder at her. "He talked Chase, Tate, and Cort into participating, too."

"Well, isn't that interesting," Marvella said, holding her hands out to Marley. The little girl climbed over her mother and plopped down on Marvella's lap. "How are you, sweet girl?"

Marley smiled at her and babbled something about doggies and candy that Tally couldn't quite understand. It's too bad she and Trevor hadn't settled down and started families because Aunt Marv would be a fun grandmother-figure.

Tally swallowed back a sigh. Today wasn't the day to think about what might never be. She turned her focus to the arena where Cooper jumped on top of the barrel and whistled loudly, drawing everyone's attention.

"Good morning, everyone!" he said into the cordless mic clipped to his shirt. "Are you ready for some fun?"

The crowd whistled, clapped, cheered, and stomped their feet, making enough noise even Marvella covered her ears.

"Some of you've probably heard of a western

pickup event, or buddy barrel pickup. Well, that's what's happening right here, right now, with the first-ever Buddy Barrel Boogie! I have twelve teams ready to participate. If you have a good time, I hope you'll drop a little cash in the donation jars on your way out of the stands. All the proceeds will go to the crisis fund and you all know how much that helps our rodeo cowboys when they get hurt." Cooper looked at someone and nodded his head. Upbeat music started playing.

"The rules are simple. Team member one comes out, climbs on top of this barrel, and busts a little move. Team member two will ride out, race around the barrel, and hope that team member one swings on the back of the horse behind him before he races across the finish line. Each ride will be timed and the team with the best score wins. The prize is a hundred-dollar gift card for each of the two winners to the Lasso Eight booth downstairs." Cooper grinned and looked around then winked at Paige when he saw her in the stands. "Without further ado, here comes our first team. Some of you might recognize Tate Morgan from his years as a world champion saddle bronc rider. He'll be the buddy on the barrel. Cort McGraw, his partner in crime, was a world champion steer wrestler before he retired."

"That's my daddy!" Grace McGraw shouted as she jumped up on her mother's lap.

"And there is one of the reasons Cort took up ranching full-time and left behind rodeoing," Cooper said. "Let's give Tate and Cort a warm welcome!"

Tate jogged into the arena, waved his hat to the crowd and blew a kiss to Kenzie before he hopped on top of the barrel.

"Hi, Uncle Tate!" Grace wildly waved both hands at him.

The crowd laughed and Cooper's grin broadened as Tate returned her wave. Celia took out her camera and started snapping photos when he broke into a dance on top of the barrel. Tally thought the knee-bending, leg-bouncing, posterior-shaking dance looked like one his daughter might have taught him. The crowd roared with laughter as music blasted over the speakers.

Cort raced past the starting point into the arena on a borrowed horse. He rounded the barrel, and Tate, who'd balanced on the balls of his feet on the edge of the barrel, hooked his arm around Cort's neck and swung behind him. They raced back across the arena while the crowd cheered.

"Not bad, especially for a couple of decrepit old men," Cooper teased. "Up next is a bull rider who has a shot at taking the world championship again this year, Mr. Chase Jarrett. His buddy today is none other than pickup man extraordinaire, Shaun Price. Give it up for Chase and Shaun!"

Chase ran across the arena and leaped onto the barrel. He executed a few running man dance steps then crouched into position when Shaun tore into the arena. Used to having cowboys swing all over him as a pickup man, Shaun rounded the barrel with hardly a blink. Chase caught him on the shoulder, swinging behind him in one smooth motion as they rushed back toward the gate.

"Woohee!" Cooper said, as he stood off to the side of the arena, clapping. "Now that was some fancy footwork and fast moves. Let's see if the next team can keep up. Trevor King retired from bareback riding a few years back, but his buddy, Gage Taggart, is one of the current top riders in the world."

Tally had hoped Gage would have enough sense to not participate in the event. If he rode the horse, odds were high Trevor might hurt his shoulder or his rib when he swung behind him. If he was the one on the barrel, it was almost guaranteed he'd stretch something that shouldn't be, and the potential for him falling and hurting his leg, rib, or who knows what else was high.

"That man is a bona fide idiot," Tally muttered.

"They all are, Tally, but we love them anyway," Brylee said as she turned around and offered her a commiserative smile. "You know how they are."

"Yes, I do." Tally held her breath until she saw Trevor jog into the arena and wave his hat to the crowd. He smiled at her and Marvella, then jumped onto the barrel. Cooper cued the music and *"Stayin' Alive"* started to play. Tally's cheeks heated as her brother broke into a disco dance, index finger pointed into the air above his head then it crossed in front of his body and pointed toward the ground on the other side.

Gage rode into the arena and Trevor hurried into position to jump on the back of the horse. Gage rounded the barrel and Trevor grabbed onto his left shoulder, obviously trying to avoid touching his right side. He almost slid off before he grabbed the back of the saddle and pulled himself on a second before Gage crossed the finish line.

"Good gracious!" Tally pressed her hands to her hot cheeks while Marvella laughed and cheered.

They watched Kash Kressley compete with his twin brother, Ransom, who'd come to town with his wife and baby to see the rodeo for the first time in years. Several other teams raced. Twice, the man on the barrel missed getting on the horse and one slid off halfway across the arena.

Tally sat up and took notice when Wyatt Nash was introduced as part of the final team. His buddy in the contest was the man she'd seen him with in Pendleton, one Cooper introduced as Cole.

"Isn't that your Wyatt, darling?" Marvella asked with a grin as Marley slid off her lap and climbed onto her mother's, whining that she was hungry.

Seven pairs of eyes turned to stare at Tally.

"Your Wyatt?" Paige asked with a surprised look.

"When did that happen?" Jessie questioned with a grin.

"Nothing happened and he certainly isn't mine. We're just meeting for ice cream later. That's all."

"I want ice cream, Mommy! Please!" Grace begged as she bounced on Kaley's lap.

"No to the ice cream, Gracie. Your daddy will ply you with enough treats later." Kaley kissed Grace's rosy cheek. "And no pouting or I'll take away all sweets today, including Daddy's."

Grace sucked in the lip that had rolled out in

pout and sighed with a huff. To her credit, though, she didn't push the matter or continue pouting.

Tally bit back a grin, thinking the child surely did put one in mind of her father and aunt Celia. She turned her attention back to the arena and watched Cole step onto the barrel. He offered a few Thriller-inspired dance moves then moved into position, waiting for Wyatt.

Wyatt raced in on a showy black horse and circled the barrel so fast, he looked like a blur. Cole leaped onto the back in one smooth motion and the two of them hit the finish line a full second ahead of anyone else's time.

"And there is our winning team, ladies and gentlemen. Let's give all these guys a hand. And don't forget, your donations help a great cause. Be sure to help out the crisis fund." Cooper led the crowd in clapping for the contestants who all came back out to the arena and took a bow. Gage looked like he was limping slightly and that worried Tally, but if he wanted to behave with less sense than a dead duck, that was his choice.

"So, what are your plans, other than ice cream with that very cute cowboy?" Paige asked as Tally gathered her things and helped Marvella to her feet.

"We're going to grab a bite to eat. Aunt Marv and I aren't quite finished shopping and then Gage has an autograph session at one."

"Want to eat together?" Ashley asked as they meandered out of the bleachers. "They have a great taco booth downstairs."

"Sure, sounds good." Tally glanced down at Marvella for approval.

"I haven't had tacos in a long time. Lead the way, my darlings." Marvella wrapped her hand around Ashley's arm. "Tell me more about your glamorous life in Los Angeles, dear. Have you met any movie stars?"

"Well, I did a campaign for..." the two of them wandered ahead while Tally walked with the other women.

"I'll text Cooper and tell him to bring the guys to the taco booth. We can go down and save seats," Paige said, pulling out her phone and sending her husband a text.

After their boisterous group ate lunch amid much laughter and good-natured teasing, Gage went off to his autograph session with Chase and Brylee, since they would be signing at the same booth. Trevor scowled at Tally when she told him of her plans and tried to forbid her to go. Marvella insisted Trevor mind his own business and yanked him down an aisle to help her with her shopping.

Tally watched Trevor skulk off with their aunt, thinking an afternoon of shopping with Marvella served him right for being so high-handed with her. He acted like an overbearing dolt anytime she had a date. That hadn't changed since she was sixteen. If she left it up to him, she'd be an old maid who still lived with him and cooked his meals, since he'd never get around to finding a wife.

Hmm. Maybe she needed to start looking for someone for her brother. Not just anyone would do. The right woman needed to enjoy ranch life, be honest, dependable, kind and sweet, but independent and strong. She had an idea the woman for Trevor would have to stand up to him and not let his tendency to take charge run roughshod over her wishes. That was a tall order.

Tally wandered through the booths thinking about women she knew, but none seemed right for her brother. Maybe she could ask around their group of friends. Surely one of them knew a girl who might be interested in Trevor. If she could help him find his happily ever after, maybe he'd give her enough breathing room to pursue hers.

Then again, from the time she was ten, she'd envisioned Gage as her knight in shining armor and that hadn't changed. If anything, every moment she spent with him only served to strengthen her love for him and make her long for him all the more.

Determined to put him from her mind, at least for the afternoon, she bought a few more gifts and slipped them inside the large tote she carried then made her way to the lobby where Wyatt greeted her with a welcoming smile.

"Are you ready for the best gelato you'll ever have?" he asked as he held the door and followed her out into the afternoon sunshine.

"Since I've only had gelato a few times, and that was at the county fair, I'm pretty sure it will be the best."

He chuckled and opened a taxi door for her. He took the heavy tote bag from her then gave her his hand as she climbed in the backseat. He slid in beside her, set the bag on the floor, and told the driver the name of the property where he wanted to go.

Wyatt made small talk on the way there. Tally

discovered he'd grown up in Pendleton on the family ranch. It was a wonder they'd never run into each other before since they'd grown up living not all that far apart.

When they arrived at the hotel, Wyatt paid the taxi driver, got out with Tally's bag in one hand, and offered her his other. He didn't let go as they walked inside the lobby.

Tally looked around at the festive holiday decorations. A tree that had to be at least forty-feet tall dominated the space, while poinsettia-festooned garlands and tartan plaid bows provided traditional accents.

"It's lovely," she said, allowing her gaze to rove around as Wyatt led her to a little gelato shop not far from the hotel's casino.

She tried not to gape as she watched the two women behind the counter form gelato into rose shapes as they filled waffle cones.

"I thought you might get a kick out of the frozen roses." Wyatt said as he stood behind her.

"It's amazing," she said, impressed he'd put that much thought into their afternoon treat.

"What's your favorite flavor?" he asked as they stepped up to the counter.

Tally quickly scanned the selections and settled on a vanilla and raspberry swirl with a raspberry macaron on top. Wyatt ordered chocolate topped with salted caramel and a chocolate macaron.

"I'm getting the idea you like chocolate," she said with a grin.

"What gave me away?" he asked with a wink as he paid for the sweets and motioned to a table in the corner.

"It just came to me," she said, taking a seat at the table and tasting the gelato. She closed her eyes and smiled. "You're right. That is the best gelato I've ever had."

"I wouldn't kid you about frozen confections. That's serious business," he said with a teasing look. "Now, tell me more about you. What do you do when you aren't rescuing cowboys in distress or shopping with your aunt?"

Chapter Twenty-One

"What's your name, darlin'?" Gage asked a child with red pigtails and freckles scattered across her pert nose. She couldn't have been much older than Grace McGraw. Chubby fingers clasped the edge of the table where he signed autographs and she looked up at him with wide gray eyes. Eyes so much like Tally's, his heart skipped a beat as he smiled at the little girl.

"Holly," she said in a quiet voice, more like a whisper.

Gage leaned forward slightly, his smile friendly and encouraging. "Holly, is it? Like Christmas holly?"

The little girl nodded so hard her pigtails swung like pendulums on either side of her head.

Gage picked up his pen and began autographing a glossy photo for her. "That's a beautiful name, Holly. Do you like Christmas?"

Another nod.

"Did you visit Santa Claus and tell him what you want for Christmas?"

"Mommy said we'd go see him when we get home from the rodeo," she said, standing on her tiptoes to watch as Gage signed his name with a flourish then blew on the ink so it would dry faster.

"I bet you've been a good girl all year." He handed the photo to her.

She clutched it to her chest and grinned. "I think so, but my brother says I'm a pest. He's ten."

"Aw, that explains it, then," Gage gave her another grin as she grabbed her mother's hand.

"Thank you, Mr. Taggart," the child's mother said.

"Thank you!" Holly echoed without being prompted.

"You're welcome. Merry Christmas!" He didn't have time to watch them walk away since there was a long line of fans waiting for him, Chase, Brylee, and a few other Lasso Eight sponsored rodeo contestants to sign autographs. They sat at a table in the middle of the Lasso Eight booth, which was Paige's idea.

As people waited, a shirt here or a pair of jeans there caught their eye and they ended up shopping along with getting an autograph. It was brilliant from a marketing standpoint, but then Paige was incredibly good at what she did. He wondered how things would roll out next year when she had a new baby.

Regardless of what happened with Lasso Eight, he wished her and Cooper every happiness in the world as they expanded their family.

A slight lull in the fans gave him a chance to people watch, something he enjoyed. A couple that had to be around his age walked by with two little ones. The cowboy carried a little girl about the size of Marley Morgan. She had on a frilly pink dress with pink cowboy boots and a darker pink ribbon in her curly blond hair. The mother held a baby with light brown hair and big blue eyes. He stared at Gage and flapped a dimpled hand and squealed.

Gage waggled his fingers at the baby and smiled. A longing unlike anything he'd ever experienced settled over him as he realized he wanted what that young family had. He wanted a wife and a couple of kids and a house of his own. He wanted Sunday pot roast and the mundane chores of everyday living. He wanted summer evenings on the porch, and he wanted, oh how he wanted, his own Christmas tree with stockings hanging by the fireplace and a home brimming with holiday cheer and love.

The face that came to mind as he envisioned the future was Tally. Yes, he wanted all those things, but not with just anyone. He wanted them with her, because of her.

He sighed and leaned back in his chair. Here he was back at the same point he'd beleaguered until he felt like his head might explode. It didn't matter how much he wanted Tally, how much he loved her. The fact remained that he could never have her. Even if, by some miracle, Trevor released him from his promise, he just wouldn't ever be good enough for her.

"Woman troubles?" Chase asked from beside

him.

Gage glared at his friend. "What gave you that idea?"

"Past experience. You do recall how Jessie and I met, don't you?"

Gage nodded. Chase had agreed to pretend to marry a fan in a fake ceremony, only the ceremony was real, and Jessie's friend had entered her. They were two strangers who knew nothing about one another, but anyone could see they were now deeply in love and completely devoted to one another.

"That's different," Gage said, glad when fans stepped into line so he didn't have to elaborate. He couldn't explain to anyone why Tally would never be his. Cooper and Paige hadn't pressed him for details when he'd shown up at their place after he left King Penny Ranch. They'd welcomed him and given him the space he needed to get his focus back onto the rodeo and off how much he missed Tally.

His shift was nearly over when Trevor showed up with Marvella. The old woman had one of the rodeo programs and went down the line, asking everyone to sign it for her.

When she got to him, she grinned. "Well, young man. Do I get your autograph, too?"

"Of course, Aunt Marv." Gage signed his name by his photo and wrote a funny little note for her, too.

She took the program he held out to her and kissed his cheek, then brushed away the smear of dark red lipstick. "Don't want the girls to get any ideas," she said, stepping back.

"We'll just look around while you finish up, if

you want to go back to the hotel with us," Trevor said.

"That would be great." Gage nodded at him and watched a few straggling fans get in line.

"Oh, Trevor!" Marvella said with a raised voice, drawing all eyes her way. "Mercy! Today is the holiday bazaar and I completely forgot about it. We've got dozens of loaves of bread in the freezer to take."

"Don't worry, auntie," Trevor said, squeezing her hand. "Tally asked Judd to haul it all into town. Nancy June is going to sell the bread at her table. And before you ask, Tally made sure our contribution to the food baskets was delivered, she donated to the lighting project, and sent over the prize for Christmas Bingo."

"Keeping Christmas," Gage muttered under his breath. Even with an unexpected trip out of town, Tally somehow managed to keep up with the Christmas traditions and obligations at home.

He signed half a dozen more autographs before he and the others stood and gathered their things. He visited with his friends a few minutes before he stowed the photographs and his pens in a leather briefcase then went in search of Trevor.

Maybe Tally was busy shopping, since Trevor had Marvella with him. When he first saw Tally that morning, he thought she looked like she belonged in some sort of Christmas advertisement. The long, pretty dark red dress she had on featured little white rosebuds and dark green leaves that gave it a festive holiday vibe. She wore the same concho belt she'd had on at the fashion show and black boots on her feet. She looked lovely, sweet, and sexy all at the same time, especially with her glorious, thick hair falling in loose waves over her shoulders and down her back.

It had taken every bit of restraint Gage possessed not to bury his hands and face in it.

He noticed Trevor and Marvella step into a jewelry booth and followed them. The vendor had high-end jewelry with everything from necklaces and earrings to wedding sets. Gage couldn't explain what drew him to one set in particular, but the platinum rings with gold acanthus scrolls around the bands made him think of Tally. The bride's ring featured a tasteful square diamond set into the band. He tried on the groom's ring and it fit perfectly. He quickly yanked it off and noticed a display full of charms.

Trevor and Marvella were busy looking at a shelf full of bracelets, so he picked out a charm for Marvella, then saw something for Tally and added it to his purchases. He checked out and tucked the gifts into his briefcase before Trevor noticed him and waved him over.

"Where's Tally?" Gage asked as he stepped beside Trevor and watched as Marvella tried on a heavy silver bracelet. It dwarfed her thin arm and made it look even more frail.

"She's on a date," Marvella said with a cheerful smile as she removed the bracelet then slipped her hand around his arm. "Such a nice boy, too."

Gage glared from Marvella to Trevor. "Date? Who?" he asked. Fury created an electrical thunderstorm in his head that threatened to short-circuit his brain, leaving him unable to speak in complete sentences.

"What's his name, again, honey?" Marvella looked to Trevor.

"Wyatt. Wyatt Nash." Trevor avoided making eye contact with Gage. "No one asked my opinion on the matter and she refused to listen to the voice of reason when I tried to put the kibosh on Tally's plans."

Marvella swatted his arm. "It's none of your business if Tally wants to go out on a date and have a little fun. All that poor girl does is work. If she isn't putting in long hours at the hospital, she's at the ranch cooking, cleaning, helping you, doing the books, and taking care of me. Don't you think she deserves a few hours of fun once in a while?"

Trevor appeared stunned and Gage understood how he felt. They all took for granted how hard Tally worked and how little she asked for or expected in return.

"I don't begrudge her a minute of fun, Aunt Marv," Trevor said. "I'm just not certain she should be with a guy she knows nothing about in a city like Las Vegas."

"She said she'll be back at the hotel by four and she didn't seem concerned about anything scandalous happening." Marvella stared up at him. "Besides, you two have met him. He comes from a good family. For goodness sakes, he just beat you at that barrel thing Cooper hosted before lunch. Is this sour grapes about losing, Trevor?"

"No, Aunt Marv." Trevor's voice held a hefty dose of frustration.

"Where did they go?" Gage asked, considering the idea of following Tally just to make sure Nash didn't do anything he shouldn't. The thought of him, anyone, touching Tally made Gage's blood boil. He didn't want anyone to date her, ogle her, or, heaven forbid, kiss her. No one but him. But he couldn't exactly expect her to live like a shut-in at a convent, could he?

"She said something about ice cream," Marvella said, pointing to a booth selling baby clothes and accessories. "I want to get something for Paige and Cooper."

While Marvella shopped, Trevor and Gage stood outside the booth where they could keep an eye on her.

"Ice cream? Any idea where they are?" Gage asked, hoping to pump Trevor for details.

"Nope. Your guess is as good as mine," Trevor said. "I don't care what Aunt Marv says, Tally shouldn't have gone out with him. Nash might be a good guy, but not good enough for my sister."

Gage stiffened. "No one fills that role, do they?"

Trevor's gaze narrowed as he stared at Gage. "Let's table this conversation until we get back to the hotel."

"Agreed."

The two of them remained silent as Marvella picked out a Pendleton blanket patterned layette set that would work for a boy or a girl.

Trevor carried her purchases while Marvella hung onto Gage's arm as they slowly made their way to the door. She bought several other things that caught her eye as they meandered past booths.

Trevor finally scowled at her. "How do you intend to get all this plunder home, Aunt Marv?"

"Tally said she'd either get a box and ship it or buy an extra suitcase. We'll manage, sweetheart." Marvella leaned heavily on Gage as he helped her up the steps and out the door. "I'm about beat, boys. Do I have time for a little nap before we need to leave for the rodeo?"

"Sure, Aunt Marv. You've got time." Gage smiled at her and helped her into a taxi then they returned to the hotel.

After Marvella went into the bedroom and closed the door, Trevor motioned for Gage to take a seat on the couch.

"It seems like you've got something you'd like to say regarding Tally," Trevor said with a disdainful look.

Gage eyed him, thinking there were times when he'd really like to punch his best friend. Today was one of those days.

"Look, Trev, you know you're like a brother to me, closer than one, in fact. I would never do anything to mess that up because you and your family mean the world to me," he finally said.

Trevor relaxed and nodded. "That feeling is mutual, bro, but…"

Gage held up his hand, cutting him off. "I made you a promise to leave Tally alone and I plan to keep it, but just so you know, my feelings for her haven't changed since October. If anything, they've evolved."

"Evolved?" Trevor frowned. "How? Explain it

to me."

Gage picked up an event guide off the table and curled the magazine in his hands, rolling it tighter and tighter. "I knew when I saw Tally in August that she was special. That was before I realized the beautiful woman was your little sister. All those weeks at the ranch, I tried to ignore my feelings for her, but I fell for her, Trev. I fell hard."

"You told me all that already. What's evolved since you left?"

"My feelings for her. They've... I don't know... Grown, I suppose. Grown and deepened, gained strength and clarity."

Trevor stared at him, face impassive. "And?"

Gage shrugged and loosened his hold on the magazine. The pages flapped as they unfurled then he started twisting it in his hands again. "I love Tally, Trev. I love her with all my heart, but I won't do anything about it. Not today, not ever. I made you a promise and I'll keep it."

"And what if I told you the promise no longer mattered?" Trevor asked.

Gage stopped playing with the magazine and tossed it on the coffee table. "What are you saying?"

"You know, the morning after you left was mighty unpleasant at my house. Tally was so fired up, I thought smoke might roll out her ears. She kicked the clothesbasket so hard it sailed from the laundry room door all the way across the kitchen. Then there was Aunt Marv." Trevor picked up the magazine and rolled it into a tight tube, then playfully shook it at Gage. "When she found out about the promise you made to me and the reason you left, she rolled up a newspaper and nearly flailed the hide right off me with it. She acted like I was that ol' flea-bitten mutt that used to come over from the neighbor's place and leave hidden treasures in her flower beds. She always accused him of being an obedience school drop out."

Gage cracked a smile. "I might have stayed just to see her whapping you like that."

Trevor grinned. "I'm sure you would have." He dropped the magazine and sighed. "Look, Gage, you are closer than a brother to me and I love my sister. I want you both to be happy."

"But?" Gage asked when Trevor fell silent. "Let me guess, you don't think I'm good enough for her and you're not convinced I'm done sowing my wild oats. Is that it?"

"Not entirely. No one is ever going to be good enough for Tally. Not ever. It's nothing personal, just the way things are. As for your wild oats, that bag is getting close to empty and I don't think you have plans to refill it," Trevor said. "However, now that Tal is off on a date with Wyatt Nash, it's got me thinking that at some point she might actually get serious about this getting married and settling down business. Whether I like it or not, she's eventually going to choose someone and leave the ranch. If I have to let her go and get stuck with a brother-in-law, I'd much rather have her marry my best friend than anyone else. After all, I've already gotten you broken in."

Gage leaned forward. "What are you saying, man?"

"I'm saying I release you from that ridiculous promise that I should never have extracted from you in the first place. There's no one I'd rather have fall for my sister than you." Trevor grinned at him. "It's up to you to get her to love you back, though. According to Aunt Marv, you shouldn't have to work too hard."

Trevor said the words Gage had hoped to hear but dreaded at the same time. Just because he had a green light from his friend to pursue Tally didn't mean he should. Not when he was convinced he'd never make her happy.

"Say something, dude. I just told you I'm okay with you marrying my sister. Isn't that the direction you want things to go?"

"It is, or it was." Gage forked a hand through his hair, making it stand up on top. "I love your sister to the very depths of my soul, and I'd do anything for her, which is why I'm not pursuing this thing with her. She could do so much better than me, man. Tally needs someone who'll be home every night. Someone with dreams aligned to hers. The last thing she needs is a rodeo cowboy who's gone far more often than he's home. I'd never ask her to give up her job and go on the road and she'd never be happy with a husband who was rarely home."

"She knows what she's getting with you, but I get the idea she doesn't care what you do for a living. You could be a butcher, baker, or the village candlestick maker. I don't think it would change how she feels about you."

"That's what I'm trying to tell you, Trev. She's

too good for me and deserves so much more than I can give her."

"Gage, don't be an idiot. Let her decide. Tell her how you feel and see where it goes. Honest, I'm okay with it. Personally, I don't think there's anyone better than you for my sister, and that's saying something, considering the fact that in my head she's still twelve and in need of my constant protection."

A grin toyed with the corners of Gage's mouth. "And here I thought you treated her like she was at least fourteen." He stood and reached a hand out to Trevor. "No matter what happens, thanks for being my friend."

Trevor pulled him into a bear hug and slapped his back. "Always, Gage."

Gage returned to his room where he changed his clothes for the rodeo and warred with himself about the best thing to do... not for his future, but Tally's.

Chapter Twenty-Two

"Head in the game, head in the game," Gage chanted to himself as he shook his arms and stretched his legs, preparing for the final ride of the national finals rodeo.

Last night, he'd been so distracted with thoughts of Tally, particularly when she came back from her date with Wyatt sporting a dreamy smile, he'd almost gotten himself tossed off the bronc he rode. He barely managed to hang on for eight seconds, but he only pulled out a seventy-six score on the ride.

One of only two cowboys who'd ridden every horse, the two of them were competing not just for the average win tonight, but the world champion title. The average win was determined based on the number of rides made over the ten nights of competition, the total number of points earned, and money won. Gage had to not only ride tonight, but he needed at least an eighty-point ride to win.

Anything less would leave him in second place, and he'd come too far to settle for that.

"You ready to win this?" Kash Kressley asked as he walked up beside Gage.

"Sure," Gage said, knowing he sounded less than convincing. Truthfully, he was so beat up, sore, and tired, he was ready for the rodeo to end. In addition to his cracked rib, multiple bruises, black eye, and shoulder that ached every time he moved it, he had a dozen stitches on his thigh from where the horse stomped on him the other night and four more on the side of his head where he ducked a flying hoof last night but wasn't quite fast enough. He was lucky to be alive, since the horse could have killed him with one well-placed kick.

On top of that, Tally had spent the morning sight-seeing with Wyatt Nash. Gage had asked around about him. The man came from a long line of ranchers in Pendleton. He was a talented tie-down roper, and all-around good guy. No one had anything bad to say about the cowboy. With Wyatt's dark, good looks, he could have been a cover model for the romances Gage knew Tally liked to read. Black hair, brown eyes, and jawline that looked like it had been chiseled from rock didn't hurt his appearance any.

Gage couldn't understand Tally's sudden interest in the guy, though. From what he'd observed and heard, she never dated. Trevor said the last steady boyfriend she'd had was her senior year of high school. Gage vaguely remembered a gangly kid with braces who seemed a little shy.

The fact that he'd seen Wyatt in the stands

talking to Tally before the rodeo began only increased his frustration and irritation. He'd asked Tally if she'd go with him for a walk after the rodeo and awards ceremony. She told him she would, then mentioned the walk she went on with Wyatt through one of the hotels to see a Flamingo habitat.

Gage had no interest in pink-feathered birds when the woman he loved was falling for someone else.

"Hey, are you okay?" Kash asked, placing a hand on Gage's shoulder as he unknowingly clenched his hands into tight fists at his sides.

"I'm fine," Gage said, relaxing his hands and shaking them again.

"It'll be okay, Gage. Just focus on being present in the moment. You can't change what's already happened and you can't predict what might come, but you can do your best right now."

Gage looked at the stock contractor and nodded. "Thanks, Kash. Those are good words of wisdom. When did you get so smart?"

Kash smirked and dropped his voice as he leaned closer. "Call it the school of experience. I've been right where you're at before, except the woman causing my misery has a head full of red hair and a temper just as fiery."

A chuckle rolled out of Gage and he felt his body relax a little. "For what it's worth, you make a great couple. When are you and Celia gonna add a little buckaroo to your family?"

Kash rolled his eyes. "When she's ready, I suppose. She wants to get in another year or two on the road as a rodeo photographer. Once we have kids, she's declared her plans to stay home and raise them."

"That's probably a good plan to travel and take photos while she can. I think it would be hard trying to raise kids on the rodeo road." Gage couldn't even figure out how to have a wife and still compete in rodeo. Well, he could marry a girl who would tag after him like an obedient puppy, but that wasn't what he wanted. He wanted Tally and if he couldn't have her, he'd remain alone. In fact, since the moment he set eyes on her, he'd felt no interest in any other females. He hadn't been on any dates, and he'd cringed inwardly at every proposal and proposition he'd been offered by fans.

When he thought of Tally, all other women seemed to pale in comparison.

"Keep focused and you can win this thing," Kash said, thumping Gage on the back as he walked off.

Gage did a few more stretches then stepped onto the catwalk behind the chutes. He looked into the stands until his gaze landed on Tally. She laughed at something Jessie Jarrett said as the two of them stood together in the aisle while Aunt Marv settled into her seat.

Tally looked like a cowboy's dream, at least to him, in snug dark blue jeans and a top that looked like it was made of fairy dust collected after a storm. The gray hue of the airy fabric was accented with black embroidery and sequins stitched in a vertical pattern along the front. The cap sleeves showed off the smooth skin of her arms and a rounded neckline made his eyes zero in on the creamy skin modestly exposed.

Although Tally would never dress like some of the girls who had every one of their feminine assets on display, she didn't need to. She could have been covered from her chin to her wrists and on down to her toes in a shapeless gunnysack and she still would have heated his blood.

He was glad she appeared to be having a good time. She needed to relax and enjoy life instead of working all the time. He supposed part of that was just her nature. Another part, he was sure, had to do with her past. Lulu, her mother, hadn't held down a job in years. She went from one man to another, gaining more money with each divorce.

No doubt, Tally wanted to prove she was nothing like the woman. It would take less than a second for anyone to see the two of them had nothing in common, but perhaps Tally didn't realize it. Even without her saying anything, he knew she sometimes felt out of place, like she didn't fit in at the ranch. She'd mentioned something to him once about feeling like an imposter pretending to be a country girl. He'd assured her she had more right to call herself a country girl than the majority of the women who flung around the title.

He wished Tally could see herself as others saw her, as he saw her. She wasn't the plump, sometimes shy, awkward girl she thought herself to be. To him she was a gorgeous, intelligent woman, and one of the genuinely nicest people he'd ever met.

Perhaps before he told her goodbye tonight, he could convince her just how amazing she really was.

For now, though, he absolutely had to focus on his upcoming ride. The horse he'd be riding, Smokebuster, wasn't known for being an easy ride. In fact, the horse's name came from the fact she busted the riders who blew smoke about their riding abilities. It took someone with grit, determination, and skill to successfully stay on the big bay mare's back until the eight-second buzzer. She wasn't a mean horse, but she was good at sending riders flying in a disgraceful heap into the arena dirt.

When it was his turn to ride, the announcer's voice boomed throughout the arena.

"Ladies and gentlemen, talk about the comeback kid! Gage Taggart was at the top of his career when an accident left him out of the game back at the end of August. He squeaked into the finals and man, oh man, has he been proving he's got the chops to be here. Depending on his score tonight, this cowboy could walk away as our average winner as well as the world champion. Let him know what you think of his performance the last nine days. He's like the energizer bunny. He's taken a lickin' but kept right on tickin'! Get 'er done, son!"

Gage took a deep breath and eased onto the horse's back. He felt her muscles twitch beneath him as he tugged on the handle of his rigging to make sure it was tight then worked his riding hand into the handle. He pulled on the thumb of his glove, then the fingers, forcing his fingers deeper into the opening of the handle. He checked the tape wrapped around his wrist over the top of the long cuff of the glove, tugged on his fingers one more time, then snugged down his hat.

With a final deep breath, he slid his butt forward, whipped back the legs of his chaps and leaned back. He raised his free hand in the air and nodded his head.

Smokebuster came out of the chute with her hind feet high in the air. Fourteen hundred pounds of determination churned beneath Gage as the horse bucked, twisted, snorted, and kicked. At one point, she kicked with her back feet and pivoted on the front two, executing a perfect ninety-degree turn without breaking her rhythm.

Centered and focused, Gage raked his spurs, kept his free hand up in the air, and rode like his future depended on it. Each time Smokebuster's hooves came in contact with the arena dirt, the vibrations it shot up his legs and into his body felt like it could have registered in the red zone of the Richter scale.

The buzzer sounded, signaling he'd made the eight-second ride. He rode through one more buck before he freed his hand from the rigging. Smokebuster crowhopped a few steps then broke into a run around the arena, as though she carried a rodeo princess on her back instead of a bareback rider.

A pickup man came up on Gage's right. He reached with his left arm and swung off the far side of the man's horse then lifted his hat and waved to the crowd.

The noise was deafening as cheers and whistles roared from the stands. Gage's gaze swiveled to the section where Tally stood, arms upraised, clapping and smiling. He waggled his fingers at her then jogged toward the gate.

"We may just have our winner, folks! Gage scored an eighty-five and a half on that ride, and boy was it a dandy! Give that cowboy another hand!" the announcer boomed.

Gage sent up a prayer of thanks as he reached the back of the chutes, grateful he'd made it through the ride unscathed and pleased he'd done well. He helped a few friends as they got ready to ride and listened to the scores. When the last cowboy had ridden, Gage remained the winner.

He made a lightning fast victory lap on a borrowed horse around the arena, then accepted the trophy saddle and buckle and posed for photographs. At the end of the rodeo, he joined the other world champions in accepting their awards. The title he'd pursued all year was finally his.

Pressed into signing autographs, a chore he typically enjoyed, he just wanted to be with Tally. It seemed to take forever before Gage wrapped up his obligations and made his way back to the hotel where the King family waited his arrival.

After he took them all out for dessert, Trevor returned to the hotel with Aunt Marv while Gage and Tally walked along the strip, taking in the lights and the sights.

Several people who recognized Gage from his Lasso Eight appearances as well as the rodeo stopped him and asked for photographs.

Finally, he took Tally's hand in his and pulled her up an escalator and onto a skywalk that spanned the street. From there, they had a wonderful view of the Bellagio's fountains as they shot water into the sky to a recording of Ella Fitzgerald singing "Sleigh Ride."

Gage watched Tally more than the fountains. Her face glowed with excitement and happiness. He knew she'd been to Las Vegas at least once with Ross and Trevor, but her dad, in an effort to shelter her from the more tasteless aspects of Sin City, only took her to the rodeo and the shopping mall. It was no wonder all the tourist attractions had enthralled her, if she was seeing them for the first time.

"That's incredible," Tally said, taking a photo of the fountains.

"Here, give me your phone." Gage took her phone from her and captured a photo of her with the fountains in the background.

"Take one of us together," she said, tugging on his arm until he moved beside her and held out the phone, snapping a few images of them together.

"Send me one of those?" he asked as he gave her the phone.

She nodded then watched the rest of the fountain show. When it ended, she browsed through the images he captured then sent one to his phone. He laughed at the silly faces they were making, but it lightened his heart.

In the middle of the skywalk wasn't the place to have the conversation he needed to with her, but he wasn't ready to tell her goodbye. Not yet.

"Where did Wyatt take you this morning?" he asked, already knowing the answer. He'd listened as Tally told Marvella they'd gone to a chocolate factory just outside of town then visited the aquarium at Mandalay Bay before strolling through a vendor show there.

"Mandalay Bay and the chocolate factory. They have the best toffee there. I have some back in the room if you want to try it," she said, taking his hand and lacing their fingers together as they walked across the skywalk and entered the Bellagio.

"Are you up to a little more sight-seeing?" he asked, guiding her toward a series of high-end shops.

"Absolutely. It's so fun to do a little exploring. When I came with Dad and Trevor, they were both convinced I'd be corrupted if I went anywhere other than the rodeo, or shopping. Apparently, Macy's is a safe haven for a teenager with body issues no matter the city."

Gage shook his head. "That teenager should have asked her brother's best friend for his opinion on how she looked. She wouldn't have had any issues after that."

Tally whipped her head around and stared at him with a shocked expression on her face.

He squeezed the hand he still held and grinned. "It's true, Talilah King. You are a beautiful woman and with a body like that, you could be quite dangerous if you decided to use it for evil purposes."

Red seared her cheeks until it looked like she'd been attacked by a Cirque de Soleil makeup artist.

Gage held back a chuckle as they made their way past the hotel's casino to the lobby.

Tally's steps slowed as she took in the elaborate holiday decorations behind the front desk and the mind-boggling blown glass display hanging from the ceiling.

"Wow," she whispered, clearly awed.

He bent close to her ear. "Just wait until you see the conservatory."

"You mean there's more?" she asked, following as he led her into a space that was transformed each season with decorations made of flowers and natural elements. It was like taking the Tournament of Roses Parade and condensing it into one small showcase. White mum polar bears slid across ice. There was a life-size gingerbread house made of real gingerbread. Gage inhaled the spicy scent and thought of all the delicious meals and treats Tally had made while he was recuperating at King Penny Ranch.

"Are you going to do any holiday baking this year?" he asked as she stopped to read a sign. Apparently, the carriage taking up the center of the conservatory had required more than a thousand pounds of tapioca pearls, flax seed, and black lentils to decorate it.

"Baking?" Tally asked, distracted by the wonder of the creations around her.

"Cookies, candy, holiday treats for good little boys?"

She glanced up at him and smiled. "If only I knew any good little boys. Maybe I'll make sugar cookies for Jacob McGraw and Gideon Morgan."

Gage gave her a disparaging look, then led her into the gift shop where she found an ornament, made of feathers and sequins she bought for Marvella.

Next door, they watched chocolate flow through a fountain, admired displays of elaborate cakes, then Gage took her on a tram to a nearby shopping center where they stared at a bedazzled Christmas tree that was three stories high. Crystals shimmered in the lights and cast refracted sparkles around them.

"I just can't believe all these decorations," Tally said, admiring a window display with a classic holiday scene of carolers and snow. "They certainly help get a person into the spirit of things."

By the time they wandered through three more hotels, shared a burger and fries at midnight, and made it back to their hotel, Gage's entire body was one aching mass of pain.

"You need some rest, Gage, instead of playing tour guide. Do you need help with anything? Any bandages that need to be changed?" she asked as they stepped off the elevator on their floor.

"I don't need help, but I do want to talk to you a few minutes, if you don't mind." He slid his key in the lock to his room then held the door open for her.

She entered his room, flicked on the light, and took a seat on the sofa. He looked at her, taking in the dark waves of her hair falling around her face to the black velvet jacket she wore that glided over her curves.

His mouth went dry while the moisture lacking there seemed to ooze out of his palms as they grew damp. He rubbed his hands up and down his jeans, then took a deep breath. It filled his nose with Tally's decadent scent, making him think of

Christmas and dreams that weren't ever coming true.

"What's going on, Gage? You look like I just offered to feed you a plate full of Brussels sprouts instead of the world champion bareback rider." She gave him a pleased smile. "Congrats, again. We're all so proud of you."

"Thanks, Tally. It means more than you can know to have you all here."

"Even Aunt Marv?" Tally asked with a teasing grin.

"Even Aunt Marv," Gage said, sitting beside her and holding back a groan as his abused body protested even the slightest movement. "She's been a trooper."

"She really has been," Tally agreed. "And she's been on her best behavior."

"I noticed. She hasn't done or said anything truly outlandish the whole time you've been here." Gage wiped his hands on his jeans again then looked at Tally. Her eyes met his and he thought he could get lost in their soft gray depths. Everything about Tally was soft and welcoming, like coming home.

But that home wasn't meant for him.

"I don't know how to say this, Tally, so I suppose the best thing to do is just spit it out." He took her hand between his then lifted her fingers and kissed the back of each one.

She drew in a sharp breath and he looked up at her. It would be so easy to just pull her into his arms, kiss those luscious lips, and forget about being an honorable, upright man.

But he wouldn't do that, no matter how much he longed to love her. She wasn't his to keep and never would be.

"What's wrong, Gage?" she asked, placing the hand he wasn't holding on his leg. He thought it might sear right through his jeans and leave his thigh branded with a handprint.

"When I kissed you back in October that night, I didn't do it because of the moonlight or because you were basically my nurse and I had that weird syndrome when you fall in love with your caregiver."

"Florence Nightingale syndrome," she said.

"That's it. I kissed you because I care about you, because I think you're about the prettiest girl I've ever held in my arms. You're an amazing, incredible person, Talilah King, and if I was a different person, a better person, I'd pursue you with everything I had."

"Gage, I don't..."

He placed his fingers on her lips to silence her and realized the mistake in that. Her lips were so soft, so tantalizing. He traced the bottom one with his index finger and leaned toward her but regained his sense before he kissed her.

"Tally, unless I'm mistaken, you have feelings for me, deep feelings. I love you, but I can't be with you. I can't be the man you're dreaming of. You need someone who'll be home every night. Someone who provides stability and dependability. I'm on the road almost fifty weeks a year. That's no life for you and I'd never ask you to give up nursing to go with me. I certainly wouldn't expect you to be happy sitting at home alone, night after night, wondering who I was with and how I was doing. I promise I won't make things awkward between us when you find a guy who'll be the kind of husband you need. Maybe it's Wyatt Nash, maybe it's someone else, but you deserve all the happiness you can find in this world, and it's not with me."

Tally yanked her hand from his and glared at him. The soft light that had glowed in her eyes earlier had segued into a dark storm. In fact, he thought he could see lightning sparks dancing in those expressive eyes as she rose to her feet and placed her hands on her hips in a stance that made him wish he could hold her, just one more time.

"Gage Taggart! You are the biggest idiot on the planet! You don't get to decide who I love, that's up to me. If I love you from now until the end of time, it's not your choice. You think you can just waltz into my life and waltz right back out without any problem at all? Well, good luck with that, buster! As for you and your promises, I know how well you keep them. In spite of being a moron, you're full of honor and duty."

His eyes widened and he leaned back when she took a step forward.

"That's right. After I read the letter you left in October, I also read between the lines. Trevor made you promise to leave, didn't he?"

"Not exactly," Gage said, rubbing the back of his neck. This was not how he'd envisioned the conversation going at all. He assumed Tally might shed a few tears. He figured she would run back to her room and slam the door. But this fury was not something he'd anticipated.

"What exactly did he make you promise?"

"That I'd leave you alone, stay away from you, romantically speaking."

Tally looked like she could rip something in two, preferably her well-meaning, albeit meddling, brother, as she stood with her chest heaving and fire snapping in her eyes.

"You know the thing about promises, Gage, is that they either make something or break something. It's long been my opinion that three things you should never break are a promise, a friendship, or a heart. Since you broke my heart and friendship back in October, you're two out of three with me. Why not go for a perfect score and break that promise, too?"

"I never meant to hurt you. I never wanted to hurt you. That's the whole reason I left in the first place," he said, rising to his feet and pacing across the room. If he didn't get a little distance from her, there was no telling what might happen. He'd forget about promises and doing what was right. Instead, he'd follow his heart and give in to the need to love this infuriating, fascinating woman.

"But you did hurt me, Gage. How do you think I felt waking up after... after we... after kisses and moonlight? I thought we had something special. Your absence the following morning made me feel like a stupid, naïve girl who'd imagined the whole thing. Seeing you these past few days made me realize you do care." Tally marched over to him. "Are you really going to walk away from what we can have together? Deny what you feel?"

"I love you, Talilah, but I won't ruin your life because of it. I have no doubt we'd be blissful newlyweds, but then you'd start to resent me for being gone all the time and I'd resent you for wanting me to stay. I'd be the biggest mistake you'd ever make." He took her arms in his hands and despite knowing better, he pulled her against him and hugged her close. "I need this to be goodbye. I can't keep seeing you, Queenie. Not when I love you so much."

"What about Christmas? We all thought you'd come to the ranch." She looked like a little girl who'd just been told Santa didn't really exist. Her eyes shimmered with tears and her bottom lip quivered. "I can't bear the thought of you spending it alone."

"It wouldn't be the first time or the last." He caught her chin with his hand and lifted it. The big, salty teardrop that ran down her cheek almost brought him to his knees, but he closed his eyes and turned away. "I'll come to visit next summer when I'm in the area. Other than that, I'll leave you alone and stay away. If you ever need me, though, all you have to do is call and I'll be there. Anytime, anywhere. All you have to do is get in touch."

When he turned to look at her again, the fury sizzled in her eyes. "If I didn't love you so much, it would be easy to hate you, Gage. When you realize you've just tossed aside a love that could last a lifetime, don't expect me to be waiting for you to come back. Maybe I'll be married with a baby on the way by then!"

"Hey, don't you do anything foolish. This isn't

the time for you to make a bad decision that will affect your future. It's not about showing me you don't need me or proving a point. I'm doing this because I care about you, Tally." He caught her arm as she stormed past him toward the door.

"If you cared about me, you wouldn't leave me! Again!" She yanked away from him. Her hand was on the doorknob when she spun around and grabbed the front of his shirt with both hands. She raised herself up and kissed him. It wasn't a soft kiss of parting. No, this was a kiss meant to haunt a man for the remainder of his days on earth. It was the most passionate, powerful, fierce, yet sweet kiss Gage had ever experienced. His arms slid around her back and he moved a step closer, mind blank of everything except how perfectly she fit in his arms and his heart.

She jerked away and opened the door. "Remember that the next time you decide what's best for someone else."

Quietly, she closed the door and left him alone in the room.

Chapter Twenty-Three

The ringing of her cell phone pulled Tally from much needed sleep. The phone continued ringing and she groggily glanced at the caller ID.

Work.

Again.

Quickly answering, she almost wished she'd ignored it when her boss asked her if she'd work a shift to fill in for someone who called in sick.

"No, it's no problem," Tally assured her supervisor. "I'll be there as soon as I can."

She disconnected the call and rushed into her bathroom to get ready. The last thing she wanted to do was spend Christmas Eve at the hospital. She'd driven home in a dense fog late last night after working four fourteen-hour shifts in a row.

Even exhaustion hadn't been able to dull the piercing ache she felt in her heart every time she thought about Gage and the conversation they'd had that last night in Vegas.

She'd endured nine of the longest days of her life since she left his room in a fury. Nine days for her to waver between despair, disappointment, and rage. Nine days to replay every word he said over and over. Nine days to think about how he held her against him, so tenderly yet what seemed desperately, too.

The thoughts chasing around and around in her head regarding the infuriating man only left her more confused, upset, and angry. Yet, she couldn't stop thinking about him, about the fact he admitted he loved her.

After the fun they had in Las Vegas before that fateful Saturday night when he bid her goodbye, she'd envisioned Gage coming home with them and spending Christmas together. Oh, she'd had such dreams to make it their best holiday ever. She'd planned the menus in her head, considered extra decorations she wanted to put out, and even thought about the type of stocking she'd make for Gage and hang by the fireplace to surprise him Christmas morning.

Then, in the length of one brief, completely unexpected conversation, he'd shattered her delusions and left her wondering why, of all the men she could have fallen for, she had to be in love with one so… so…maddening. And noble. And good. And kind.

"Agh!" Tally picked up her toothpaste and squeezed it so hard it squirted out on her mirror. She wiped up the mess, brushed her teeth, pulled her hair into a bun, and added a swipe of mascara to her eyelashes. After tugging on a pair of scrubs and her comfortable work shoes, she hurried downstairs.

Trevor wandered into the kitchen as she filled a sparkly pink travel mug with coffee. Wyatt Nash had sent it to her. On the side of the cup it said, "Forget the glass slippers, this princess wears scrubs."

Tally thought it was funny and had thanked Wyatt for the gift by sending him an ornament she found that looked like a little cougar. A switch on the bottom, when turned on, made a roaring sound. He'd called her when he got it and laughed about the first time they met, when she rescued him from the prowling women at the rodeo. She and Wyatt, by mutual unspoken agreement, knew they had no romantic future, but they had become friends.

"Hey, what are you doing up? I thought you didn't have to go back to work until Monday since you've been covering extra shifts." Trevor yawned and poured himself a cup of coffee while Tally snatched a muffin from a batch Aunt Marv had made yesterday.

She cut it in half and took a bite then rummaged in her purse for her car keys. She hit the remote starter for her car. Although it hadn't yet snowed, the weather had been bitterly cold the last several days.

"The hospital called this morning and they need a hand. The boss promised I'll be off work by four at the latest."

Trevor shook his head. "So that means you'll be home by, what, nine? We both know that means a minimum of four more hours of work after your supposed quitting time."

"Too bad my boss's promises aren't like those of someone else we know," Tally muttered as she ate the last of her muffin then rinsed the crumbs from her hands.

Trevor tried to hide his grin behind his coffee cup, but Tally noticed it. At her scowl, he cleared his throat. "You might not remember, but Dad used to say people with good intentions make promises and people with good character keep them. No matter how mad you are at Gage for being a certifiable dunce, he's still one of the good guys."

"I know that, Trev. It's just…" A frustrated sigh escaped her. "What you and Gage failed to take into consideration is that I'm not a little girl who can't think for herself. I'm all grown up with a mind of my own. Neither one of you get to make decisions for me, which is exactly what Gage is trying to do. Rather than give me the option of deciding what I want, he ran off with his noble intentions. I hope they make miserable company for him."

Trevor chuckled and set down his coffee cup. He wrapped Tally in a hug then stepped back. "I know we've both been idiots and I'm glad you decided to forgive me. Maybe, with enough time, you'll forgive Gage, too. Don't be too mad at him, Tal. He really does love you."

"I know that. Why do you think I'm so upset? If he didn't love me, it wouldn't be an issue." She glanced at the clock and hurried to the door, yanking on her coat and wrapping a scarf around her neck. "You and Aunt Marv enjoy the day. I'll see you this evening. Happy Christmas Eve, big brother."

"Happy Christmas Eve to you, Tal. Have a good day and try to focus on only the good stuff today."

"Right. Morons who burn their arms while frying turkeys. Kids overstuffed on candy suffering from horrible tummy aches. People who get into family brawls and come in with claw marks. 'Tis the season for spreading joy far and wide."

His laughter followed her out the door as she hurried to her car. The cold air made her eyes sting and her nose feel like icicles might be freezing in her nostrils. She opened the car door, slid inside, and turned the heater on full blast. By the time she reached the end of the lane, she was starting to warm up.

Her thoughts wandered in a hundred directions as she headed toward Echo. It was still dark as she drove through the little town, but she slowed to take in the lights hanging from city hall, around houses and businesses. Although they were in Las Vegas for the holiday bazaar and the assembling of food baskets, Aunt Marv insisted they all attend the annual Christmas bingo fundraiser. Tally had no interest in it, but Trevor had made it fun by whispering snarky comments in her ear that Nancy June Ledbetter and Betty Brewster might exchange if they actually spoke to each other. The two women sat on opposite sides of the room, staring daggers at one another the entire evening.

Tally had tried, she really had, to keep Christmas in her heart every day. Nevertheless, the holes left behind by Gage leaving her, again, made it hard to hold onto the holiday spirit. She half-heartedly baked cookies and made candy. She'd even watched a handful of holiday movies with Aunt Marv, but she couldn't get interested in them.

Regardless of her sullen mood, it was hard not to feel a little flickering of Christmas cheer as lights twinkled through the pre-dawn darkness and frost coated everything like confectioner's sugar.

Tally drove to work and spent the morning running from one patient to the next. Her mother called from Barbados where she'd gone with her new husband. Tally hadn't even known she'd divorced the last one. Lulu wished her a happy holiday and said she'd try to get by to visit sometime soon. They both knew Lulu had no intention of setting foot back at the ranch or the area, which suited Tally just fine.

At noon, she took a quick break to eat a bite of lunch in the cafeteria. Although there were festive options on the day's menu, she chose a salad with turkey, dried cranberries and feta cheese. Trevor would have turned up his nose at it, but Tally thought it was delicious.

She'd just finished eating when her phone chimed with a text. A smile played on her mouth as she read the message from Elliott Flynn, fashion designer and owner of Lasso Eight apparel. He'd texted her, called her, mailed a handwritten letter, and sent an enormous bouquet of red and white roses with Christmas greens that Tally had taken to the church for the pastor to use for the Christmas Eve service because it was so pretty.

Apparently, after watching her model the

clothes from his new Wyld Roads line for women with curves in Las Vegas, Elliott had decided she had to be a model in an upcoming photo shoot for spring. He'd offered a ridiculous amount of money if she'd just agree to be a model.

Tally had been terrified to walk out on the runway in Las Vegas, but between the encouragement of her friends and the reactions of those in attendance, she realized that her perception of herself and that of others were entirely different things.

When she got home from Las Vegas, she'd spent a while one evening studying herself in her bedroom mirror. Maybe, just maybe, she wasn't the chubby, awkward girl she'd always imagined herself to be. Perhaps, with the right clothes and attitude, she really could pull off modeling for the company.

She read Elliott's text with a smile.

Miss King, sending you wishes for the most spectacular Christmas ever. Please call me, text me, send a courier pigeon or smoke signals — whatever works for you — after the New Year to discuss the possibility of modeling. Truly, you are the perfect model for the Wyld Roads line from Lasso Eight. I'll fly there and beg if it will help. We'll talk soon. Merry Christmas!

Tally realized it was time to believe in herself and step beyond the borders of her comfort zone. Modeling in a photo shoot was so far out of her realm of norm, it might be considered entering alien territory, but she knew it would be good for her to do it.

Before she could change her mind, she sent Elliott a text.

Happy Christmas Eve, Mr. Flynn. Thank you, again, for the beautiful flowers and kind words. No pigeons or smoke signals will be necessary. I'm willing to give modeling a try. Have a Merry Christmas and a Happy New Year. I'll connect with Paige next week to get the particulars.

Before she could rise from the table and toss her trash in the garbage, her phone chimed again.

Excellent news, Miss King! You are going to make my apparel look fantastic! Can't wait to work with you. Merry, merry Christmas!

Tally grinned. "Merry Christmas to me," she said, tossing her trash and heading back to work. An hour later, her phone rang as she stood in the back of the elevator waiting for a woman with two wailing children to step off.

She glanced at the caller ID and answered immediately. "Aunt Marv? What's wrong? You never call me at work. Are you okay?"

"I'm fine, darling. Marvelous, in fact. Happy Christmas Eve, sweetheart."

"Happy Christmas Eve to you. What's going on?" Tally asked, still worried something was wrong at the ranch.

"I have the most exciting news." Marvella's

voice increased in both volume and excitement. "I sold the farm today!"

Tally almost dropped the phone as the elevator stopped on her floor. She scrambled to grab it before it fell to the floor and stepped off the elevator.

"You what?" she asked, hurrying around the corner and moving into the stairwell where it was quiet. Hardly anyone used the stairs unless they were in a huge rush.

"I said I sold the farm today. A buyer approached me this morning and it felt right," Marvella said. "You know I always said I'd sell it when the right buyer came along and that was today."

Tally heard a sigh from Marvella that sounded so content, she couldn't argue with her aunt's decision. Secretly, she'd always hoped her aunt might sell her the farm. Trevor had the ranch, but Tally had always longed for a place of her own. A place where she didn't have to worry about ever leaving or fitting in. A place where she'd set her roots so deep, they'd keep her there until the day she died.

Regardless of her dreams, it was Marvella's place to do with as she wished.

"That's wonderful, Aunt Marv, but what kind of weirdo buys a farm on Christmas Eve?"

"A determined one, I do believe," Marvella said with a laugh. "The buyer offered cash and I took it. We'll complete all the paperwork after Christmas, but I turned over the key after walking through the house with them this morning. My, but it's been an interesting day."

"I'm sure it has been," Tally said, rubbing a hand over her forehead, realizing she suddenly had a throbbing headache. "So, what did you need me to do?"

"The reason I called is because in the excitement this morning, I completely forgot there's a box of Christmas things, special memories, you know, at the back of my old bedroom closet. I hate to leave it there because the buyer plans to move in right away. Would you be a dear and pick it up for me on your way home? Please, darling?"

Marvella rarely asked for favors and Tally didn't have it in her to tell her aunt no.

"Will the buyer be there?"

"I don't think so. The spare key is still under the flowerpot by the back door. Just go in and get the box. Come to think of it, there's a vase in the kitchen in the back of the pantry I'd like you to have. My sweet Richard gave it to me for our eighth anniversary. You'll know it when you see it."

"Thank you, Aunt Marv. I'll stop by as soon as I leave work then head home. I should be there by five-thirty at the latest. Are you sure you don't need me to bring home something for dinner?"

"No, darling. Your brother is grilling steaks and I'm handling the rest. It will be ready at six on the dot. Don't be late. We'll see you then!"

Tally stared at the phone a moment after her aunt hung up then shoved it back into her pocket. What a strange Christmas Eve this was turning out to be.

A lull arrived mid-afternoon. Tally looked up

in surprise when her supervisor approached and told her to leave while she could.

"But what if you need help later?" she asked.

"We'll be fine. I have someone coming in at five. We've got this, Tally. You get out of here while the getting is good. Have a merry Christmas and I don't want to see you here before your next scheduled shift. Understood?"

Tally grinned at her boss. "Understood. Thank you and merry Christmas to you." She wasted no time in gathering her things, wishing her friends a merry Christmas, and hurrying out to her car.

The sky, at least what she could see of it through the light fog, was a gunmetal hue. The temperature had dropped during the day instead of rising. She started her car and took out an ice scraper to remove the frost that coated her windshield.

She left the hospital parking lot at a few minutes past three and headed toward Marvella's farm. In an effort to drum up more of her own Christmas cheer, Tally turned on the radio and listened to a local country station. They played all Christmas songs and Tally enjoyed hearing some of her favorite artists perform holiday tunes.

"It's Christmas Eve, folks," the DJ said as the notes of the last song faded. "The next hour, we'll be playing Christmas songs from decades past. To kick it off, here's a great old Alan Jackson tune."

Tally listened as Alan sang "I Only Want You For Christmas." The upbeat tune had her tapping her fingers on the steering wheel until she thought about the words. All she'd really wanted for

Christmas was Gage. Maybe she'd been naughty and didn't know it and having Gage walk away from her was the equivalent of a life sentence of coal in her stocking.

The next song was one from John Michael Montgomery, one she hadn't heard before. He sang about something missing, being sentimental and it being regrettable.

"Isn't that the truth," Tally mumbled as she listened to the song.

The song went on to mention the holiday not seeming right and Tally could relate on so many levels. In spite of trying to pretend everything was fine, it wasn't. And it wouldn't be. Not when her heart felt so raw, wounded, and sore from Gage's goodbye.

When the song segued to moonlight and old man winter helping draw them together, Tally's eyes burned and emotion clogged her throat.

The song ended and she took a deep, calming breath. Then Ricky Van Shelton started singing "Please Come Home for Christmas," and Tally couldn't hold back the tears.

There was nothing she wanted more than to have Gage with her for Christmas. Nothing.

By the time Ricky sang, "tell me you'll never more roam," Tally could barely see the road.

Thankfully, she was nearly to the farm. She'd been there so many times, she could have found her way with one eye closed in a blinding blizzard.

At the end of a lane surrounded by now-empty fields, Tally drove past a rusty sign hanging from a rotting fence post. "Roamin' End Ranch," she said, smiling through her tears. How fitting the song she'd just been listening to talked about roaming no more.

Tally glanced at the big red barn that stood in bright contrast to the gray, hazy day then parked in front of the yellow house. The white trim looked cheery and she was glad they'd painted it in the spring when the new roof had been installed.

Suddenly, Tally realized there were lights hanging on the house. Christmas lights. And they glowed through the darkening afternoon sky with soft bursts of color. The big, old bulbs were probably a major fire hazard, but it was fun to see them hanging off the front porch and wrapped around the five porch posts.

"They didn't waste any time making themselves at home," Tally grumbled as she got out of the car and stared at the house. She'd planned to spend a few minutes sitting in the swing that hung from one of the big maple trees in the backyard, but now she'd just get Marvella's things and go.

A wave of nostalgia swept over her as she thought of all the happy hours she'd spent at the farm with Uncle Rich and Aunt Marv. They'd been so good to her, always made her feel so welcome and loved.

Slowly, she made her way down the slate walk, noticing a big gray pickup parked on the side of the house. Most likely, it belonged to the new owner. She walked up the steps, but lingered a moment, recalling a summer afternoon when she and Trevor had sat on the top step and cranked the handle to make ice cream while Uncle Rich told them stories from life in Alaska.

Fighting her emotions, she stared at the ceiling of the porch until she thought she could knock on the door without bursting into tears.

She raised a hand and rapped on the wood then waited. Frost had created a lacy pattern on the glass of the window closest to the door. It looked like Jack Frost had waved a wand and transformed the world into his own special wonderland. Even if she longed for snow, the frost was almost as good.

Tally glanced over her shoulder, admiring how pretty everything looked in the gathering dusk. There were even old lights strung along the fence by the barn.

She turned back to the door and knocked again. Aunt Marv had told her to go right in, so maybe whoever bought the place was running errands. If it was a couple, it made sense they might have brought two vehicles and taken one into town.

Tally tried the knob and it turned beneath her hand. She pushed the door open and stuck her head inside. "Hello? Anyone here?" she called. The sound of Nat King Cole crooning carols provided a pleasing background noise.

When no one answered, she walked inside and closed the door behind her. The scent of bayberry mingled with pine, taking her back to a wonderful Christmas in her childhood that she spent in this house with Aunt Marv and Uncle Rich. She breathed deeply, letting the scent evoke sweet memories.

She turned to face the room and sucked in a startled gasp to see many of Aunt Marv's Christmas decorations in the bookcases that flanked the marble fireplace. Flames danced with inviting warmth. She would have thought the new owners foolish to go off and leave a fire unattended if she hadn't known it was a gas fireplace. Trevor had arranged to have it installed a few years before Aunt Marv moved out of the house.

A towering fir tree in front of the window had been decorated with antique ornaments. Tally recognized several that belonged to Uncle Rich's parents and wondered just who these new owners thought they were to use her aunt's things. They most certainly did not come with the house.

Annoyed at how they'd rifled through her aunt's belongings, Tally looked around and realized Aunt Marv's old Christmas records sat in a stack by a record player that hadn't worked in years. The old player was the source of the Christmas music that filled the house.

On the table by the record player, she noticed a bouquet of roses filling a large etched crystal vase. She walked across the room and studied the vase with a scene of pine trees in the background and two little birds, cozied up together in the snow. That was the vase Aunt Marv told her to gather from the pantry.

It was then she noticed the roses weren't real but made of playing cards. What kind of people had flowers made from a deck of cards? Gamblers? Reprobates?

Between the songs and the scents and the vase, Tally went from mildly irritated to livid. How dare these people take her aunt's things, her cherished treasures, and use them like their own.

Tally hurried into the kitchen to find the china hot chocolate pot and matching cups that Uncle Rich's grandmother had received as a wedding gift sitting on the table. Hand-painted with holly berries and poinsettias, the chocolate set had been one of Aunt Marv's favorite holiday possessions. The new owners had the gall to serve hot chocolate in it. The pot was hot when she touched it. Next to it a dish, one of Aunt Marv's, held little marshmallows.

"Of all the nerve!" Tally yanked off her coat and left it with her scarf on a kitchen chair. She wasn't leaving until she'd boxed up every single one of her aunt's things and taken them with her.

She marched into the living room and over to the tree. Her fingers caressed a glass ball she knew had belonged to her great-great grandmother. And there was the little pointy-eared elf Uncle Rich would hide in the tree for her to find. Precious memories flooded over her and left her in a state of what Aunt Marv would call overwhelming happy-sad.

Her gaze settled on a new ornament. She picked it up and stared at it. Tiny little bareback riders made of silver formed a heart. A red ribbon ran through a small ring at the top and served as a hanger. Tally held the ornament on her finger and studied it. She'd purchased one exactly like it for Gage when they were in Las Vegas. Since Gage wouldn't be joining them for Christmas, Trevor had boxed up the gifts they'd all purchased for him and mailed them to Cooper James. Last Trevor had heard, Gage planned to spend Christmas with

Cooper, Paige, and Nick.

She draped the ornament back onto a branch and sighed. Nothing seemed right and at that moment, the whole world felt out of place. Like something fundamental had shifted a degree and left everything off kilter.

A floorboard creaked behind her. Every hair on the back of her neck prickled. Evidently, she wasn't alone in the house. A decidedly masculine scent surrounded her, one she recognized, as it mingled with the fragrance of the tree and bayberry candle.

"Have some chocolate, Queenie. Maybe it will bring you a little cheer. Aren't you supposed to be keeping Christmas alive in your heart? Instead, you look like you could shoot Santa and all eight of his reindeer without blinking then wipe out all the elves, too."

Tally spun around and gaped at Gage as he held out one of the delicate china cups, filled with hot chocolate and miniature marshmallows. When she failed to accept it, he took a sip then set it on a side table by the tree. "Mmm, that is good. Aunt Marv told me exactly how to make it."

"Aunt Marv?" Tally asked, confused. Why was her aunt consorting with the enemy? And why was the enemy in the house her aunt had just sold that morning? "What are you doing here?"

"Getting ready to settle in, settle down, and settle my affairs." Gage grinned at her and lifted the cup again, holding it out to her.

So distracted by his presence, by how wonderful he looked in a bright blue shirt that accented his incredible eyes, she sipped the rich, hot liquid. He grinned, took the cup, and placed his lips in the exact spot hers had been. He took a drink before returning the cup to the table.

Tally blinked twice and would have taken a step back from him, but he had her hemmed in with the Christmas tree. "I don't understand what you said. Why are you here?"

Gage reached out to her, but she sidestepped and moved across the room. Suddenly, she felt chilled to the bone. She turned her back to the fire and pinned Gage with a glare. "I thought you promised to stay away from me and not come back until next August. The mighty Gage Taggart wouldn't dare break a promise, would he?"

With determined steps, he walked over to the table that held the vase and picked up the bouquet of flowers made from cards. He closed the distance between them until he stood so close the tips of his boots touched the toes of her shoes. She noticed his gaze travel from them, up her navy scrub pants and across her top that featured a reindeer flying through a swirl of snow, to her face.

When his eyes tangled with hers, he grinned. "Just this once, I think it's gonna be okay to break a promise, because it was one my heart never intended to keep anyway, Queenie."

"You don't get to call me that anymore, Gage."

"Oh, I think I do." He held the bouquet out to her. "You've always been the queen of King Penny Ranch, which is why I gave you the nickname in the first place. But since August, you've been the queen of my heart, Talilah King. You always will be."

Tally looked at the roses and realized each one

of them had been formed from a queen of hearts playing card. There had to be at least two dozen roses in the bouquet, and each rose appeared to be made of several cards. Gage must have gone through more than a hundred decks of cards for the bouquet.

She took the roses from him but refused to acknowledge how much the gift impressed her. "You still haven't answered my question. Why are you here, at Roamin' End Ranch?"

Gage took the bouquet from her and set it back in the vase then clasped both her hands between his. Tally knew she should pull her hands free and walk away from him, but she couldn't seem to move. Didn't really want to. Not when glimmers of hope for her Christmas dreams coming true began to flicker.

"I'm here because this morning your aunt agreed to sell me the place."

Tally couldn't believe what she was hearing. Why would Gage want to buy her aunt's farm when the man had made it abundantly clear he didn't want to be tied down anywhere? It made no sense. None at all.

"Why on earth would you buy it?"

"Because, Queenie, I'm fixin' to get domesticated," he said in a teasing drawl. He inched closer. "It's time for me to settle down and set down roots, and there's no one I'd rather do that with than you. My roaming days are numbered. The moment I stepped into this house it felt like home."

"It's always felt like home to me," she admitted, glancing around the room. "I loved coming here when I was a little girl. Other than the ranch, it was the only other place I felt loved. Here, I felt like I belonged."

"I know, baby," Gage wrapped his arms around her and pulled her against his solid chest.

Tally breathed in the delicious scent of him and let herself rest against his strength. She should be angry with him. She should walk out the door and not look back. She should tell Gage exactly what she thought of him leaving her due to his stupid promise to Trevor.

But she didn't. Not when all she wanted was to love him, be loved by him. She slid her arms around his waist and held him close.

"I'm sorry for being an idiot, and a jerk, and whatever other names you can think to call me," he said, leaning back and looking down at her. That darn half-grin that never failed to weaken her knees greeted her when she stared up at him.

She smiled. "I have a long list that grew daily."

He chuckled. "I believe that, and I deserve it. Tally, the dumbest thing I've done is try to turn away from what we have together, from a love so special and true, I could live a hundred lifetimes and not find it again. I'm sorry."

Tally continued holding his gaze, not quite ready to speak her heart, even if she had decided to forgive him.

"I realized after some intense soul-searching and a long lecture from Cooper and Paige that I needed to get my head on straight and do what's right, even if it means breaking an idiotic promise I never should have made."

Tally nodded. "Had you bothered to ask my thoughts on the matter, you could have saved us both some trouble and heartache."

"I know, and I'm sorry, more than you can know. Yesterday, I called Trevor and Aunt Marv. They agreed to my plans and met me here this morning. Your aunt must have called in favors from every person she knows. There was a whole busload of little old ladies who cleaned the house, top to bottom. Trevor rounded up a crew who helped me put up the tree and hang the lights. Kaley and Kenzie stocked the fridge while Brylee and Jessie brought candles and set out decorations. And your aunt sat there on the couch, overseeing everything. I think it was the most fun she's had in a while."

"You have great friends, Gage."

He shook his head and lifted her hand, kissing her fingers. "No, baby. *We* have great friends. The girls all told me I was the biggest lunkhead on the face of the earth for walking away from you in Las Vegas. I couldn't disagree, since they are right."

"They're a group of smart women."

Gage chuckled and kissed her cheek. Butterflies took flight in her stomach and she wondered how long her wobbly knees would hold her. Just being in the same room with Gage left her lightheaded and full of longing, but she needed more than an apology. She needed a promise for the future.

"You said your roaming days are numbered. What do you mean by that? Are you giving up rodeo?" she asked.

Gage kissed her fingers again then held her

hand against his chest. She could feel his heart beating rapidly beneath her palm.

"I'm planning to retire at the end of next year. I need to ease into the idea of leaving behind a career I enjoy for the woman I love."

Tally gave him a wide-eyed look and he brushed his fingers tenderly across her cheek. "I do love you, Tally, more than anything in this world. For the next year, I can't promise to be home every night, but I will be starting next December, right after the finals in Vegas."

"Is that so?" she asked, warming to the idea of Gage living on her aunt's ranch, especially if he thought it might one day be a home for them both.

"That is so. In fact, I plan to cut back on my rodeo schedule this year. I'll enter fewer rodeos and just work on winning those I do enter. It might help if I had someone there to cheer me on. Someone who looks completely adorable in a pair of reindeer scrubs."

"So, you've got another nurse you've been seeing?" she asked in an impassive tone, trying to keep from smiling.

Gage grabbed her around the waist and swung her around in his arms, making her laugh.

"You are a pill. There's no one but you. There hasn't been since I saw you leaning against the ticket booth at the rodeo."

"What? You saw me standing there? I thought I was completely invisible to you until I tapped you on the shoulder."

Gage grinned and swung her into his arms like a bride. "No, Tally. You've never been invisible to me, even when you were Trevor's little sister tagging after us. I always saw you and I think there's a part of me that always loved you. But that summer evening when I looked through the crowd and noticed you leaning against the ticket booth, I lost my heart to you."

"Gage," she whispered and bracketed his face with her hands. Their lips collided in an eager, hungry kiss that cleared any doubts from her mind about blending their lives together. Somehow, she knew they'd find a way to make it work.

Gage kissed her once more with such gentle sweetness, tears burned the backs of her eyes as he set her on Marvella's old couch and dropped down to one knee beside her. He took her hands between his and looked into her eyes. In his, she saw acceptance, hope, and deep, abiding love. The kind that came with promises of forever.

"Talilah Jade King, I can't promise to be here every night, but I'll always provide a home for you, a place you feel loved and accepted. I promise to cherish and treasure you, to give you the very best that I have to give. And I promise to love you with all that I am and all that I hope to be. You make me a better person, Tally. I never dreamed it was possible to feel this way about another human being, but I do. I love you so much it's beyond the boundaries of reason. I'll go right on loving you until the day I die, which I hope is when we are both very old, still living right here in this beautiful little house that we're going to make into a haven and our home. Will you please, please say you'll marry me, Queenie? I can't imagine any better gift this Christmas than your love."

"Of course, I'll marry you, Gage. Today, tomorrow, a year from now. I've been waiting for you since I was ten years old. When you're ready, I'll be here."

He took a small box from his pocket, opened the lid and showed her a set of silver wedding bands with gold acanthus scrolls. The smaller of the two had a gorgeous square diamond set into the center. She looked from the rings to him in question.

He smiled and took the smaller ring out of the box, sliding it onto her finger. It fit perfectly.

"I bought these in Las Vegas. At the time it seemed like an insane thing to do, but I had to buy them. Right now, I'm glad I did."

Tally held out her hand, studied the ring on her finger, how right it looked there as the diamond refracted the colorful lights on the tree.

She looped her arms around Gage's neck and kissed him with all the love she held in her heart.

In one smooth motion, he scooped her up and sat down on the couch with her on his lap, continuing their amorous interlude.

When the clock on the wall chimed five, Gage lifted his head and smiled at her. "I promised Aunt Marv we'd be there for dinner. If we're gonna make it on time, we better get going."

"Then let's go," she said, sliding off his lap and hurrying to turn off lights and switches, rinse out the hot chocolate pot, and lock the door. Gage held her hand as they stepped outside and looked up to see big, fluffy flakes drifting down from the evening sky.

Tally laughed and rushed down the steps, holding out both hands and tipping up her face to catch snowflakes.

"Merry Christmas, Queenie," Gage said, wrapping his arms around her from behind and nuzzling her neck. "I hope we keep the joy and love of this special Christmas Eve in our hearts every year."

"Always and forever, Gage. We'll always keep Christmas in our hearts."

Epilogue

"Look what's in the paper today," Trevor said as he hurried inside the kitchen and handed the newspaper to his aunt.

Marvella took the pages from him and pushed her black-framed glasses up on her nose. "Oh, she looks beautiful and Gage is so handsome." She handed the paper back to Trevor. "Read the article for me, darling."

Trevor cleared his throat. "'Gage Ethan Taggart and Talilah Jade King were united in marriage on New Year's Eve in a private ceremony at the home of her brother, Trevor King. In attendance were immediate family and close friends including Elliott Flynn, owner of Lasso Eight apparel. The designer created the bride's gown, the first in a line he plans to launch under the Wyld Rose label.'"

He stopped reading and looked at his aunt. "I still can't believe Paige and Elliott talked Tally into modeling. Or that he just happened to have that dress to bring at a moment's notice since Gage and Tal only gave everyone a few days to plan the wedding. I don't understand how Tally went from wanting to throttle Gage to agreeing to marry him in a matter of hours."

"No one can explain the heart, sweetheart," Marvella said, reaching out to pat his hand "Now, go back to reading, please."

Trevor read about the decorations, the bridal party, and the couple's plans to take a honeymoon trip in February to San Antonio where Gage would compete in the rodeo.

"It ends with, 'Mr. and Mrs. Taggart will make their home in Kennewick at the Roamin' End Ranch, recently purchased by the couple from Mrs. Taggart's aunt, Marvella Hawkins.'" Trevor smiled at her. "You did good, Auntie, selling the farm to Gage. I think they'll be happy there."

"I know they will be, darling. The house is already brimming with love from all the years of happiness that have already taken place there." Marvella sat back and sipped her tea. "Now, we just need to find you your happily-ever-after."

"Aunt Marv, don't you go getting any ideas," Trevor warned, wary of the look in her eye.

She grinned and his wariness turned to fear.

"No way, Aunt Marv. Not a chance…"

Recipe

The first time I made this doughnut recipe, you would have thought we'd never tasted a doughnut before because we couldn't stop eating them! (Good thing I only made a half-batch!) They are so soft, and light, melt-in-your-mouth delicious, you'll have a hard time eating only one! If you make a full batch, you'll get about 24 doughnuts. Enjoy!

The Best Doughnuts:
2 packets of yeast (1/4 ounce each)
¼ cup warm water
1 ½ cups milk
½ cup sugar
1 teaspoon salt
2 eggs
½ cup shortening
5 cups all-purpose flour
4 cups vegetable oil
Glaze:
2 ½ cups confectioners' sugar
¼ cup milk
1 teaspoon vanilla extract

Heat milk in a heavy saucepan over medium heat until scalded. Cool to lukewarm (think baby bottle temperature).

Add water and yeast together in a mixing bowl and set aside for 10 minutes. Add in the milk, sugar, salt, eggs, shortening and 2 cups of the flour.

Mix for two minutes on medium speed then add in the rest of the flour and mix until just combined.

Cover the bowl with a clean towel and allow dough to rise for an hour. I like to set the bowl someplace warm (not hot). When you can push down on the dough and your finger leaves an indentation, the dough is ready. Divide the dough in half and roll on a floured surface to about ½ inch thick. Dip a doughnut cutter in flour (a drinking glass will work, too, in a pinch), and cut out a dozen doughnuts with each half of the dough. Set on waxed paper or parchment paper sprayed with non-stick spray, cover, and allow to rise for about 30 minutes.

Mix confectioners' sugar, milk, and vanilla extract for the glaze and set aside.

In a deep saucepan, heat oil to 375 degrees. Fry doughnuts for approximately 90 seconds on each side. Drain on a cooling rack then dip them in the glaze.

Eat while warm for the best experience. Your taste buds will thank you.

Author's Note

Thank you for reading Keeping Christmas. I hope you enjoyed meeting Gage and Tally and watching them fall in love. For those who have read all the books in the Rodeo Romance series, I hope you also enjoyed catching up with old friends!

When I first started working on this series, the thought of a cowboy who traveled to rodeos on a motorcycle instead of in a pickup intrigued me. It would have to be a rodeo athlete who didn't need to have a horse, so that narrowed it down to the roughstock events. Since I've already written about a saddle bronc rider (*The Christmas Cowboy*) and a bull rider (*Chasing Christmas*) that left bareback riding.

One of the most physically demanding events in rodeo, bareback riding is exciting to watch and proved to be so fun to write about.

I truly enjoyed creating Gage's character, imagining him rolling from one rodeo to the next on his bike, free and unfettered as he could be.

Tally is such a wonderful contrast to Gage. She's deeply rooted, a little shy, yet determined and strong. And I have to say to anyone who is a nurse – you have my admiration and my gratitude for what you do. Thank you!

Some of the things that happened to Tally came from personal experiences.

When the frog jumped out and "attacked" her that was something that happened to me. I went into our storage barn to grab something and this little frog jumped out of nowhere at me. It was totally harmless, but it scared me half to death. A few days later, I had to get something else from the barn. I'd already forgotten about the encounter with the frog as I opened the door and stepped inside. And the frog leaped out of nowhere again. I'm sure he was aiming for my head, but he landed on my neck, moving with lightning speed as I screamed and slapped at it. By that time, Captain Cavedweller came running to see what was trying to kill me only to find the tiny green frog hopping away like his life depended on a mad escape. Which it did. Of course, my husband laughed and relocated the frog to a safe place (for the frog and me!).

Another thing that happened last summer that didn't seem quite as amusing at the time was a day that began with the stench of skunk so heavy in the air you could taste it. I cowered in the house for hours, convinced the skunk had to be right outside the front door for as bad as it smelled. That very evening, I was outside, minding my own business and watering my flowers when a snake slithered right over my foot. To say I freaked out would be mildly understating the circumstances. Apparently, the ruckus of me trying to bring about the snake's demise drew Captain Cavedweller from the cool of the house where he'd settled after a long day's work. When he finally realized what was happening and the reason I was blowing a hole in my cinnamon pinks with the hose was to keep the snake from making a getaway, he rolled his eyes and asked why I was trying to destroy a worm. I assure you, the snake was bigger than a worm. Slightly bigger. Maybe. Regardless of size, when something slithers across my bare toes, it's done for. Although CC didn't start humming "Stayin' Alive," that song was stuck in my head for days afterward!

Oh, and I have to tell you about the inspiration for Aunt Marvella. Isn't she a hoot? I was flipping through a magazine and there was a photo of an elderly woman in a pea-green and white polka-dot dress with a bright raspberry-hued flower in her hair swinging a hula hoop around her waist and smiling like a delighted child. I knew right then that a fun-loving, slightly quirky character had to be included in the story. I'm sure we all know at least one person who saves everything, which is where I got the idea for having her wear all the clothes from decades past.

The idea for Tally redoing her bedroom is one I got from doing a surprise redecoration of my mom's guest bedroom last year! She'd mentioned one day when I was visiting that she wanted to get new bedding for the guest room. She prefers a particular style of bedspread (which is nearly impossible to find!), so I started searching. And searching. And searching some more. I finally found something online I thought she would like, added pillow shams and matching curtains to my shopping cart, and was all set to check out. Only the website wouldn't let me. I tried, and tried, and finally called to place my order. Let me tell you... I spent almost an hour on the phone trying to place a simple order. If that bedding hadn't been just "the thing" that I knew Mom would love, I would have given up after the first five minutes. As it was, the order was finally placed and arrived. I let Dad in on my plans to make a quick visit for Mom's birthday and redecorate the room. We coordinated for him to take her out of the house for a few hours so I could make the transformation. Only I got stuck in road construction and they were back at the house by the time I got there. But it turned out to be fun anyway because Mom and my aunt sat in chairs by the door, excitedly watching as Dad helped me hang the curtains, make the bed with the new bedding, and do a little redecorating in the room. Mom was so excited and pleased, I'm glad I sat through the agony of placing the order!

Special thanks to Shauna, Leo, Katrina, and my Hopeless Romantics for their help in making this book the best it can be. I so appreciate each one of you!

Thank you, again, for coming along on another Rodeo Romance adventure. If there are characters you'd like to see in future stories, please let me know! To see more of my inspiration for the book, check out my Pinterest board.

Thank you for reading *Keeping Christmas*. I hope you enjoyed meeting Tally and Gage and reading their story. If you have just a moment, would you please leave a review so others might discover this book? I'd so appreciate it! And I hope, too, that as you celebrate this season, you'll be *#KeepingChristmas* in your heart!

If you haven't yet read them, check out the other books in the *Rodeo Romance* series!

Please hop over to my website and read more about the Justin Cowboy Crisis Fund and how your book purchase helps a rodeo athlete in need of a hand up.

Also, if you haven't yet signed up for my newsletter, won't you consider subscribing? I send it out when I have new releases, sales, or news of freebies to share. Each month, you can enter a contest, get a new recipe to try, and discover details about upcoming events. When you sign up, you'll receive a free digital book. Don't wait. Sign up today!

Shanna's Newsletter

And if newsletters aren't your thing, please follow me on BookBub. You'll receive notifications on pre-orders, new releases, and sale books!

BookBub

Rodeo Romance Series

Hunky rodeo cowboys tangle with independent sassy women who can't help but love them.

The Christmas Cowboy (Book 1) — Among the top saddle bronc riders in the rodeo circuit, easy-going Tate Morgan can master the toughest horse out there, but trying to woo Kenzie Beckett is a completely different story.

Wrestling Christmas (Book 2) —Shanghaied by his sister and best friend, Cort McGraw finds himself on a run-down ranch with a worrisome, albeit gorgeous widow, and her silent, solemn son.

Capturing Christmas (Book 3) — Life is hectic for rodeo stock contractor Kash Kressley. The last thing Kash needs is the entanglement of a sweet romance, especially with a woman as feisty as Celia McGraw.

Barreling Through Christmas (Book 4) — Cooper James might be a lot of things, but beefcake model wasn't something he intended to add to his resume.

Chasing Christmas (Book 5) — Tired of his cousin's publicity stunts on his behalf, bull rider Chase Jarrett has no idea how he ended up with an accidental bride!

Racing Christmas (Book 6) — Brylee Barton is racing to save her family's ranch. Shaun Price is struggling to win her heart. . . again.

Keeping Christmas (Book 7) — A promise made is one Gage Taggart will never break, even if it costs him the woman he loves.

Roping Christmas (Book 8) —All he wanted was to keep his sponsor happy. He sure didn't intend on letting that woman capture his heart.

Remembering Christmas (Book 9) — Romance swirls like December snowflakes in this sweet holiday romance.

Savoring Christmas (Book 10) — Will the holiday season lead a hungry cowboy and an ambitious chef to realize what they really need is each other?

Taming Christmas (Book 11) — Will his two left feet lead to a ring on her left hand?

Between Christmas and Romance — When the bright lights and big city lost its luster, former model Carol Bennett returns to her Montana hometown disillusioned and ready to embrace a simple, quiet existence.

On a day when she's sure nothing could get worse, she encounters a cowboy too handsome for his own good and too insightful for hers. Although she adores his grandmother, rancher Tim Burke is stubborn and opinionated, declaring the only thing more wasteful of his time than the holidays is romance.

In spite of her determination to detest the man, the sparks sizzling between them make Carol wonder if being brave and latching onto happiness isn't far better than staying safely tucked away in her store.

Will two such opposite people be able to find love somewhere between romance and Christmas?

The jangle of spurs mingles with the jingle of sleigh bells in this celebration of Christmas— cowboy style!

Welcome home to a western holiday with *A Cowboy Christmas*. A collection of unique holiday décor, traditions, recipes, and guides for entertaining with ease make this your go-to resource for an amazing western Christmas. Filled with stories of real-life ranch families and rodeo cowboys, get a glimpse into their traditions, try their family recipes, and experience their lifestyles. From preserving memories of the past to tips for wrapping presents, discover the special touches incorporated throughout this book that make it a holiday keepsake you'll cherish for years to come.

About the Author

PHOTO BY SHANA BAILEY PHOTOGRAPHY

USA Today bestselling author Shanna Hatfield is a farm girl who loves to write. Her sweet historical and contemporary romances are filled with sarcasm, humor, hope, and hunky heroes.

When Shanna isn't dreaming up unforgettable characters, twisting plots, or covertly seeking dark, decadent chocolate, she hangs out with her beloved husband, Captain Cavedweller, at their home in the Pacific Northwest.

Shanna loves to hear from readers.

Connect with her online:

Website: shannahatfield.com

Made in the USA
Middletown, DE
18 August 2023